Praise for *The Killing Hour*:

'With tight plotting, an ear for forensic detail and a dash of romance, this is a truly satisfying sizzler in the tradition of Tess Gerritsen and Tami Hoag' *Publishers Weekly*

'Gardner keeps us guessing . . . She also keeps us on edge' *LA Times*

Praise for *The Survivors Club*:

'A high-octane, nerve-jangling tale of suspense' Harlan Coben

'When it comes to suspense, nobody does it better' Jayne Ann Krentz

Praise for *The Third Victim*:

'Riveting, hold-your-breath suspense' Iris Johansen

'A suspenseful, curl-up winter read, this thriller teems with crisp, realistic dialogue and engaging characters' *Publishers Weekly*

Praise for *The Other Daughter*:

'Sheer terror . . . A great read' *Booklist*

'Once again, Gardner serves up suspense at a furious pace' *Publishers Weekly*

Praise for *The Perfect Husband*:

'A dark, powerful tale of nerve-shattering suspense' Tami Hoag

'An unforgettably evil villain and a throat-gripping climax make *The Perfect Husband* a real page-turner!' Tess Gerritsen

By Lisa Gardner

The Perfect Husband
The Other Daughter
The Third Victim
The Next Accident
The Survivors Club
The Killing Hour
Alone
Gone
Hide
Say Goodbye
The Neighbour
Live to Tell
Love You More
Catch Me

LISA GARDNER

the Next Accident

Accident

headline

First published in Great Britain in 2002 by Orion Publishing Group

This paperback edition first published in 2012 by
HEADLINE PUBLISHING GROUP

6

Cataloguing in Publication Data is available from the British Library

ISBN 978 0 7553 9643 6

Typeset in Sabon by Avon DataSet Ltd,
Bidford-on-Avon, Warwickshire

Printed and bound in Great Britain by Clays Ltd, St Ives plc

Headline's policy is to use papers that are natural, renewable and
recyclable products and made from wood grown in sustainable forests.
The logging and manufacturing processes are expected to conform to
the environmental regulations of the country of origin.

HEADLINE PUBLISHING GROUP
An Hachette UK Company
338 Euston Road
London NW1 3BH

www.headline.co.uk
www.hachette.co.uk

the Next Accident

Acknowledgments

For most of my career as a suspense author, I've been repeatedly greeted by the comment, 'Wow, you look so nice for someone who writes such twisted books'. For once I'd like to agree. I really am a dull, ordinary person leading a dull, ordinary life. The only real background I have is as a business consultant, and while I suppose characters could die from process reengineering efforts gone horribly awry, I'm not sure anyone other than Dilbert enthusiasts would appreciate that.

Thus I have enlisted the help of the following experts to give my plot especially devious twists and my characters especially evil deaths. Please bear in mind that these people patiently and accurately answered all my questions. That does not mean, however, that I used their information in a patient or accurate way. I am a firm believer in artistic license, plus I possess a warped mind. We all have our talents.

That said, my deepest gratitude and appreciation to:

Dr Greg Moffatt, PhD, Professor of Psychology, Atlanta Christian College, for generously answering my steady stream of questions and offering such fabulous insights into the criminal mind.

Phil Agrue, Private Investigator, Agrue & Associates,

Portland, OR, who in three hours convinced me that I want to be a defense investigator when I grow up.

Gary Vencill, Consultant-Legal Investigation, Johnson, Clifton, Larson & Corson, PC, whose delight in creating an auto accident/murder scenario was equaled only by his diligence in personally showing me how to tamper with seat belts.

Dr Stan Stojkovic, Professor of Criminal Justice, University of Wisconsin-Milwaukee, for his insights on prison protocol and communication.

Dr Robert Johnson, American University, who was gracious enough to allow me to use his honest academic study as a model for conducting various forms of criminal mayhem.

Larry Jachrimo, custom pistolsmith, whose ongoing assistance with firearm details and ballistics techniques enables me to be more diabolical than I ever hoped. He provides me with wonderful information; I do make some mistakes.

Mark Bouton, former FBI firearms instructor and fellow writer, for helping bring my FBI agents into the new millennium.

Celia MacDonell and Margaret Charpentier, pharmacists extraordinaire, who also have a very promising future as poisoners. Nothing personal, but from here on out, I'm bringing my own food.

Mark Smerznak, chemical engineer, great friend, and extraordinary cook.

Heather Sharer, wonderful friend, jazz enthusiast, and general shoulder to cry on.

Rob, Julie, and Mom for the tour of the Pearl District and steady stream of café mochas.

Kate Miciak, editor extraordinaire, who definitely made this a better book.

Damaris Rowland and Steve Axelrod, agents extraordinaire, who encourage me to always write the book of my heart, and even better, allow me to pay my mortgage while doing so.

And finally to my husband, Anthony, for the supply of homemade chocolate champagne truffles and chocolate mousse cake. You know how to keep a writer motivated, and I love you.

the Next Accident

Accident

Plan A

Prologue

Virginia

His mouth grazed the side of her neck. She liked the feel of his kiss, whisper-light, teasing. Her head fell back. She heard herself giggle. He drew her earlobe between his lips, and the giggle turned to a moan.

God, she loved it when he touched her.

His fingers lifted her heavy hair. They danced across the nape of her neck, then slid down her bare shoulders.

'Beautiful, Mandy,' he whispered. 'Sexy, sexy, Mandy.'

She giggled again. She laughed, then she tasted salt on her lips and knew that she cried. He turned her belly-down on the bed. She didn't protest.

His hands traced the line of her spine before settling in at her waist.

'I like this curve right here,' he murmured, dipping one finger into the concave curve at the small of her back. 'Perfect for sipping champagne. Other men can have breasts and thighs. I just want this spot here. Can I have it, Mandy? Will you give that to me?'

Maybe she said yes. Maybe she just moaned. She didn't know anymore. One bottle of champagne empty on the bed.

Another half gone. Her mouth tingled with the forbidden flavor, and she kept telling herself it would be okay. It was just champagne, and they were celebrating, weren't they? He had a new job, the BIG job, and oops, it was far away. But there would be weekend visits, maybe some letters, long-distance phone calls . . .

They were celebrating, they were mourning. It was a farewell fuck, and either way champagne sex shouldn't count with the nice folks at AA.

He tilted the open bottle of bubbly over her shoulders. Cool, sparkling fluid cascaded down her neck, pooling on the white satin sheet. She lapped it up helplessly.

'That's my girl,' he whispered. 'My sweet, sexy, girl . . . Open for me, baby. Let me in.'

Her legs parted. She arched her back, the whole of her focusing down, down, down, to the spot between her legs where the ache had built and now only he could ease the pain. Only he could save her.

Fill me up. Make me whole.

'Beautiful, Mandy. Sexy, sexy, Mandy.'

'Pl-pl-please . . .'

He pushed inside her. Her hips went back. Her spine seemed to melt and she gave herself over to him.

Fill me up. Make me whole.

Salt on her cheeks. Champagne on her tongue. Why couldn't she stop crying? She tilted her head down to the sheets and sipped champagne as the room spun sickeningly.

Suddenly the bed was gone. They were outside. In the driveway. Clothes on, cheeks dry. Champagne gone, but not the thirst. Six months she'd been dry. Now she craved another drink horribly. One bottle of champagne still unopened. Maybe she could get him to give it to her for the drive home. One for the road.

Don't go . . .

'You okay, baby?'

'I'm okay,' she mumbled.

'Maybe you shouldn't be driving. Maybe you should stay the night . . .'

'I'm okay,' she murmured again. She couldn't stay, and they both knew it. Beautiful things came, beautiful things went. If she tried to hold on now, it would just make it worse.

He was hesitating, though. Looking at her with those deep, concerned eyes. They crinkled at the corners. She had loved that when she first met him. The way his eyes creased as if he was studying her intently, really, truly seeing her. Then he'd smiled a split second later, as if merely finding her had made him so very happy.

She'd never had a man smile at her like that before. As if she were someone special.

Oh God, don't go . . .

And then: *Third bottle of champagne. All full. One more for old times' sake. One more for the road.*

Her lover took her face between his hands. He stroked her cheeks with his thumbs. 'Mandy . . .' he whispered tenderly. 'The small of your back . . .'

She couldn't answer anymore. She was choking on her tears.

'Wait, baby,' he said suddenly. 'I have an idea.'

Driving. Thinking really hard because the narrow road curved like a snake and it was dark and it was so strange how early she could have a thought, and how late her body would be in responding. He sat beside her in the passenger's seat. He wanted to make sure she got home safe; then he'd take a cab. *Maybe she should take a cab. Maybe she was in no shape to drive. As long as he was coming with her, why was she the one at the wheel?*

She couldn't hold on to that thought long enough to make it work.

'Slow down,' he cautioned. 'The road is tricky here.'

She nodded, furrowing her brow and struggling to concentrate. *Wheel felt funny in her hand. Round. Huh.* Pressed on the brakes. Hit the gas instead. The SUV lurched forward.

'Sorry,' she muttered. World was beginning to spin again. She didn't feel well. Like she was going to throw up, or pass out. Maybe both. *If she could just close her eyes . . .*

Road moved on her again. Vehicle jerked.

Seat belt. Needed a seat belt. She groped for the strap, got the clasp. Pulled. Seat belt spun out toothlessly. *That's right. Broken. Must get that fixed. Someday. Today. May day. Stars spinning away, sky starting to lighten. Sun going to come up. Now she just needed a little girl singing, 'Tomorrow, tomorrow, there's always tomorrow—'*

'Slow down,' he repeated from the passenger's seat. 'There's a sharp turn ahead.'

She looked at him numbly. He had a strange gleam in his eyes. Excitement. She didn't understand.

'I love you,' she heard herself say.

'I know,' he replied. He reached for her kindly. His hand settled on the wheel. 'Sweet, sexy, Mandy. You're never going to get over me.'

She nodded. The dam broke, and tears poured down her cheeks. She sobbed hopelessly as the Ford Explorer swerved across the road, and the gleam built in his eyes.

'I'm as good as it gets,' he continued relentlessly. 'Without me, Mandy, you'll be lost.'

'I know, I know.'

'Your own father left you. Now, I'm doing the same. The weekend visits will stop, then the phone calls. And then it will just be you, Mandy, all alone night after night after night.'

She sobbed harder. Salt on her cheeks, champagne on her lips. *So alone. The black abyss. Alone, alone, alone.*

'Face it, Mandy,' he said gently. 'You're not good enough to keep a man. You're nothing but a drunk. Christ, I'm breaking up with you, and all you can think about is that third bottle of champagne. That's the truth, isn't it? *Isn't it?*'

She tried to shake her head. She ended up nodding.

'Mandy,' he whispered. 'Speed up.'

'Why didn't Daddy come home for my birthday? But I want Daddy!'

'Sweet, sexy Mandy.'

Fill me up. Make me whole.

So alone . . .

'You hurt, Mandy. I know you hurt. But I'll help you, baby. Speed up.'

Salt on her cheeks. Champagne on her lips. Her foot settling on the gas . . .

'One little push of the accelerator, and you'll never be lonely again. You'll never have to miss me.'

Her foot . . . The approaching curve in the road. *So alone. God, I'm tired.*

'Come on, Mandy. Speed up.'

Her foot pressing down . . .

At the last minute, she saw him. A man on the narrow shoulder of the country road. Walking his dog, looking startled to see a vehicle at this time of the morning, then even more surprised to have it bearing down on him.

Turn! Turn! Must turn! Amanda Jane Quincy jerked frantically at the wheel . . .

And it remained pointed straight ahead. Her lover still gripped it, and he held it tight.

Time suspended. Mandy looked up without comprehension at the face she had grown to love. She saw the rushing dark through the window behind him. She saw the seat belt strapped tight across his strong, broad chest. And she heard him say, 'Bye-bye, sweet Mandy. When you get to hell, be sure to give your father my regards.'

The Explorer hit the man. Thump bump. A short-circuited cry. The vehicle plowed ahead. And just as she was thinking it would be okay, she was still in one piece, they were still in one piece, the telephone pole reared out of the darkness.

Mandy never had time to scream. The Explorer hit the thick wooden pole at thirty-five miles per hour. The front bumper drove down, the back end came up. And her unsecured body vaulted from the driver's seat into the windshield, where the hard metal frame crushed the top of her skull.

The passenger had no such problems. The seat belt caught his chest, pushing him back into his seat even as the front end of the Explorer crumpled. His neck snapped forward. His internal organs rushed up in his chest, momentarily cutting off his air. He gasped, blinked his eyes, and seconds later, the pressure was gone. The SUV settled in. He settled in. He was fine.

He unfastened his seat belt with his bare hands. He had done his homework and he wasn't worried about prints.

Nor was he concerned about time. A rural road in the early hours of dawn. It would be ten, twenty, thirty minutes before someone happened by.

He inspected beautiful, sexy Mandy. She still had a faint pulse, but she was now missing most of the top of her head. Even if her body was putting up a last-ditch fight, her brain would never recover.

A year and a half of planning later, he was satisfied. Amanda Jane Quincy had died scared, died confused, died heartbroken.

He and Pierce Quincy were still not even, the man thought, but it was a start.

1

Monday afternoon, private investigator Lorraine Conner sat hunched over her paper-swamped desk, punched a few more numbers into her old, cagey laptop, then scowled at the results shown on the screen. She tried the numbers again, got the same dismal results, and gave them the same dark look. The Quicken-generated budget, however, refused to be intimidated.

Damn file, she thought. Damn budget, damn heat. And damn circular fan that she'd purchased just last week and was already refusing to work unless she whacked it twice in the head. She stopped now to give it the requisite double-smack and was finally rewarded with a feeble breeze. Christ, this weather was killing her.

It was three in the afternoon on Monday. Outside the sun was shining, the heat about to crest for another record-breaking July day in downtown Portland, Oregon. Technically speaking, Portland didn't get as ridiculously hot as the East Coast. Nor, in theory, did it get as humid as the South. These days, unfortunately, the climate didn't seem to realize that. Rainie had long since traded in her T-shirt for a white cotton tank top. It was now plastered to her skin, while her elbows left rings of condensation on the one clear spot on her desk. If it got any hotter, she was taking her laptop into the shower.

Rainie's loft offered central air, but as part of her 'belt-tightening' program, she was cooling her vast, one-room condo the old-fashioned way – she'd opened the windows and turned on a small desk fan. Unfortunately, that little matter of heat rising was conspiring against her. The eighth-floor condo wasn't magically getting any cooler, while the smog content had increased tenfold.

Bad day for belt-tightening programs. Especially in Portland's trendy Pearl District, where iced coffee was served on practically every street corner, and all the little cafés prided themselves on their gourmet ice cream. God knows the majority of her upwardly mobile neighbors were probably sitting in Starbucks right now, basking in air-conditioned glory while trying to choose between an iced Chai or nonfat mocha latte.

Not Rainie. No, the new and improved Lorraine Conner was sitting in her trendy loft in this trendy little neighborhood, trying to decide which was more important – money for the Laundromat, or a new carburetor for her fifteen-year-old clunker. On the one hand, clean clothes always made a good impression when meeting a new client. On the other hand, it didn't do her any good to land new cases if she had no means of carrying them out. Details, details.

She tried a fresh round of numbers in her Quicken file. Showing a gross lack of imagination, the file spit back the same red results. She sighed. Rainie had just passed the

Oregon Board of Investigators' test to receive her license. In the good news department, this meant she could start working for defense lawyers as a defense investigator, à la Paul Drake to their Perry Mason. In the bad news department, the two-year license cost her seven hundred bucks. Then came the hundred dollars for the standard five-thousand-dollar bond to protect her against complaints. Finally, she got to fork over eight hundred dollars for a million dollars in errors-and-omissions insurance, more CYA infrastructure. All in all, Conner Investigations was moving up – except she was now out sixteen hundred dollars and feeling the crunch.

'But I like eating,' she tried to tell her computerized business records. They didn't seem to care.

A buzzer sounded. Rainie sat up, dragging a hand discouragingly through her hair, while she blinked twice in surprise. She wasn't expecting any clients today. She peered into the family room, where her TV was tuned in to the building's security cameras and now broadcasted the view from the main entrance. A well-dressed man with salt-and-pepper hair stood patiently outside the locked front doors. As she watched, he buzzed her loft again. Then he glanced up at the camera.

Rainie couldn't help herself. Her breath caught. Maybe her heart even stopped. She looked at him, the last person she expected to see these days, and everything inside her went topsy-turvy.

She ran a hand through her newly shorn hair again. She was still getting used to the look, and the heat made it flip out like a dark, chestnut dish mop. Then there was her tank top – old and sweat-soaked. Her denim shorts, ripped up, frayed, and hardly professional. She was just doing paperwork today, no need to dress up, and oh God had she put on deodorant this morning, because it was really hot in here and she could no longer tell.

Supervisory Special Agent Pierce Quincy remained gazing up at the security camera, and even through the grainy image, she could see the intent look in his deep blue eyes.

Rainie's scattered thoughts slowed. Her hand settled at the hollow of her throat. And she studied Quincy, nearly eight months since she'd last seen him and six months since even the phone calls had stopped.

His eyes still crinkled in the corners. His forehead still carried deep, furrowed lines. He had the hard, lean features of a man who spent too much time dealing with death, and damn if she hadn't liked that about him. Same impeccably tailored suit. Same hard-to-read face. There was no one quite like SupSpAg Quincy.

He pressed the ringer for a third time. He wasn't going away. Once he made up his mind about something, Quincy rarely let it go. *Except her* . . .

Rainie shook her head in disgust. She didn't want to think that way. They'd tried, they'd failed. Shit happened. Whatever Quincy wanted now, she doubted it was personal. She buzzed him in.

Eight floors later, he knocked at her front door. She'd had time for deodorant, but nothing in the world could save her hair. She swung open the door, balanced one hand on her denim-clad hip, and said, 'Hey.'

'Hello, Rainie.'

She waited. The pause drew out, and to her satisfaction, Quincy broke first.

'I was beginning to worry that you were out on a case,' he said.

'Yeah well, even the good guys can't be working all the time.'

Quincy raised a brow. His dry tone made her positively nostalgic as he said, 'I wouldn't know anything about that.'

She smiled in spite of herself. Then she swung the door open a bit wider, and truly let him in.

Quincy didn't speak right away. He walked around her loft casually, but Rainie wasn't fooled. She'd blown the majority of her savings on the loft just four months ago and she knew the kind of impression it made. The eleven-foot ceilings of a converted warehouse space. The open, sunny layout with nothing but a kitchen counter and eight giant support columns to carve out four simple spaces: kitchen, bedroom, family room, and study. The huge expanse of windows, filling the entire outer wall with original 1925 paned glass.

The woman who had owned the condo before Rainie had finished the entranceway with warm red brick and painted the living space with rustic shades of adobe and tan. The result was the shabby chic look Rainie had read about in magazines, but knew better than to try on her own.

The loft had nearly bankrupted her, but the minute Rainie had seen it, she couldn't have gone without it. It was fashionable, it was upscale, it was beautiful. And maybe if the new and improved Lorraine Conner lived in this kind of place, she could be that kind of person.

'It's nice,' Quincy said finally.

Rainie scrutinized his face. He seemed sincere. She grunted a reply.

'I didn't know you did sponge painting,' Quincy commented.

'Don't. The previous owner.'

'Ahh, she did a nice job. New hairdo?'

'I cut off the length and sold it to buy the loft, of course.'

'You always were clever. Not organized, as I can tell by looking at the desk, but clever.'

'Why are you here?'

Quincy paused, then smiled grudgingly. 'I see you still know how to cut to the chase.'

'And you still know how to dodge a question.'

'Touché.'

She arched a brow, signaling that, too, wasn't an answer. Then she propped up her hip on the edge of her desk, and knowing Quincy as well as she did, she waited.

Supervisory Special Agent Pierce Quincy had started his career as an FBI profiler, back in the days when that division was called the Investigative Support Unit and he was known as one of the best of the best. Six years ago, after a particularly brutal case, he'd moved to the Behavioral Science Unit, where he focused on researching future homicidal practices and teaching classes at Quantico. Rainie had met him a year ago, in her hometown of Bakersville, Oregon, when a mass murder had ravaged her quaint community and garnered Quincy's attention. As the primary officer, she had walked that crime scene with him, having met him just an hour before and already impressed by how impassive he could keep his face, even when looking at the chalk outlines of little girls.

She hadn't had his composure in the beginning. She had earned hers the hard way, over the following days of the investigation, when things in her town had gone from bad to worse, and she'd realized just how much she had to fear. Quincy had started as her ally. He'd become her anchor. By the end of the case, there'd been the hint of more.

Then Rainie had lost her job with the sheriff's department. Then the DA had charged her with man one for a fourteen-year-old homicide, and she'd spent four months waiting for her day in court. Eight months ago, without warning or explanation, the charges against her were dropped. It was over.

Rainie's lawyer had the impression that someone might have intervened on her behalf. Someone with clout. Rainie had never brought it up, but she'd always suspected that person was Quincy. And far from drawing them together, it was one more thing cluttering the space between.

He was Supervisory Special Agent Pierce Quincy, the man who'd brought down Jim Beckett, the man who'd discovered Henry Hawkins, the man who probably did know what had happened to Jimmy Hoffa.

She was simply Lorraine Conner, and she still had a lot to do to get her life on track.

Quincy said, 'I have a job for you.'

Rainie nearly snorted. 'What? The Bureau's no longer good enough for you?'

He hesitated. 'It's . . . personal.'

'The Bureau's your life, Quincy. It's *all* personal for you.'

'But this more so than most. Could I have a glass of water?'

Rainie furrowed her brow. Quincy with a personal mission. She was hopelessly intrigued.

She went into the kitchen, fixed two glasses of water with plenty of ice, then joined him in the family room. Quincy had already taken a seat on her overstuffed blue-striped sofa. The couch was old and threadbare, one of the few remnants of her life in Bakersville. There, she'd lived in a tiny ranch-style house with a back deck surrounded by soaring pine trees and air filled with the mournful cries of hoot owls. No sounds of sirens or late-night partyers. Just endless evenings crammed full of memories – her mother drunk, her mother raising her fist. Her mother, missing most of her head.

Not all of the recent changes in Rainie's life were bad.

Quincy took a long sip of water. Then he removed his jacket and carefully draped it over the arm of the sofa. His shoulder holster stood out darkly against his white dress shirt.

'My daughter – we buried Mandy last month.'

'Oh Quincy, I'm sorry,' Rainie responded instinctively, then fisted her hands before she did something awkward such as reaching out to him. She knew the story behind Mandy's automobile accident. Last April, Quincy's twenty-three-year-old daughter had collided head-on with a telephone pole in Virginia, causing permanent brain damage as well as shattering her face. At the hospital, she'd immediately been put on life support, though that had only been intended to sustain her organs long enough to gain permission for harvest. Unfortunately, Quincy's ex-wife, Bethie, had confused life support with life, and refused to have the machines turned off. Quincy and Bethie had argued. Finally, Quincy had left the bedside vigil to return to work, a decision that had alienated his ex-wife even more.

'Bethie finally gave permission,' Rainie supplied.

Quincy nodded. 'I didn't think . . . In my mind, Mandy has been dead for well over a year. I didn't think it would be this hard.'

'She was your daughter. It would be strange if it were easy.'

'Rainie . . .' He appeared on the verge of saying something more, maybe caught up in this moment when they seemed like old friends again. Then the moment passed. He shook his head. He said, 'I want to hire you.'

'Why?'

'I want you to look into my daughter's accident. I want you to make sure that it was an accident.' Rainie was too flabbergasted to speak. Quincy read her doubt and rushed on firmly: 'Some things have come up. I want you to investigate them.'

'I thought she was drunk,' Rainie said, still trying to get her bearings. 'Drunk, hit a man, a dog, and a telephone pole. End of story.'

'She was drunk. The hospital confirmed that she had a blood alcohol level of twice the legal limit, but it's how she came to be drunk that has me concerned. I met a few of her friends at the funeral, and one of them, Mary Olsen, claims that Amanda spent most of the evening at Mary's house, playing cards and drinking Diet Coke. Now, I hadn't spoken with Mandy in a bit. You . . . you know I haven't had the closest relationship with her. But apparently, Amanda had joined AA six months before her accident and was doing very well. Her friends were very proud of her.'

In spite of herself, Rainie frowned. 'Did something happen during the card game? Get her upset, make her drive straight to a bar?'

'Not according to Mary Olsen. And Amanda didn't leave until nearly two-thirty in the morning, after the bars were closed.'

'Was she alone?'

'Yes.'

'Maybe she drove home and got drunk.'

'And then got back into her car to drive where?'

Rainie chewed her bottom lip. 'Okay, maybe she had liquor stashed in her car and started drinking the minute she left the party.'

'No containers were found in her vehicle or in her apartment. Plus, the liquor stores would all be closed, so she couldn't have purchased it that night.'

'Maybe she'd bought it before arriving at her friend's, then she threw away the empty containers on her way home. You know, to cover her tracks.'

'Amanda crashed fifteen miles from her apartment, on some back road that bears no direct relationship to Mary Olsen's house or hers.'

'As if she was just out driving . . .'

'Drunk, at five-thirty in the morning, with no obvious supply of alcohol,' Quincy finished for her. 'Rainie, I'm concerned.'

Rainie didn't answer right away. She was still turning the facts over in her mind, trying to make the pieces fit. 'She could have gone to someone else's house after leaving Mary's.'

'It's possible. Mary said Amanda had met a man a few months before. None of Amanda's friends had met him yet, but he was supposedly a very nice man, very supportive. My daughter . . . Amanda told Mary that she thought she might be in love.'

'But you never met this guy?'

'No.'

She cocked her head to the side. 'What about at the funeral? Surely he attended the funeral?'

'He didn't attend the funeral. No one knew his name or how to contact him.'

Rainie gave Quincy a look. 'If he's that great, he would've

found *you* by now. Surely Mandy mentioned her father, and given the amount of press you've received on various cases . . .'

'I've thought of that.'

'But no sign of Mr Wonderful.'

'No.'

Rainie finally got it. 'You don't think this was an accident, do you? You think it is Mr Wonderful's fault. He got your little girl drunk, then let her drive home.'

'I don't know what he did,' Quincy replied quietly, 'but somehow, Amanda got access to alcohol between two-thirty and five-thirty in the morning, and it cost her her life. She was troubled. She had a history of drinking . . . Yes, I would like to hear his side of things.'

'Quincy, this isn't a case. This is one of the five stages of grief. You know – denial.'

Rainie tried to utter the words gently, but they came out bald, and almost immediately, Quincy was pissed off. His lips thinned. His eyes grew darker, his features harsher. For the most part, Quincy was an academic, prone to approaching the world as a puzzle to be analyzed and solved. But he was also a hunter; Rainie had seen that side of him, too. Once – their final evening together – she had fingered the scars on his chest.

'I want to know what happened the last night of my daughter's life,' Quincy uttered firmly, precisely. 'I'm asking you to look into it. I'm willing to pay your fees. Now, will you take the case or not?'

'Oh for God's sake.' Rainie bolted out of her chair. She paced the room a few times so he wouldn't see how mad he'd just made her, then said sourly, 'You know I'll help you, and you know I won't take your damn money.'

'It's a case, Rainie. A simple case, and you don't owe me anything.'

'Bullshit! It's another bread crumb you're tossing my way and we both know it. You're an FBI agent. You have access to your own crime lab; you have one hundred times the number of contacts I do.'

'All of whom will want to know why I'm asking questions. All of whom will pry into my family's life and will sit in judgment of my concerns, even if *they* are too polite to accuse me of denial.'

'I'm only saying—'

'I know I'm in denial! I'm her father, for God's sake. Of course I'm in denial. But I'm also a trained investigator, just like you, Rainie, and something about this stinks. Look me in the eye and tell me it doesn't stink.'

Rainie stopped. She mutinously looked him in the eye. Then she wished she hadn't, because his jaw was tight and his hands were clenched into fists, and dammit she liked him when he was like this. The rest of the world could have composed, professional Pierce Quincy. She wanted this man. At least she had.

'*Did you ask the DA to drop the charges against me?*' she demanded.

'What?'

'Did you ask the DA to drop the charges against me?'

'No.' He shook his head in bewilderment. 'Rainie, I'm the one who told you to go through with the trial, that it was probably the best way to put the past behind you. Why would I then interfere?'

'Fine, I'll take your case.'

'What?'

'I'll take your case! Four hundred dollars a day, plus

expenses. And I don't know beans about Virginia or motor vehicle accident investigation, so no accusing me later of not having enough experience. I'm telling you now, I'm inexperienced, and it's still going to cost you four hundred dollars a day.'

'There you go with that charm again.'

'I'm a fast learner. We both know I'm a fast learner.' She said that more savagely than she'd intended. Quincy's face nearly softened, then he caught himself.

'Deal,' he said crisply. He picked up his jacket, drew out a manila envelope and dropped it on her glass coffee table. 'There's the accident report. It includes the name of the investigating officer. I'm sure you'll want to start with him.'

'Jesus, Quincy, you shouldn't be reading that.'

'She's my daughter, Rainie; it's the only thing I can do for her anymore. Now, come on, I'm buying.'

'Buying what?'

'Dinner. It's too damn hot in here, Rainie, and you really need to put on some clothes.'

'Just for that, I'm wearing the tank top to dinner. And as long as you're buying, we're going to Oba's.'

2

Pearl District, Portland

One night out on the town, and it was easy to slip into old
roles. Quincy sweeping into town and taking her out to an
extravagant restaurant. Eating great food, tropical shrimp
ceviche, rare ahi tuna, butternut squash enchiladas. Quincy
drank two world-famous marionberry daiquiris, served in
chilled martini glasses. Rainie stuck to water, because in a
place like Oba's she was too embarrassed to conduct her
little ritual of ordering – but not drinking – a Bud Light.

They talked a little. They talked a lot. God it was good to
see him again.

'So how is the investigative business?' Quincy asked
halfway through dessert, when they had exhausted small
talk and settled in.

'Good. Just got my license. Number five hundred and
twenty-one, that's me.'

'Doing private work?'

'Some. I got in with a few defense attorneys; they're the
ones who convinced me to get licensed. Now I can do more
work for them – background checks on witnesses, crime-
scene reconstruction, police report analysis. Still a lot of

24

sitting at the desk, but it beats chasing down the cheating husband or wife.'

'Sounds interesting.'

Rainie laughed. 'Sounds dull! I spend my time logged on to the Oregon Judicial Information Network. On a really exciting day, I might access my Oregon State Police account to peruse criminal history. It takes intelligence, but we're not talking adrenaline rush.'

'I read lots of reports, too,' Quincy said, sounding mildly defensive.

'You fly places. You talk to people. You get there while the blood's still fresh.'

'You miss it that much, Rainie?'

She avoided his gaze to keep from answering, wished she did have a bottle of Bud Light, and switched topics. 'How's Kimberly?'

'I don't know.'

Rainie arched a brow. 'I thought she was the daughter who liked you.'

Quincy grimaced. 'Tact, Rainie. Tact.'

'I strive to be consistent.'

'Kimberly needs some space. I think her sister's accident hit her harder than the rest of us. She's angry, and I don't think she's comfortable with that yet.'

'Angry with Amanda, or angry with you and Bethie?'

'To be honest, I'm not sure.'

Rainie nodded. 'I always wanted a sister. I figured that must be something special, to have a genetic ally in the world. Someone to play with. Someone to fight with. Someone who had your parents, too, so she could tell you if your mom really was nuts, or if it was all in your head. But it doesn't sound like Mandy has been much of an ally for

Kimberly. Instead, she's been the major source of family stress.'

'The rebellious older sister, getting all the attention,' Quincy agreed.

'While Kimberly behaves as the model child, the born diplomat.'

'Bethie hates for me to say it, but Kim will make a terrific agent someday.'

'She's still pursuing criminology?'

'Psychology for her BA. Now she's looking at sub-matriculating into a master's program for criminology.' The lines in Quincy's forehead momentarily smoothed away. He was very proud of his younger daughter, and it showed on his face. 'How's Bakersville?' he asked presently.

'Okay. Moving on the best you can after these things.'

'Shep and Sandy?'

'Still together.' Rainie shook her head as if to say, who understood. 'Shep's working for a security company in Salem. Sandy's gotten active in revamping juvenile law.'

'Good for her. And Luke Hayes?'

'Making a fine new sheriff, or so he tells me. I visited five, six months ago. The town's in good hands.'

'I'm surprised you went back.'

'Luke had some business for me.'

Quincy gazed at her curiously; she finally gave up the information with a shrug. 'He was getting inquiries about my mom.'

'Your mom?' Quincy was surprised. Rainie's mother had been dead for fifteen years, murdered by a shotgun blast to the head. Most of the people in Bakersville figured Rainie had pulled the trigger. That's what happens when you leave a house with brains dripping down your hair.

'Some guy was calling around town, trying to find her. Luke thought I should know about it.'

'Why after all this time?'

Rainie grinned; she couldn't help herself. 'The guy had just gotten out of prison. Released after serving thirty years for aggravated murder. Yeah, my mom knew how to pick 'em.'

'And apparently she knew how to make an impression,' Quincy added drolly, 'if the man was still thinking about her thirty years later.'

'Luke gave him the score. Ran a background check to be sure nothing was funny. Passed it along to me, and that's that.'

Quincy had that strange look on his face again. Rainie thought he might be about to say more, then he apparently changed his mind.

The waiter came with the bill. Quincy paid it. And just like old times, Rainie pretended it didn't bother her.

The sensible thing would've been to end the night there. Quincy had flown in, handed her some desperately needed business, and taken her out on the town. She should quit while she was ahead. But it was only seven o'clock, the temperature was just beginning to cool, and her ego still felt raw.

Rainie walked him through the Pearl District. Look at this gorgeous antique store, complete with a Porsche illegally parked out front. Here's another coffeehouse, here's an art gallery, here's a showroom for unique, handmade furniture. She led him by rows of recently converted warehouses, their facades now redone in creamy yellows and warm brick reds, modest exteriors for half-a-million-dollar condos and luxurious penthouse suites. People sat in tiny square gardens that dotted each front door. More than a few J. Crew-clad couples walked their prized black Labs down well-manicured streets.

Look at this place, Rainie thought. Look at me. Not bad for a small-town Bakersville girl.

Then she glanced down at her ripped-up shorts and ratty tank top, and that quickly, the euphoria left her. She wanted this world, with its pretty, pretty things. She hated this world, with its pretty, pretty things. She was thirty-two years old, and she still didn't know who she was or what she wanted out of life. It made her angry, but mostly with herself.

She made an abrupt about-face, and headed for the hills. After a confused moment, Quincy followed.

Touché was a local place. It had stood when poor college students were the only ones who found the declining warehouse district inhabitable. It would stand long after the SUV crowd got tired of cavernous lofts and fled for greener pastures. The downstairs of the building was a restaurant. Not bad. The upstairs was a pool hall. Much better.

Rainie handed over her driver's license and a wad of cash at the bar. In return, she got a rack of billiard balls, two cue sticks, and two Bud Lights. Quincy arched a brow, then took off his jacket. He wore the only suit in a dimly lit room filled with half a dozen bikers and two dozen college kids. He was now the fish out of water, and he knew it.

'Eight ball,' Rainie said. 'Junk balls count the same as a scratch. Hit the eight in first and you die.'

'I know the game,' he said evenly.

'I bet you do.' She racked up the balls, then handed him the cue stick to break. He offered her the first pleasant surprise by rolling the stick on the table to test for warp.

'Not bad,' he commented.

'They run a good show here. Now stop stalling and break.'

He was good. She'd expected that. In their time together, she hadn't found his weak spot yet, something that both irritated her and held her attention. But Rainie had been living in the Pearl District for four months now, and Touché was still the only place that felt like home. The tables were scuffed from use, the carpet well worn, the bar beat up. The place had taken its lickings, just like her.

Quincy hit two balls in on the break and went on a six-ball run before missing. Leonard, the bartender, stopped by long enough to watch, then shrugged indifferently. Touché attracted its fair share of pool sharks and he'd seen better.

Rainie took over with a swagger. She felt good now. Adrenaline in her veins, a pleasant hum in her ears. She was smiling. She could feel it on her face. A light was beginning to burn in Quincy's eyes. She could feel it on her bare arms as she bent over the table. His shirt collar was open, his sleeves rolled up. He had chalk on his hands and another light blue smudge on his cheek.

They were on dangerous ground now. She liked it.

'Corner pocket,' she said, and the game truly began.

They played for three hours. He won the first game when she got cute and tried to hop the cue ball over the eight. She missed. He won the second game when she got aggressive and tried a triple bank shot to close out the table. She missed again. Then she won the third, fourth, and fifth games by nailing those same shots and giving Quincy's meticulous nature something to consider.

'Give up yet?' she asked him.

'Just warming up, Rainie. Just warming up.'

She gave him a huge grin and returned to the table. Game six, he surprised her by exchanging some of his finesse for power. So he'd been holding out on her. It only made things more interesting.

He got her game six; they settled in for game seven.

'You've been playing a lot,' he observed halfway through a four-ball run. His tone was mild, but his brow was covered with a sheen of sweat and he was taking more time to line up his shots than he had in the beginning.

'I like it here.'

'It's a nice place,' he agreed. 'But for real pool, you need to go to Chicago.'

He went after the eight ball and missed. Rainie took the cue stick from him.

'Fuck Chicago,' she told him and cleared the felt-lined table.

'What now?' Quincy asked. He was breathing hard. She was, too. The room had grown hot. The hour was late. She was not so naïve that she missed the nuances in his question. She looked around inside, at the poor, beat-up room. She looked outside, where streetlights glowed charmingly. She thought of her beautiful, overpriced loft. She thought of her old fifties-style rancher in Bakersville and the soaring pine trees she still missed.

She looked at Quincy then, and . . .

'I should go home now,' she said.

'I thought as much.'

'I got a big job in the morning.'

'Rainie . . .'

'Nothing's really changed, has it? We can fool ourselves for a bit, but nothing's changed.'

'I don't know if anything changed, Rainie. I never knew what was wrong to begin with.'

'Not here.'

'Yes here! I understand what happened that last night. I know I didn't handle it as well as I could've. But I was willing to try again. Except next thing I knew, you were too busy to see me when I came into town, then you were so busy you couldn't even return a phone call. For God's sake, I know what you're going through, Rainie. I know it's not easy—'

'There you go again. Pity.'

'Understanding is not pity!'

'It's close enough!'

He closed his eyes. She could tell he was counting to ten so he wouldn't give in to impulse and strangle her. There was irony in that, because physical abuse was something she would have understood better and they both knew it.

'I miss you,' he said finally, quietly. 'Eight months later, I still miss you. And yes, I probably came here and offered you a job for that reason as much as anything—'

'I knew it!'

'Rainie, I won't miss you forever.'

The words hung in the air. She didn't pretend to misunderstand them. She thought of Bakersville again, the house she grew up in, that big back deck, those gorgeous towering pine trees. She thought of that one day fifteen years ago, then that one night, fifteen years ago, and she knew he must be thinking of them, too. Quincy had told her once that getting the truth out would set her free.

One year later, she wasn't so sure. She lived with the truth these days, and all she could think was that there were still so many things cluttering the space between.

'I should go home now,' she said again.

And he repeated, 'I thought as much.'

Rainie walked home alone. She turned on the lights of her cavernous loft alone. She took a cool shower, brushed her teeth, and climbed into bed alone.

She had a bad dream.

She was in a desert in Africa. She knew the place from some wildlife show she'd watched one night on the Discovery Channel. In her dream, she half recognized the scenes as part of that TV program, and half felt they were unfolding in real time in front of her.

The desert plains. A horrible drought. A baby elephant born to a sick, exhausted mother. He rose shakily to his feet, covered in goo. His mother sighed and passed away.

Sitting too far away to help, Rainie heard herself cry, 'Run little guy, run.' Though she didn't know yet why she was afraid.

The hour-old baby leaned against his mother, trying to nurse a corpse. Finally, he staggered away.

Rainie followed him through the desert. The air shimmered with heat, the hard-baked earth cracked beneath their feet. The orphaned elephant uttered little moans as he searched for food, for companionship. He came to a grove of sagging trees and rubbed his body against the thick trunks.

'*The newborn pachyderm mistakes the tree trunks for his mother's legs,*' Rainie heard an unseen narrator report. '*He rubs against them to announce his presence and seek comfort. When none comes, the exhausted creature continues his search for badly needed water in the midst of this savage drought.*'

'Run little guy, run,' Rainie whispered again.

The baby lurched forward. Hours passed. The baby began to stumble more. Collapsing into the unforgiving ground. Heaving himself back up and continuing on.

'*He must find water,*' the narrator droned. '*In desert life, water means the difference between life and death.*'

Suddenly, a herd of elephants appeared on the horizon. As they neared, Rainie could see other young calves running protectively in the shade of their mothers' bulk. When the herd paused, the babies stopped to nurse, and the mothers stroked them with their trunks.

She was relieved. Other elephants had arrived, the orphan would be saved.

The herd came closer. The baby ran to them, bleating his joy. And the head bull elephant stepped forward, picked up the infant with his trunk, and hurtled him away. The nine-hour-old baby landed hard. He didn't move.

The narrator commented again. '*It is not uncommon for a herd of elephants to adopt an orphan into its midst. The aggressive behaviour you see here is indicative of the severity of the drought. The herd is already under stress trying to sustain its own members, and thus is not willing to add to their group. Indeed, the bull elephant sees the newborn as a threat to his herd's survival and acts accordingly.*'

Rainie was trying to run to the downed infant. The desert grew broader, vaster. She couldn't get there. 'Run little guy, run.'

The baby finally stirred. He shook his head, climbed unsteadily to his feet. His legs trembled. She thought he was going to go down again, then he bowed his head, pulled himself together, and the shaking stopped.

The passing herd was still in sight. The baby ran after them.

A younger bull elephant turned, paused, then kicked the tiny form in the head. The baby fell back. Cried. Tried again. Two other male elephants turned. He ran to them. They slammed him to the ground. He staggered back up. They slammed him back down. The baby kept coming, crying, crying, crying. And they pummeled him into the hard, cracked earth. Then they turned and ponderously moved on.

'Run little guy, run,' Rainie whispered. She had tears on her cheeks.

The infant crawled wearily to his feet. There was blood on his head. Flies buzzed around the torn flesh. One of his eyes had swollen shut. Nine hours of life, all of it cruel, and still he fought to live another.

He took a step. Then one more. Step-by-step, he followed the main elephant herd, no longer bothering to cry and no longer getting near enough to be charged.

Three hours later, the sun sank low and the herd found a shallow pool of water. One by one, the elephants went into the water. According to the narrator, the newborn orphan was waiting for them to be done, then he would have his turn.

Rainie finally breathed easier. It was going to be all right now. The animals had found water, they would feel less threatened, they would help the orphan. He had persisted, and now everything would be all right. That's the way it works. You bear the unbearable. You earn the happily-ever-after.

She thought that right up to the moment when the jackals appeared and in front of the uncaring bull elephants, jumped on the overwhelmed newborn and methodically ripped him to shreds.

Rainie awoke with a start. The plaintive sounds of the

dying baby's cries were still ringing in her ears. Tears washed down her cheeks.

She got out of bed unsteadily. She walked through her darkened loft to the kitchen, where she poured herself a glass of water and took a long, long drink.

There was no sound in her loft. Three A.M., still, dark, empty. Her hands were trembling. Her body didn't feel as if it belonged to her.

And she wished . . .

She wished Quincy was here.

35

3

South Street, Philadelphia

Elizabeth Ann Quincy had aged well.

She'd been raised being told that a woman should always take care of herself. Plucked brows, coiffed hair, moisturized face. Then there was flossing, twice a day. Nothing aged you as fast as bacteria trapped in the gums.

Elizabeth had done as she was told. She plucked and coiffed and moisturized. She put on a dress to run errands. Off the tennis court, she never wore tennis shoes.

Elizabeth prided herself on playing by the rules. She'd grown up in an affluent family outside of Pittsburgh, riding English-style every weekend and practicing her jumps. By the age of eighteen, she could dance *Swan Lake* and crochet a tea cozy. She also knew how to use beer to set her dark brown hair in curlers and how to use a flatiron to straighten it out again. Girls today considered her generation frivolous. Let them stick their heads on ironing boards first thing every morning, and see if they still thought the same.

She had a tough streak. It had taken her to college when her mother had disapproved. While there, it had drawn her to a man quite outside of her family's experience – enigmatic

Pierce Quincy. He was from New England originally. Her mother had liked that. (*Mayflower* maybe? Does he still have ties to the motherland? He didn't. His father ran a farm in Rhode Island, owning hundreds of acres of land, and apparently few words or sentiments.) Quincy was pursuing a doctorate in psychology. Her mother had liked that, too. (An academic then, nothing wrong with that. Dr Quincy, yes very good. He'll settle down, open a private practice. There's a lot of money to be had in troubled minds, you know.)

Quincy had been drawn to troubled minds. In fact, it was his years on the Chicago police force that had convinced him to pursue dual degrees in criminology and psychology. Apparently, even more than the guns and testosterone inherent in police work, he was fascinated by the criminal mind. What made a deviant personality? When would the person first kill? How could he be stopped?

She and Pierce had had long talks on the subject. Elizabeth had been mesmerized by the clarity of his thoughts, the passion in his voice. He was a quiet, well-educated man and positively shocking in his ability to step into the shoes of a killer and assume his path.

The darkness of his work gave her a secret thrill. Watching his hands as he talked of psychopaths and sadists, picturing his fingers holding a gun . . . He was a thinker, but he was also a doer, and she had genuinely loved that.

In the beginning, when she had still thought they'd marry, settle down, and lead a normal life. In the beginning, before she'd realized that for a man like Pierce, there was no such thing as normal. He needed his work, he breathed his work, and she and their two little girls were the ones who became out of place in his world.

Elizabeth was the only member of her family to get a divorce, be a single mom. Her mother had not liked it, had told her to stick it out, but Elizabeth had found her tough streak again. She had Amanda and Kimberly to think about, and her daughters needed stability, some sort of sane suburban life where their father was not buzzed away from soccer games to look at corpses. Amanda, in particular, had had difficulties with her father's career. She never did understand why she only saw her dad when the homicidal maniacs were through for the day.

Elizabeth had done right by her children. She told herself that often these days. She'd done right by her children.

Even when she'd pulled the plug?

At the age of forty-seven, Elizabeth Ann Quincy was a beautiful woman. Cultured, sophisticated, and lonely.

This Monday evening she walked down South Street in Philadelphia, ignoring the laughing throngs of people who were enjoying the quirky mix of high-end boutiques and sex-toy shops. She bypassed three heavily tattooed teens, then sidestepped a long black limo. The horse-drawn carriages were out in full force tonight, adding the strong scent of horse manure to South Street's already distinct odor of human sweat and deep-fried food.

Bethie resolutely ignored the smell, while simultaneously refusing to make eye contact with any of her fellow Philadelphians. She just wanted to get back to her Society Hill town house, where she could retreat into a comforting shell of ecru-colored walls and silk-covered sofas. Another night alone with cable TV. Trying not to watch the phone. Trying not to wish too badly for it to ring.

She jostled against the man unexpectedly. He was walking out of the gourmet grocery store just as she was passing and knocked her square in the shoulder. One moment she was striding forward. The next she was falling sideways.

He grabbed her arm just before she hit the manure-splattered street.

'Oh, I'm so sorry. Clumsy, clumsy me. Here you go. Up again. Right as rain. You are okay, aren't you? I would hate to think I'd knocked the stuffing out of you.'

Elizabeth shook her head in a daze. She started the obligatory *I'm okay*, then actually saw the man who'd collided with her, and felt the words die in her throat. His face . . . Strong European features with merry blue eyes, while a generous dollop of silver capped the dark hair at his temples. Older, forties or fifties, she would guess. Well-to-do. The fine linen shirt, unbuttoned enough to reveal the distinctive column of his throat and a light smattering of graying chest hairs. The well-tailored tan slacks, belted by Gucci and finished with Armani loafers. He looked . . . He was gorgeous.

She was suddenly much more aware of his hand still on her arm. She started to babble. 'I wasn't looking . . . lost in my own little world . . . ran right into you. Not your fault, no apology necessary.'

'Elizabeth! Elizabeth Quincy.'

'What?' She peered up at him again, feeling even more flustered and not at all like herself. He was tall, very tall, broad shoulders, handsome. And an absolute stranger. She was sure of it.

'I'm sorry,' he said immediately. 'Here I go again, making a mess of things. I know you, but you don't know me.'

'I don't know you,' Bethie told him honestly. Her gaze fell to his hand, still on her arm. He belatedly released her, and to her surprise, he blushed.

'This is awkward now,' he stammered, obviously discon-
certed and somehow all the more charming for it. 'I don't
know quite what to say. Maybe I should never have
mentioned your name, never brought it up. Well, in for a
penny, in for a pound. I've seen you before, you see. Had
you pointed out to me. Last month. In Virginia. At the
hospital.'

It took Elizabeth a moment to put those facts together.
When she did, her whole body stilled. Her face paled. Her
arms wrapped around her waist defensively. If he'd been at
the hospital, had her pointed out . . . She thought she knew
where this was going now, and something inside her felt ice
cold. She closed her eyes. She swallowed thickly. She said,
'Maybe, maybe you'd better tell me your name.'

'Tristan. Tristan Shandling.'

'And how do you know me, Mr Shandling?'

His answer was as she feared. He didn't say a word. He
simply pulled his finely woven shirt from the waistband of
his slacks, and bared his right side to her.

The scar wasn't too big, just a few inches. It was still a
raw, angry red, fresh out of surgery. Give it another month
or two, however, and it would fade, the swelling would go
down. It would become a fine white line on a broad, tanned
torso.

She reached out a trembling hand without ever realizing
what she was doing, and touched the incision.

A sharp gasp brought her back to reality. She blinked her
eyes, then realized her hand was on a stranger's stomach and
he was still holding up his shirt for her and now people were
stopping to stare.

And she was crying. She hadn't realized it, but there were
tears on her cheeks.

'Your daughter saved my life,' Tristan Shandling said quietly.

Elizabeth Quincy broke down. She wrapped her arms around his waist; she pressed herself against the man who carried Mandy's kidney. And she held him as tight as she'd ever held her daughter, held him as if finding him would bring Mandy back to her. A mother should never have to bury her own child. She had pulled the plug. Oh God, she had given permission and they had taken her baby from her . . .

Tristan Shandling's arms went around her. In the middle of bustling South Street, he patted her shoulders awkwardly, then with more assurance. He let her cry against his chest and he said, 'Shhhh, it's all right. I'm here now, Bethie, and I'll take care of you. I promise.'

41

4

Pearl District, Portland

Rainie crawled out of bed at five A.M. Tuesday morning. To satisfy her masochistic streak for the day, she proceeded to run six miles in 90 percent humidity. Interestingly enough, she didn't die.

Upon returning home forty minutes later, she went straight into an ice cold shower where she wondered idly what Virginia would be like.

She'd never left the state of Oregon. Every now and then, she'd thought of taking a trip to Seattle, but it never quite happened, so now at the age of thirty-two she was a complete neophyte to the broader United States. She wasn't the only Oregonian like that either. Oregon was a big state. It offered beaches, mountains, deserts, lakes, upscale cities, and small frontier towns. You could gamble, windsurf, rock climb, ski, hike, sunbathe, shop, golf, sail, fish, race, white-water raft, and horseback ride, sometimes almost all at the same resort. So sure you could visit other states, but what would be the point?

She toweled off, chose loose-fitting cotton clothes for the plane, then officially kicked off her new assignment by coughing up two thousand dollars for a last-minute flight across the country. The car rental agency had even more fun with her credit card. Thank God for AmEx.

Her next issue was how to conduct business out of state. As a private investigator, she didn't technically have jurisdictional boundaries. Most state agencies, however, required a local PI license number on all requests for information. Thus, if she wanted to pull DMV records, conduct a title search, anything in Virginia, she'd be out of luck. On the other hand, this was hardly a new problem in the business, and PIs had worked out a way around it.

Rainie pulled out her *Private Investigator Digest*, located a PI in Virginia and gave the guy a call. Fifteen minutes later, after providing her Oregon license number for credibility and explaining her mission, Rainie had a pseudo-partner. She'd pass along her information requests to Virginian PI Phil de Beers, who'd pull the records in return for a nominal fee. The sixteen hundred dollars it had cost her to be licensed had now paid off.

Rainie packed three days' worth of clothes and, given her last case with Quincy, threw in her stainless-steel Glock. She headed out the door.

Three hours later, airborne and finally relaxed enough to let go of the armrests, Rainie read the official report of Amanda Jane Quincy's death.

The first officer at the scene was a Virginia state trooper, responding to a call made from the cell phone of a passing trucker. The call was logged at 5:52 A.M., and the caller, who was very shaken, reported seeing a body along the side of the road. When he'd stopped, he found an older man whom he thought was dead, a small dog that was definitely dead, and deeper in the underbrush, a Ford Explorer crumpled against a telephone pole. Steam still poured out of the smashed hood. The caller said he'd tried to verbally rouse the driver without success. He didn't attempt to touch or move her, however, as he thought that was a bad thing to do in a car accident – might cause further injury.

The trucker was still at the scene when the state trooper arrived. He led the officer straight to the pedestrian, whom the state trooper agreed was DOA. They moved on to the Explorer, where the state trooper was able to force open the driver-side door and check the female motorist for a pulse. He found signs of life, which he passed along to dispatch, while the trucker, having finally seen the full extent of damage to the woman's head, turned around and threw up.

In the good news department, the report provided a great number of details, mostly thanks to the state trooper beating EMS to the scene. As Rainie knew from her own experience, no one ruined a crime scene faster than EMTs, except maybe firemen.

She studied the Polaroids, as well as a small diagram indicating where the pedestrian and dog were found, and then the position of the vehicle against the utility pole. Records showed the vehicle to be a green 1994 Ford Explorer, registered to Amanda Jane Quincy, and purchased used three years earlier. It was a no-frills model, lacking automatic transmission, and more unfortunately for Mandy, a driver-side airbag.

At the time of the crash, the driver was not wearing her seat belt. According to a note made by the trooper, it was found to be 'nonoperative'. Rainie didn't know what that meant and when she flipped through the pages, she didn't find any follow-up notes.

A designated auto-accident investigator had not been called, which disappointed her. In Oregon, the state police had a separate unit that specialized in analyzing and reconstructing motor vehicle accidents (MVAs). Either Virginia didn't have one, or they didn't feel it was necessary in this case. At least the trooper had run through the basics. No sign of skid marks going into the curve, indicating that the driver never made an attempt to brake. No signs of damage or paint on the rear or side of the Explorer, which would've signaled the involvement of another vehicle. No signs of other tire tracks or impressions at the scene.

The trooper's conclusion was blunt: Single-car accident, at-fault driver lost control of vehicle, check for drugs and alcohol.

At the emergency room, the trooper got to add to his summary: Blood tests confirm blood alcohol level of .20. At-fault driver sustained massive head injury, not expected to live.

The file contained no more notes. The at-fault driver had never regained consciousness to be presented with criminal charges. Over a year later, she'd died. Case closed.

Rainie felt a chill.

She put away the notes, though the photos remained in her hands. Pictures of that poor man, out walking his dog. Pictures of the poor fox terrier who hadn't had a long enough leash. Pictures of the twisted front end of a massive vehicle, which had crumpled like paper upon impact.

The EMTs had whisked Mandy to the emergency room, sparing everyone those images. The state trooper had captured the front windshield, however, including the shattered upper left quadrant, which bore a macabre mold of Amanda Quincy's face.

Quincy had studied these photos. Rainie wondered how long it had taken him to look away.

45

She sighed. The report didn't give her much hope. No evidence of any other vehicles involved. The lack of braking, which might bother an untrained investigator, was also consistent with DUI incidents. Also, no evidence of anyone else at the scene. The state trooper had written up a straightforward report, and at this juncture, Rainie had to agree.

But there was the issue of how Mandy came to be drunk at five-thirty in the morning when her friends had seen her sober just three hours before. And there was the 'nonoperative' seat belt that had turned what should have been a survivable crash into tragedy. Finally, there was the mystery man, the supposed love of Amanda Quincy's life, whom no one had ever met.

'Still not much of a case,' she murmured. But Quincy must be getting to her, because she no longer sounded convinced.

Greenwich Village, New York City

Kimberly August Quincy was having one of those spells again. She stood on the corner of Washington Square in the heart of New York University's campus. The sun was shining brightly. The sky gleamed a vast, vast blue. The grass around the square's signature arch was a deep, deep green. Residents strolled by, tidy in trendy suits and tiny John Lennon sunglasses. Summer students clad in ripped denim shorts and shrink-wrapped tank tops lay out on the green, ostensibly doing homework, but half of them sound asleep.

A nice July afternoon. A safe, charming place, even by New York City standards.

Kimberly was breathing too hard. Panting. She had a bag, once slung over her shoulder, now in a death grip in her hands. She had been on her way somewhere. She couldn't remember where. Sweat poured down her face.

A man in a business suit walked briskly down the sidewalk. He glanced casually at her, then came to a halt.

'Are you all right?'

'Go . . . away.'

'Miss—'

'*Go away!*'

The man hurried away, shaking his head and no doubt sorry he'd tried to do a good deed in New York when everyone knew the city was full of nuts.

Kimberly wasn't nuts. Not yet at least. The logical part of her mind, which had taken enough psych classes to know, understood that. She was having an anxiety attack. Had been having them, in fact, for months now.

She'd go days, even weeks, when everything was perfectly normal. She'd just wrapped up her junior year at NYU and with two summer courses, an internship with her criminology professor, and volunteer work at a homeless shelter, she had places to go and people to see. Out the door at six forty-five A.M. Rarely home before ten P.M. She liked things that way.

And then . . .

A strange sensation at first. A tingle running up her spine. A prickle at the nape of her neck. She'd find herself stopping abruptly, halfway down a street. Or whirling around sharply in the middle of a crowded subway. She'd look for . . . She didn't know what she looked for. She'd just suffer the acute sensation that someone was watching. Someone she couldn't see.

Then it would go away as swiftly as it had come. Her pulse would calm, her breathing ease. She'd be fine again. For a few days, a few weeks, and then . . .

It had been worse since the funeral. At times almost hourly, then she'd get two or three days to catch her breath before bam, she'd step onto the subway and the world would close in on her again.

Logically she supposed it made sense. She'd lost her sister, was battling with her mother, and God knows what was going on with her father. She'd consulted Dr Marcus Andrews, her criminology professor, and he'd assured her it was probably stress related.

'Ease up a little,' he'd advised her. 'Give yourself some time to rest. What you don't accomplish at twenty-one, you can always accomplish at twenty-two.'

They both knew she wouldn't slow down, though. It wasn't her style. As her mother loved to tell her, Kimberly was too much like her father. And in many ways that made the anxiety attacks even worse, because just like her dad, Kimberly had never been afraid of anything.

She remembered being eight years old and going to some local fair with her father and her older sister. She and Mandy had been so excited. A whole afternoon alone with Daddy, plus cotton candy and rides. They could barely contain themselves.

They'd gone on the Tilt-A-Whirl, and the spider, and the Ferris wheel. They'd eaten caramel apples, two bags of popcorn and washed it down with well-iced Coke. Then, positively buzzing with sugar and caffeine, they'd rounded up their dad to continue the adventure.

Except their father wasn't paying attention to them anymore. He was studying some man who stood off to the side by the kiddy rides. The man wore a long, grubby overcoat and Kimberly vividly remembered Mandy crinkling her nose and saying, 'Oooh, what smells?'

Their father gestured for them to be quiet. They took one look at the intent expression on his face and didn't dare disobey.

The strange man had a camera around his neck. As they all watched, he took picture after picture of little kids on the rides.

'He's a pedophile,' their father murmured. 'This is how he starts. With photos, lots of photos of what he wants but can't have. He's still fighting it, or he'd have his own stash of porn by now and not be into fully dressed targets. He's fighting it, but he's losing the war. So he's setting himself up to be a situational offender. Going places where there are lots of children. Then when he finally gives in to his depravity, he'll tell himself it was their fault. The kids made him do it.'

Standing beside Kimberly, Mandy faltered. She looked at the strange man, snapping away furiously, and her lower lip began to tremble.

Their father continued, 'If you ever see someone like him, girls, don't be afraid to leave the area. Always trust your instincts. Head straight to the nearest security booth, or if you feel that's too far away, duck in behind a woman walking with children. He'll assume she's your mother, too, and give up the chase.'

'What are you going to do?' Kimberly asked him breathlessly.

'I'm going to pass along his description to security. Then I'm going to come back here tomorrow and the day after that and the day after that. If he's still coming around, we'll find an excuse to arrest him. That'll at least give him pause.'

'I want to go home!' Mandy wailed and started to cry.

Kimberly looked at her older sister without comprehension. Then she turned back to her father, who was sighing at having set off good old Mandy again. Kimmy didn't blame him. Mandy always got upset. Mandy always cried. But not Kimberly.

She gazed up at her father proudly, and in September, when her new teacher asked each child what her parents did for a living, Kimberly declared that her daddy was Superman. The other kids teased her for months. She never did recant.

Her father protected happy children from horrible strange men. Someday, she wanted to do that, too.

Except for this afternoon, when she merely wanted her pulse to slow and her breathing to ease and the bright spots in front of her eyes to disappear. Dr Andrews had suggested trying biofeedback. She did that now, focusing on her hands and imagining them getting warm, warmer, hot.

The world slowly opened up. The sky became blue again, the grass green, the streets bustling. The hair was no longer standing up at the nape of her neck. The sweat cooled on her brow.

Kimberly finally relaxed her grip on her book bag. She let herself conduct a slow, sweeping circle of everything around her.

'See now,' she murmured to herself. 'Everyone's just going about their business, having a perfectly usual day. There's no one watching, there's nothing to fear. It's all in your head, Kimmy. It's all in your head.'

She resumed walking, but at the intersection she hesitated again. She paused. She turned. She felt that chill. And even though it was a hot July day. Even though she was smart and rational and the strong member of the Quincy family, she started running and she didn't stop for a long, long time.

5

Driving through Quantico, Quincy approached the FBI Academy's guard post, located behind the Marines' facilities, and finally slowed his car. He waited for the young security officer to spot his identifying window sticker, then nodded when the officer signaled for him to proceed. Quincy waved his thanks, but didn't take it personally when the security officer remained grim. It was the guard's job to appear intimidating at all times, he knew. On the other hand, it made an interesting start of work each day.

Not much of a sleeper, Quincy had risen at three A.M. to drive to Seattle and catch a direct flight to DC. He'd spent so many years flying all over the country that layovers had become unbearable to him and he'd do just about anything to hasten the trip. Cars, he liked, and his new thing was to avoid planes altogether and drive. He'd thought that might change after Mandy's accident. It hadn't.

Reaching the outdoor lot next to the firing ranges, Quincy parked his car, then walked across the street to the back entrance of the building. He swiped his security card through the electronic reader. It graciously let him in.

Taking the stairs down two flights to the BSU offices, he passed a fellow agent. Quincy nodded in greeting. Special Agent Deacon nodded back while judiciously avoiding his gaze. It had been like that for the last four weeks; Quincy barely noticed anymore. His daughter had died tragically, which was awkward in the best of circumstances, let alone when you worked with people who made their living trying to thwart, and thus control, untimely death. Quincy now stood as a reminder that bad things could happen close to home, that crime-scene photos weren't always of some stranger's daughter. How rude of him to show his face in the office and rock their carefully compartmentalized worlds. Quincy had even heard rumblings that he was wrong to have gone from Mandy's funeral straight to work. What kind of father could be so cold?

He didn't bother addressing those comments. When their own children died, they could figure it out for themselves.

Quincy opened the metal fire door and walked into the BSU offices.

Contrary to Hollywood images, the offices at the FBI Academy were purely functional, and the BSU offices even more so than most. Located in the second sublevel below the facility's indoor firing range, the walls were comprised of cinder blocks painted an appropriate bone-white. As the offices were carved deep into the earth, there were no windows.

The office of the Special Agent in Charge sat in the middle; the remaining offices formed a square perimeter around it. The floor plan reminded Quincy of most major prisons – central control office surrounded by maximum-security cells. Maybe the powers-that-be figured the ambience would help them enter the criminal mind.

The BSU boasted one impressive feature. Its state-of-the-art technology room, closely resembling a TV studio, enabled the agents to do teleconferencing as well as make major presentations with as many bells and whistles as the individual agent could dream up. It always amused Quincy that his working space could be so dull, and his speaking space so sleek. The Bureau did have its priorities.

Quincy hadn't always worked with the BSU. He was one of the rare agents who'd crossed an unspoken line by going from the Child Abduction/Serial Killer Unit (CASKU) to the BSU years ago. It made him something of a novelty in both worlds. An academic who'd entered the glamorous world of profiling, to a glamorous profiler who'd entered the academic world of behavioral science. Both sides used his work. Neither side knew what to make of him.

He hadn't told anyone yet, not even Rainie, but he was considering rocking the boat once more. A month ago, he'd been approached about switching again. He would join what was now called the National Center for Analysis of Violent Crime (NCAVC) as a profiler. At nearly the age of fifty, he would resume working active cases and return to the field.

Honestly, he'd missed it.

When Quincy had first joined the Bureau, he'd told himself he was doing it for the greater good. He'd spent two years as a private-practice psychologist, and while the money was good (Bethie's concern) and the work was interesting (his concern), it left him feeling restless. He'd quit policing to pursue an advanced degree because he felt it was psychology that held his primary interest. Now, he discovered that he genuinely missed detecting. The thrill of the chase, the camaraderie of fellow police officers, the comforting weight of his gun. When a friend in the Bureau approached him later that year, it wasn't a hard sale.

The next thing Quincy knew, he was working one hundred and twenty cases a year. He routinely traveled to four cities in five days. He carried a briefcase filled with photographs of the most savage crimes imaginable. He gave advice that saved lives, and sometimes, he missed clues that cost lives.

While his girls grew up. And his marriage fell apart. And the man who'd once testified in custody hearings was so knee-deep in dead bodies he was the last one to see it coming.

By the time Jim Beckett broke out of a Massachusetts prison by slaughtering two prison guards, Quincy was already a walking advertisement for burnout. By the end of that case, when he was done burying the bodies of various law enforcement officers he'd known and respected, he knew it was time for a change.

He'd transferred to the BSU where he could scale back his travel schedule and make more time for his daughters. He'd missed their childhood. Now, he belatedly tried to catch their high school years.

He designed and taught classes at Quantico while watching soccer games and school plays. He took up researching past cases, including the notorious child killer Russell Lee Holmes, for entry into the FBI's database. He attended Mandy's graduation from high school. He revisited the cold case files, examining records of serial killers who had never been caught. He helped Kimberly select the right college. He created a checklist for identifying potential mass murderers. He got a call to come to a hospital in Virginia, where he watched his older daughter die.

Time had given Quincy regrets. It had also taught him

honesty. He understood now that he no longer did what he did to save the world. He worked as an agent for the same reason people worked as accountants and lawyers and corporate clerks. Because he was good at it. Because he liked the challenge. Because when the job was done right, he felt good about himself.

He had not been the husband he had wanted to be. He had not been the father he had hoped to be. Last year, however, he'd connected three mass murders that local officials had thought were one-off crimes.

He was a damn good agent. And year by year, he was working on becoming a better person. He had honestly tried connecting with Mandy not long before the accident. He was definitely trying to connect with Kimberly now, though she seemed hell-bent on ignoring his calls. Last month, he'd even gone to the Rhode Island nursing home and spent an afternoon with his eighty-year-old father, who was so stricken with Alzheimer's that he didn't recognize Quincy anymore and had started the visit by ordering Quincy to go away. Quincy had stayed. Eventually, Abraham Quincy had stopped yelling. Then, they sat in silence, and Quincy worked on remembering the other moments that they had shared, because he knew his father could not.

Quincy was learning the hard way that isolation was not protection, that no number of crime scenes ever prepared you for the death of your own child, and that no matter how many nights passed, it was never any easier to sleep alone.

Rainie had once accused him of being too polite. He had told her that there was enough ugliness in the world without him having to add to it, and he'd meant it.

He had genuinely loved Mandy.

And he was so sorry now that she never knew.

Virginia

When Rainie's plane touched down at Ronald Reagan National Airport, she felt a little giddy. She grabbed her bag from the overhead compartment, collected the small suitcase containing her Glock .40 from baggage claim, and proceeded straight to the car rental agency where she secured the world's tiniest economy car without a hitch. Not bad for her first trip – Dirty Harry, eat your heart out.

Her stomach was rumbling; she hadn't trusted the mystery meat they'd tried to serve her on the plane. It was already four o'clock however, rush hour traffic would be a bear, and she didn't want to miss the change of shifts at the state police barracks. Dinner would have to wait.

She headed straight for the Virginia state police station that had handled Mandy's case, and hoped she got lucky.

An hour and a half of cursing and swearing later, she found state trooper Vince Amity just striding out the door.

'Officer Amity?' she called out, as the desk sergeant waved vaguely in his direction, then went back to reading the latest edition of the *FBI Law Enforcement Bulletin*.

The officer in question paused, realized he was being waved down by an attractive young woman, and halted with more interest.

Rainie seized the opportunity to give him her most charming smile. The smile didn't get much practice, but it must have been good enough because Officer Amity walked back toward her. At six five, he was a big boy with broad shoulders, thick neck, and a jawline only Jay Leno would love. Rainie was guessing Swedish ancestors and football. Lots of football.

'Can I help you, ma'am?' Big Boy had a southern drawl.

Damn, she liked that. Before things got all warm and cuddly, however, Rainie flashed her PI's license. Officer Amity's face promptly fell. Another fine romance nipped in the bud.

'I have some questions regarding an MVA homicide,' she started off. 'You worked the case about a year ago.'

No response.

'The case is closed now – driver died at the hospital, but I'm clarifying some of the details for the family.'

Officer Amity said, 'I gotta go on patrol now.'

'Great. I'll go with you.'

'No, ma'am. Civilians can't accompany officers on patrol. Too much liability.'

'I won't sue.'

'Ma'am—'

'Officer. Look, I flew all the way here from Portland, Oregon, to get answers to my questions. The sooner you start talking, the sooner we can both move on with our lives.'

Officer Amity scowled. Given his size, the look really worked for him. Rainie figured the minute he stepped out of his patrol car, most perps dropped obediently to the pavement and held out their wrists for the bracelets. As a woman, she'd never had his advantage. She'd had to wrestle most of her hostiles to the ground. The thing about that, however, was it meant she'd built her career by always being ready for a fight.

Officer Amity was still working the scowl. She folded her arms. Waited. Waited. Big Boy caved with a sigh.

'Let me check in with dispatch,' he said. 'Then I'll meet you at my desk.'

Rainie nodded. Not being a dummy, she followed him to dispatch – police stations had back doors. Five minutes later, they sat across from each other at a beat-up desk, both armed with hot cups of coffee, and got into it.

'April twenty-eight,' Rainie said. 'Last year. Single-car accident. SUV versus man walking a dog versus a telephone pole. The SUV got the man and dog. The telephone pole got the SUV. Kind of like an obscene version of rock, paper, scissors.'

'Female driver?'

'Yep, Amanda Jane Quincy. The accident put her in a coma. Last month, her family pulled the plug. I have a copy of the police report right here.'

Officer Amity closed his eyes. 'Her father's the fed, right?'

'There you go.'

'I should have known,' he muttered, and sighed again, a rumbling sound deep in his chest. He opened his desk, drew out a spiral notebook bearing last year's date, and began flipping through the pages.

Rainie waited for him to refresh his memory with his personal notations, then plunged in. 'You were the only officer at the scene?'

'Yes, ma'am.'

'Why?'

'Everybody was pretty much dead. There's not a whole lot police officers can do about that.'

'The driver wasn't dead. Plus, you have at least one fatality and preliminary signs that the driver was operating a vehicle while impaired. In Oregon, that's already the makings of neg homicide if not manslaughter. Surely that's worth calling out a traffic investigation team.'

Officer Amity shook his head. 'Ma'am, with all due respect, the driver wasn't wearing a seat belt. She'd hit the rim of the windshield and lost half her brain. While she might not have been DOA, even I could tell it was only a matter of time. Now I don't know how it is in Oregon, but in Virginia it doesn't do us any good to build the case when we got no one left alive to charge with the crime.'

Rainie eyed him shrewdly. She said two words. 'Budget cuts.'

Amity's eyes widened in surprise. He nodded slowly, studying her with fresh interest. In most states, the minute an accident involves a fatality, particularly a pedestrian fatality, an accident investigation team will be called out regardless of the condition of the driver. But in the wonderful world of policing, accident investigation teams were the first to feel the sting of budget cuts, even though police officers spent the majority of their time dealing with MVAs and not homicides. Apparently, society couldn't stand the thought of death by stranger, but demise by automobile was okay. Merely the cost of living in the modern age.

'Tell me about the seat belt.' Rainie switched gears.

'She wasn't wearing one.'

'In the report, it says the strap was "nonoperative." What does that mean?'

Amity frowned, scratched his head, and flipped through his notes. 'When I was checking for a pulse, I brushed against the seat belt and it pooled out onto the floor. No tension. Gears probably busted.'

'The seat belt was defective?'

'It was nonoperative.'

'No kidding.' Rainie's voice gained an edge. 'Why was it nonoperative?'

'I haven't the foggiest idea,' Amity drawled evenly.

'You didn't examine it, disassemble it? Come on, Officer, if that seat belt had been working, it might have saved the driver's life. That ought to make it worth some attention.'

'A defective seat belt is a civil, not criminal, matter, ma'am. Being underworked cops with an unlimited budget, we would love to focus on things outside of our jurisdiction, of course, but that would entail spitting in the face of standard investigative procedures.'

Rainie blinked twice, then scowled when she finally detected the sarcasm underlining his amiable drawl. Here was the difference between formal and informal police practices, she thought not for the first time. If she'd come across an accident like Mandy's when she'd been a small-town cop, she would've checked out the seat belt. But small sheriff's departments didn't rigidly follow things like standard investigative procedures. Hell, half of their volunteer staff probably couldn't spell investigative, let alone procedures.

'I made a phone call,' Officer Amity said abruptly. His face remained expressionless, but his voice dropped, as if he were about to confess a sin.

'About the seat belt?' As long as they were being coconspirators, Rainie lowered her voice, too.

'I didn't like the fact that lack of seat belt made it a fatality,' Amity said, 'and it just so happened that the seat belt was broken. So I called the garage that serviced the Explorer. Seems that the broken seat belt wasn't new; it happened a month before. The driver called about having it replaced. Even made an appointment. But she never came in.'

'When was the appointment?'

'A week before the crash.'

'Did the garage know why she canceled?'

'She called to say something had come up, she'd

reschedule shortly.' He shrugged. 'So now we got a driver running around for four weeks without a proper harness system. Then she crawls behind the wheel dead drunk. I don't know about suspicious, ma'am, but in my book the accident is looking stupider all the time.'

Rainie chewed her bottom lip. 'I still don't like the *nonoperative* seat belt.'

'Makes Daddy nervous,' Officer Amity shrewdly guessed.

'Something like that. What about the pedestrian victim, the old man?'

'Oliver Jenkins. Lived one mile from the crash site. According to his wife, he always walked his dog along the road and she always told him it was dangerous.'

'Any chance this had something to do with him?'

'Mr Jenkins was a retired Korean War vet. He lived on a small pension from the state and loved butter pecan ice cream. No, I don't think he did anything to deserve being run over by a Ford Explorer. The dog, on the other hand, had a long history of eating shoes.'

Big Boy's face remained so impassive, Rainie almost missed the sarcasm again. Were all Southern boys so charming, or was she just in for a special treat?

'No sign of braking,' she tried, still working the suspicious angle.

'Never met a drunk who did.'

'Could've gotten tapped by a second vehicle,' she rallied.

'No fresh scratches, dents, or paint chips on the SUV. No marks on the tire walls. No additional sets of tire tracks. Look at your photos, *ma'am*.'

Rainie scowled. Competent policemen could be such a pain in the ass. 'What about a second person in the vehicle? A passenger?'

'I didn't see one.'

'Did you look?'

'I looked in the passenger's seat. There was no one there.'

'Did you dust for prints?'

Amity rolled his eyes. 'What the hell would you gain by printing a car? First off, the dashboards and most side panels are too rough to yield a print. Second, the smooth surfaces that would work, such as seat belt clasps, door handles, or steering wheels, have been handled by so many Tom, Dick, and Harrys, you'd never get clean ridges. Again, I refer you to standard investigative procedures—'

'I get the point. You're the greatest police officer that ever lived and there is no evidence of a second person at the scene.'

'Why, yes ma'am, I think we're finally in agreement.'

Rainie smiled thinly at him. Then she leaned forward. 'Did you happen to try the passenger-side door?'

Amity's eyes narrowed. She knew he followed her train of thought, because he started to nod. 'As a matter of fact . . .'

'The door was operable, wasn't it?'

'Yes ma'am.'

'And you looked down for footprints?'

'Too much undergrowth. Couldn't get a sign of anything.'

'But you were looking, Officer. Why were you looking?'

Officer Amity grew silent. He said finally, 'I don't know.'

'Off the record.'

'I don't know.'

'Way off the record. You followed up on this case, Officer, even after you knew the driver was dying. As you kindly pointed out, you state boys are much too overworked to randomly do such a thing. Something bothered you.

Something's still bothering you. I'm even willing to bet that you're not that surprised I'm here.'

Officer Amity remained silent. Just when she thought he was going to continue to play hard to get, he said suddenly, 'I didn't think I was alone.'

'What?'

His lips thinned. He continued in a rush. 'I was standing at the vehicle staring at that poor, poor girl and this guy is puking out his guts behind me and I swore . . . I swore to God I heard someone laughing.'

'*What?*'

'Maybe it was all in my head. Jesus, the sun wasn't all the way up yet and it gets kind of hinky on those rural routes. All the trees and brush, half of it hasn't been cleared in the last fifty years. Million and a half places for someone to hide, if they had the mind to. I looked around, checked things out. Never saw a thing. Probably was all in my head. The puking Samaritan didn't help much either. He almost got my leg.'

'I want to see the car.'

'Good luck.'

'Come on, just a quick peek in the impound lot.'

Amity shook his head. 'It's been fourteen months. Sure the vehicle started in our lot, but only until the insurance company settled. They took it away months ago, probably towed it to some salvage yard where it's already been broken down for parts.'

'Shit,' Rainie muttered. She worried her lower lip again, not expecting this and trying to think of more options. 'I thought there was some rule that seat belts from a wrecked vehicle couldn't be resold as parts. They're no longer guaranteed after the first accident.'

'Yes, ma'am.'

'So in theory, the salvage yard should at least still have the seat belts.'

He shrugged. 'If they haven't tossed them into a dumpster by now.'

'I'll take my chances. Name of the salvage yard?'

'Hell if I know. The insurance company handles all that.'

'Officer . . .'

She gave him an intent look. He sighed heavily. 'I suppose I could make a call . . .'

Rainie summoned her charming smile again. Officer Amity was a smart boy, though, because this time he merely grunted and shook his head.

'You should've opened with that, you know,' he told her.

'With what?'

'That you used to be a cop.'

'I was just a local. I'm surprised you could even tell.'

'I got a good head for these things.'

She nodded grimly. 'Yeah, that's what I'm afraid of.'

6

Society Hill, Philadelphia

Bethie was nervous. She shouldn't be doing this. She liked her solitary lifestyle; she was comfortable spending her evenings alone. What had she been thinking? And did these earrings go with this dress? Maybe the earrings were too nice. Maybe the dress was too nice. Oh God, she was going to have to start over again and she was already five minutes late.

She changed from her little black dress to a below-the-knees black skirt with an electric blue satin top. More coverage; she liked that. But she kept the same tall, strappy heels. At her age she was proud of her calves and figured it didn't hurt to show them off. God knows she had a few extra pounds tucked in other locations, let alone what gravity had done to her butt. She had aged well, but on the eve of her first date in over two years, she still felt bitter about Father Time. How is it that men fill out with age, while women fall down?

Earrings. Which pair of earrings? Come on, Bethie, it's just a date. She grabbed the first gold pair she came to, told herself firmly that they were perfect and headed for the door.

She had not expected to have dinner with Mr Shandling. It had started out as coffee yesterday evening. He felt so bad at having upset her, and she was too topsy-turvy to resist. So he took her to one of South Street's little cafés, plied her with cappuccino, and told her stories until the tears dried on her cheeks and she began to smile.

She stopped looking at his side so much. She started listening to his words more. Tales of travel to Ireland, England, Austria. Scuba diving off the coral reefs of Australia, shopping for precious gems in Hong Kong. He had a rich baritone voice, perfect for spinning fabulous tales and in the end, while she wasn't sure if one man could have really done all those things, she found that she didn't care. She liked listening to him talk. She liked watching the corner of his sparkling blue eyes crinkle every time he grinned. She liked the way he looked at her, as if his sole purpose in life was to make her happy.

He'd asked her to dinner the very next night. She hemmed and hawed. It was moving so fast, she really didn't know . . .

He was only in town for a week. Surely one dinner couldn't hurt . . . She'd caved in with a yes. He'd chosen Zanzibar Blue, a renowned jazz club and one of her favorite restaurants. She'd promised to meet him there.

Bethie was not a complete neophyte to dating; she read *Cosmo*. On a first date, always arrive on your own, therefore you can leave anytime you choose. Don't give out too much personal information, such as your home address, right away. Get to know the person first. Just because a man was well dressed and charming didn't mean he was safe. Just ask her ex-husband, Pierce.

Bethie flagged down a taxi, and took the short ride up to Zanzibar's.

Tristan Shandling was waiting for her outside the club. Tonight he wore black pleated slacks with a plum-colored shirt and strikingly patterned silver and turquoise tie. In deference to the hot, muggy weather, he'd eschewed a jacket. With his hands tucked comfortably into his pockets, one foot crossed over the other, he looked dignified, handsome, and totally in control. Bethie took one look at him and promptly wished she'd gone with the little black dress. This man shouldn't be dating some middle-aged mother. A man like him should be meeting some bubble-gum blonde, some little bit of arm candy.

She got out of the cab, self-consciously fingering her matronly skirt. Tristan turned, spotted her, and promptly beamed. 'Elizabeth! I'm so happy you made it.'

For the life of her, she couldn't think of a thing to say. She stood there silently, clutching her small black purse while his eyes crinkled and he held out his arm to her. Her breath had caught in her chest.

He was still smiling, his blue eyes patient and kind. He knew, she realized abruptly. He understood that she was nervous and by grinning so effusively, he was trying to make things easier for her.

'I'm sorry I'm late,' she managed.

He waved away her apology, taking her hand and tucking it into the crook of his elbow. He patted her fingers, which she knew must feel like ice. 'Jazz is my favorite,' he told her amiably as he escorted her to the doors and the first notes of bluesy horns washed over them. 'I hope you don't mind.'

'I love jazz,' she volunteered. 'It's always been my favorite as well.'

'Really? Davis or Coltrane?'

'Davis.'

Lisa Gardner

' "'Round Midnight" or "Kind of Blue"?'
' "'Round Midnight," of course.'
'Ahh, I knew from the first moment I saw you that you were a woman of impeccable taste. Of course, then you agreed to go out with me and cast my whole theory in doubt.' He winked.

She found herself finally smiling back. 'Well, there's no rule that says you can't enjoy water as well as wine,' she said more gamely.

'Dear heavens, have I just been insulted?'

'I don't know. Depends if you're water or wine. I guess I have the whole evening to find out.'

'Elizabeth,' he said heartily, 'we are going to have a smashing good evening!'

And she said with the first real emotion she'd felt in months, 'Honestly, I would like that.'

Later, over plates of steaming mussels and vegetarian pasta, and a bottle of a very fine Bordeaux, she asked the question that was burning in her mind.

'Does it hurt?' Her eyes drifted to his right side. She didn't have to say more for him to understand.

Slowly, he nodded. 'Not as bad as it did, though. Just no more jumping jacks for a while.'

'But you're feeling better?'

He smiled at her. 'I was born with two bad kidneys, love. The first one failed when I was eighteen. The second one started going last year. I spent sixteen long months on dialysis. That felt bad. Now, as far as I am concerned, things can only feel good.'

'Is there . . . is there still a chance of rejection?'

'In life, love, and organ transplants. But I take my

68

truckload of meds like a good dooby and say my prayers at night. I don't know why God gives second chances to old rascals like me, but as long as I have one, I hate to complain.'

'Your family must be very relieved.'

He smiled again, but this time she caught a trace of sorrow in his gaze. 'I don't have much family, Bethie. One older brother. He went away a long time ago and I haven't seen him since. There was a woman once. She said she carried my child. I was young though, and I'm afraid I didn't take it too well. When I learned I needed a kidney – well, that hardly seemed the time to call. I don't have patience for fair-weather friends, let alone fair-weather fathers.'

'I'm sorry,' she said honestly. 'I didn't mean to dredge up bad times.'

'Not to worry. I've made my mistakes and taken my licks and I still think a quiet life is overrated. I'm going to die with my boots on.' He grimaced. 'Probably once again hooked to a dialysis machine.'

'Don't say that. You've come this far. Besides, you still have plenty of things to do. Like finding your child.'

'You think I'm going to find my long-lost child?'

'Yes.'

'Why?'

'Because you brought it up in a conversation with a woman you've just met, so obviously you've been thinking about it.'

He grew silent. His fingers thrummed the curve of his wineglass. He said seriously, 'You're an extremely astute woman, Elizabeth Quincy.'

'No, I'm just a parent, too.'

'Ah, I don't know . . .' He backed off from the conversation, picking up his glass and taking a sip. 'I don't even know if the child is a boy or girl, let alone if it's mine. And even at my age . . . I'm running around the world most of the time. Hardly father-of-the-year material.'

'What is it you do?'

'I specialize in doohickeys.'

'Doohickeys?'

'Doohickeys,' he chuckled. 'I scour the globe for the cute, the strange, the interesting, and most of all, the cheap. Wooden boxes from Thailand, black lacquer from Singapore, paper kites from China. You go into a gift shop, fall in love with some hopelessly overpriced, crudely carved figurine, and that's me, Bethie. I found that just for you. At a hundred percent markup, of course.'

She shook her head in mock protest. 'And you can make a living at this?'

'I make a very fine living at this. Bring things in by the container loads. Volume is the key.'

'You must have a fine eye.'

'No, just lots of experience as an impulse shopper.' He grinned at her. 'And yourself?'

He'd meant the question kindly. He had just volunteered more than a little about himself. Still she flinched, and the instant she did, the smile faded from his face.

'I apologize,' he said immediately. 'I'm sorry, Bethie. I have this habit of speaking before thinking. I swear I've been meaning to quit—'

'No, no. It's a logical question and you've been very generous about sharing your life—'

'But things are difficult for you, now. I know and I shouldn't have pried.'

'It's not . . . it's not that,' she ventured.

He nodded for her to continue, his expression patient, his

crinkling blue eyes sincere. It was easy to talk to him, she discovered. Much easier than she would've thought.

'I was raised to be a wife,' she told him. 'A high-society wife. To create a beautiful home, throw lovely parties, always wear a smile when my husband is at my side. And be a good mother, of course. Raise the next generation of high-society wives.'

Tristan nodded gravely.

'And then . . . then I got divorced. It's funny, I didn't notice it right away. I had Kimberly and Amanda to think about, and in all honesty, things had been rough for them. They needed attention. I needed to give it. I guess I went from being an extension of my husband to being an extension of my daughters. It seemed so natural at the time.'

'Except little girls don't stay little girls forever,' Tristan filled in.

'Kimberly went away to college three years ago,' Bethie said quietly. 'Things haven't been the same since.'

She looked down at her lap. She couldn't help it. The music was blues jazz tonight, some older woman belting out the aching strains of 'At last, my love has come along . . .' and Bethie felt the melancholy all the way down to her bones.

Her beautiful, empty brick town house. Room after room of so much silence. Four separate phones that rarely rang. Hallways lined with framed photographs that were all she had left of the people she loved.

And standing on that hillside a month ago, staring at that freshly dug, gaping black grave. *Ashes to ashes, dust to dust.*

She was forty-seven years old, and she didn't know who she was anymore. She was forty-seven years old, no longer a wife, no longer Mandy's mother, and she didn't know where she belonged.

Tristan's hand reached over, tangled with her own. He drew her gaze up and she saw he wasn't grinning anymore. Instead he wore a somber expression, not unlike her own. For an uncanny moment she had an image of him, waking up in the hospital after his transplant surgery, and discovering no one at his side. No wife or children to hold his hand. He knew, she thought. He knew.

Her fingers curled around his. The woman continued to sing, 'My love has come along . . .' and the moment went on and on.

'Bethie,' he said gently, 'let's take a walk.'

Outside, the air was heavy and hot, but the sun was beginning to set and Bethie had always loved this time of day. The world became muted, velvety, offering less color but also fewer sharp lines and hard objects. It comforted her.

They walked in silence, not heading anywhere in particular, but by some mutual understanding of the city, working their way toward Rittenhouse Square.

'My turn to ask a question,' Tristan said abruptly. He had loosened his tie and rolled up his shirtsleeves in deference to the wet-wool humidity. He still looked elegant, and Bethie was aware of other people casting them covert glances.

'Ask,' she prodded, becoming aware that Tristan was still studying her.

'You promise not to be insulted?'

'After two glasses of wine, you have to work very hard to get me insulted.'

He stopped walking in the middle of the block, then turned her so she'd have to face him. 'It's not just the kidney, is it?'

'What?'

'This. It's not only about me having your daughter's kidney, is it? I know it's a rude question, and I don't want to upset you, but this evening is going even better than I imagined, and well, I need to know. Some people think when you get someone's organ, you get a piece of her soul as well. Is that what this evening is about? Am I just a proxy for your daughter?' He added in a rush, 'Because I'm seriously considering kissing you, Elizabeth Quincy, and I don't think a proxy for your daughter should be doing that.'

Bethie felt dazed. Her hand fell free of his, fluttered at the base of her throat, toyed with the collar of her satin shirt. 'I don't . . . Of course not! That's . . . that's foolishness. An old wives' tale. Silly superstition.'

Tristan nodded with satisfaction. He seemed ready to resume walking, when she ruined her own argument by saying. 'You don't . . . You don't feel any differently, do you?'

'Pardon?'

'We did run into each other by chance,' she continued hastily, 'and yet you knew who I was right away, even though I'd been pointed out to you only once before. That's a little odd, don't you think? God knows when I go to parties I have to meet someone three or four times before I can put a name to a face.'

'You helped save my life. That's a bit more significant than some stuffed suit at a black-and-white soiree.'

'There's something else.'

'What?' He looked genuinely concerned now. The evening had been so beautiful. It pained her to say what she had to say next.

She whispered, 'You know my nickname.'

'What nickname?'

'Bethie. You've called me Bethie. Many times. Always

73

Bethie, never Liz or Beth. I never told you that was my nickname, Tristan. And how many Elizabeths do you know who go by Bethie instead?'

The blood drained out of his face. His eyes widened, and for a moment, he appeared so horror-struck she wished she could recall her words. Simultaneously, both of their gazes slid to his side, where the scar still puckered pink and raw beneath the protective cover of his shirt.

'Blimey,' he breathed.

Bethie had a chill. The night was hot, the humidity oppressive, and still she rubbed her arms for warmth.

'This was a bad idea,' she said abruptly.

'No—'

'Yes!'

'Dammit, no!' He reclaimed her arm, his grip firm but not painful. 'I'm not your daughter.'

'I know that.'

'I'm fifty-two years old, Bethie . . . Elizabeth. My favorite food is steak, my favorite drink Glenfiddich straight up. I run my own business. I enjoy fast cars, fast boats. Lord be praised, I have a deep and abiding love for *Playboy*, and it's not for the articles. Does any of that sound like a twenty-three-year-old girl to you?'

'How did you know Amanda's age?'

'*Because the doctors told me!*'

'You asked questions about her?'

'Bethie . . . love, of course I asked questions. Someone had to die for me to live. I think about that. Hell, half my nights I lie awake thinking of nothing but that. I am not your daughter; I swear I'm not even the ghost of your daughter. But I am a man who's grateful.'

Bethie was silent. She needed to think about this. Then,

she nodded. 'It's possible,' she offered, 'that someone once referred to me as Bethie. You know, in the hospital.'

His grip loosened on her arm. 'Yes, probably that's how it happened.'

She had to know. 'Did they tell you about the crash?'

'I know she was drunk, if that's what you mean.'

'She'd been doing so well,' Bethie said softly. 'She'd joined AA just six months before the accident. I had such hopes for her.'

He didn't say anything, but his expression gentled. He tucked a strand of her hair behind her ear, his fingers lingering on the curve of her cheek. His thumb stroked her jawline.

'She was so sensitive,' Bethie murmured. 'Even as a little girl. Nothing fazed Kimberly, nothing scared Kimberly, but my Mandy was always different. Shy. Timid. Bugs scared her. Thanks to Hitchcock, birds scared her. One year, she was terrified of the slide at the school playground. We never knew why. She slept with a night-light on until she was twelve.'

'You must have worried about her a great deal.'

'I wanted her to feel safe. I wanted her to see herself as strong, independent, and capable. I wanted her to be able to dream bigger than I ever did.'

'What happened to her isn't your fault,' Tristan said.

'That's what I try telling myself.' She gave him a halfhearted smile. 'I blame my ex-husband instead.'

'Why?'

'His job. He joined the FBI when the girls were little, became a profiler, and for all intents and purposes, disappeared. Granted, he did important work, but I've always been a bit biased – I thought our children should come first.

Silly me.' She heard the bitterness in her voice and grimaced. 'Sorry. You didn't need to hear all that.'

'Hear what?'

She smiled again, with none of the gaiety of before when the evening was new, but still a smile. 'You're very kind to listen to me,' she murmured.

'Ah Bethie, I stand by what I said before. This is the nicest evening I've had in ages. Good things can come from bad, you know. It's taken me fifty-two years and one extremely dangerous surgical procedure to learn that, but I did.'

'Are you really only here for a week?'

'This time. But I could arrange to return.'

'For business?'

'If that's what you'd like to call it.'

She ducked her head, a slow blush creeping up her cheeks. The telltale warmth betrayed her, and his thumb slowly tilted her chin back up. He had moved closer to her. She could feel the heat of his body just an inch away. He was going to kiss her, she realized. He was going to kiss her. She leaned forward.

'Bethie,' he murmured right before his lips touched hers, 'let me take you for a drive.'

7

Quincy's House, Virginia

It was after ten P.M. before Quincy finally returned to his darkened home. He juggled his black leather computer case, a cardboard box of manila files, and his cell phone as he fought with his key. The moment he opened the door, his security system sounded its warning beeps.

He crossed the threshold quickly and in movements born of years of habit, he punched in the entry code without ever having to look at the keys. A minute later, when the front door was closed and locked again, he rearmed the outside sensors while leaving the internal motion detectors disabled. Welcome home.

Quincy valued his security system. Ironically enough, it was probably the only object in his house worth real money.

He went into the kitchen, dropping his computer case and box of files on the counter, then opening his refrigerator for no good reason. It remained empty, having not magically grown any food from the last time he checked. He closed the door, drew himself a glass of tap water, and leaned against the counter.

The kitchen was sizable, modern. It had hardwood floors,

a massive stainless steel stove with an impressive stainless steel hood. The refrigerator was industrial-sized and stainless steel. The cabinets were made of cherry wood, the counter-tops fashioned from black granite. Five years ago, the real estate agent had assured him that this was a kitchen perfectly suited for entertaining. Now Quincy looked at the yawning bay windows of the empty breakfast nook, which still didn't contain a kitchen table.

He traveled a lot. His place looked it.

He pushed away from the counter and roamed the space restlessly. Another long day completed. Another home-coming to . . . what?

Maybe he should get a pet. Fish, parakeet, cat, something that didn't take too much care but would at least greet him at the end of the day with cheerful noise or even howling racket. He was not someone who needed a lot of creature comforts. He could handle the absence of furniture, the lack of artwork on his walls. His mother had died when he was very young, and most of his life had been lacking in softer touches. But silence . . . Silence still got to him.

He found himself thinking of dinnertime with his father, two people sitting at a scarred pine table, sharing a simple meal, and never saying a word. The farm had required a lot of physical effort. Abraham would be up and out at the break of day. He'd return at sunset. They'd eat. Watch a little TV. Read. Each night, the two of them in separate patched-up recliners, plowing their way through separate novels.

Quincy shook his head. His father had raised his only child the best way he knew how. Abraham had worked hard, put food on the table, and given his son an appreciation for the written word. Quincy could respect that now. He considered himself at peace with things. At least he had until a month ago. Grief played horrible tricks on the mind, and not even he knew what sort of demons were going to leap out of his subconscious next.

He was rattled these days, self-doubt stoked by lunchtimes no one knew of, when he went to Arlington and stood by his daughter's grave; nerve endings eroded by weeks spent working with people who would no longer meet his eye.

He wasn't used to feeling like this, as if the world were an uncertain place and he needed to feel his way carefully or risk plunging into an unknown abyss. Some nights he jerked awake, his heart hammering in his chest with the frantic need to call Kimberly and make sure she was okay, that he still had one daughter left. Ironically enough, some evenings he was consumed by the desire to call Bethie, because while his ex-wife hated his guts, she was someone who had loved Mandy. She was a connection to his daughter, and with each day that went by, there were fewer and fewer of those connections left.

Quincy had not thought it would be this hard. He was an academic, a PhD who'd studied the five stages of grief and the resulting physical and emotional turmoil. You should eat plenty of fresh fruits and vegetables, engage in some sort of vigorous exercise, and avoid alcohol – it never helps. He was a professional, an FBI agent who'd been present numerous times when the word came down that some wife, husband, brother, sister, child would not be coming home again. You should maintain focus, revisit the last days of your loved one's life as objectively as possible and avoid hysterics – they never help.

He was a man after all, an arrogant father who'd assumed tragedy would strike someone else's family and never his. He was not eating plenty of fruits and vegetables. He was not objective about the last few days of Mandy's life. Some days he desperately craved alcohol. And some nights he knew he was dangerously close to hysterics.

The great Supervisory Special Agent Pierce Quincy. Quantico's best of the best. How low the mighty have fallen, he thought, and it disturbed him to find himself still so egocentric, even when dealing with his daughter's death.

He wished Rainie would call. He had thought that he would've heard from her by now, and it bothered him that he hadn't. He rubbed his temples wearily, feeling the low beat of a headache that never really went away these days. And as if on cue, the cordless phone on his kitchen counter began to ring.

'Finally,' Quincy muttered and scooped it up. 'Hello.'

Silence. Strange background noises, like metal clanging against metal.

'Well, well, well,' a voice said. 'If it ain't the man himself.'

Quincy frowned. The voice stirred memories, something in the back of his head. 'Who is this?'

'You don't remember me? Aw, and here I thought I was your *loco simpatico*. You fed boys break my heart.'

All at once, the voice clicked with a name. 'How did you get this number?' Quincy asked sternly, while his palms began to sweat and his gaze flew to his security system to assure himself that it was still armed.

'You mean you don't know yet?'

'*How did you get this number?*'

'Amigo, relax. I just wanna talk. Revisit old times on this fine Tuesday evening.'

'Fuck you,' Quincy said without thinking. He hardly ever swore, and a moment later he wished he hadn't done so now, because the caller simply began to laugh.

'Ah, Quincy, *mi amigo*, you even swear like a suit. Shit, man, we're hardened criminals here, you gotta do better than that. Fuck your mother, maybe. Fuck your mother up her mother-fucking ass. Yeah, that's a good one. Or maybe,' the voice turned silky, 'fuck your dead daughter in her dead-fucking grave with a white fucking cross. Yeah, I'd like that.'

Quincy gripped the phone harder as the words penetrated, and the first wave of anger washed over him like a tidal wave. He wanted to smash the phone. He wanted to smash it against his bare hardwood floor or black granite counter-top. He wanted to smash it over and over again and then he wanted to fly to California just so he could beat the crap out of Miguel Sanchez, thirty-four years old and already sentenced to death, and he had never felt himself this angry, the rage throbbing in his temples and his whole body rigid with the need to lash out.

Then he saw his answering machine. The red blinking light indicating that there were messages. And the red digital display screen giving him the new-message count: 56. Fifty-six new messages on what should've been his unlisted telephone line.

He amazed himself with how calm he could keep his voice. 'One call from me, Sanchez, and you'll be sent straight to solitary. And remember, I'm the one who knows how much you hate to be alone.'

'That mean you don't like talking about your daughter? Pretty, pretty girl, Quincy. How nice you gave her my favorite name.'

'—weeks in the hole. No one to brag to, no one to boost your ego, no one to rape when you realize you're never ever going to even touch a woman again.'

'Do me a favor, fed. Next time you listen to my tape,

picture your daughter's face for me. Oh, and give your second daughter a kiss. Because someday, I'm gonna find a way out of this joint, and it makes me *real* happy to know that you've still got one daughter left.'

'One last time,' Quincy said tightly, his gaze locked on his blinking security system, 'how did you get my unlisted number?'

And Sanchez drawled, 'Unlisted? Not anymore.'

Quincy had no sooner set down his phone, than it rang again. He snatched it back up.

'What?' he demanded harshly.

There was a moment of silence, then his ex-wife's uncertain voice. 'Pierce?'

Quincy closed his eyes. He was unraveling. He would not unravel. He would not permit himself to do such a thing. 'Elizabeth.'

'I was wondering if you could do me a small favor,' Bethie murmured. 'Nothing major. Simply run a background check. You know, as you did before.'

'Your father hiring more contractors?' Quincy worked on loosening his grip on the phone and taking a deep breath. His father-in-law had built an addition on his home last year. He'd made his only daughter call her ex-husband to request background checks on the entire crew. According to his former father-in-law, it was the least Quincy could do.

'The name is Shandling. Tristan Shandling.'

Quincy found a piece of paper and wrote down the name. His heart was finally beginning to slow, the darkness receding at the edge of his vision. He felt more and more like his former self, and not some beast about to burst its chains. The red digital counter still glowed on his answering machine. Fifty-six messages. Something had gone wrong. He would deal with it, however, as he'd dealt with everything before. All in good time.

'Time frame?' he asked his ex-wife.

'Ummm, no rush. But soon. I think he has a place in Virginia if that helps.'

'All right, Bethie. Give me a few days.'

'Thank you, Pierce,' she said, and for once it sounded as if she meant it.

Quincy didn't hang up the phone right away. Neither did she.

'Have you . . . have you heard from Kimberly lately?' he found himself asking.

Bethie seemed surprised. 'No, but I'd assumed that you had.'

'Ah, so we're equally shunned.'

'Maybe she tried to call you when you were gone . . .' Bethie's voice trailed off. She seemed to realize how that sounded and added hastily, 'I tried to reach you earlier in the week, but you weren't home and I didn't feel like leaving a message.'

'I was in Portland visiting someone. An old friend.' He wasn't sure why he offered the information, and the minute he did, he wished he could call it back. An old friend? Who was he trying to kid? When Bethie spoke, however, she didn't sound angry or tense, which surprised him.

'Maybe I should pay Kimberly a visit,' she said. 'She's just an hour away, I could tell her I was in the area. It's been a month.'

Quincy almost said no, then caught himself. Once, Rainie had accused him of taking his job too far. Even in his personal life, he showed up, gave his expert opinion, and left.

Lisa Gardner

'Perhaps Kimberly just needs some space,' he tried neutrally.

'I don't know why. We're the only family she has left. Frankly, I thought she'd strive to be closer to us, not further away.'

Quincy rubbed his temples. 'Bethie, I know that you're sad. I'm sad, too.'

'Pierce, you're speaking to me as if I were five.'

'We tried so hard for her. I know we don't always agree on each other's role as a parent, but we both loved Mandy. We wanted the best for her. We would've . . . We would've given her the world if such a thing were possible. Instead she got drunk, crawled behind the wheel of her vehicle and killed two people. I love her. I miss her. And some days . . . Some days, I'm just so *angry*.'

He was thinking of Sanchez's call again, and the way his hands had fisted and his body had gone rigid. He was still angry, he realized. He was furious in places way down deep where it would take years to weed it all out and begin to feel normal again.

'Bethie,' he tried one last time, 'don't you get angry, too?'

His ex-wife didn't speak right away. Then she asked quietly, in a strange tone, 'Pierce, do you think if someone gets an organ transplant, that maybe they get more than just the other person's tissue? Maybe . . . maybe they also get part of the other person's being, some part of her soul?'

'An organ transplant is a medical procedure, nothing more.'

'I thought you would say that.'

'Returning to Kimberly for a moment—'

'She's angry, she needs space. I got it, Pierce. I'm not as dumb as you think.'

84

'Bethie—'

The phone clicked off. His ex-wife had hung up on him.

Quincy slowly recradled the cordless phone on its base. And that, he thought tiredly, concluded one of the more civil conversations of his day.

Five minutes later, Quincy sat down at the kitchen counter. The scrap of paper with Tristan Shandling's name had been pushed aside. Now, he had out a fresh spiral notebook and three black ink pens. He pressed the play button on his answering machine.

Then he began the two-page list of all the nice felons who'd called his unlisted telephone number simply to wish him dead.

The light on his security panel indicated his system was fully operational and armed. He watched it for a long time, thinking of Kimberly, remembering Mandy.

Shortly, he went into the front room he used as an office. He dug through a stack of cardboard boxes marked Criminology: Basic Theories, until he found a small cassette tape labeled 'Miguel Sanchez: Victim Eight'. The original tape sat in an evidence storage locker in California. This was Quincy's personal copy, used in several of his classes.

He placed the tape in an old cassette recorder. He hit play. He sat alone in the dark, while his office filled with sounds of a young girl's pleading wails.

Amanda Johnson, fifteen years old and eight long hours from death.

'Nooooooooooo,' she cried. '*Oh God, noooooooooooo.*'

Quincy put his head in his hands. And he knew he was in trouble, because one month after his daughter's funeral, he still couldn't weep.

8

Motel 6, Virginia

'Who is Miguel Sanchez?' Rainie asked an hour later. She was propped up against the headboard of her mud-brown motel room, having just treated herself to a late dinner of blueberry pancakes at the nearby Waffle House. The Motel 6 had been highly visible from the highway and seemed as good a stopping point as any. Besides, at fifty dollars a night, no one could question her expense account.

She'd found the motel. She'd found the neighboring Waffle House. She'd eaten her blueberry pancakes alone, thinking of Officer Amity's take on the accident scene and wishing she didn't have a chill. Then she'd wasted ten minutes watching other diners, burly, working-class men out with their girls. In some cases, tables crowded with entire families. She was three thousand miles away from home. Funny how nothing seemed that different.

She'd walked back to the motel knowing she should call Quincy and deliver a report on her day. Instead, she'd turned on the TV and perused the modern miracle of fifty-seven channels and still nothing to see. She told herself she didn't have much to report, anyway. Besides, she didn't want to seem anxious to hear Quincy's voice. She wanted to ensure that she was treating this as business, purely business. Quincy the client.

There had been nothing good on TV. She had spent the day in a strange state thinking, this is where Quincy lives, and she had been anxious to hear his voice. She'd called. And it had taken her all of one second to realize that she should've called sooner. Quincy sounded tired, nearly flat, as if he had no emotions left. She had never heard him sound like that before.

'Miguel Sanchez was my first case,' he told her now. 'Worked out of California in the mid-eighties, with his cousin, Richie Millos. They specialized in sadistic rape-murders of young prostitutes. Eight total. Sanchez liked to tape his work.'

'Nice guy,' Rainie commented. She turned off the TV and set down the remote. 'So you were instrumental in catching Sanchez?'

'I formulated the strategy used by the police for Sanchez's arrest. A witness had reported seeing two men dragging the eighth victim into a white van twenty-four hours before her corpse was found mutilated alongside I-5. At this point, we already knew we were dealing with an organized killer. As I explained to the LAPD, partnerships are rare for psychopaths, but in the few occasions we've encountered them, the partner has generally been subservient – a weak sidekick who merely fulfills the psychopath's desire for an audience. My advice, therefore, once the police had identified two likely suspects, was that they focus their attention on the weaker member of the pair. Turn Richie to give up Miguel, who was the real instigator and threat.'

'I'm guessing this was easier said than done.'

'Yes. Richie idolized his older cousin. He was also terrified of him. For good reason. Six months after Richie handed over Miguel in return for a reduced sentence, he was found in the prison showers with his penis cut off and shoved down his throat. Miguel never believed in being subtle.'

'Ah. So this fine piece of humanity called your personal line tonight?'

'Him, and forty-seven of his fellow deviants. Then I had eight calls from various prison officials, who thought I should know that my unlisted telephone number is currently being circulated in prison yards in everything from scraps of paper to packs of cigarettes. Oh, and in one prison, my number is now scratched into the shower wall.'

'Quincy—'

'By my count, the forty-eight inmates represent twenty-one different correctional facilities, so I imagine I will be hearing from more prison officials in the morning.'

'Quincy—'

'But don't worry,' he continued, his voice no longer flat, but gaining an edge, 'most corrections departments have the right to monitor an inmate's calls, so I'm sure the new members of my fan club will be suitably punished. Maybe have a disciplinary ticket written up or receive ad seg – administrative segregation. You know, penalties I'm sure more than compensate for the sheer thrill a bunch of psychopathic lifers can get by toying with a federal agent.'

'Change your number.'

'Not yet.'

'Quincy, don't be an ass!'

'I'm not. I'm being patient.'

Rainie grew silent, then she got it. 'You want to keep everyone calling in case you can trick one of them into revealing the original source of your phone number.'

'In the morning, I will report the incident to my SAC. The Bureau takes the protection of its agents very seriously. I'm sure my line will be tapped and monitored in no time at all. Calls will be going out to the various prisons. Perhaps even a personal visit to one Miguel Sanchez. I would like that.'

'Do you have a theory of who did this? It has to be somebody who knows you.'

'Maybe. Then again, it could be some bored college flunkie who hacked into the telephone company's records in order to have a little fun.'

'But you don't think so.'

'No. I think it's personal. And I think the mysterious practical joker gave out more than just my private number, Rainie. Think of what Mr Sanchez said. That he wanted to fuck my daughter in her fucking grave with a white fucking cross. Why a white cross? What's the first thing you think of when you picture a white cross?'

Rainie closed her eyes. She pictured a white cross, and her stomach went hollow. She shouldn't be at this stupid motel, she realized. She shouldn't be sitting here pretending that business was just business. She should be at Quincy's home. She should be holding him the way he had once so kindly held her. And she should be putting her hands over his ears to spare him from what she knew he would say next. He had always been too brutally clever.

'Arlington,' Quincy continued relentlessly. 'The instigator didn't just give out my home telephone number. He told at least one convicted sadist where to find my daughter's grave. The son of a bitch.' His voice finally cracked. 'He gave away Mandy.'

* * *

Rainie waited. On the other end of the phone, the sound of Quincy's breathing grew less ragged. She could feel him pulling himself back together, becoming once more the cool, composed federal agent he so prided himself on being. He needed his masks, she thought, just as she needed hers. It surprised her how much that realization hurt her.

For no good reason, she was thinking about the baby elephant again, his desperate run across the desert. Kicked down, getting back up. And still the jackals shredded him in the end.

'Do you think they're connected?' she asked him shortly.

'What?'

'The phone calls. With Mandy's accident. Seems rather interesting that you've no sooner hired someone to investigate Mandy's death, than you're getting a bunch of threatening calls.'

'I don't know, Rainie. It could simply be opportunity. There are enough people out there who have nothing better to do than hate me. Maybe they heard about my daughter's funeral and decided it was their chance to have some fun. We've had incidents in the past where someone has gotten an agent's personal information. Nothing on this big of a scale, but then again, we're now in the computer age.'

'I don't like it,' Rainie said flatly. 'Plus the fact that Sanchez evoked Mandy in the phone call . . . Seems a rather pointed message.'

'I . . . I don't know.' Quincy sounded tired again. 'I think they must be connected. Then I think I'm paranoid. Then I think I'm merely being diligent. I don't . . . I'm not myself at the moment.'

Rainie fell silent. She kept thinking there was something comforting she should say. She had not grown up in a house big on comfort. Thirty-two years old. It was kind of funny all the things she didn't know how to do.

'I spoke with the investigating officer,' she said, since like Quincy, business was what she handled best. 'He did a good job at the scene. I couldn't find anything he'd overlooked.'

'What about the seat belt?'

'The driver . . .' She stuttered immediately, shocked by her coldness at using that impersonal word.

Quincy didn't say anything and the silence loomed huge this time, a giant black void between them. They couldn't get this right, Rainie thought suddenly, desperately. Even when they were trying, they couldn't get this right.

'Mandy reported the seat belt broken a month before the accident,' she tried again, her voice meek now, humbled by her mistake. 'She made an appointment with the garage that serviced her vehicle, then canceled at the last minute.'

'She'd been driving without a working seat belt for a month?'

'It would appear so.'

'Why didn't someone pull her over? I thought there were seat belt laws in this state!'

Rainie didn't reply to his outburst. She knew he didn't expect her to.

'What had happened to the seat belt?' he redirected his line of questioning. 'How did it break?'

'We don't know yet. Officer Amity is helping me locate the vehicle so I can examine it, but fourteen months later makes things difficult. Most likely the Explorer has already been broken down for parts at some salvage yard.'

'I want to know what happened to the seat belt.'

'I'll find it, Quincy. You know I'll find it.'

'And the man, the one she was supposedly seeing?'

'First thing tomorrow morning, I meet with Mary Olsen. Hopefully she can point me in his direction. I'll also check in with Mandy's local AA group. They probably know more about her personal life.'

'AA has policies about giving out information.'

'Then I'll just have to turn on my charm again.'

'Rainie—'

'I'm on top of the case, Quincy. Things are beginning to happen and I know you need answers. I'll get them.'

His silence was subdued now, a long soft spell where they both sat not too many miles apart and yet still too far away. She wondered if he was sitting in a darkened room. She wondered if he'd skipped dinner again, the way he'd probably skipped lunch before that and breakfast before that. She wondered how many hours he'd pace before finally falling in a restless, exhausted sleep. And then she wondered how they could know each other so well, and still have this chasm between them.

'I should go,' Quincy said. 'I want to speak to Everett first thing in the morning.'

'Everett?'

'Special Agent in Charge. He'll want to know about the phone calls, assuming he doesn't already. Plus, I need to type up this list of names.'

Rainie glanced at the clock. It was now after midnight.

'Quincy,' she began.

'I'm fine.'

'I'm not that far away. One hour tops, I can be at your front door.'

'And then what, Rainie? Then everything's all right, because now I'm *your* charity case?'

'Hey, it's not like that at all!'

'Yes? And what do you think it is I've been trying to say? Understanding is not pity. Oh, but excuse me, in your world it is.'

'Quincy . . .'

'Thank you for the update, Investigator Conner. Good night.'

The phone punctuated his sharp sentence with a click. Rainie thinned her lips, shook her head, and replaced her own receiver much more slowly.

'But my case was different,' she muttered.

Her motel room remained silent. She figured that was an appropriate enough reply.

Later, six hours later, the motel alarm clock beeped to life and Rainie crawled blearily out of bed. Jet lag had caught up with her. She gulped down twelve ounces of Coke for breakfast and still felt half dead.

She hit the four-lane street, running for thirty minutes through the concrete maze of a seemingly endless strip mall tucked conveniently off Interstate 95. Middle-aged men in rumpled suits poured out of the motel. A line of cars sat impatiently at a McDonald's drive-through.

Rainie ran through parking lot after parking lot, dodging reckless cars and people already fed up with their morning commute. Tall maple trees and dark waxy magnolias beckoned lushly in the distance. Wild honeysuckle grabbed at cement barriers lining the parking lots as if the vine would reclaim the urban jungle as its own. Rainie coughed on diesel fumes from spewing trucks and fought her way back to Motel 6, wishing the green landscape didn't make her think of Bakersville again and long for the feel of salty ocean air upon her face.

She took a five-minute shower, towel-dried her hair, and combed in mousse. Expecting another long day, she donned a pair of worn jeans and a clean white T-shirt, the official uniform of the aspiring PI. She checked her phone messages on her home answering machine while lacing up her shoes. The weather was already brutally hot outside. Man, what she would give to wear sandals and shorts.

She blew the thought aside while hearing that she had six new messages, a personal record. She grabbed the motel pen and pad of paper.

First two messages were from clients wanting updates. She really should do that. The next three messages were all hang ups, received in hourly intervals. If the person couldn't be bothered to leave a message, she decided, she couldn't be bothered to wonder about who they were. The final message was from some lawyer she'd never heard of, requesting a basic information packet.

She eyed the clock, judged it to be four A.M. Pacific Coast time, and shrewdly called back the law firm to tell the lawyer that her secretary would send him something in the mail. Then she left her number at Motel 6, just in case the lawyer wanted a more immediate reply. She now felt industrious and exceedingly clever and it was not even noon.

Rainie finished lacing her shoes. After a moment's hesitation, she slid her Glock .40 into a shoulder holster. A simple black jacket covered the bulge.

Seven A.M., she picked up her notes and headed out the door. The sun glared harsh white, causing her to blink. Her tiny rental car felt like it was two hundred degrees inside. Damn, she thought. It was going to be a killer of a day.

9

Quantico, Virginia

'The first call arrived at two thirty-two P.M., Tuesday afternoon.' Back in the bowels of the earth, Quincy reported last night's events in his crispest voice to Special Agent in Charge Chad Everett, while the SAC nodded attentively and a fluorescent bulb buzzed ominously overhead. 'At ten-eighteen P.M., I personally handled a call from Miguel Sanchez. There have been more calls since; given the circumstances, I've been letting the machine pick up.' Quincy handed over copies of the freshly made case file to the assembled agents. They accepted the information while continuing to regard him gravely.

'Enclosed you will find a complete list of caller activity and the corrections departments currently involved in the situation,' he continued. 'Eight officers checked in with me, which you will see noted. In some cases, they reported my personal information being passed along from inmate to inmate in the yard. More interesting, however, is the last two officers, who identified the source of the information as being an ad currently running in their local prison newsletters. In one newsletter, I'm a producer looking to interview inmates for an upcoming documentary on prison life. Interested parties are encouraged to contact me directly at the number listed below. In another newsletter, I'm eagerly seeking a prison pen pal, again, please contact me at the number listed below.'

Quincy smiled tightly. 'I'm still waiting to hear back from a few sources, but it would appear that similar ads just appeared in at least six other newsletters, including *Cellpals*, *Freedom Now*, and my personal favorite, *Prison Legal News*, which has a monthly circulation of over three thousand. Then there are the Web sites, such as PrisonPenPals. com, which apparently has been paid to e-mail my ad to dozens of prisoners "seeking a new friend." Look at me. I'm a groupie.'

Quincy shut the case file and sat down grimly. All eyes were still on him, but he had nothing more to add. This was his life. Now it had been violated. Phone call after phone call, message after message promising a slow, tortured death. He could not remember the last time he had slept.

At least the Bureau was taking the situation seriously. A small case team had been assembled in Everett's office. A younger man with a mop of sandy brown hair, Special Agent Randy Jackson, represented the Technical Services Division, in charge of wiretapping. From NCAVC were Special Agent Glenda Rodman, an older woman with a penchant for severe gray suits, and Special Agent Albert Montgomery, whose bloodshot eyes and hound-dog face already made Quincy uncomfortable. The agent had either taken a red-eye flight last night, or he'd been drinking heavily. Perhaps both. Then again, who was Quincy, with his own wan features, to judge?

'For the record, who has access to your personal

telephone number?' Everett asked, while Special Agent Rodman sat up straighter and positioned her pen over her yellow legal pad of notes.

'My family,' Quincy replied immediately. 'Some professionals, including fellow agents and members of law enforcement. Some friends. I've included as complete a list as possible in my notes. In all honesty, I've had that number for the past five years, and even I was surprised by how many people now have it.'

'You've worked over two hundred and ninety-six active cases,' Glenda spoke up.

Quincy nodded. Frankly, he was surprised the number was not higher. As profilers served a consulting role, each routinely juggled over one hundred cases at a time.

'That's a lot of people who may feel they have the right to be unhappy with you.'

'Assuming they ever knew I was involved.' Quincy shrugged. 'Be honest, Glenda. For a fair amount of our cases, we receive a request by phone, get the case file by mail, and return our report via fax or FedEx. In those incidents, I have a hard time believing the perpetrator's focus ever leaves the local homicide detectives who actively work the case.'

'So weeding out those cases . . .' she prodded.

Quincy did the math in his head. 'Maybe fifty-six convicted inmates.'

'What about open cases?'

Quincy shook his head. 'I haven't worked an active case in six years.'

'Last year,' she began.

He said quietly, 'Henry Hawkins is dead.'

Montgomery leaned forward, his elbows resting on the knees of his rumpled pants. The fluorescent light flickered, jaundicing his jowls, and Quincy found himself pondering the agent's presence once again. Montgomery's expression was sullen, almost as if he was here against his will, and yet what kind of agent begrudged helping a fellow agent in trouble? That hardly boded well.

'Aren't we putting the cart before the horse?' Montgomery grumbled. 'You got a bunch of calls. Whoopdee doo.'

Special Agent in Charge Everett replied sternly, 'The fact that an agent's personal telephone number was disseminated to over twenty correctional facilities *is* whoopdee doo. We don't need any more whoopdee doo than that.'

Montgomery turned to the SAC. Quincy thought the disheveled agent would quit while he was ahead; he was wrong. 'Bullshit,' Montgomery snapped, making them all blink. 'If this was something personal, if this was someone *serious*, the instigator would do more than pass along a private number to a bunch of schmucks behind bars. He'd visit the house. Or he'd arrange for someone else to visit the house. Phone calls? This is fucking child's play.'

Everett's face darkened. A thirty-year veteran of the Bureau, he was a throwback to the days when an FBI agent dressed, spoke, and carried himself a certain way. Agents were the good guys, the last bastion of protection against gangsters, bank robbers, and child molesters. Agents did not arrive on the job in wrinkled suits and they did not go around saying things like 'fucking child's play.'

'Special Agent Montgomery—'

'Wait a minute.' Quincy surprised them all by raising his hand and saving Montgomery from a lecture that wouldn't be career-building. 'Say that one more time.'

'Phone calls,' Montgomery drawled as if they were all daft. 'The question is not who, but *why* phone calls.'

Glenda Rodman sat back. She was nodding her head now. Randy Jackson yawned.

'Montgomery's right,' the techie agreed. 'If it's a hacker, guy could get your home address from the phone company just as easily as your unlisted number. If it's just some person who happened to snag your number, they could still call information and get your street address from a reverse directory. Either way, home phone number equals home address.'

'Wonderful,' Quincy said. Somehow, he hadn't put those pieces together, another sure sign he was not himself these days. The dull ache was back in his temples. Morning, noon, and night. Grief was like a hangover he couldn't shake.

Why phone calls? The obvious answer was that someone was out to get him. Probably someone from an old case. Psychopaths were like sharks. They probably viewed his daughter's death as blood in the water and now they were moving in for the kill. So why not keep it simple? Move in. Attack. Finish him off. Hell, he definitely wasn't in any kind of shape for a fight.

Was that why he had gone to Rainie? Because he knew he was becoming too isolated? Or because he wanted to remember how to fight the good fight? Rainie never gave an inch, not even when backed into a corner. Not even when she should.

Focus, Quincy. Why phone calls?

'This is serious,' Everett pronounced. 'I want an immediate follow-up with the newsletters and Web sites involved to determine the origin of these ads. Furthermore, we need to figure out just how many inmates now have this information. We ought to be able to trace something.'

Quincy closed his eyes. 'So many grassroots newsletters,'

he murmured. 'Big ones, little ones, and for all we know, he placed ads in all of them, which is a lot of work. So why . . .' His eyes popped open. He had it. Dammit, he should've thought of this last night. 'Cover,' he said.

'What's that, Agent?'

'Cover,' Montgomery repeated for him, then grunted. He stared at Quincy with red-rimmed eyes that appeared reluctantly impressed. 'Yeah, probably. Let's say this guy has your home address right now – which, by the way, he probably does. He goes after you tomorrow, we can hunt him down through process of elimination. But he spreads that info to dozens of prisons where the inmates will pass it along to dozens more . . . Now we gotta look at superfelons A, B, and C, their pals on the outside, and the pals of their pals on the outside. It's like a fucking criminal spider web. We'll be tracking down nasties for years after your funeral.'

'Why thank you,' Quincy said evenly.

'It's true,' Glenda chimed in, though she had the courtesy to look at him with more concern than Montgomery. 'If something had happened to you yesterday, standard procedure would have been to investigate personal acquaintances as well as people from prior cases. Not an easy feat, but certainly a manageable one. Now, however, entire prison populations have your personal information. You could be targeted by any neo-Nazi who hates federal agents, any gangster looking to build a rep, or any psychopath who's simply bored. If something should happen to you now . . . The playing field is wide open. No matter how many agents were assigned to the task, we'd never wrap our arms around a suspect list this big. Frankly, it's a brilliant strategy.'

'This is serious,' Everett pronounced again.

As the one who was being targeted by some unknown

stalker, Quincy thought he already knew that.

Glenda flipped through the file Quincy had put together. 'In the good news department,' she reported, 'some of these newsletters are more reputable than others. If they ran an ad, it was because they received specs and payment by mail. If they've kept the original letter and envelope, we're in luck. We can trace the postmark back to city of origin, test the envelope for DNA and fingerprints, plus test the whole package for chemical residues, dirt, debris. On the other hand . . .' She hesitated, glancing at Quincy apologetically. 'Prison newsletters are mostly grassroots journalism. It could take us weeks simply to track down every publication carrying the ad. And even then . . .'

She didn't have to say the rest. They all knew. Not all prison newsletters were really about journalism and not all were reputable. In the sixties, information was smuggled into prisons in packs of cigarettes. When the drug problem grew too big, however, correction departments across the country cracked down on all contraband by universally banning outside packages, including ones bearing tobacco products. Prisoners were allowed to receive only money, which they could then use to purchase cigarettes from the prison commissary. While it was unknown if this policy truly limited the drug problem, it did cut off the information flow.

Which brought the underground information network into the nineties and the miracles of constitutionally protected free speech. Prisons got computers, complete with desktop publishing software, and prison newsletters sprang up across the country. While some were small, many garnered national distribution. And the coded ad was born. Got some information you want to disseminate? Disguise it as a request for a pen pal, and pay five, ten, one hundred bucks to bring your message to the masses. Financially constrained? Some Web sites would now run pen pal ads and even build personal Web sites for inmates, free of charge. Just because you murdered eight people doesn't mean you shouldn't have a voice in society. Or a pretty blond writing correspondent named Candi.

'A lot of these newsletters probably didn't require much in the way of payment,' Quincy filled in for Glenda. 'And most of them probably did destroy the original letter of request, as a matter of protocol.'

'*Prison Legal News* is a good one,' she offered. 'We can focus our efforts there.'

'Good.' Everett nodded approvingly.

'I can call the phone company,' Jackson volunteered. 'See if Verizon has had any breaches of security lately. You know, that they'll admit to.'

Everett nodded again, looking pleased. Quincy, however, rubbed his temples. 'I doubt you'll find the original letter and envelope,' he said quietly. 'And even if we do, there won't be any DNA evidence. There won't be fingerprints. Nobody takes the time to think of such an elaborate ruse, then forgets something as simple as fingerprints on the envelope and saliva on the seal. Whoever we're looking for, he's smarter than that.'

'You think it's personal,' Glenda said.

Quincy gave her a look. 'What kind of stranger would bother?'

'We got another strategy,' Montgomery spoke up. He threw out baldly, 'Monitor the grave.'

'No!' Immediately, Quincy was out of his chair.

'It's standard procedure—' Montgomery began.

'Fuck procedure!' Quincy told him coldly, the second time in as many days he'd been driven to swear. 'It's my daughter. You are not using my daughter!'

Montgomery lumbered to his feet. His eyes were small and dark in the folds of his face. They reminded Quincy of the eyes of a bird, and he suddenly wondered if this was how he, too, appeared to victims' families. Not as a man, but as some bird of prey, swooping down after the kill.

'You said Sanchez implied he knew where your daughter was buried,' Montgomery said flatly.

'I was wrong.'

'Wrong my ass. He *knew*. Which means the UNSUB thought to look up where your daughter was buried, which means he's been considering her grave for quite some time. Guy's gotta know by now we'll be watching your house. So if he wants to feel close to you . . . have a private little laugh . . .'

'I do not want cameras at my daughter's grave. I do not give permission!'

But Glenda was nodding now, Jackson, as well. Quincy turned slowly toward Everett. The SAC's face was kind, sympathetic. But he was nodding, too.

Time spun away from Quincy. He was remembering an afternoon he hadn't thought of in years. At the state fair, Mandy and Kimberly in tow. Father-daughter day, he'd promised them, and taken them on as many rides as their young stomachs could handle. Then, right after buying them cotton candy, he'd turned and seen a man snapping photo after photo of children on the kiddy rides.

He remembered the smile fading from his face, a chill seeping into his body. He watched a pedophile capture rolls of film of laughing little children and all he could think was that his girls were only a few feet away. His sweet, beautiful, healthy little girls with their mother's striking dark blond hair.

He had spoken to them urgently, angrily. Look at that man, he had instructed them, his heart hammering wildly in his chest. Know what he is, he had told them. And don't be afraid to run.

Kimberly had nodded solemnly, absorbing his words with fierce concentration. Mandy, however, had started to cry. Weeks later, she still had nightmares about a man in a smelly overcoat who came with a camera to take her away.

'No,' he said hoarsely now. 'I won't allow cameras. Try and I swear I'll move Mandy's grave.'

The other agents were looking at him curiously. Everett said, 'Maybe it's time to think about taking a few sick days . . .'

'I'm fine!' Quincy tried again, but his voice still sounded odd, not like him. He sounded desperate, he realized. He sounded like a desperate father. And then he had a strange thought. It came to him as instinct, something he understood better than truth. *This is what the stalker wanted.* The UNSUB had set up this first wave of attack not just to make his identity harder to pinpoint, but to have some fun. To identify Quincy's deepest wound and rip at it savagely.

Quincy licked his lips and sought once more for control. 'Listen to me. This is not about my daughter. The UNSUB could care less about my daughter. He gave out that information just to get a cheap thrill.'

'So you know who it is then?' Glenda Rodman seemed intent on pinning him down.

'No, I don't know who it is. I'm simply theorizing based upon the company I keep.'

'In other words, you don't know shit,' Montgomery declared.

'Agent, you are not turning my daughter's grave into some obscene stakeout.'

'Why?' Montgomery pushed. 'It's not like it's something you haven't asked of other families.'

'You son of a bitch—'

'Quincy!' Everett interrupted sharply. Quincy stilled as they all drew up short. He was slightly surprised to find that his hand was raised in midair, his index finger jabbing at Montgomery as if he would do the man harm.

'I know this is difficult,' the SAC said quietly, 'but you're still a federal agent, Quincy, and breaches of security are a threat to all of us. Take a few days. The case team will monitor your house and apprise you of any new developments. In the meantime, you can make yourself comfortable in a nearby hotel or perhaps take a visit to see family.'

'Sir, listen to me—'

'Agent, how long has it been since you've slept?'

Quincy fell silent. He knew he had bags beneath his eyes, he knew he had lost weight. When Mandy had died, he had told himself that he was too smart to let it eat away at him. He'd lied.

The other agents were still staring at them. He could read their judgments on their faces. *Quincy's losing it. Quincy's strung too tight. Told you he shouldn't have returned to work so soon after the funeral . . .*

The FBI and animals in the wild, he thought: all culled the weak from their herd.

'I'll . . . I'll find a hotel,' he said brusquely. 'I just need to pack a few things.'

'Excellent. Glenda, you and Albert will be in charge of setting up surveillance of Quincy's house.'

Glenda nodded. 'I'll send you daily reports,' she offered Quincy, her tone even, but her eyes kind.

'I'd appreciate that,' he said stiffly.

'We're on top of things,' Everett concluded firmly, and nodded at the group. 'You'll see, Quincy. It'll be all right.'

Quincy simply shook his head. He walked back to his office in silence. He watched the play of stale fluorescent light over industrial-cream cinder block. He wondered again what kind of man chose a job that denied him daylight.

When he was inside his office, he closed the door. Then he called the one person who might be able to help him now, who might still be able to protect Mandy's grave.

He called Bethie, but somewhere in Philadelphia the phone merely rang and rang and rang.

10

Greenwich Village, New York City

Kimberly left her apartment walking fast. She'd gotten up early – Wednesday was her weekly shooting lesson – and lately she'd come to really need her time on the firing range. She'd donned jeans and a casual T-shirt, stuck her fine long hair into a ponytail, then headed out to catch the commuter train to Jersey. Just like clockwork, she told herself. Wednesday morning just like any other Wednesday morning. Breathe deep. Inhale the smog.

It wasn't like any other Wednesday morning. For starters, she no longer had to show up for work. She had been so pale and jumpy yesterday afternoon, Dr Andrews had grumpily ordered her to take the rest of the week off, her first vacation since Mandy's funeral. She could take her time today. Stop and smell the roses. Ease up a little, as her professor had instructed her to do.

Her footsteps remained compulsively quick, more of a run than a walk. She glanced over her shoulder more than any normal person should. And even though she absolutely, positively knew better, she was carrying her Glock .40 fully loaded and with the safety off. *Don't be this freaky*, she kept telling herself.

She was doing it anyway.

Funny thing was, she didn't even feel that bad at the moment. No hairs standing up at the nape of her neck. No cold chills creeping down her spine. No sense of doom, which almost always preceded the anxiety attacks. The weather was balmy. The streets possessed enough people so that she was not isolated, while also being few enough people for her to maintain a large safety zone around herself. And even if someone did try to attack her, she found herself thinking, she was fully trained in self-defense as well as heavily armed. Kimberly Quincy a victim? Not likely.

Yet she was grateful to arrive at Penn Station. She took a seat on the commuter train, scrutinized her fellow passengers, and finally concluded that none of them appeared the slightest bit interested in her. People read magazines. People watched the scenery go by. People ignored her in favor of their own lives. Who would've thought?

'You're a fucking psycho,' she murmured, which finally did earn her a look from the guy sitting next to her. She thought of telling him that she was carrying a loaded gun, but given that he was heading into Jersey, he was probably carrying one, too. As Dr Andrews liked to say, normality was a relative term.

The train slowed for her stop. Just for the hell of it, she gave the guy next to her a big huge grin. He immediately broke eye contact and assumed the submissive position. That made her feel better for the first time in days.

She got off the train with a lighter step and was immediately assaulted by 100 percent humidity. Ah, another lovely Jersey day.

Reaching into her shoulder bag, she adjusted the Glock's safety to the on position, and started walking at a much more normal pace. New York City was behind her. The shooting range was only a few blocks away. New Jersey was hardly safer than Greenwich Village, but she did feel better here. Lighter. Free from some burden she couldn't name.

Kimberly had loved shooting from the first moment she'd cajoled her parents into letting her go. She'd started begging at eight. Her father had done the expected thing and told her to talk to her mother. Her mother had done the expected thing and said, absolutely not. Kimberly, however, had been possessed. Every time her father headed for the practice range, she started badgering. Four years later, on her twelfth birthday, her mother finally caved.

'Guns are loud, guns are violent, guns are evil. But if you won't take my word for it, fine! Go shoot yourself silly.'

Mandy had wanted to go, too, but for a change their parents both agreed that handling guns would not be in Mandy's best interest. That suited Kimberly just fine. Mandy cried. Mandy got upset. Mandy was a big baby, and Kimberly was more than delighted to have an afternoon with her father all to herself.

She wasn't sure what her father thought. It was always hard to know what her father thought.

At the firing range, he carefully explained the basic rules for gun handling and firearms safety. She learned how to take apart a .38 Chief's Special, name all the parts, clean all the parts, and then put them back together again. Then came lectures on always keeping the gun pointed at a safe target. Always keep the gun unloaded until ready to fire. Always keep the safety on until ready to fire. Always wear earplugs and eye protection. Always listen to the range officer. Load when he says load, fire when he says fire, and cease firing when he says cease fire.

Then at long last, her father let her aim the .38 Chief's Special at a paper target and practice dry firing, while he stood behind her and adjusted her aim. She remembered the muffled sound of his voice next to her ear, more like a deep rumble than words. She remembered being anxious to get to live ammunition after two hours of straight lectures, and her father, exhibiting his typical, maddening calm.

'*A gun is not a toy. On its own, a gun is not even a weapon. It's an inanimate object. It is up to you to bring it to life and use it responsibly. Whose job is it to use it responsibly?*'

'*Mine!*'

'*Very good. Now let's go through it one more time . . .*'

It had taken four trips to the firing range before he let her fire live rounds. He placed the target at fifteen feet. She hit it with a respectable six shots, four clustered in the middle. She promptly dropped her pistol, jerked off her goggles, and threw her arms around her father's neck.

'I did it, I did it, I did it! Daddy, I did it!'

And her father said, 'Don't ever throw down your firearm like that! It could go off and hit someone. First put on the safety, then set down the gun and step away from the firing line. Remember, you must treat your pistol responsibly.'

She had been deflated. Maybe even tears flooded her eyes. She didn't remember anymore. She just recalled the curious change that came over her father's face. He looked at her crestfallen expression and perhaps he finally heard his own words, because his features suddenly shifted.

He said quietly, 'You know what, Kimmy? That was great shooting. You did a wonderful job. And sometimes . . .

sometimes your father is a real ass.'

She had never heard her father call himself an ass before. She was pretty sure that was one of the words she was never supposed to repeat. And she liked that. That made it special. Their first real father-daughter moment. She could shoot a gun. And sometimes Daddy was a real ass.

She went with him to the firing range from then on out, and under his patient tutelage she graduated from a .38 Chief's Special to a .357 Magnum to a 9mm semiauto. As a form of silent protest, her mother enrolled her in ballet. Kimberly attended two lessons before coming home and announcing, 'Fuck ballet! I want a rifle.'

That got her mouth washed out with soap and no TV for a week, but was still worth every syllable. Even Mandy had been impressed. In a rare show of support, she'd spent the next few weeks saying fuck everything, and together they went through two bars of Ivory soap. A curious, delirious month, back in the days when the four of them had been a family.

Funny the things she hadn't thought about in a while. Funny the way the memory made her breathe hard now, like someone had socked her in the stomach, like someone was slowly squeezing her chest.

Dammit, Mandy. You couldn't stay out of the driver's seat? Sure, quitting drinking is hard, but you could've at least stayed off the roads!

No more fucking ballet. No more fucking anything. Just a white cross in beautiful, prestigious Arlington cemetery because her mother's family was loaded with military connections and had somehow earned Bethie and her children the honor. Mandy and war heroes. Who would've thought?

Kimberly had barely been able to make it through the

funeral. She had thought the irony might drive her mad, and she didn't think her mother could take it if she had started laughing hysterically, so Kimberly had spent the whole service with her lips pressed into a bloodless line. And her father? Once again, it was so hard to know what her father thought.

He'd been calling her lately. Leaving gently inquiring messages because she wouldn't pick up the phone. She didn't return his calls. Not his calls, not her mother's calls. Not anyone's calls. Not now. Not yet. She didn't know when. Maybe soon?

She didn't like the anxiety attacks. They shamed her and she didn't want to speak to her overly perceptive father when he might catch the fear in her voice.

Guess what, Dad? I couldn't teach Mandy to be strong, but apparently she's inspired me to be a flake. Whoo-hoo! Lucky you. Two fucked-up daughters.

She arrived at the shooting club. She pushed through the wooden door into the dimly lit lounge area, and the cooler air swept over her like a welcoming breeze. The club boasted a small, utilitarian lounge, empty this early in the morning, then the door leading to the cavernous shooting range. Kimberly didn't look at the threadbare sofa or the tall display case filled with shooting medals or the line of animal-head trophies mounted on the wall. She was looking for him. Even as she told herself that wasn't why she'd been so excited to get here first thing this morning, she was looking for the new gun pro, Doug James.

Thick brown hair, sprinkled with silver at the temples. Deep blue eyes, crinkled with laugh lines at the corners. A tall, well-toned body. A broad, hard-muscled chest. Doug James had started at the rifle association six months ago, and Kimberly wasn't the only female who was suddenly very interested in lessons.

Not that she thought about him that way. She wasn't like Mandy, always on the lookout for a man. She wasn't like her mom, incapable of defining herself except through a man's eyes. Anyway, Doug James was almost as old as her father. A happily married man, besides. And he was a terrific shot, of course. Had won a lot of shooting competitions, or so the rumors went.

All in all, he was a highly capable instructor, who was working wonders with her stance.

And a patient man. Kind. Had a way of looking at her, as if he was genuinely interested in what she was saying. Had a way of greeting her, as if he was made happier by her simply entering the room. Had a way of talking to her, as if he understood all the things she didn't say . . . the nightmares she still had of her sister where she was in the car with Mandy, grabbing desperately at the wheel . . . the sense of isolation that would sweep down upon her suddenly, with her sister gone, her parents fragmented, until she felt like a speck of sand in a vast, uncaring universe.

The need she had today, to come here and fire a mammoth stainless steel firearm at a puny paper target as if that would bring her world back together again. As if that would make her strong.

She walked up to the counter, where the head of the rifle association, Fred Eagen, was bent over a stack of paperwork.

'I'm ready for Doug,' she said.

'Doug's not here today. Called in sick.' Fred flipped over the next document, signed the bottom. 'He was going to try you at your apartment. You must've already left.'

Kimberly blinked. 'But . . . but . . .'

'I guess it came on quick.'

'But . . .' She sounded like an idiot.

Fred finally looked up. 'If a guy gets sick, a guy gets sick. He'll see you next week.'

'Next week. Of course, next week,' she murmured and struggled to recover her bearings. Sick. It happened. Why should she feel this bereft? He was just a gun instructor, for God's sake. She didn't need him. She didn't need anyone. Why oh why were her hands suddenly shaking so badly. And why, oh why, did she suddenly feel so desperately, keenly alone?

She took her gun. She went out to the firing range and set up. Earplugs and protective eye gear. Box of ammunition. Smell of cordite in the air. The fragrance of her youth, the comforting weight of her stainless steel Glock, loose in her hand.

She set up targets fifty feet back. She annihilated paper hearts, she shredded paper heads. But she already knew now, that it wouldn't be enough. She had not come here for the practice. She had come here for a man.

And more than anything else that had happened in the last month, that proved to her that something wasn't right anymore. Strong, logical Kimberly wasn't the person she had always thought herself to be.

When she left, she was walking too fast again, and even though it was ninety-five degrees out, she fought a chill.

Society Hill, Philadelphia

Bethie was nervous. No, she was giddy. No, she was nervous. Okay, she was both.

Standing outside her stately brick town house in Society

Hill on a sunny Wednesday morning, she ran a quick hand over her sundress and picked imaginary lint from the tiny purple flowers that patterned the gold silk. Next she inspected her freshly painted toenails, now colored Winsome Wine, whatever that meant, and peeking out from strappy gold sandals. She didn't detect any signs of smudging. She glanced at her hands. Fine, as well.

She'd risen at five A.M.; for the first time in months, anticipation of good things had brought her instantly awake and eager to start the day. With Tristan not due to arrive for another two hours, she'd celebrated her morning with a long overdue bubble bath followed by an impromptu pedicure. She'd even done her fingernails, and it still shocked her to look down and see two well-groomed hands. It had been a while, longer than she wanted to think.

Now she had a large wicker picnic basket slung over her left arm. She'd bought it years ago on a whim, one of those impulse buys based more upon the life she wished she was leading than the life she truly led. She had thought of it immediately when Tristan had suggested they go for a drive, and had dedicated twenty minutes of her morning to locating the basket in the back of her kitchen pantry. She'd then stocked it with crackers and Brie, grapes and caviar, a fresh French baguette and a bottle of La Grande Dame champagne. Tristan struck her as a man of refined tastes, and yes, she was definitely trying to impress.

She glanced at her watch. Ten past seven. She grew nervous again. What if he didn't show? She was leaping to conclusions. After all, last night she'd been nearly twenty minutes late, but she'd still kept their date.

She wanted him to arrive. She wanted to go on a drive, far away from this house that was too big and this city that held too many memories. She wanted one afternoon when she stepped out of a middle-aged, divorced woman's skin and lived with the sun on her face.

Last night, coming home from her first date in years, she had realized that it was time to move forward again. Not easy, but time.

A short beep-beep broke into her thoughts. Bethie looked down the narrow street to see a little red convertible with New York plates dart around the corner and come flying down the lane.

'My goodness, what is this?' she asked as Tristan came to a screeching halt, ran a hand through his hair, and beamed.

'Your carriage, my lady.'

'Yes, but what *is* it?'

'The Audi TT Roadster two twenty-five Quattro,' he announced with pride, 'based loosely on the 1950s Porsche Boxter. Cute, isn't she?'

He swung open the driver-side door and came bounding around the front, looking somehow flushed, windblown, and dashing all at once.

Bethie held out her basket, thinking now would be a good time to say something clever, but distracted by the bright, burning light in his eyes, the impact of his smile. 'I fixed a picnic lunch,' she stated and instantly felt foolish for the obvious comment.

'Wonderful.'

She nodded, still feeling self-conscious. She returned her attention to the picnic basket. 'Champagne, caviar, Brie. I didn't know what you liked.'

'I like champagne, caviar, and Brie.' He reached for the basket, and his hands lingered on hers. He stood very close, handsome this morning in tan slacks and a deep blue cable-knit sweater. Sandalwood and lemon, she thought and wondered if she'd given herself away by inhaling too deeply.

'Did you sleep well?' he asked, his fingers lightly brushing hers.

'Yes. And you?'

'I didn't sleep a wink. I was too busy looking forward to seeing you.'

She flushed, but couldn't repress her smile. 'Very smooth,' she conceded.

'Is it? I practiced all the way over.' He grinned. Then, without warning, he leaned over and kissed her full on the mouth. She was still reeling when he straightened again and took the picnic basket from her arm.

'In all seriousness,' he said as he popped the trunk, 'I have not looked forward to a day as much as I've been looking forward to this one in a very long time. We are going to go someplace marvelous, Bethie. We are going to have an ungodly amount of fun. Are you with me?'

'I could do ungodly amounts of fun.'

'Perfect!'

He closed the trunk, then returned to get her door. The little red roadster really was commanding. Beautiful rounded lines on the outside. A striking black-and-chrome color scheme on the inside. It looked like something a movie star should drive, say Marilyn Monroe or James Dean. Bethie was almost afraid to touch it. Tristan, however, took her hand and without hesitation, helped lower her into the low-slung black leather seat.

'You know what?' he said suddenly. 'You should drive.'

'Oh, no. I couldn't—'

'Yes, yes, absolutely. Everyone needs to drive a sports car once in her life and today, it's your turn.'

He helped her back out of the car. She was still protesting when she found herself in the driver's seat, holding a small, rectangular key fob and wearing a very silly grin. The sleek chrome gauges winked at her. The rounded chrome gear stick felt warm and smooth beneath her palm. Tristan climbed into the passenger's seat. She barely looked at him. She hadn't even pulled away from the curb, and she was already in love with this car.

'See the little silver button?' He pointed to a small button on the corner of the key fob in her hand. 'Push it.'

She did and the tiny silver key shot out of the side of the box like a switchblade. She startled, almost dropped the key, then laughed. 'Oh my goodness, who thought of that?'

'Probably somebody in marketing. Pure gimmick, but highly effective. Now love, put it in the old ignition. Here's the lights, here's the windshield wipers, and here's the hand brake. Give it a whirl.'

She stalled the car in first. Jerked them into second as she tried to get a feel for the clutch, then finally spluttered down the road. It had been years since she'd driven a standard, not since her college days. But she quickly discovered that some part of her had missed the feel of a gear stick in her hand, the sense of controlling the vehicle as if it were a high-spirited horse, the surge of power as she felt the zippy car respond. She went around the block, grinding the gears painfully, but Tristan didn't seem to care and she found herself laughing breathlessly. She liked this car. She liked this man. She could do this.

'Listen to this, Bethie,' Tristan said. 'I got it just for you.'

He pushed a silver panel on the dash. It rose to reveal a

myriad of stereo buttons. Two more jabs with his finger, and Miles Davis's ''Round Midnight' poured out of discreet Bose speakers and flowed all around her.

'You remembered.'

'Bethie, of course.'

Miles Davis's trumpet began to wail. She found the proper rhythm for the gears, and the roadster began to purr. Tristan was right, she thought. Everyone should drive a little red sports car once in her life, and this car drove like a dream.

She took the on-ramp to I-76, feeling the roadster gather beneath her feet. First, second, third, pushing the tachometer all the way up into the red zone. The second turbo kicking in and pressing her back against her seat. Twenty, forty, eighty miles per hour, and still as smooth as silk.

'There you go,' Tristan said approvingly. 'That's how you drive, Bethie. Go after the road like a speed racer, don't let anything hold you back.'

She smiled. She pressed on the gas. She hit one hundred miles per hour and let the wind gather up her dark blond hair and the sun beat down on her upturned face.

'We're off like a herd of turtles!' Tristan roared over the rushing air.

She laughed, she drove faster, and she never bothered to mention that that was one of Mandy's favorite expressions. *I love you*, she thought. *God, I am so happy!*

Tristan was still watching her with that intent look in his eyes. He had pulled on a pair of black leather driving gloves. He ran one gloved finger down her cheek.

'Bethie,' he said after a moment. 'Tell me about your second daughter. Tell me about Kimberly.'

11

The Olsen Residence, Virginia

It took Rainie four tries to find Mary Olsen's house. The first time, she didn't even notice the narrow driveway off the heavily wooded road. The second time, she spotted the driveway, but couldn't see any sign of a house through the trees. The third time, knowing she had to be close, she drove halfway up the driveway, saw a freaking mansion perched on top of a circular drive, and hurriedly backed down before some butler loosed the Dobermans on her. The fourth time, she parked alongside the road, got out of her car, and went over to the discreet black mailbox on its ornate wrought-iron post to read the house number.

'You're kidding me,' she said to no one in particular, then flipped open the file of background information she had gathered on Mary Olsen, and scanned the material one last time. 'Huh. Who the hell is a twenty-five-year-old unemployed waitress sleeping with to get a house like that? And does he want a mistress?'

Who, turned out to be a neurosurgeon, which Rainie learned when she drove back up the driveway and made it to the front door. Dr Olsen had already left for the day, but an oil portrait of his grandfather was the first thing she was shown when the butler – yes, the butler – led her into the cavernous marble foyer. He left her to stare while he went to fetch Mrs Olsen.

Rainie amused herself by price-checking the interior. One gigantic round crystal table, centered in the middle of the foyer, bearing a Lalique stamp. She figured twenty grand. One highly polished side table constructed from bird's-eye maple with black walnut trim and legs straight out of a Louis XIV wet dream – probably fifteen grand. Sixteen-foot draperies of peach velvet with gold satin lining and miles of gold cord. Twenty thousand, maybe even thirty; custom window dressings weren't her strong suit.

At any rate, the room seemed to have a fifteen-grand minimum, which put Rainie way out of her league, as the last she knew her entire body was worth a whopping buck eighty-two, or something like that.

'Would you like some coffee?'

Mary Olsen stood at the top of the circular staircase, looking down into the foyer. As she was half-expecting Scarlett O'Hara at this point, Rainie found her first impression of Mary disappointing. No hoop skirt. No big hair. Just a frightfully young-looking girl in a blue-and-yellow flowered Laura Ashley dress, leaning over the gilded railing and looking at Rainie expectantly.

'I could handle coffee,' Rainie said at last, her voice booming off the marble.

'Decaf or regular?'

'Never saw the point to decaf.'

Mary Olsen smiled. Rainie thought the expression appeared tight on her face. She was nervous, Rainie realized. Little Mrs Doctor Olsen was frightened of her.

Wow, she felt good for the first time in days.

Mary descended the stairs. She held on to the railing with both hands, which Rainie found interesting. So the former waitress was now living in a mansion, but obviously still not comfortable about it. When Mary hit floor level, Rainie got her second surprise. The woman was three inches taller than Rainie and had the dark eyes and sultry features of a Super-model. That explained Dr Olsen's interest, but he was dressing her all wrong. Screw Laura Ashley. Mary should be running around in V-neck dresses colored deep, sinner's red. Then again, the Olsens would probably go through a lot more butlers that way.

'We'll go into the front parlor,' Mary said, her features carefully blank. 'Follow me.'

Rainie dutifully followed. The front parlor turned out to be bigger than her whole loft, crowded with white-painted French antiques, and decorated with more pale colors, this time blue and cream. When Mary sat on the delicate loveseat, her dress blended right into the silk-covered cushions. One minute Rainie was with a person, next minute it looked like she was interviewing a sofa with a head.

'As I mentioned on the phone,' Rainie said, 'I have a few simple questions about Amanda Quincy.'

Mary held up a hand. 'The coffee, please.'

Rainie blinked, feeling gauche. Then she realized that good old Jeeves was hovering with a silver tray bearing an antique coffee urn and two tiny china cups. He set the serving tray down on a side table and did the honors of pouring the first dose. Rainie accepted hers with genuine trepidation. The paper-thin china looked old, rare, and highly fragile. She was guessing that it held approximately three sips of coffee, at which time she'd be forced to refill the cup herself from the heavy silver pot. Maybe she'd just nurse this batch.

'Nice place,' Rainie tried, attempting to balance the teacup on her knee while still trying to figure out why Mandy's best friend appeared so nervous.

'It's been in my husband's family for generations.'

'He's a doctor?'

'Yes.'

'Works lots of hours?'

'Of course. He's one of the best neurosurgeons in the country and his patients need him.'

Rainie was getting a few things now. 'Older?'

'In his forties.'

'Met him where you used to work, huh? Went from best tipper to permanent meal ticket. Not bad.'

Mary flushed. 'I suppose you could look at it that way.'

'Oh no, trust me, I admire you. Wouldn't mind meeting a neurosurgeon, myself.'

'Mark's a wonderful husband.' Mary was still in defensive mode.

'Mark and Mary. Oh yeah, those Christmas cards have got to be killers.'

'I thought you said you were working on Mandy's accident.'

'You're right; I'm getting off track. So about the night in question—'

'What about that night?' Mary interrupted. 'I'm afraid I don't understand the reason for this interview. The accident happened over a year ago. Mandy got drunk, she drove. She did that sometimes, you know. I don't see any point in you being here.'

'Well, I heard about the coffee, thought I'd stop by.'

Rainie sighed at the confused look on Mary's face. Sarcasm was definitely lost on the woman. 'So, about that night. You told Mandy's father that she had come over to play cards.'

'That's right. We always played cards on Wednesday night. At least we did.'

'Who's we?'

'Mandy, myself, Tommy, and Sue.'

'You knew each other from . . .'

'We used to work together, at the restaurant, before I met Mark. Why is this relevant?' Mary had that tight look on her face again.

'Just asking,' Rainie replied lightly. 'So the four of you are playing cards.'

'Hi-low-jack,' Mary supplied.

'Great. Hi-low-jack. Party starts at . . .'

'I wouldn't call it a party,' Mary said immediately. 'We were drinking soda, you know. I told Mr Quincy that we were drinking Coke.'

'I got that. Playing cards, drinking Coke. You started at?'

'Nine, maybe ten. Sue's still a waitress and she had the dinner shift.'

'You guys started that late on a weeknight?'

'Sue and Mandy waitressed, Tommy's a bartender. So they don't have to be at work until noon at the earliest. And I . . . well, hours don't really matter much for me anymore.'

Rainie thought she detected a trace of bitterness there. All was not well with Cinderella and Prince Charming. 'You played cards until?'

'Two-thirty.'

'Drinking soda the whole time.'

'Yes,' Mary said quickly. Too quickly. She looked down

at her lap, where her fingers were now intertwined. Here we go, Rainie thought.

'You told Mandy's father that she didn't have anything to drink other than Diet Coke.'

'I said I didn't see her drink anything other than Diet Coke.'

'You didn't see?'

'I didn't see.'

Rainie stood up. She put her cup back on the silver tray, happy to be rid of breakable objects. Then she turned back on Mary, and this time her gaze was hard. 'Didn't see, Mary? *Didn't see?* Now why does that seem to imply that Mandy might have been drinking after all, but you don't want to admit it?'

Mary's gaze had become fixated on her lap. She untangled her fingers, twisted the three-carat rock on her left hand, then tangled her fingers back up again.

'I swear I didn't know,' she whispered.

'Do us both a favor, Mary. Spit it out.'

Mary's head jerked up. Her eyes were growing darker; maybe Mrs Doctor Olsen had some fire in her after all. 'She carried the Diet Coke can with her everywhere, okay? I didn't think much of it at the time, but Mandy kept the can with her everywhere. You know, even when she went into the bathroom.'

'You think she might have been mixing her own drink on the side. Looks like Diet Coke, smells like Diet Coke, oops so I added a little rum.'

'It wouldn't have been the first time.'

'Alcoholics do learn some good tricks,' Rainie agreed, though personally she'd never been one for mixed drinks. For her, it would always be beer. 'Well, let's think about this, Mary. Amanda is doing a little bartending of her own. You say she got here ten at the latest, and didn't leave until two-thirty. That's at least four and a half hours of spiked Diet Coke. Couldn't you tell?'

'No,' Mary said immediately. There was a clarity to her voice now, certainty that had been previously lacking. Interesting. 'That was the thing with Mandy,' Mary continued earnestly. 'No matter how much she had to drink, she always seemed fine. Functional. Back when we were working, she used to brag about her tolerance. We all believed her. We never thought . . . never would've thought, that she had a problem.'

'So her joining AA was news to you?'

'Yes. Though later, when we all looked back on things, it made sense. There were some nights after closing that she'd sit in the bar and down eight drinks before heading home. Even if she seemed all right, how right could she be? She wasn't much bigger than me and alcohol doesn't exactly evaporate from your bloodstream.'

'So she could've been sneaking drinks that night and you wouldn't have known?'

'Yes.' Mary nodded her head emphatically. 'That's true.'

'What about this mystery man?'

'Mystery man?' Mary blinked.

'At the funeral, you implied to Quincy that Mandy had met someone. The new love of her life.'

'No, I didn't.'

'You didn't?'

'No. I'm not sure where Mr Quincy got that idea. I don't remember saying any such thing. Why would I say such a thing?' Mary spoke in a rush.

Rainie cocked her head to the side. She regarded Mary intently. 'Maybe Quincy misunderstood you.'

'Maybe.' Mary nodded vigorously. 'It was a funeral. He wasn't in the best shape. None of us . . .' Her voice choked for the first time, her head bobbed back down. 'None of us were.'

'Mary, are you sure you want to stick with this story? That your best friend got loaded on her own. Drove home on her own. Mowed down an old pedestrian on her own.'

'I'm telling you what I know to the best of my knowledge—'

'It's not what you said four weeks ago at the funeral.'

'It is, too! Mr Quincy got it all wrong! I don't know, maybe he's even more grief stricken than we thought so now he's grasping at straws and twisting what I said. Who knows what grief-crazed fathers do!'

'Grief-crazed?' Rainie echoed skeptically.

Mary finally flushed. She looked away. On her lap, however, her fingers were tangling and untangling furiously. Rainie figured it would be a miracle if they didn't end up with whiplash. Rainie took a deep breath. She nodded at Mary thoughtfully. She took her time and paced the room.

'Beautiful furniture,' she commented.

Mary didn't say anything. She looked now as if she would cry.

'Must have cost your husband a lot of money.'

'Mark inherited most of it,' she murmured.

'Still makes quite an impression. Must have blown you away the first time you saw all this. Cinderella, entering the castle.'

'Please, I'm telling you the truth about Mandy.'

'Fine. All right, you're telling the truth. I haven't denied it. I mean, I wasn't around a year ago. How do I know what your best friend drank on your last night together? How do I know if she laughed honestly while playing cards with you, or if it was some kind of drunken stupor? Hey, I don't even know if she hugged you before she left, thanked you for a great evening and for keeping her busy on the long nights when she was doing her best not to drink. Quitting cold turkey is tough. I've been there. It's tough and good friends make all the difference.'

Mary bowed her head again. Her shoulders had started to shake.

'You're pretty lonely, aren't you, Mary?' Rainie said bluntly. 'You're sitting in the house you always thought you wanted, and it's a prison cell. The proverbial gilded cage.'

'I don't think I want to talk to you anymore.'

'Your best friend's dead, your husband works all the time. Yeah, if I were you and I met the right man, someone who told me I looked pretty, someone who complimented my smile, I'd pretty much do whatever he wanted.'

'This is crazy! I don't know what it is you think you're doing, but we're through. I mean that.' Her head came up. She said sternly, 'Get out.'

And Rainie replied with the same artlessness Mary had employed before: 'You mean you're not looking for a new best friend, Mary? You're not looking for anyone new to betray?'

'Damn you!' Mary sprang to her feet. 'Harold!' she yelled. 'Harold!'

The butler came scurrying into the room, his eyes wide at the hysteria percolating through his mistress's call. Rainie feigned a yawn, while Mary stabbed a shaking finger in her direction and screeched, 'Get her out. Out, out, *out*!'

The butler looked at Rainie. He was middle aged, and his bald head and gaunt features really didn't make him the intimidating type. Rainie, on the other hand, lounged against yet another side table with her right hand positioned strategically on a heavy gold candelabrum. Poor Harold didn't know what to do.

'Do you miss her?' Rainie asked Mary. 'When Wednesday night rolls around, do you miss Mandy at all?'

'*Get out!*'

'The irony is,' Rainie persisted softly, 'that Mandy was the drunk, but I'm willing to bet she would've missed you. If your positions had been reversed, she would've missed you badly.'

'*Harrrrrooooold!*'

The butler finally edged his way over to Rainie and put a hand on her arm. His touch was light, but firm, and she gave him credit. He managed to hold himself with regal dignity, when God knows the rest of the situation had clearly moved beyond that.

Rainie gave in to the light pull of his hand, and let him lead her back into the foyer toward the door.

Mary, oddly enough, followed right behind them, her features still distorted and her right hand pressed protectively against her belly.

'Thank you for the coffee,' Rainie said politely to Harold. 'I'm sure I'll be in touch,' she added to Mary, before heading down the broad steps.

Her last view, as she opened the door of her rent-a-wreck, was Mary Olsen standing in the grand entrance of her enormous mansion, screaming, 'You have no idea what you're talking about, lady. You have no fucking idea!'

* * *

Two miles from the Olsen residence, Rainie pulled over her car and killed the ignition. Despite her earlier composure, her hands had started trembling. The adrenaline was ebbing from her bloodstream, leaving her light-headed in its wake.

'Well,' she murmured, all alone in her tiny car, 'that wasn't what I expected.'

She thought of Mary Olsen's furious features and final taunting remark. She thought of Quincy, and the host of phone calls he'd received last night. She heard an all-too-familiar ringing in her ears.

Rainie leaned forward and rested her forehead against the steering wheel. She was suddenly very tired. Last time she'd heard ringing in her ears, small children had died. And things had gotten even worse from there.

She took a moment. Then two and three. Okay, she had a plan. She pulled back onto the windy country road and since she hadn't had the funds to buy a cell phone yet, she drove until she found a gas station with a pay phone. From there, she called her new partner in crime, Virginia PI Phil de Beers. She was lucky that he was in. She was even luckier that he was currently in between cases, and if she was willing to pay his rate to tail Mary Olsen, he was more than willing to do the work. That took care of merry Mary for a bit.

Hoping her luck would hold out, Rainie tried Officer Amity next. The officer on duty informed her that Big Boy was on patrol. Rainie asked to be switched to dispatch, whom she sweet-talked into transferring her to Amity's car. Dispatch did her the honor of introducing her, and Officer Amity picked up the radio receiver already sounding unhappy.

'What d'you want?'

'Officer Amity! How's my favorite state trooper?'

'What d'you want?'

'Oh, just thought I'd see if you'd had any luck locating that vehicle we spoke of.'

'You mean in the twelve hours since we talked?'

'That would be what I'm going for.'

'I have a job, ma'am.'

'So the answer is no? Officer, you're breaking my heart.'

'I sincerely doubt that,' Amity said dryly.

'What are the chances of getting that information sometime today?'

'I don't know. Ask the broader civilian and criminal community. If enough drivers promise not to rear-end each other and enough reprobates cease breaking and entering, I may have a shot.'

'So if I douse the entire state in Valium . . .'

'I like the way you think.'

Rainie sighed heavily. Apparently that was the right tactic; Officer Amity sighed heavily as well.

'Thursdays are my day off,' he told her. 'If it doesn't happen today, I'll make sure I get to it tomorrow.'

'Officer Amity, you're super!'

'Wonderful,' he grumbled. 'I finally impress a woman and she lives three thousand miles away. Talk to you later, ma'am.'

He clicked off before Rainie had a chance to reply, which also saved her from dealing with that last statement.

She returned to her car. She got out the police reports of Mandy's crash. Then she got out her newly purchased Virginia state map.

Forty minutes later, she found the bend in the road where the accident had happened. Quincy had been right. This wasn't on any direct route from Mary Olsen's mansion and

Lisa Gardner

it wasn't on any direct route from Mandy's apartment. In fact, this place wasn't any direct route to anywhere. It was a narrow country road leading from nowhere and going to nowhere with lots of twists and turns in between.

The bend in question was deep and arching, forming a sixty-degree curve complete with dense brush, thick trees, and a single telephone pole. Off to one side there was a small unpainted cross. Recently decorated with plastic flowers, probably by Oliver Jenkins's widow.

Rainie parked her car. She got out and for a long time, she simply stood there, feeling the wind on her face. The road was quiet, no other cars in sight. The trees rustled overhead, and in her current frame of mind, the sound reminded her of dry, clicking bones.

She had to walk seventy feet to the telephone pole. A long enough distance to stop a car, she thought, or at least start to brake. She put her hand on the telephone pole. Then she ran her fingers down the violent scar slashing into the wood. Splinters stood straight out, the raw wood of the wound still lighter than the weathered exterior. She pressed the shards of wood gently back into place, as if that would somehow make things right.

The wind rose. The trees rustled and for a moment, it was very easy to believe she'd just heard someone laugh.

Rainie's heart was thumping loudly. She was suddenly keenly aware of how alone she was in this place. And just how thick the underbrush, and just how dark the depths of the wood.

Five in the morning, Mandy had hit this post. Five in the morning, the trees barely kissed by sun, and the wind still cool. Five in the morning, dark, isolated, and terribly, terribly deserted.

Rainie had to get back to her car. She got in the driver's side and locked the doors with shaking hands. Her shoulders were hunched. She could feel her heart loud and insistent in her chest.

She sat there. She wondered how many times Quincy had come to this mournful place. And then she started to drive because she didn't care what anyone said. Standing next to that telephone pole, she'd been certain she was not alone.

12

Pennsylvania Dutch Country

Bethie was having a marvelous time. The sun was bright, the sky was blue, the wind was cool against her neck. She loved the feel of the car beneath her hands. She loved the sound of Tristan's voice as he regaled her with story after story. And she liked telling him her stories, of her mother, her daughter, even her ex-husband, Pierce, whom she now suspected had a girlfriend in Portland, Oregon.

Time rolled by as easily as the miles. They headed west at first, no location in mind, then, on a whim, shifted south and drove into southern Pennsylvania with its lush expanse of verdant fields and the beautiful old farmhouses. They spotted women walking down dusty roads wearing quaint white bonnets. They passed horse-drawn carriages. They saw a man in his stone barnyard, bent over a woodpile and raising a blunt ax.

Tristan told her the histories of the various Germanic religious groups who'd settled here. She nodded, inhaling the scent of fresh mowed hay and thinking this was the most alive she'd felt in years.

They came to a narrow, twisty road shooting off into the fields.

'Let's take it!' Tristan declared. So she did.

The road turned to gravel, then dirt. It grew narrower and the crop grew taller. A mile later, sheafs of wheat flowed along the side of the bright red car like a golden river.

'Keep going,' Tristan urged her eagerly. So she did.

The tide of wheat broke. They emerged into the low grass of a riverbank and Bethie hit the brakes right before they hit the water. She laughed breathlessly. Tristan clambered out of the car.

'Get out,' he told her. So she did.

'Come on, we're going to have our picnic,' he informed her. 'Look, I also brought champagne.'

They drank champagne. They ate caviar. They devoured the rich old cheese. Bethie sat in the curve of his body, with her arm pressed against his right side and the scar she thought of so protectively. He brushed bread crumbs from her knee. Then he lowered her down into the sweet-smelling grass, and covered her mouth with his as his fingers found her breast.

Afterwards, she stroked his right side tenderly. Then they both got up and without speaking, got dressed.

'Isn't it wonderful out here?' she murmured. 'So peaceful and isolated. I wonder how many cars must whiz by on the highway without ever thinking of taking this turn. There's probably not anyone around for miles. Think of it: it's our own special little place.'

Tristan turned back toward her. In the aftermath of making love, his blue eyes seemed especially fierce.

'Let's go for a walk,' he told her. So she did.

13

Virginia

Rainie was in trouble. She was thinking dangerous thoughts. And she was in the middle of doing a very dangerous thing. She wasn't heading back to the Motel 6. Instead, she was driving to Quincy's.

He would want a full report of her investigation, and she had news at this point, or maybe not really news, more of a feeling that she didn't want to deliver by phone. He would want to analyze everything. That was his way. And she did not want to picture him sitting in the dark again, contemplating horrible things all alone like his daughter's murder.

Then there were all the questions. Maybe Mary Olsen was simply a little batty, a high-strung gold-digger desperate for attention. Perhaps the torrent of phone calls to Quincy's house were purely coincidence, a bunch of bored felons looking for sick entertainment. And maybe Mandy's accident was still an accident, and everyone else was merely seizing the opportunity to mess with a reputable FBI agent's mind.

Or maybe there was a mystery man. Maybe he'd helped Mandy get drunk that night, guessing from her past behavior where that would lead. And maybe he understood what Mandy's subsequent death would do to Quincy. Leave him feeling off balance, distracted, alone. Leave him vulnerable as the real plan began to unfold, the real threat to emerge . . .

There had been a time when Rainie would have dismissed such a theory as outlandish. Too cold, too callous to be possible. But that was before what had happened in Bakersville last year. Now she had the same fundamental training Quincy did. She understood the worst men could do, and she no longer considered anything to be too cruel to happen. Most people thought murderers killed out of some sort of necessity. Those were the easy cases. Far worse were psychopaths who considered murder to be not only a hobby, but a recreational sport.

Quincy had been there for her once. She planned on returning the favor.

Rainie consulted her map again, blew by her turnoff, and after thirty-six hours of practice, executed a perfectly brilliant and highly illegal U-turn. She went down the desired street.

The road was wide here, boasting a gracefully curving sidewalk and tons of freshly planted magnolia trees. New neighborhood, she decided. New money. She turned into a cul-de-sac and tried to keep her eyes from popping out of her head. Huge brick colonials sat up on vast expanses of emerald lawn. Big houses. Big yards. Fenced-in properties and gated drives.

She had figured Quincy's security-conscious nature would place him in some type of gated community, but she hadn't planned on this. She followed the house numbers down to the end, where a smaller, more discreet brick house was tucked back from the road. Rainie knew it was Quincy's without having to check the address; it was the only home where every single bush had been removed, eliminating places for the discriminating intruder to hide.

She looked at his denuded lot and sighed. 'Quincy, Quincy, Quincy,' she murmured. 'You have got to take a vacation.'

She pulled up to the black, wrought-iron gate and pushed the intercom button. It was only four P.M. and she really didn't expect Quincy to be home, so she was surprised when someone answered her buzz. She was even more surprised that it was a woman's voice.

'Name and business,' the woman asked evenly.

'Uhhhh, Lorraine Conner. I work with Quincy.' Not quite a lie.

'Please look into the camera and show your ID.'

Run now, Rainie thought, or forever hold your peace. Gamely, she stared into the mounted camera and flashed her PI's license.

Moments later, the gate began to rumble, then slide slowly back. Rainie drove up the sweeping drive to find the front door open and a woman standing there. Rainie got out of her car, feeling not nearly so good about things.

The woman in question was middle-aged. Probably forty, but maybe thirty – the severe hairstyle and stern gray suit didn't do her any favors. She stood stiffly, her arms folded over her chest and her feet clad in sensible black shoes.

Didn't look like a housekeeper, Rainie decided. Not Quincy's type so she couldn't be his ex-wife. On the other hand, she'd make one hell of a governess.

Shoulders back, head up, Rainie marched up to the entrance.

'Who are you?' she asked Dour Chic.

'The question is, who are you?'

'I already gave at the camera. Plus, I asked you first.'

Dour Chic smiled, but it came out as a grim line. 'Maybe, honey, but my ID is bigger than yours.' Dour Chic flashed her creds. The FBI emblem did carry a bit more weight than Rainie's puny PI's license. Rainie scowled and tried to figure out what was going on.

'I'm here to see Quincy,' she said.

'Why?'

'That would be Quincy's business, not yours.'

'At the moment, his business is my business.'

'Are you sleeping with him?'

Dour Chic blinked. 'I believe you misunderstand the nature of my business—'

'So you're not sleeping with him. Then my business and his business isn't your business.'

Rainie let the female agent sort that out. She knew the instant the woman had arrived at the implied conclusion, because she blushed.

'I thought you said you were a private investigator,' Dour Chic said with a scowl.

'Yeah, well, I thought you might be his ex-wife,' Rainie lied. 'Now, if you don't mind, I've given my name and I've traded IDs, so where's Quincy?'

The woman seemed to be debating with herself. 'You might be able to find him at Quantico,' she allowed brusquely. 'That's all I'm at liberty to say.'

'You don't expect him to come home tonight?'

'That's all I'm at liberty to say.'

'Oh, I get it,' Rainie said. 'The phone calls. You're the cavalry.'

The agent didn't answer right away. Then she gave a slow

nod. Rainie nodded back. She looked at the woman with new interest, and what she saw now made her feel small and more than a bit bad. Not a stern suit, but a professional suit fashioned to hide a handgun. Not a severe hairstyle, but one suitable for running down master criminals. Not a dour face, but the intelligent face of a smart, successful woman. In short, a genuine, certified one hundred percent well-trained federal agent. And then there was Rainie, a freshly hatched PI who had been fired from the policing job she'd loved because she'd once been driven to kill.

This was Quincy's world. And that quickly, Rainie was sorry that she'd intruded.

'Well, I'll be going now,' she said.

'I'll tell him you came.'

Rainie bit her lower lip. Of course the agent would tell him. That was her job, and Dour Chic obviously lived for her job.

'You do that. In the meantime, I'll try him at his office—'

'Quantico.'

'Yeah, Quantico—'

'It's a Marine base.'

'I know it's a Marine base!'

Dour Chic formed another thin-lipped smile. She was giving Rainie a fresh perusal as well, and her first impression was clearly sliding downhill.

Fuck it. Rainie didn't bother with goodbye. She turned around, climbed back into her car and tried not to let the gate hit her ass on the way out.

'Goddamn know-it-all,' she muttered a moment later, but she was driving too fast. She was thinking again of nights much too long ago to change. And she was thinking again that admitting to your past still didn't allow you to escape it. Some people grew up to be federal agents. And other people?

'Fuck it,' she said again.

Rainie should've quit while she was ahead. She found the turnoff to Quantico, then drove for fifteen minutes through a heavily wooded road where Marines jogged in formation along the edge of the blacktop and the air was repeatedly split by the crack of gunfire. She passed a number of indistinguishable buildings, heading deeper into the Marine base and feeling more and more like an interloper at Uncle Sam's private club. No one stopped her. No one asked for ID. She wasn't sure whether to be grateful or worried.

She had just started to relax when the Marine base ended, and a guard post abruptly loomed ahead. Apparently, someone had decided that the Marines could take care of themselves. The FBI Academy, however, required a great deal of protection. She halted at the guard post, where a stony-faced security officer took her name, studied her PI's license and told her she was not permitted to enter. She gave her name again. She flashed her ID. He told her that she was not permitted to enter.

'Look, I'm an associate of SupSpAg— er, Supervisory Special Agent Pierce Quincy,' she tried.

The grim guard was not impressed.

'I don't need full access or anything,' she attempted next. 'Don't you guys offer a visitor's pass?'

She learned she could indeed be a visitor. If her name had been given to him ahead of time. With appropriate clearance.

'So what the hell do I do now? Wait, wait,' she held up a hand upon seeing the firm expression on his chiseled face. 'I remember: I am not permitted to enter.'

After a little more wrangling, she finally agreed to wait in her car under the officer's tight scrutiny. In turn, he agreed to contact the BSU office and inquire if Supervisory Special Agent Pierce Quincy would like to come out and see a guest.

Fifteen minutes later, Quincy's car appeared. He looked tired, stressed, and not at all happy to see her. So much for the reunion scene where they ran to each other with open arms. Instead, she meekly followed his car off the Marine base into the nearby little town where he pulled into the parking lot of a restaurant.

'I want some coffee,' he said as he climbed out of his car.

'Hello to you, too,' she replied.

'You crash government facilities often?'

'I didn't realize it would be so hard.'

'Rainie, it's the *FBI* Academy. We have procedures and protocol. If just anyone could walk in, it would ruin the point.'

'Fine. Next time I'll wear my best cocktail dress.'

'Christ,' he said. 'You really can be childish.'

He headed for the restaurant. She stood rooted in the parking lot, stunned by the coldness in his voice. Then the shock wore off, and she went after him.

'What the hell is with you?' Rainie demanded, catching up with Quincy as he approached the cashier and grabbing his arm.

'Two coffees,' he ordered. 'One black, one with way too much cream and sugar.'

'I don't need coffee. I want an explanation.'

'Coffee's easier,' he told her, and wouldn't say another word until the amused cashier delivered both cups. Then he made Rainie follow him back outside, to a picnic table in a grove of trees she hadn't noticed before. The walk was long and didn't do a thing to calm her temper.

'Okay,' she announced the instant he sat at the table. 'What the hell is going on, Quincy? And you'd better start talking or you'll be wearing this coffee with "way too much cream and sugar."'

Quincy blew on his black, steaming brew. She could see now that the shadows had deepened under his eyes and his cheeks had gained the hollowed look of a man not sleeping at night. It was funny, she thought. Last year, she had been the one looking like walking death, and Quincy had been the one lecturing her to eat and sleep anyway. Stress is an even better reason to take care of yourself, he'd told her. Taking care of the body helps take care of the mind. If she repeated his own lecture back to him now, she wondered, how childish would *that* be?

'Have you heard of something called identity theft?' Quincy asked tersely.

Rainie sat down. She sipped her coffee. She nodded.

'A person steals someone's identity. Not too hard to do in this day and age. Gets the person's Social Security number and mother's maiden name, then uses that information to get a copy of the birth certificate and voilà, becomes the new person. It's amazing all the things you can do once you have basic documentation. Get a valid driver's license. Open a bank account or apply for a credit card. Buy a car, a red Audi TT roadster, I take it, registered and financed in the unwitting victim's name.'

'Someone used your name to buy a sports car?'

'In New York. Two weeks ago. In theory, I currently owe a Westchester dealership forty thousand dollars, payable in convenient monthly installments of eight hundred and eleven dollars over the next five years.'

'Someone stole an *FBI agent's* identity?'

'Why not? He's already given out my personal information to half the hardened criminals in the country. After that, what's one high-performance vehicle?' Quincy paused. He added grudgingly, 'At least the man has good taste.'

Rainie still couldn't believe it. 'Identity theft . . . Doesn't the Bureau have specialists in this area?'

'The Bureau has specialists in every area,' Quincy told her, but didn't sound encouraged. He set down his coffee cup, and Rainie was shocked to see that his hands were shaking.

'They took over my house, Rainie,' he said quietly. 'This afternoon fellow agents set up cameras on my daughter's grave. It's ironic. I'm an expert. In fact, I'm an expert in precisely these kinds of cases, and as of seven oh-five this morning, no one cares about my opinion anymore. As of seven oh-five this morning, I became a victim, and I have never hated anything more.'

'They're idiots, Quince. I've told you that before. If FBI agents were so smart, they wouldn't still be running around in such god-awful suits after the rest of the world has gone business casual. What kind of man starts his day by tying a noose around his neck anyway?'

Quincy glanced down at his burgundy tie, today's choice offering tiny navy blue and dark green geometric patterns and looking suspiciously close to the tie he wore the day before that and the day before that.

'I can't stand this,' he said baldly. 'Someone is taking over my life. I don't even know why.'

'Sure you do. You're the good guy. By definition, all the bad guys hate you.'

'Agents Rodman and Montgomery are working on the phone calls. They're staking out my house, and trying to trace ads placed in various prison newsletters, as if that will amount to anything. They're also working on tracking the Audi. I don't know what that has to do with anything, unless it's simply one more way for the UNSUB to thumb his nose at me – I'm still stuck in basic investigative strategies while he's shopping for luxury automobiles. He may have a point.'

Quincy sighed. He dragged a hand through his hair. 'Today, I amused myself by pulling all my old case files and building a database of anyone I've ever ticked off. The bad news is that there's a lot of them. The good news is that an amazing number of them are either in jail or dead.'

'That's what I like about you, Quincy. Your ability to network.'

He nodded absently. 'I'm eighty percent sure I'm a target, Rainie. I have no idea whose. I can't even be sure why. Revenge is the obvious answer. Why not? But for whatever reason, someone has started weaving a very complex web, and no matter what I do, I think I'm already stuck right smack in the middle of it.'

'You have friends, Quincy,' she said quietly. 'We'll help you. *I'll* help you.'

'Will you?' He looked her in the eye. 'Rainie,' he said softly, 'tell me what you learned about Mandy. Tell me what we both already know in our gut.'

Rainie looked away. She finished her coffee. She set the empty paper cup on the picnic table, then spun it between her hands. She didn't want to answer his request, and they both knew it. She also understood, however, that she couldn't soft-pedal the news. One more thing she and Quincy had in common – they preferred their bad news

Lisa Gardner

direct. Get it out. Get it over. Get it done.

'You're right,' she said shortly, 'something's rotten in Denmark.'

'It was murder?'

'I don't know that,' she countered immediately, her voice firm. 'What's the number one rule of investigating – no jumping to conclusions. At the moment, we have no physical evidence that suggests murder.'

'On the other hand . . .' he said for her.

'On the other hand, something's up with Mary Olsen.'

'Really?' Quincy seemed genuinely surprised. He frowned, rubbed his temples, and she could tell he'd gone straight to self-doubt about his impression of sweet little Mrs Doctor Olsen because he already appeared dazed.

'I spoke with her this morning, Quince, and Mary recanted everything. Mandy *looked* like she was drinking Diet Coke all night, but *maybe* she was spiking it with rum. You might have gotten the impression from Mary that Mandy had a boyfriend, but Mary now says that wasn't the case at all. Furthermore, Mandy had been known to drink and drive before, so it probably was as simple as that.'

'Mandy spiked her own Coke at a friend's house, then made it all the way to the middle of nowhere before suddenly being so drunk that she crashed?'

'I didn't say Mary had a good story, I just said she had a new story.'

'Why? She was my daughter's best friend. *Why?*'

Rainie could hear the deeper question behind those words. Why was this happening, to Mandy, to him? Why would someone hurt his daughter? Why wouldn't the world stay controlled and rational, the way all behavioral scientists wanted it to be?

146

'I think Mary's a lonely little princess,' Rainie answered softly. 'I think for the right kind of attention, she could be manipulated very easily.'

'The UNSUB got to her? Made her change her story?'

'Or the UNSUB got to her and had her make up the story in the first place. We don't really know that someone hurt Mandy. We do know that Mary said things at the funeral, however, that made you *think* someone hurt Mandy.'

'I'm being played,' Quincy filled in slowly. 'Harassing phone calls, illegal automobile purchases, rumors about my daughter . . .' He sat up a little straighter. 'Shit, I'm being played like a fucking violin!'

Rainie blinked. 'Since when did you take up swearing?'

'Yesterday. I'm finding it highly addictive. Like nicotine.'

'You're *smoking*, too?'

'No, but I haven't lost my deep and abiding love for metaphors.'

'I'm serious, Quince, you're letting yourself fall apart.'

'And apparently, you haven't lost your deep and abiding love for understatement.'

'Quincy—'

'What's wrong, Rainie?' he quizzed with that new edge in his voice. 'Can't stand for me to be so *human*?'

She was up from the picnic table before she knew what she was doing, her hands fisted at her side and her heart hammering in her chest. 'What is that supposed to mean?'

'It means . . . it means I'm tired,' Quincy said more quietly, his voice already conciliatory. 'It means I'm under pressure. It means probably, that I'm looking for a fight. But you're not the person for me to fight with. So let's not do this now. Let's forget I said anything, and simply not do this now.'

'Too late.'

'You looking for a fight, too, Rainie?'

She knew she shouldn't say it. She knew he was right and they were both stressed and now was not the time. Six long months without even one damn phone call. She brought up her chin and said, 'Maybe.'

Quincy got up from the picnic table. He dusted off his hands. He stared at her, and his gaze appeared a lot more composed than she felt. He'd always been so good at remaining in control.

'You want to know where we went wrong?' he said crisply. 'You want to know why it started out seeming so right, and then the world ended, not with a bang, but a whimper? I can tell you why, Rainie. It ended because you have no faith. Because one year later, the new, improved Lorraine Conner still doesn't believe. Not in me. And most certainly not in yourself.'

'I don't have faith?' she countered. '*I* don't have faith? This from the man whose only way of coming to terms with his daughter's death is to turn it into murder.'

Quincy recoiled sharply. 'Strike one to the woman in blue jeans,' he murmured, his expression growing hidden, growing hard.

Rainie wouldn't back down, though, couldn't back down. She'd only learned one way to deal with life, and that was to fight. 'No hiding behind your wry observations, Quincy. You want me to see you as human? Then act human. For God's sake, we're not even having a real argument yet, because you're still too busy lecturing me!'

'I'm simply saying you have no faith—'

'Stop psychoanalyzing me! Be less therapist, more man—'

'Man? Last time I tried being a man, you looked at me as

if I was going to hit you. You don't need a man, Rainie. You need either a blow-up doll or a damn saint!'

'Son of a bitch!' Rainie opened her mouth to yell further, then suddenly froze. She knew what he was talking about. That night, their last night together nearly eight months ago in Portland. Going to Pioneer Square. Sitting outside at Starbucks and listening to some a capella group perform. Talking, relaxing, having a nice time. And afterwards, going to his hotel because she still had the dingy apartment. She'd been thinking that she'd been so lonely. She'd been thinking that it was so good to see him again.

She'd moved closer. Inhaled the scent of his cologne. How much she loved that fragrance. And she'd felt him grow still, his body nearly breathless as if he understood that even exhaling might frighten her away. He'd gone still, so she'd kept approaching. She'd smelled the skin at his throat. Explored the curve of his ear. And then, something had taken hold of her. Desire maybe – she had so little experience with the real thing. She'd just wanted to touch him, more and more, if he'd stay, just like that, not moving, not breathing. She'd unbuttoned his shirt. She'd smoothed it from his shoulders. He had a hard chest, sculpted by a lifetime of running. The whorls of chest hair felt spongy against her palm. She placed her hand over his heart and felt it race against her touch.

On his collarbone and upper arm. Three small scars. Souvenirs of a shotgun blast, not all of which had been absorbed by his vest. Tracing those scars with her fingertips. Quincy, the super agent. Quincy, the superhero. Marveling . . .

His hand had suddenly snapped around her wrist. Her gaze jerked up. For the first time she saw his expression, dark and glittery with lust.

And the moment flew away from her. Her body froze, her mind rocketed back and she was thinking of yellow-flowered fields and smooth-flowing streams. She remained touching his body, but it was harsh now, a sick imitation of the real thing. The way she'd been taught in the very beginning.

Quincy had pushed her away. He'd told her to give him a minute. But she hadn't. She'd been humiliated, embarrassed, ashamed. And being Rainie, she'd told him it was all his fault, then left without saying another word. In the following months, it had been easier for her to simply let the phone ring. If he did catch her at home, she was always too busy to talk.

He was right; she was the one who'd stopped returning his calls. But he was supposed to know better. He was supposed to understand and still come after her. Except he hadn't.

'I'm supposed to be patient,' Quincy said, as if reading her mind. 'I'm supposed to be persistent. I'm supposed to be tolerant of your mood swings, your temper, your troubled past. I'm supposed to be everything, Rainie, but frustrated and angry—'

'Hey, I'm dealing with a lot of things—'

'And so am I! We're all dealing with things. Unfortunately, you seem to think you're the only person who's allowed to be petty. Well, I have news for you. I buried my daughter last month. My coworkers are now conducting surveillance on her grave. And no matter what I do, I can't reach my ex-wife, whose family connections might have enough power to call it off. I'm not just mad, Rainie. I'm pretty damn pissed off.'

'Well, there's your problem, Quincy – you're mimicking me when we both know I should be mimicking you.'

'I can't be perfect for you right now, Rainie.'

'Dammit, I am not that needy!' Rainie scowled at him. Quincy merely shook his head.

'You have to have faith,' he said quietly. 'I know it's hard, but at some point, you have to believe. Some people are evil, some people will hurt you, but not everyone will. And trying to stay safe by going at it alone doesn't work in the end. Isolation is *not* protection. I know. I thought it would be easier if I never opened up to my family, if I never got too close. Then I lost my daughter, and it hasn't been any easier at all. I am falling apart.'

'Quincy—'

'But I am going to put myself back together,' he continued as if he hadn't heard her. 'I am going to find the son of a bitch who did this. And if I have to be angry to do that, I'll be angry. And if I have to stop sleeping and start swearing and behave like an utter jerk, I'll do that, too. I'm coping, Rainie, and nobody ever said coping had to be pretty. Now if you'll excuse me, I need to try to reach Bethie again.'

Quincy turned away. He started walking back to his car. Rainie knew she should say something, but what came out didn't make much sense.

'Just because you survive, doesn't mean you'll end up happily-ever-after,' she yelled at him. 'Just because you cope, doesn't mean you'll win. Bad things can still happen. There's the jackals, you know. And, and . . . jackals everywhere . . .'

'Good night, Rainie.'

He wasn't going to stop. It was her turn to make the effort; fair was fair. Funny, she'd never thought about it until now, but in her family, no one was ever encouraged to stay.

'It's hard to teach an old dog new tricks,' she muttered in

her own defense. But Quincy was already gone and there wasn't anyone else left to hear.

The hour was growing late, dusk beginning to fall. In his car, Quincy used his cell phone to call his ex-wife. But once more he got the machine.

Rainie didn't have a cell phone. She went into the restaurant and used the pay phone in the lobby.

'Hey, Big Boy,' she said a moment later. 'Let me buy you a drink.'

14

Virginia

By nine P.M., Rainie was edgy and tense. She'd returned to her motel for a quick shower before meeting Officer Amity – who was now suggesting that she call him Vince. In her room, she discovered a phone message from the same lawyer who'd called that morning. Some attorney named Carl Mitz was all hot and bothered to get in touch with her. He'd left numbers for his pager and his cell phone. Rainie studied the numbers without calling any of them.

Prospective clients were never this eager. Prospective clients made it their business to make you find them.

Rainie put the message aside. She showered. She washed her hair. She stood for a long, long time with the hot water beating down on her neck and shoulders. Then she put on the same old clothes and headed for the bar.

Officer Vince Amity was already there. He'd also showered and now wore a black western dress shirt tucked into a faded pair of jeans and finished with a pair of scuffed-up boots. The shirt stretched across broad shoulders. When he stood, the jeans barely contained the bulge of his thighs.

A fine specimen of a man. The proverbial hunk of burning love.

Rainie ordered her bottle of Bud Light and told herself she did not miss Quincy.

'Ribs here are really good,' Vince said.

'Okay.'

'And the sweet potato fries. Ever had sweet potato fries? Worth every minute of the ensuing open-heart surgery.'

'Okay.' The waitress came by. They placed their twin orders for ribs and sweet potato fries and the minute the waitress was gone, Vince gamely tried again.

'So how long do you think you'll be in Virginia?'

'Don't know. Right now, I have more questions than answers, so at this rate it could be a while.'

'Where are you staying?'

'Motel Six.'

'Virginia has more to offer than Motel Six, you know. Ever have some free time, feel like seeing any of the sights . . .'

He let the invitation trail off politely. She nodded with equal politeness. Then he surprised her by saying quietly, 'I ran a background check, Rainie. You don't have to pretend for me.'

She stiffened. She couldn't help herself, even if she was supposedly now at peace with her past. Old habits died hard; she found she was relentlessly stroking the icy cold bottle of unconsumed beer.

'You run background checks on all your dates?' she asked finally.

'Man can't be too careful.'

She gave his muscle-bound build a meaningful look and he rewarded her with a grin.

'You found me at work, asked a lot of questions, and kept following up,' he told her. 'Call me old-fashioned, but I like to know more about the women chasing me. Besides, your friend Sheriff Hayes sang your praises from here to the Mississippi—'

'He tell you I was indicted for man one?'

'Charged but never tried.'

'Not everyone sees the difference.'

'I'm from Georgia, honey. We consider all women dangerous; it's part of their charm.'

'The open-minded men of the South. Who would've thought?'

Officer Amity grinned again. He leaned over the old wood table and planted his thick forearms. 'I like you,' he said bluntly, 'but don't play me for dumb.'

'I don't know what you mean—'

'I'm not who you want to have dinner with tonight.'

'Luke,' Rainie declared grimly, 'has a big mouth!'

'Sheriff Hayes is a good friend. It's nice to see they grow them right in Oregon, too. By the end of this evening, however, I'm gonna be an even bigger friend for you.'

'Oh yeah?'

The waitress interrupted them with heaping platters of food. The minute she was gone, Vince said, 'Eat your ribs, ma'am. Then I'll take you to Amanda Quincy's car.'

Society Hill, Pennsylvania

Bethie was humming when they finally pulled up to her darkened town house. It was nearly ten o'clock; the moon was full and the humidity a soft, fragrant caress against her wind-burned cheeks. It had been a wonderful day, a glorious day, and while the hour was growing late, she still wasn't ready for it to end.

'What a fabulous evening,' she said gaily.

Tristan smiled at her. Three hours ago, as the day cooled and slid into a purple-hued dusk, he'd taken off his sweater and tucked it around her shoulders. Now she snuggled in soft, cable-knit cotton, inhaling the scent of his cologne and finding it as poignant as his touch earlier in the afternoon. He'd retrieved a navy-blue blazer from the trunk for his own warmth. The jacket was finely cut but there was something about it that nagged at her. Giggling, she'd finally gotten it. He looked like an FBI agent, she teased him. He'd become a G-man. Fortunately, the comment seemed to amuse him.

'What now?' she asked.

'I believe that's your call, love.'

'Are you playing hard to get?'

'I thought it would be an interesting change of pace.'

Bethie giggled. She was probably still feeling the effects of the champagne, she decided, because she'd never been the giggling schoolgirl type, not even when she'd been a giggling schoolgirl. Today, however, they'd had one bottle of champagne in Pennsylvania Dutch country, then another bottle back in Philadelphia, sitting down at the waterfront after a superb lobster dinner at Bookbinder's. She'd been worried about driving home, but fortunately the champagne didn't seem to affect Tristan at all. He was a solidly built man, and one who could apparently hold his liquor.

Interesting, she thought absently, but should a man who'd just had a kidney transplant be able to hold his liquor? She wondered when he took all his pills.

'I don't think we're alone anymore,' Tristan murmured.

'What? Where?' She looked around her quiet street wide-eyed. Tristan had his arm draped casually around the back of her seat. She leaned her head closer to him.

'I don't see anyone,' she said in an exaggerated stage whisper.

'Your neighbor. Through the lace curtains.'

'Ah, good old Betty Wilson. Old bat. She's always watching me. About time I had something good to show her.' Bethie draped her arms around Tristan's neck and kissed him full on the mouth. He complied readily, his other arm curling around her back and trying to draw her closer only to have the gearshift get in the way. They broke apart breathlessly, thwarted by bucket seats, and she was struck once more by the taste of him on her lips, and her own desperate hunger for more.

His eyes had grown dark again. She loved it when they held that intense, burning gleam.

'Bethie . . .' he said thickly.

'Oh God, come inside!'

He smiled. 'I thought you'd never ask.'

Virginia

The salvage yard was dark and deserted, but Officer Amity had come well equipped. He handed out two high-powered flashlights, then strapped a fanny pack filled with tools around his waist. Rainie was impressed.

'I didn't take you for the breaking and entering type,' she told him.

Amity shrugged. 'When I called earlier, the owner wasn't big on cooperation. Salvage yards can be that way. They've paid for the vehicles and they're afraid to have their new-found property seized as part of a police case. Understandable maybe, but why should you and I keep beating our heads against a wall, when we're both so capable of scaling a chain-link fence?'

'I can do fences,' Rainie assured him. 'Dobermans have me a little more concerned.'

'No dogs. I drove by earlier.'

'No dogs? What kind of self-respecting salvage-yard owner doesn't have a dog?'

'The kind who's been turned in to the humane society twice and could no longer afford the cruelty-toward-animal fines. Now he has a security company that drives around in hourly intervals. You see headlights, duck.'

'Cool,' Rainie said and started whistling 'We're off to see the Wizard, the wonderful Wizard of Oz.'

Five minutes later, they'd scaled the eight-foot-high fence and were making their way through the final resting place for thousands of cars. Compacted cubes of metal were piled into rusted-out heaps. Back ends, front ends, bumpers were scattered about like dismembered limbs. The newer acquisitions sat quietly in long lines, fully formed skeletons still awaiting their fate.

'Sheee – it.' Amity whistled, looking out at two football fields' worth of wrecked vehicles and untold numbers of tires.

'I'd say look for an SUV,' Rainie murmured, 'but that doesn't exactly limit our options.'

'America's love for the big automobile,' he agreed. 'Kind of ironic that we're about to compare a Ford Explorer with the proverbial needle.'

'Split up?'

'No.'

Rainie nodded and pretended not to hear the concern in

his voice. The moon was full, visibility great for a nighttime rendezvous. Still she was conscious of the total hush, the unnatural still of a cemetery-like place. In the dark, abandoned metal took on lifelike shapes, and it was hard not to turn shadowy corners and feel the hairs prickle at the nape of her neck.

They walked in silence, flashlights slicing through the twisted heaps. Every few feet they'd come to an SUV, check for make and model, then keep on moving. One dozen down, five hundred to go. They stumbled upon one particularly crushed compact car and Rainie recoiled at the stench of dried blood.

'Jesus!' she cried, then stuffed a fist into her mouth to keep from saying more.

Vince swept his flashlight over a four-door sedan that had forcefully become a convertible. The cloth seats had once been blue; now they were stained with ugly splotches of brown.

'I'm guessing car versus semi,' he said.

'I'm guessing decapitation,' Rainie moaned and quickly moved on.

The sound of an approaching engine rumbled through the silence. Rent-a-Cop. They ducked swiftly behind a mountain of twisted chassis, still too close to the bloody convertible and Rainie pinched her nose with her fingers to block out the smell. She was thinking of the medical report now, the one Quincy had no doubt read time after time after time. How Amanda Quincy had struck the telephone pole at approximately 35 miles per hour. How the force of that impact pushed the front bumper down and the rear bumper up, launching her unsecured body into the air. Her body had hit the steering wheel first. The column had crumpled as it was designed to do, sparing her internal organs but doing nothing to halt her flight. Next had come the dashboard, bending her body like a rag doll at the waist. Finally came the metal frame of the windshield, not designed to crumple on impact, and now driving deep into Mandy's brain while the unyielding glass crushed all the bones in her face.

The security guard finally moved on. Amity and Rainie stood. She said, 'I know how to find the Explorer.'

'The windshield?'

'Yeah.' And maybe it was horrible, but things moved much faster from there.

They finally found the dark green remnant at the very edge of the salvage yard; Rainie called it a remnant because it certainly didn't resemble a vehicle anymore. The entire back end had been clipped off, no doubt soldered together with some rear-ended SUV's front end by the auto world's equivalent of Dr Frankenstein. The runners were gone. Both doors and the front seats stripped. The tires shed. What was left looked like a gutted fish head, lying on the gaping back hole where its body used to be while its crushed bumper smiled obscenely in the dark.

'Spooky,' Amity muttered.

'Let's not linger.'

'I'll second that.'

Officer Amity opened up his fanny pack and spread out his wares. He was the proud owner of two pairs of latex gloves – a little late to protect the evidence now, Rainie thought, but what the hell. He'd also brought a penknife, a screwdriver, a wrench, four Baggies, and interestingly enough, a magnifying glass.

He handed her the screwdriver, and wordlessly they went to work. First they took off the trim piece of the B-pillar, exposing the plastic casing around the driver-side seat belt. Rainie tested the strap with her hand, and true to Amity's report, it spooled toothlessly onto the floor. He held up the flashlight to provide better lighting and before they went any farther, she got out the magnifying glass. She held it up to the casing. Then she looked somberly at Amity. The plastic casing bore deep scratch marks: they were not the first to pry it open.

'I hereby do solemnly swear,' he murmured, 'to disassemble all "nonoperative" seat belts in all auto accidents to come.'

Rainie exchanged the magnifying glass for the penknife and cracked the mechanism open. Inside was a giant white plastic gear, with one main white plastic paw and one small back-up lever in case the primary failed. In theory, when the seat belt was pulled forward, it turned the gear, which then caught on the lever and froze. Except that in this case, the main paw had been filed down and the back-up lever clipped off. Rainie pulled on the seat belt again, and they both watched the white gear spin around and around and around.

'If she'd taken it in,' Amity said after a moment, 'the mechanic guy would've caught it.'

'So our guy had to make sure she didn't have the vehicle serviced.'

'Isn't that risky, though? If you're going to tamper with a seat belt, why do it a whole month before? Seems like you'd do it day of, or maybe I've just been watching too much *Murder, She Wrote*.'

'Prejudices,' Rainie said. 'Yours, mine, any cop's. She knows the seat belt is broken, so she doesn't even put it on. And when you arrive at a scene where the driver is drunk and hasn't even bothered to strap in . . .'

'You think she's pretty stupid,' Amity said quietly. 'You think, whether you mean to or not, that she got what she deserved. And then you don't ask too many questions.'

'Nobody looks too closely,' Rainie agreed. She was frowning though, chewing on her bottom lip. 'It still seems risky. I mean, if you wanted to kill someone and have it look like an accident, would you simply tamper with a seat belt and hope fate sooner or later takes its course?'

'Victim has a history of drinking and driving. Perp provides the alcohol, then lets her get behind the wheel. Chances are she won't make it home.'

'Are they? A shocking number of people drink and drive every day without crashing. Look at Mandy, she'd already done it dozens of times before.'

'Maybe he wanted an out. Think of it this way: even if we'd caught on right away, how are you going to prove who tampered with the seat belt weeks before a collision? That just leaves us with looking at who got her drunk. Victim was of age. Serving her isn't a crime, and letting her drive is back to being a civil matter, not criminal.'

'Someone who wanted to plan a murder, but wanted to be cautious,' Rainie murmured, then firmly determined, 'no, I don't buy it. If you're going to go to this much trouble to kill someone, you're going to see it through. You're going to make sure you got the job done. Oh shit, we're idiots!'

She grabbed the magnifying glass and before Amity could react she was around the mutilated hunk of metal to the passenger's side. She pulled on the seat belt. It caught and held. Perfectly good, of course. It would need to be.

'You son of a bitch,' Rainie said. And then Amity was holding the flashlight and she was running over the tight weave of the strap with the magnifying glass. 'There! Right there!'

The fabric buckled and warped, a two-inch span where the fibers had been stretched as the SUV hit the pole, the seat belt caught, and a body flew against the strap.

'Meet passenger number two!' Rainie cried triumphantly, and then a heartbeat later, 'Oh, Quincy, I am so sorry.'

15

The minute Bethie opened her front door, her security system sounded a warning beep. She crossed the threshold and worked the keypad. As was her custom, she entered in the disarm code first, then requested a survey of the various security zones. All quiet on the western front.

Tristan shut the front door behind her. Then locked it.

'Nice system,' he commented.

'Believe it or not, as part of our divorce decree, my ex-husband must provide basic security for the girls and me for the rest of our lives. Not that he minds. Quincy has been at his job a little too long; he sees homicidal maniacs everywhere.'

'You can never be too sure,' Tristan said.

'Perhaps.' Bethie set down the picnic basket next to the entry table. It needed to be cleaned out, but that could wait until morning. She started humming, thinking about waking up with Tristan and the various possibilities for breakfast in bed. When was the last time she'd made omelets or biscuits or crêpes suzette? When was the last time she'd started her day with anything more than black coffee and a boring piece of toast? She was so happy she'd gone out with Tristan today. And she was even happier that she'd taken these first few baby steps back into the land of the living.

She glanced absently at her answering machine and was surprised to see that she had eight new messages.

'Do you mind?' she asked, nodding her head toward the digital display. 'It will only take a minute.'

'By all means. Do you have some sherry? I can pour us each a glass while I wait.'

Bethie directed him toward the small wet bar in her dining room, hoping her cleaning woman had been conscientious about checking the crystal decanter for dust; Bethie had last had a glass of sherry five years ago. Well, this was a night for new beginnings.

She picked up a little spiral notepad and hit play.

The first message was a hang up, from seven-ten that morning. The caller had just missed her: she'd left with Tristan only moments before. Then came another hang up. Then another. Finally, a person: Pierce calling shortly after noon. 'We need to talk,' her ex-husband said in that crisp manner of his. 'It's about Mandy.'

Bethie frowned. She felt the first prickle of unease. Another hang up. Another hang up. Then another one. The muscles in her abdomen tightened. She realized now that she was steeling herself for something bad, preparing her body for the blow.

It came at precisely 8:02 P.M. Pierce, once more on the machine. 'Elizabeth, I've been trying to reach you all day. I'll be honest, I'm very worried. When you get this message, please call me immediately on my cell phone, regardless of time. Some things have come up. And Bethie – maybe we need to talk about Tristan Shandling because I tried to run a background check on him today and no such person exists. Call me.'

Bethie's gaze came up. She fumbled with the volume switch on her answering machine but it was already too late. Tristan stood in the doorway, holding two tiny glasses of sherry and gazing at her curiously.

'You asked Pierce to run a background check on me?'

She nodded dumbly. The blood had drained out of her face. She felt suddenly light-headed, unsteady on her feet.

'Why, Elizabeth Quincy, you have finally surprised me.'

Tristan set down the two glasses on a side table. *Run*, Bethie thought. But she was in her own house, she didn't know where to go. And then she was thinking of all those textbooks Pierce used to have in his office. The day she'd come home and found her girls staring wide-eyed at a pile they'd pulled down from the bookshelf, color photo after color photo of mutilated female flesh, naked, tortured bodies with hacked-off breasts.

'Who . . . who are you?'

'Supervisory Special Agent Pierce Quincy, of course. I have a driver's license that says so.'

'But . . . but you have the scar. I touched it, I know!' Her voice was rising.

In comparison, he sounded increasingly serene. 'Did it myself, the day you pulled the plug on Mandy. A sterile knife, a steady hand with the needle. There are certain things you should never leave to chance.'

'Mandy . . . You knew Mandy . . . Her expressions, my nickname . . .'

'Have you seen me take any pills, Bethie? Haven't you wondered if a man with a brand-new kidney should drink two bottles of champagne? My cover is never perfect, you know. I like to leave the person a sporting chance. But you women insist on seeing only what you want to see – at least while you're falling in love. We all know it changes after that.'

'I don't understand.'

'Your understanding is not important to me.'

'Pierce is a high-ranking FBI agent. You won't get away with this!'

He smiled thinly. Then he reached into his pocket and pulled out his black leather gloves. 'That's what I'm counting on. You know, I wasn't going to do this so soon. I was going to wait until the night you came to me, hysterical about what had happened to Kimberly. And then I was going to tell you how much she always hated you. Kimberly and Mandy. It was never their father who traumatized them, Bethie. It was you, weak, overprotective, unforgiving you.'

'Don't hurt my daughter. Don't you touch Kimberly!'

'Too late.' He pulled on the gloves. 'Run, Bethie,' he murmured. '*Run!*'

Greenwich Village, New York City

In the middle of the night, Kimberly bolted awake. Her breathing was harsh and sweat had glued her T-shirt to her skin. She was shivering. Bad dream. She didn't remember of what.

She waited, focusing on breathing again until her heart finally slowed in her chest. Then she turned on her bedside light and padded silently into the kitchen. The door of her roommate's bedroom was closed. She could just make out the low undertones of Bobby's rhythmic snores. The sound soothed her. Bobby had a new girlfriend and hadn't been around much lately. That was his business, of course, but tonight she was glad that he was here. Someone else shared the tiny apartment. She was not alone.

She sat down at the kitchen table. She knew from prior experience that it would be a while before she would go back to sleep. Even then, she could not be sure that she wouldn't dream. Sometimes it was Mandy driving her Explorer while Kimberly tried desperately to grab the steering wheel. Sometimes it was herself, running through a long dark tunnel, seeing her father far ahead but never able to catch up with him. Once she dreamed of her mother. Bethie was dancing ballet in a beautiful white tutu and no matter what Kimberly did, she could not get Bethie's attention. Then a rift opened up in the floor, and Kimberly watched her mom dance right over the edge.

Anxious dreams from an anxious subconscious. Kimberly glanced at the phone. She should just pick it up. Call her mother. Call her father. Get over whatever it was she needed to get over.

But she didn't do it. She sat at the kitchen table. She listened to the deep sound of silence that exists only after midnight. And then, after minutes turned into an hour, she made her way back to bed.

Motel 6, Virginia

Rainie had just returned from her salvage-yard rendezvous, when the phone in her motel room shrieked to life. She glanced at the clock. Three A.M. She looked back at the phone. She wondered if the caller was Quincy or the hotshot lawyer Carl Mitz. Then she wondered which would be worse. She picked up the phone.

It was Quincy. 'I'm in Philadelphia. At Bethie's house. She's dead.'

Rainie said, 'I'll be right there.'

16

Society Hill, Pennsylvania

Rainie made the nighttime drive to Philly in just over two hours. She ignored speed limits, rules of the road, and most standard courtesy. And she arrived in full-warrior mode.

Elizabeth Quincy's elite town house was not hard to find. Rainie simply drove into Society Hill and followed the garish display of flashing lights. A white medical examiner's van was illegally parked up on the sidewalk. A cluster of three police cruisers represented the ground troops. One older unmarked sedan would be the pair of homicide detectives; they'd had the decency to also park up on the sidewalk, trying to leave enough room for traffic to squeeze by on the narrow lane. Three larger, dark sedans, however, lined up as a single clog in the space the detectives had tried to leave. They would be the feds. Too many chiefs, not enough Indians, Rainie thought immediately, and wondered how Quincy was faring.

She parked a block back and walked up as the sky was just beginning to lighten with the first tinge of dawn. Half a dozen neighbors hovered in overpriced doorways, wearing silk dressing robes and Burberry overcoats and gazing at

Rainie cautiously as she passed. The neighbors looked scared. The tall, narrow town houses sat shoulder to shoulder, and for all their impression of discreet wealth, they weren't that different from one long apartment complex. Now, a very bad thing had happened down the hall, and not all the money in the world could put enough distance between that and them.

Rainie arrived at Bethie's residence. Inside the hastily roped off perimeter, a young officer was guarding the scene, sipping coffee from Wawa's and yawning every two or three seconds. Rainie flashed her PI's license.

'Nope,' he said.

'I'm working for FBI Agent Pierce Quincy,' she countered.

'And I'm working for Mayor John F. Street. Fuck off.'

'You kiss your mother with that mouth?' She arched a brow, then dropped her voice to deadly serious. 'Hey rookie, go inside. Find Supervisory Special Agent Quincy and tell him Lorraine Conner is here.'

'Why?'

'Because I work with him, because he personally called me to this scene, and because you don't want to start your day getting your ass kicked by a girl.'

'Like I'm going to start my day taking orders from one—'

'Officer.'

Both Rainie and the young officer jerked their attention to the open doorway. Of all people, Special Agent Glenda Rodman stood there, wearing the same stark gray suit from the day before, except as she'd also been dragged out of bed in the middle of the night, her dark hair was a bit more mussed around her face. Rainie thought the hairstyle was kinder, but mostly she was mortified at being caught in yet another losing battle.

'Special Agent Quincy has requested Ms Conner's presence,' Glenda informed the officer. 'Do allow her in, and don't mind what she says. I understand that she's not a morning person.'

'Oh, I like mornings just fine. It's people I can't stand.'

'If you will follow me . . .'

Officer I'm-in-Charge grudgingly raised the police tape. In turn, Rainie flashed him a gloating smile, then immediately blanked her features before entering the scene. She had no sooner followed Special Agent Rodman into the foyer, when she was assaulted with the stench of blood.

She recoiled, caught herself, and for a moment, simply had to stand her ground. Special Agent Rodman had stopped as well. Her expression was patient, perhaps even kind. At that moment, Rainie understood just how bad it was going to get.

Blood was everywhere. Streaked across ecru-colored walls, splattered onto oil canvases, pooled on parquet floors and century-old silk carpets. In the foyer, the table had been toppled, the phone yanked out of its socket, and the answering machine dashed against a massive gold-framed mirror. Shards of glass riddled the floor, and the sweet smell of alcohol mingled with bodily fluids.

Jesus, Rainie thought. She couldn't get beyond that. Jesus.

Special Agent Rodman was moving. She led Rainie into the dining room, where crime-scene technicians were now dusting a gleaming cherrywood table for prints, while another pair of officers were rolling up the oriental rug to be shipped to the lab. Glenda paused again. She was providing a tour of the scene, Rainie realized. Giving discreet but effective highlights of events.

It would appear that the attack started in the foyer. Given

the spray pattern, the weapon was maybe a knife or blunt object. Elizabeth is ambushed. Elizabeth fights back. Elizabeth runs into the dining room. A gilded French lamp. Rainie saw it ripped out of the wall and flung across the room. The base bore a small round mark of blood and hair. His? Hers? She supposed it depended on who grabbed the lamp first. More spray patterns on the far wall. Someone had taken another solid hit, probably Elizabeth.

Bloody footprints on the oak parquet floor. Rainie and Glenda followed them into the Spanish-style kitchen, where a large butcher's block of knives had been overturned on the tiled counter. The smaller knives, paring knives, steak knives, had been knocked on the floor as someone – again him, her, who got here first? – reached frantically for the butcher blades. It had not gone well. More blood, smeared along the vast expanse of deep blue tiles, a larger print on the floor.

Rainie could see it now. Quiet, refined Elizabeth Quincy attacked, wounded, already dizzy from terror and blood loss, racing into the kitchen. Knowing she was overpowered and outmaneuvered. Desperate to even the odds. Then seeing her collection of knives. And making a desperate gamble.

Poor, poor, Elizabeth. Knives were always a bad choice for a woman. Blades required skill, strength, and reach, attributes better suited to a man. It was one of those things police officers got to analyze in case studies. Women who ran into the kitchen for a knife, almost always had it used on them instead. Bethie should have gone after a cast iron skillet. Something big and heavy that could punish an opponent without a great deal of accuracy.

Had she realized that as he caught her at the end of the counter? Had she considered her other options as she went down on the hardwoods, her bloody fingers scrabbling at the cupboard handles, desperate for support?

On the floor was a clear imprint of her hip and her thigh as she'd fallen on her side. But somehow she'd managed to fight him off, because the blood trail kept going. She had been tough. Or he simply hadn't wanted it to end.

'It's trickier in here,' Special Agent Rodman murmured. 'Follow the tape.'

For the first time, Rainie noticed the masking tape forming a thin, zig-zagging line through the debris field. Smart, she decided, having once worked a large, complicated crime scene herself. By the time all was said and done, dozens of people would have walked through this house, searching for evidence and providing their individual areas of expertise. It would takes weeks to sort it all out, and months to write it all up. Best to try and corral the intrusion from the very start, versus trying to sort out all the sources of contamination later, as she had needed to do.

Rainie tiptoed along the masking tape, following it into the hallway, where the burgundy runner carried wet splotches and the walls bore a cacophony of bloody hand-prints. The prints ran the length of the tight, claustrophobic space, an obscene version of sponge painting. *Jesus*, Rainie thought again.

'We think he did this postmortem,' Glenda said.

'But the palm prints are too small to be his.'

'They're not his.'

'Quincy walked through all this?' Rainie asked sharply.

'Many times. At his own request.'

They came to the master bedroom. Rainie didn't look at the bed right away. The ME and his assistant were standing over there and she did not want to see what they were studying that had already caused the assistant to turn an unnatural shade of green. She looked at the perimeter first. More shattered mirrors. Two lamps ripped from the wall. Another phone jerked from a nightstand. Pillows had been gutted, strewing feathers across the deep-pile rug. Perfume bottles had been shattered, leaving the horrible, cloying scent of flowers in a blood-ravaged room.

'Somebody had to have heard something,' Rainie said, her voice no longer quite sounding like her own. 'How could all of this go on without someone calling the police?'

'The previous owner was a concert pianist,' Glenda said. 'When he had the town house redone twenty years ago, he soundproofed the walls so he wouldn't disturb his neighbors.'

'Who . . . who finally called the police?'

'Quincy.'

'He was here?'

'He claims he drove here shortly after midnight, when he still couldn't reach his ex-wife by phone. He was worried about her safety, so he took a ride.'

'He claims?' Rainie didn't like that phrase. 'He *claims?*'

Special Agent Rodman wouldn't meet her gaze anymore. 'There is a stained-glass window broken in the master bathroom,' she murmured. 'One theory is that the UNSUB broke into the house earlier in the evening, and surprised Mrs Quincy when she came home.'

'One theory?'

'This house is equipped with a state-of-the-art alarm system. It never went off.'

'Was it armed?'

'We are working with the security company now to

determine that information. They should be able to provide us with a record of the system's most recent activity.'

'So one theory is that a stranger broke in and ambushed her. The second would be that the attacker was someone she knew and trusted.' Rainie could no longer contain herself. 'You're looking at Quincy, aren't you? Goddammit, you suspect him!'

'No, I don't!' Special Agent Rodman spoke up in a low hush. Her gaze darted toward the ME, then she quickly bent closer. 'Listen to me, Ms. Conner. It is not in my nature to share information about a case. And it is certainly not in my nature to needlessly provide details to some out-of-state pseudo-cop. But it would appear that you and Special Agent Quincy are friends, and he's going to need friends. We – meaning the Bureau – are behind him right now. Personally, I have spent all day listening to various sexual sadists leave not-very-subtle messages on his answering machine. We understand that there is more to this situation than meets the eye. We cannot, however, say the same for the locals.'

'You're the feds, pull rank!'

'Can't.'

'Bullshit!'

'Honey, there's this thing called law. Look it up sometime.'

Rainie scowled. 'Where is he? Can I talk to him?'

'Detectives willing, you can try.'

'I want to see him.'

'Then follow me.'

Glenda headed back toward the hallway. Passing through the doorway, Rainie made the mistake this time of looking at the bed. She could not quite contain the gasp that rose up in her throat.

Glenda glanced at her grimly. She said once more, 'Quincy needs friends.'

Two plainclothes detectives had Quincy sequestered off in the one room that appeared spared in the attack. At any other time, Rainie might have laughed at the incongruous sight. This room had obviously been one of the girls', the walls papered in a soft yellow with tiny pink and lilac flowers, the twin bed covered in a matching comforter, and the canopy top draped with yards of dreamy white gauze. A white wicker makeup table sat against one wall, topped by an oval mirror and still bearing small photos marking a young girl's major passages in life – leaping in cheerleading practice, arms wrapped around a best friend, attending the prom. A dried corsage hung from a ribbon on the mirror, and a collection of brightly colored stuffed animals sat on the dresser top.

The room offered only a dainty, lilac-covered wicker bench, now occupied by one burly detective whose chin was nearly resting upon his knees. The other detective stood, while Quincy sat on the gauze-draped bed with a ruffled yellow pillow tucked against his thigh. *The Gestapo does Laura Ashley*, Rainie thought, and wished the sight of Quincy's pale, tightly shuttered face didn't twist her heart painfully in her chest.

'What time did you say you arrived again?' the seated detective was asking. He had a single fierce, bushy brow that overshadowed his eyes – Cro-Magnon man in a cheap gray suit.

'A little after midnight. I did not glance at my watch.'

'The neighbor, Mrs Betty Wilson, claims she saw the victim return home with a man fitting your description shortly after ten P.M.'

'I was not here at ten P.M. As I've stated already, I did not arrive here until after midnight.'

'Where were you at ten?'

'By definition, Detective, I was in my car at ten P.M., driving here, so I could arrive after twelve.'

'Got any witnesses to that?'

'I drove here alone.'

'What about toll receipts?'

'I never asked for any receipts. At the time, I didn't realize that I would need an alibi.'

The two detectives exchanged glances. Victim's ex-husband appears evasive and unnecessarily hostile. Let's get the thumbscrews and brass knuckles.

Rainie figured now was a good time to interrupt. 'Detectives,' she said quietly.

Three pairs of eyes swung toward her. The two detectives scowled, obviously assuming she was a lawyer – who else would turn up at this time of night/morning? Quincy, on the other hand, registered no reaction at all. He had obviously seen his ex-wife's remains on her feather-strewn bed. After that, any further emotion would be superfluous.

'Who the hell are you?' Cro-Magnon did the honors.

'Who do you think? Name is Conner, Lorraine Conner.'

She held out her hand authoritatively, and with the long-suffering sigh policemen reserve just for lawyers, Cro-Magnon conceded to shake her hand – with a crushing grip. 'Detective Kincaid,' he muttered. Rainie turned to his part-ner, a slightly built man with intense blue eyes. 'Albright,' he supplied and shook her hand as well while giving her a more appraising assessment. Rainie pegged him as the brains behind the operation. Cro-Magnon rattled the beehive. Smaller, less threatening guy took excellent notes.

'Where are we?' Rainie asked, plopping down on the bed as if she had every right to be here. In the doorway, Special Agent Rodman wore a small smile.

'Trying to establish an alibi—'

'Are you saying that an FBI agent is a *suspect?*' Rainie gave smaller, less threatening guy an imperious stare.

'He is the ex-husband.'

Rainie turned to Quincy. 'How long have you been divorced?'

'Eight years.'

'Do you have any current legal proceedings against your ex-wife?'

'No.'

'Do you stand to gain any money upon her death?'

'No.'

Rainie turned back to the detectives. 'Is it just me, or is there a total lack of motive here?'

'Is it true that you purchased a red Audi TT coupe two weeks ago in New York?' Detective Albright asked Quincy.

'No,' Rainie answered for him.

'Counselor, we have a record of the vehicle's registration, bearing the agent's name.'

'Fraudulent purchase. A man *posing* as Supervisory Special Agent Quincy made that purchase, as the FBI is already aware of and actively investigating. Isn't that correct, Special Agent Rodman?'

'We are actively investigating,' Glenda provided dutifully from the doorway.

Rainie addressed the detectives once more. She took a page out of Quincy's book, keeping her voice crisp and manner perfectly relentless. 'Are you aware that someone is currently stalking Supervisory Special Agent Quincy? Are you aware that his personal telephone number has been made available to prisoners all across the country? In addition, someone has used his name to make a series of purchases' – slight lie, but it sounded better – 'all of which is currently being investigated by reputable agents at the Bureau. Perhaps you should consider that before you proceed.'

'And are you aware,' Detective Albright replied in her same cadence, 'that Agent Quincy has logged eight calls to his ex-wife's house in the last twenty-four hours?'

'As he said, he was worried about her.'

'Why? They've been divorced eight years.'

Oh, score one for the homicide detective.

'Elizabeth had asked me to run a background check.' Quincy spoke up quietly. Rainie wished he wouldn't. He sounded too composed, too professional, like someone who had walked through such scenes hundreds of times and made his living by reviewing them hundreds more. She understood his detachment. She even heard the subtle, more dangerous thread of anger beneath his words, while noticing that his right hand was clenched too tightly on his lap and his left hand clutched the edge of the mattress as if he was trying to keep himself from spinning away. She wished she could touch him. She was afraid of how savage his reaction might be. So she merely sat behind him, pretending to be his lawyer so she could stay at his side, and wishing he'd trust her more, because his FBI composure was only going to sink him further with the local boys.

'However,' Quincy was continuing, 'I could find no record of the name Bethie gave me. Coupled with the incidents going on in my own life, I grew concerned about who this person was and what he might do.'

'Name?'

'Tristan Shandling.'

'How did she meet Shandling?'

'I don't know.'

'When did she meet him?'

'I don't know.'

Detective Albright arched a brow. 'So, let me get this straight. You're conscientious enough to run a background check, but you didn't ask your ex-wife any questions?'

'As you said, Detective, we'd been divorced eight years. Her personal life is not my business anymore.'

'Personal life? So you suspected he was a new love interest—'

'I didn't say that,' Quincy interjected sharply. But it was too late. Detective Albright was already making fresh notes. And now, Rainie thought with a sigh, they had motive – the ever-classic, ever-popular, jealous ex.

'Detectives,' she said crisply. 'While I'm sure we all have nothing better to do at five in the morning than continue this conversation, aren't you missing the obvious?'

Detective Albright cocked his head and regarded her curiously. Cro-Magnon went with the more obvious, 'Huh?'

'Look at this house. Look at this scene. There is blood everywhere; there are indications of a savage fight. Now behold Supervisory Special Agent Quincy: His suit is immaculate, his shoes are polished, and his hands and face don't bear a single mark. Doesn't that tell you anything?'

'He took lessons from O. J. Simpson,' Cro-Magnon declared.

Rainie sighed. She appealed to Albright, who seemed to have more common sense. She was honestly surprised to realize that even smaller, less threatening guy was not convinced. What the . . . ?

Her gaze flew to Quincy. He would not return her stare, his gaze locked somewhere on the far wall where flowers bloomed pink and lilac amid a sea of yellow. She turned to Glenda Rodman, and that agent, too, glanced away.

The feds knew something. At least Quincy and Glenda did, but they were not yet volunteering it to the locals, which could only mean one thing. How bad could one night get? And what would Quincy do, when she told him that the same person who had murdered Bethie tonight, had most likely started by killing his daughter fourteen months ago?

A tall, thin man appeared in the doorway. He was wearing a white doctor's coat. The medical examiner's assistant. 'I . . . uh. We thought you should see this.'

With gloved hands, the man held up a plastic bag. Glenda didn't take it. Instead, Detective Albright accepted the marked evidence bag, held it up to the light, and promptly said, 'Jesus Christ!' He dropped the bag on the lilac-colored rug, where it resembled a fresh pool of blood.

'It was . . .' The medical assistant wasn't doing so well. His face still carried a tinge of green and he was staring at the plastic bag with the horrified fascination of someone who knew he really should look away. 'We found it . . . abdominal cavity . . .'

Cro-Magnon wasn't moving. On the bed, Quincy's hand was gripping the floral comforter so tight, tendons stood out like ridges. Very slowly, Rainie reached down. Very slowly, she picked up the bag. She held it by the corner gingerly, as if it were a snake with the power to strike.

It looked like a piece of Christmas wrapping paper. Bright red with swirls of white. Shiny veneer. Except . . .

It was paper, she realized dizzily. At least it had been. Cheap, white paper, probably like the kind used in any copy machine. Except now it was soaked bloody red. And those were not pretty swirls. They were letters, forming words, written in some kind of white wax, in order to come to light as it sat, according to the assistant, in Elizabeth Quincy's insides.

'It's a note,' she said.

'Read it,' Quincy whispered.

'No.'

'*Read it!*'

Rainie closed her eyes. She had already made out the words. 'It says . . . it says, "You'd better hurry up, Pierce. There's only one left."'

'Kimberly,' Glenda Rodman said from the doorway.

A strange sound came from the bed. Quincy was finally moving. His body rocked back and forth. His shoulders started to shake. And then a low, dreadful sound came from his lips. Laughter. A dry, bone-chilling chuckle spewing from his lips.

'A message in a bottle,' he singsonged. 'A message in a fucking bottle!'

His shoulders broke. He bowed his head. The laughter turned to sobs.

'Kimberly . . . Rainie, get me out of here.'

She did.

17

Rainie closed her eyes. She had already made out the

Greenwich Village, New York

They drove toward New York City in silence, Rainie at the wheel, Quincy leaning against the passenger-side window. His eyes were closed, but she knew he wasn't asleep. They would arrive at his daughter's apartment in about an hour. She didn't like to think about how that conversation would go. Poor Kimberly, who had just buried her older sister. Poor Kimberly, who would now learn that her mother had been savagely murdered, and that most likely, she was next in line.

Quincy needed to regain his composure, Rainie thought, for the clock was ticking now and in this kind of game you couldn't afford a time-out.

'Talk,' he said shortly.

'We found Mandy's SUV. I was going to call you in the morning with the news.'

'The seat belt was tampered with.'

'Yes. And someone else was in the vehicle at the time of the crash. We found warping on the passenger's seat belt that proves it. In the good news department, Officer Amity recovered hairs from the cloth visor on the passenger's side.

If we can find the man, we can use the hairs to tie him to the crime.'

'What crime? Sitting in the passenger's seat of a sports-utility vehicle?'

'We'll work on it, Quincy. Officer Amity is a good guy; he can build a case. Now tell me this: Why did you go to your ex-wife's house on tonight of all nights?'

'I was worried. Elizabeth . . . Bethie never went out much. It was unusual not to be able to reach her all day.'

'I wonder if he knew that.'

'Probably.' Quincy finally turned in his seat. His face bore the stamp of freshly etched lines. In a matter of hours, his dark pepper hair seemed to have gained more salt at the temples. He was an experienced FBI agent, a man who made his living seeing the most horrible of horrors. Rainie wondered if that helped at a time like now, when he was desperate to save his remaining daughter, or if the intimate knowledge of what men could do only made things worse.

'It's obvious this Tristan Shandling is trying to frame you,' she said quietly. 'The car purchase in your name. Disguising himself to look like you when he showed up at Bethie's house. And there's more, isn't there? Things you and Dour Chic have already picked up on, but aren't volunteering to the local boys.'

'The scene was staged. When the crime-scene techs examine the broken bathroom window, they'll discover it was broken from the inside out.'

'But the broken glass was on the inside of the house, on the bathroom floor.'

'True. But if you fit one of the broken shards back into the window, the angle of the break reveals the blow came from the inside. Moving glass is easy. You can't, however, disguise the fragments. The UNSUB was already inside the house when he broke the window. And I'm sure when the police get the report back from the alarm company, they'll find it was properly disarmed.'

'He entered with Elizabeth,' Rainie murmured. 'The man fitting your description the neighbor saw at ten.'

'That would be my guess. Then there is the crime scene itself. The level of destruction is out of proportion with the crime. Each room appears destroyed, but the blood trail is actually extremely contained. My guess is the initial struggle was fast, focused. The rest of the damage occurred post-mortem.'

'He wanted it to look bad?'

'He wanted it to look horrific, terrifying, demoralizing. He's very good at what he does.'

'The body,' Rainie whispered.

'The body,' Quincy repeated, his voice detached again, overly analytical. 'When the medical examiner finishes with the autopsy, he'll know the victim was killed fairly quickly – at least on a relative scale. There won't be any evidence of rape, despite how he posed the body. There aren't any abrasions on the wrists and ankles, indicating that hog-tying occurred postmortem. I suspect the disembowelment and other mutilation occurred postmortem as well.'

'But why?'

'To make it look like a sexual-sadist attack. But a *posed* sexual-sadist attack. Such as what an expert in violent crimes might do to try and cover the cold-blooded murder of his ex-wife.'

'Parlor tricks,' Rainie said. 'The police will see through them soon enough.'

'I wouldn't be so sure about that.'

'There's still the fact the police saw you hours after the murder without a trace of blood or bruising on your body.'

'They'll simply argue that the crime was more controlled than it originally appeared to be. They'll find traces of blood in the sink pipes, indicating the murderer cleaned up afterwards. As knowledgeable as our UNSUB has been, I wouldn't be surprised if he didn't follow washing his hands by pouring a sample of blood that is the same type as mine into the sink. Or maybe he has the same blood type as me. At this point, how would I know?' His voice started out cool, but ended bitter.

'There's still the note,' Rainie persisted. 'That proves it was done by somebody out to get you.'

'The note's not going to help me.'

'Sure it will.'

'No.' Quincy shook his head. An odd smile curved his lips. 'The note . . . the handwriting. Rainie, it's mine. I don't know how, but it's as if this man . . . it's as if he's really me.'

Kimberly was sitting at the battered kitchen table, sipping a cup of coffee and trying to figure out what to do with her second day off, when the buzzer rang. Her roommate, Bobby, after announcing that he would stay tonight at his girlfriend's, had left for work. That left Kimberly with a whole day to kill and a whole apartment to kill it in. She should take a long nap. Exercise. Eat lots of fresh fruits and vegetables. Screw her head on straight.

Kimberly sipped black coffee, felt the weight of another sleepless night on her shoulders, and wondered how many city blocks she'd have to run to feel human again.

The buzzer repeated its whine. She finally got up and pressed the intercom button. 'What?'

'Kimberly, it's your dad.'

Oh no, she thought instantly. She hit the front-door button and let him in.

The old, eight-story apartment building didn't offer an elevator. It would take her father a few minutes to mount the stairs. She should do something. Gain ten pounds. Sleep four days straight. Down a bottle of vitamins to get some luster back in her too-long, too-dirty blond hair. Her old FBI sweats bagged on her frame. Her threadbare T-shirt hung low enough to reveal the gaunt line of her collarbone.

She stood trapped in the middle of the tiny kitchen until her father finally rapped on the door. She didn't want to answer it. She couldn't explain why. But she didn't want to open that door.

A second round of knocking. Her heart was pounding too hard in her chest. She slowly crossed the kitchen. She slowly opened her apartment door. Her father stood gravely in front of her, accompanied by some woman Kimberly had never seen before.

'I'm so sorry,' he said hoarsely.

He took her in his arms. She started to cry and she didn't even know what bad thing had happened yet.

Thirty minutes later they sat in the TV room, Kimberly Indian-style on the floor, her father and his friend, Rainie Conner, on the sofa. Kimberly had gone through the first box of Kleenex. Somewhere in the middle of her crying jag, things had gone from unbearable to horrible to simply numb. Now she sat, staring at the worn blue berber carpet and struggling to get the words to make sense in her head.

Your mother is dead.

Your mother has been murdered.

Someone is stalking our family. He's killed Mandy. He's killed Bethie. He will most likely come after you next.

'You don't . . . you don't know who's doing this?' she asked finally, working on forming the words, working on getting herself to think, working on keeping herself from splintering apart. She was the strong one. Her mother had always said so.

Your mother is dead.

Your mother has been murdered.

Someone is stalking our family. He's killed Mandy. He's killed Bethie. He will most likely come after you next.

'No,' her father answered quietly. 'But we're working on it.'

'It's probably someone from an old case, right? Someone you caught, or nearly caught, or you caught his dad, his son, his brother.'

'Probably.'

'Then you build a database! You build a database and you fill it with all the old names, and then . . . then you figure out who got out from jail when and you arrest his ass! Process of elimination, then arrest his ass!' Her voice was high, she didn't sound anything like herself.

Her father repeated, 'We're working on it.'

'I don't understand.' Her voice broke. She was close to weeping again. 'Mandy . . . Mandy was always attracted to the wrong sort of men. But Mom . . . Mom was careful. She didn't talk to strangers, she wouldn't let some guy sweet-talk her into entering her home. She was too smart for that.'

'Had you spoken to your mother recently?'

'No. I've been . . . busy.' Kimberly bowed her head.

'She called me two days ago. She was worried about you.'

'I know.'

'I've been worried about you, too.'

'I know.'

He waited. An expert pause, she'd always thought. But she'd been studying and learning things, too. That was the hard part of following in her father's footsteps. Once he'd seemed almost God-like to her. Lately, however, no longer a neophyte, she watched him perform the old tricks and could see him pulling the strings. The first time it had happened, she'd been proud of her new insight. After Mandy's funeral, however, it only left her feeling empty.

He got off the sofa. Paced the room the way he did when he was tense or working on a particularly baffling case. He was pale, she realized. Thinner, nearly gaunt. Then it hit her. He looked like her. She nearly started crying again.

Her mother, yelling: 'You're just like your father!'

Herself, yelling back: 'I know, Mom, and Mandy's just like you!'

'Why don't we walk through this from the beginning,' the chestnut-haired woman said from the sofa. Her father turned and frowned at her, his favorite intimidating look. The woman, however, wasn't impressed. 'Quincy, she's part of this now. She might as well know as much as we know. Information may be the only defense we have left.'

'I don't—'

'Yes!' Kimberly interrupted from the floor. 'I am part of this. I need to know . . . There has to be something we can do.'

'Dammit, you're my daughter—'

'And I'm his target.'

'You're only twenty-one—'

'I've been trained in martial arts and firearms. I am not helpless!'

'I never wanted this. If there was anything I could do . . .'

'I know.' Her voice quieted. She said more sincerely, 'I know. But here we are. There must be something I can do.'

Her father closed his eyes. For a moment, she thought she might have glimpsed tears in them. Then he sighed, returned to the sofa, and sat down. When he spoke again, he sounded cool, composed, like an FBI agent instead of a father. She wasn't sure why that comforted her.

'We'll start at the beginning,' Quincy said. 'It would appear that someone is seeking revenge against me for some perceived wrong. We don't know who, but as you suggested, Kimberly, process of elimination should be able to tell us more. For now, what we do know is that this person has been planning this for a long time. At least a year and a half, more likely two years.'

'Eighteen to twenty-four months?' Kimberly was genuinely shocked.

'We think he started with Mandy,' Rainie said. 'Maybe targeted her through an AA meeting. Things progressed from there.'

'Her new boyfriend,' Kimberly filled in. 'She mentioned something once, but I didn't pay much attention. Boyfriends . . . There were a lot of them.'

'It would seem that he positioned himself to be someone very special,' Quincy agreed. 'They dated for months. Mandy trusted him. Maybe she even fell in love.'

'But the accident,' Kimberly protested. 'She'd been drinking, she was behind the wheel. She'd done that kind of thing before. What did it have to do with him?'

Rainie spoke up. 'We think he was with her that night. According to one friend, Mandy may have started drinking early in the evening. I'm not sure I trust the "friend," however, so Mandy may have still been sober when she met up with her boyfriend, and he was the one who got her intoxicated. Either way, our mystery man tampered with her seat belt so it wouldn't work. Then, he got in the vehicle with her, strapped himself in so he'd be all right, and . . . and either let nature run its course or physically helped her hit the telephone pole.'

'He was with her when she crashed?'

'Yes.'

'Oh my God, he killed that old man!' Kimberly slapped a hand over her mouth in horror. She didn't know why, but somehow that was worse. Mandy was Mandy. She'd built an entire lifestyle on poor decisions and high-risk behavior. When her mother had called her the morning after the accident, Kimberly hadn't even been surprised. Instead, she remembered thinking, *finally*, as if part of her had been waiting for that phone call for years. Mandy was always on a course for heartbreak and disaster. That poor old man, however, had just been out walking his dog.

'She didn't die, though,' Kimberly said after a moment, pulling herself together. 'Mandy didn't actually die. Not then. Shouldn't that have panicked him?'

'Even if she came out of the coma, what would she know? What would she remember?' Rainie shrugged. 'Her body might have recovered, but her brain . . .'

'So he was safe.'

'I think things pretty much went as he planned.'

'But what about Mom? I can see Mandy being sweet-talked, but not Mom. Definitely not Mom.'

'Think of the circumstances,' Rainie countered. 'Bethie's just buried her older daughter. She's feeling lonely, struggling to cope. Then we have this man, Tristan Shandling, who dated your sister for months. Consider all the things he could have learned about your mother from Mandy in that amount of time. Her taste in music, food, clothes. Likes, dislikes. It becomes a pretty simple equation. Vulnerable, grieving mother. Well-informed, charming man. I doubt she had a chance.'

'I think he went a step further to gain Bethie's trust,' Quincy said. 'I think . . . I think he might have pretended to have received an organ transplant. From Mandy.'

'What?' Both Rainie and Kimberly stared at him.

'The last time I spoke with Bethie, she asked me about organ donation. Was there any chance the recipient received more than just tissue? Couldn't he maybe get some of the person's habits or feelings or soul? At the time, I dismissed it. It was only today when I had to wonder why she asked.'

'My God,' Rainie murmured. 'Elizabeth gave permission to terminate her daughter's life just weeks ago, and now here comes this man, claiming to have part of Mandy inside of him.'

'It's very clever,' Quincy said.

'It's the domino theory,' Kimberly declared. 'He started with the weakest one – Mandy. Got to her, then used the trauma of her death to get to Mother and now . . . now—' She looked at her father and knew his grim face was a match for her own.

'Shit!' Rainie abruptly bolted off the sofa, staring at them both wildly. 'The frame-up, Quincy. What we were talking about earlier. Even if it's not perfect, it doesn't matter – it still gets the job done. Think about it! Bethie's been murdered. As her ex-husband, you're already on the cops' radar screen, give them a few more lab results and you'll be their number one man. There you go. Mandy's death to access Bethie, Bethie's murder to lead to your arrest, and then boom – Kimberly's all alone. It's perfect!'

'But . . . but you can make bail, right?' Kimberly asked desperately.

Quincy was staring at Rainie. He looked stunned. 'It doesn't matter,' he whispered to his daughter. 'Rainie's right. The minute I become a lead suspect, they'll notify the Bureau. And following standard protocol, the Bureau will place me on desk duty, ask for my creds and confiscate my weapon. Even if I stay out of jail, what will I be able to do to protect you? My God, he's done his homework.'

'*Who the fuck is this person?*' Kimberly screamed.

Nobody had an answer.

18

Things got worse. Quincy wanted his daughter shipped to Europe. Kimberly yelled that she wouldn't go. Quincy told her now was not the time to be arrogant. Kimberly started laughing, accused the pot of calling the kettle black, then her laughter dissolved into tears, which seemed to hurt Quincy more. He stood in the middle of the dingy TV room, looking stiff and uncomfortable while his daughter wept.

Finally, Rainie sent Quincy to bed. In the past forty-eight hours, he'd had four hours of sleep and he was no longer close to fully functional. Then she brewed a fresh pot of coffee and sat with Kimberly at the kitchen table. The girl was a chip off the old block; she took her caffeine jet black. Rainie found skim milk in the fridge, then a bowl of sugar.

'Don't laugh,' she told Kimberly, as she added scoop after heaping scoop to the brew. 'I hate for the caffeine to be alone in my bloodstream.'

'Has my father seen you do that?'

'Couple of times.'

'How disparaging were his remarks?'

'On a scale of one to ten, I'd rate them a twelve.'

Lisa Gardner

'Oh that's not bad. My grandfather's comments would've hit fifteen.'

'Your grandfather's still alive?' Rainie was surprised. Quincy never spoke of his father. For that matter, he never mentioned his mother, though Rainie had a vague memory of him saying once that she'd died when he was young.

Kimberly was blowing clouds of steam off the top of her coffee. 'He's still alive. At least technically. Alzheimer's. He was hospitalized when I was ten or eleven. We used to visit him several times a year, but we haven't even done that in a while. He doesn't recognize any of us anymore, not even Dad, and well . . . Let's just say Grandpa isn't that fond of strangers.'

'That's gotta be hard. What was he like before?'

'Tough. Quiet. Funny in his own way. We used to drive up to Rhode Island to visit his farm. He had chickens and cows, horses, an apple orchard. Mandy and I loved it. Plenty of space to run around, plenty of things to get into.'

'And your mother was okay with this?' Rainie asked skeptically.

Kimberly smiled. 'I wouldn't say that. I remember one day this hot air balloon comes crashing down from the sky. Some tourist outing or something. And this little guy is yelling at the passengers to grab the branches to help brake as the balloon plows through the apple trees then plunks down in the middle of my grandfather's field. Mom comes rushing out, all excited. "Oh my goodness, did you see that? Oh my goodness." Then Grandpa comes out of the chicken coop, stands in front of the balloon holding five embarrassed people and gives them the complete up and down, never saying a word. The guide gets nervous. He holds out this bottle, going on and on about how sorry he is and the tracking vehicle will be here any minute and oh yeah, here's a bottle of wine for his trouble. Grandpa just looks at the guy. Finally, he says, "It's God's country." Then he walks back to the chicken coop. That's Grandpa.'

'I like him.' Rainie said it sincerely.

'He was a wonderful grandfather,' Kimberly said. She added more astutely, 'But I wouldn't have cared for him as a father.'

They both returned to their coffee.

'Are you and Dad dating?' Kimberly asked after the silence had stretched on too long.

'That's it, start with the easy questions.' Rainie sipped her coffee more earnestly.

Kimberly, however, had also inherited her father's probing stare. 'You're pretty young,' she said.

'I'm aware of that.'

'How old?'

'Thirty-two.'

'Mandy was twenty-four when she died.'

'All the more reason not to let a silly thing like age hold you back.'

'So you are dating?'

Rainie sighed. 'In the past, we have dated. What we are now . . . I don't know. When Quincy wakes up, do me a favor and ask him.'

'How did you meet?'

'Last year. The Bakersville case.'

'Oh,' Kimberly said with feeling. 'That was a bad one.'

'You could say that.'

'You're the one who lost her job.'

'That would be me.'

Kimberly nodded with a freshly minted psych major's knowing confidence. 'I see the problem.'

'Great. Want to explain it to me?'

'Age alone wouldn't be reason enough, but now you two are at different phases of the life cycle, which makes the gap even more extreme. You have to rebuild, which puts you back at infancy. He's established, keeping him middle-aged. That's a tough gulf to bridge. I think figuring out how to have a successful relationship in the face of such complex career issues will be the challenge of the new, dual-income generation.'

'You're working on your thesis, aren't you?'

'My thesis is on "Challenges of Modernity: The Growth of Urbanization and Its Impact on Disrupted Personalities", thank you very much.'

'Oh. Mine was on attachment disorder. You know, why good families can still breed little fucking psychopaths.'

Kimberly blinked. 'Attachment disorder. That's one of my favorite subjects.' She looked at Rainie more appraisingly. 'I didn't realize you were a psych major.'

'B.A. I never went back for my master's.'

'Still, that's pretty cool.'

'Thanks.'

They both returned to their coffee. After a moment, Kimberly said softly, 'Rainie, could you keep talking? In all honesty, it's easier to dissect your life than to think about my own.'

'I'm really sorry, Kimberly.'

'Who's going to help me plan my wedding? Who will I call when I'm expecting my first child? Who will hold my hand, when I give birth to a baby girl and see Mandy and my mother in every curve of her face?'

'We'll find out who's doing this. We'll find him, and we'll make him pay.'

'And will that make things better? Look at you and what happened last year. You found the guy who did it. You and my father killed him. Are you better off?'

Rainie didn't say anything. After a moment, Kimberly said, 'I thought as much.'

Quincy dreamed. In his dream he was back in Philadelphia, walking through Bethie's beautiful, ravaged town house. He held a pillowcase in one hand. He was trying to capture all the feathers and stuff them back in. Then he was standing over the bed, his hands now holding Bethie's intestines, and trying frantically to pile them back in her body.

Don't, his subconscious told him in his dream. *Don't let him win by remembering her the way he intended.*

His dream spiraled backwards, his mind seeking happier times. Bethie, mussed hair, sweating face. No makeup, no pearls, but a smile that could light up a city as she lay in the white hospital bed and held out their firstborn child. Himself, touching their baby girl delicately. Marveling at the ten perfect fingers, ten perfect toes. Then touching his wife's cheek. Telling her how beautiful she looked. And vowing that he would be a better father than his own dad had been. Fresh family. Fresh start. His heart, so big in his chest.

Bethie sixteen years later, coming into the family room with a dazed look on her face. She'd been cutting up carrots in the kitchen. The knife had slipped. She now carried her finger in her other hand. Himself, fresh from a California crime scene, twenty-five corpses found in a hillside, fifteen of them young women, two of them babies. Telling his wife, 'Oh honey, it's just a scratch.'

Bethie yelling, 'I can't take it anymore! How did I end up married to a man who is so goddamn *cold*?'

Time fast-forwarding. He was in Massachusetts, keeping watch on human bait, Tess Williams returning to her old house in the hopes that it would lure her homicidal ex-husband out of hiding. Everything going wrong. Himself now inside the house as shots erupted down the street. Telling Tess not to go near the door. Promising he would keep her safe. Jim Beckett appearing, and blasting him back with a close-range spray from his double-barrel shotgun.

Himself thinking, *Wow, I feel so hot, for someone who is so cold.* Later, out of the hospital, paring back his work hours, trying to find some balance, picking up the girls for a weekend visit.

'How are you?' he asked Bethie.

'Better.'

'I miss you.'

'No you don't.'

'Bethie . . .'

'Go back to work, Pierce. Who needs to be a mere husband, when you can play at being God?'

In his daughter's two-bedroom apartment, Quincy jerked awake. He lay in the darkened room, watching threads of light from the closed blinds dance with dust in the air, listening to the sounds of the huge city below. 'I'm sorry, Elizabeth,' he said.

Then he got up and went to the TV room, where the last living member of his family sat watching M*A*S*H. Rainie was by her side. Her short, reddish-brown hair contrasted with his daughter's long, dusky blond locks. Her big gray eyes and wide cheekbones rebuffed Kimberly's own finely patrician face. Yin and yang, he thought, and both so beautiful the sight of them nearly broke his heart. For a moment, he simply stood there, wishing he could stop time, wishing he could take this moment and hold it safe forever in his hand.

'Ladies,' he said. 'I have a plan.'

19

Quincy's House, Virginia

It was early evening on Thursday, and Special Agent Glenda Rodman had yet to return to bed from the night before when she looked at the security monitor and saw Quincy standing outside his front gate. She had slept two hours before receiving the call to come to Philadelphia last night, but that now seemed a lifetime ago. The two hours of sleep were the aberration. The rest of the time, touring the Philadelphia crime scene, then returning to Quincy's home to listen to message after message promising sick, perverse death, was the norm.

They were up to three hundred and fifty-nine callers. Some Quincy had personally put in jail. Others simply hated feds. Still others were merely bored. Either way, word was definitely out that the thinly disguised ad circulating in so many prison newsletters contained an FBI profiler's home number. Everyone felt compelled to call. Some, she had to admit, were more imaginative than most. One artistic soul had gone so far as to compose a death rap. It wasn't half bad.

Glenda hit the button and let Quincy into his own property. The agent wore the same suit from the night before. His features were pale. On the camera, they were also hard to read. Whether he knew it or not, Pierce Quincy was a legend around the Bureau. These days, Glenda felt sorry for the agent. But she felt even more curious about what would happen next.

He knocked on his front door. She kindly let him in.

'I need to gather a few things,' he said.

'Certainly.'

'I'll check in with Everett next, then I'm leaving town.'

'The Philadelphia P.D. aren't going to like that.'

'My daughter comes first.' He disappeared into the master bedroom. Moments later, Glenda heard the sound of closet doors opening, as he began to pack a bag.

She wandered into his home office, not sure what to do with herself. It was interesting, she'd been in this house two days now and there wasn't much here to give a sense of the man who technically occupied the space. Several of the rooms were completely empty. The majority of the walls were bare; the kitchen couldn't feed a rat. The only room with any atmosphere was this room, the office, and she found herself coming here again and again, if only to escape the starkness of a vast, overwhelmingly white space.

Here was an old sound system that offered mediocre comfort in the shape of classical jazz tapes. A state-of-the-art fax dominated the corner of a beautiful, antique cherry desk. Gold-framed diplomas and academic certificates leaned against one wall, still not hung, but at least unearthed, while cardboard boxes were piled in each corner. The desk chair, black leather, was supple and distinctly expensive. Quincy obviously spent time in this room. Sometimes she caught a whiff of his cologne.

She sat in his chair, feeling like an intruder, as the phone once more began to ring. Following protocol, she let the answering machine pick it up.

'Hey baby,' a voice crooned. 'Heard you were trying a new policy of accessibility. I dig that. God knows there isn't anyone interesting to talk to in here. Bad break about your luscious daughter. Not so sorry about the frigid ex, though. Word on the street is that somebody's got your number. The hunter has become the hunted. Don't worry, Quince baby, I got my money on you in the prison pool. Hundred to one odds is just my style. You go, girl. Life hasn't been this entertaining in ages.'

The caller hung up. It was a good call, Glenda thought, probably long enough to trace. Not that wire-tapping had helped them much; it only proved that lots of prisoners read their local newsletters. For that matter, half the callers were only too happy to leave their names and prison facility.

She left the office and spotted Quincy standing in his kitchen, holding a small black travel bag, and staring at the answering machine.

'We're taping them all,' she said by way of explanation.

'One hundred to one odds.' He gave her a sideways glance. 'Considering how many of them I put in prison, I think I deserve better than that.'

'I have a copy of the ad if you would like to see it,' Glenda said, feeling the need to sound professional. She went to fetch it from the office. When she returned, Quincy had set down the traveling bag. He was standing in front of the empty refrigerator with the look of a man who'd opened it many times before and still kept expecting something different. She understood. Her own fridge held only water and low-fat yogurt and yet she continuously checked it for a fried-chicken dinner.

She handed Quincy the fax.

The ad was already typeset, a simple four-by-four square. It read, *Reporter from BSU Productions seeks inside information on life at death's door. Interested inmates should contact head agent, Pierce Quincy, at daytime number printed below. Or, contact his assistant, Amanda Quincy, at the following address.*

'Not very subtle,' Quincy commented with that same unnerving calm. 'BSU Productions. Head agent. Life at death's door.'

'Codes can be more elaborate. From what I understand, the inmates generally disguise their communications as ads for pen pals. Then they play around with the letters. You know, instead of SWM/L for Single White Male/Lifer, they do things like BPO/M, which stands for Black Power Organization/Message. Members of the gang then know to piece through the ad for relevant information.'

'Ah, the power of grassroots journalism. And people with too much time on their hands.'

'From what we can tell, this ad ran in four major publications: *Prison Legal News*, *National Prison Project Newsletter*, *Prison Fellowship*, and *Freedom Now*. Combined circulation reaches over five thousand subscribers. That number isn't high given total prison population, but the four newsletters basically account for at least one ad reaching every major corrections department. We think word of mouth took over from there.'

'Quilting bees have nothing on the average prison for sheer amount of gossip,' Quincy murmured. 'I take it what we theorized before still stands. My phone number, and thus access to my address, has been spread so far and wide we'll never be able to pare it down. Who knows where I live? Who doesn't?'

'The *National Prison Project Newsletter* has the original hard copy of the ad,' Glenda said. 'We're having it couriered to the crime lab now. The Document Section should have more information for us in a matter of days. Also, Randy Jackson is still working on how the UNSUB got your unlisted number. I'm sure he'll have something shortly.'

'The UNSUB got my phone number from Mandy. He used my daughter.' Quincy set down the fax. For the first time, he turned and fully met her gaze. She was immediately shocked by the hardness in his eyes, the cool expression on his face. Dissociation, the professional part of her deduced. Events of the past eighteen hours had left him in a state of shock, and his mind was coping by keeping him detached. The rest of her felt an unexpected tingle at the back of her neck. She had seen that remote gaze before. Old photos of Ted Bundy. Some people believed there was only a thin line between profilers and their prey. At this moment, in Quincy, that line didn't exist. The tingle on the back of her neck grew into a shiver.

'My daughter's death wasn't an accident,' he said. 'Rainie Conner has evidence that the UNSUB tampered with her seat belt.'

'Oh no,' Glenda said immediately, and meant it.

'We believe he befriended her, gained her trust. There is no telling what he knows. Hobbies, likes, dislikes, personal habits, personal quirks. Friends of mine, where they live. He most certainly has the address and phone number of this house. You shouldn't be here alone.'

'I'm not,' she said automatically, for the Bureau would never send an agent alone in the field. 'There's Special Agent Montgomery . . .'

Quincy merely looked at her. Then he let his gaze roam the empty rooms.

'Montgomery's been busy,' she said defensively.

'Why is he on this case? He doesn't exactly seem the cavalry type.'

'He requested it. You're one of us. It's important to get to the bottom of this, so we can all be safe.'

Quincy looked at her again. She was beginning to understand his reputation now. That direct, probing stare. Those hard, compelling eyes. She broke, her gaze skittering away.

'Montgomery . . . Montgomery was on the Sanchez case. First.' She didn't have to say anything more. It was common knowledge that the first agent had botched the Sanchez case fifteen years ago. He'd insisted that they were looking for a single, charismatic sociopath, à la Ted Bundy, when the police already had evidence that more than one killer was involved. Further, the presence of cement dust had the LAPD wanting to check out blue-collar workers, not the local law schools. The police had finally thrown a fit. Montgomery had been removed. Quincy had come in. The rest was now law enforcement history.

'That would explain his language and dress in front of Everett,' Quincy commented.

She smiled thinly. 'No point in auditioning for the Bureau fast track when your career has already been derailed.'

'His mistake. Apparently he's made a few. Don't let the next one involve you.'

'I'm fine here. You have a wonderful security system, plus

we've taken the liberty of upgrading. Let me show you.' She led Quincy to the front door, where a new security box had been installed next to his doorbell. His old system had been a simple four-by-four keypad inside the entry. Now the system entailed a significantly sized plastic case boasting a keypad, scanner, and multicolor digital display located outside the front door.

'It combines a pin code with fingerprint technology,' Glenda explained. 'Instead of unlocking the front door, then rushing in to enter the security code, this box controls the front door. You enter in your personal pin number twice, then hold your index finger over the scanner to be read. If you match the print on file, the system automatically disarms and allows you into the house. The minute you close the door, it automatically resets for the next guest. In other words, the house is always protected and it now takes more than a simple sequence of numbers to gain access.'

'It's set up for multiple people?'

'Yes. We've entered your fingerprints, Montgomery's, and mine into the system. More can be added as necessary. This way, we can come and go as we please. Plus, it eliminates having a key, which frankly poses another security risk as keys can be stolen or copied.'

Quincy nodded. 'What about lifting someone's fingerprint? The UNSUB has already stolen my name. Perhaps he got my fingerprints off a piece of mail I sent to my daughter.'

'No good,' Glenda said. 'The scanner not only looks at ridges, but also analyzes the fingerprint for temperature and electrical properties. A lifted print wouldn't register the right temperature or have electrical properties.' She smiled tightly. 'Nor for that matter, would a severed digit.'

Quincy nodded again. She could tell that he liked that.

'What about override protection? There must be ways to circumvent the scanner. After all, a homeowner might end up with his hand in a cast, or cut his finger, temporarily altering his own fingerprint. The security company must also consider those things.'

'The security company has thought of them, and is even more devious than you are, Quincy. All ten digits are on file. As long as the homeowner has one available finger, he can enter his home.'

Quincy rocked back on his heels. He finally looked impressed. 'Why didn't I buy this before?' he murmured.

'You weren't a corporation. It's just now becoming available for private residences.' Glenda punched in her pin number twice, placed her index finger on the scanner, and opened the front door. Walking back into the house, she said, 'So we have a state-of-the-art security system, cameras monitoring most rooms, and wiretaps on your phone lines. And if by some chance our mysterious UNSUB makes it through all that, I always have this.' She patted her trusty 10mm, snug in its shoulder holster.

'Fair enough. But bear in mind that my ex-wife also believed her security system would keep her safe, she had taken night classes in self-defense, and she was most certainly nobody's fool.'

'She didn't know to expect trouble. I do. Don't underestimate me.'

'I won't underestimate you, if you promise not to underestimate him.' Quincy offered her a half smile. Instead of lightening the mood, however, the twist of his lips made him look sad. He was worried, she realized for the first time. Worried and truly hurting. She wondered if even he knew how badly.

Lisa Gardner

'Where are you going?' she asked more gently.

'Out of town. My daughter is wrapping up her affairs now. Rainie is attending to a last few details. First thing tomorrow morning, we'll depart. He knows too much about us here. Our homes, our family, our friends. In a fresh location, I hope to negate that advantage.'

'That's not a bad idea.'

'Well, I am an expert. Just ask Bethie. Or Mandy.'

'Quincy—'

'I need to get going.'

'What should we tell the Philadelphia PD?'

'Tell them I'm tending to my daughter, but that I'll be in touch.'

'The crime scene,' she tried again. 'You know there are issues.'

He didn't say a word.

'Quincy, it's staged. You know it's staged, I know it's staged, but the homicide detectives . . . They're going to interpret that fact as yet another indication that you did it. After all, who better to stage a crime scene than a federal agent?'

'I know.'

'And that note . . . Left in the victim's abdominal cavity. That's cold, Quincy. It's also very personal, and that won't help you.'

'You have word on the note?' he asked sharply.

She shook her head. 'No, it's too soon. I mean simply that I don't think it convinces them that you're a target. At least it doesn't convince them enough. You are the ex-husband, after all; it's easier to make you their primary suspect.'

'I didn't kill Elizabeth.'

'Of course not!'

'I mean that, Glenda. You're a good agent. And I didn't murder my wife.'

She faltered. She would have to be dense not to catch the undercurrents in his voice and she had not advanced so far in the Bureau by being dumb. 'There's more, isn't there?'

'This person' – Quincy's voice sounded almost far away – 'he's very, very good.'

'He may be good, but we've gone up against good before. We'll find him.'

'Really? Because I've been going through my old cases and I haven't seen a hint of him yet. Glenda, for the last time, don't stay here alone.'

'I'll be fine.'

'I don't think you understand. I'm removing my daughter from the playing field. With her out of reach, it's anybody guess where he'll strike next.'

20

New York University, New York City

'I can't believe she's dead.'

Kimberly sat in Professor Andrews's office as the last rays of daylight gave way to a slinky gray dusk. Day One, Kimberly called this Thursday. Day One without her mother. She gripped the edge of the old maple seat harder, as if that would keep this day from ending. Day One would only be followed by Days Two, Three, and Four, then Months One, Two, and Three, then Years . . . Tears slid down her cheeks.

She had come here with the intention of being professional. She had to leave town. She would provide a rough sketch of the last few days for her professor. She would end by calmly stating that circumstances now warranted the resignation of her coveted internship position. Dignified. Firm. In control. Those were her goals. She was nearly a master's student, for heaven's sake. She had buried her sister and had now lost her mother. If she had been a young woman once, she wasn't anymore.

She had stepped into the warm, crowded office with its hodgepodge mix of precariously stacked papers and dying plants and her composure had instantly dropped like a rock.

Her eyes welled up. She stood in front of a man she respected almost as much as her father, and bits and pieces of the last few days burst out of her mouth before her throat finally closed up on her.

Dr Andrews had led her to the chair. He had brought her a glass of water. Then he had sat patiently on the other side of his cluttered desk, his hands folded and his expression steady while he waited for her to recover. He didn't offer any platitudes or comforting noises. It wasn't his style.

In his ten years at NYU, Dr Marcus Andrews had garnered a reputation for reducing even the most brilliant PhD candidates to tears with his unwavering blue stare. Speculation placed his age anywhere between sixty and older than dirt. He had thinning gray hair, a perpetual scowl, and a penchant for tweed. While in reality he was an average-sized man, trim from a lifelong devotion to yoga, he had an uncanny ability to seem four times his natural size as he stood at a podium and railed at his students to try harder, think broader, and for heaven's sake, be *smarter*.

According to the grapevine, he'd started his career as a psychiatrist assigned to the fabled San Quentin prison. The work had intrigued him so much, he'd gotten a PhD in criminology and made a name for himself doing ground-breaking work on the institutionalization of criminals, and how the very nature of prisons guaranteed further acts of brutality when hardened inmates were released back into society.

He was hard, gruff, and demanding. He was also brilliant, and Kimberly respected him immensely.

'Maybe you should start at the beginning,' he told her.

'No. I don't want to go through it again. It's painful, and I can't afford to be in pain right now. It's funny, I never

Lisa Gardner

understood how my father could come home from his job and look so composed. All the cops on TV, they came back from crime scenes and they drank, or smoked, or cursed, or raged. My sister and I, we understood that. It made sense to us. Then my father would come home again, and it was . . . He was like a pool of still water. No matter how long you studied his face, you never saw a thing beneath the surface. I get that now. The job is war. And you can't afford any emotion. It's your enemy.'

'What do you think your father would feel right now if he could hear you?' Dr Andrews asked.

'He would be hurt.'

'And this person who is targeting your father, what is his goal?'

'To hurt him,' she replied, then bowed her head as she saw his point.

Dr Andrews gave her his lecturer's stare. 'If this is war, Miss Quincy, which side is currently winning?'

'My mother hated his job.'

'Law enforcement has a disproportionately high rate of divorce.'

'No, she *hated* his job. The violence. The grit. The way he seemed to belong more to it than to us. She created a beautiful home. She produced two beautiful daughters. And still he'd rather live in the shadows.'

'It's a calling. You understand that.'

'But that's my whole point. My mother is dead and I'm sad and I'm furious but I'm also . . . motivated. For the first time in months, I feel awake. One moment I was existing in some sort of fugue state, and now . . . I want to *find* the bastard. I want to read the crime-scene reports. I want to trace this monster's steps, I want to tear apart every little facet of his personality and unmask him. And I am thinking about him more than I'm grieving for my mother. Dr Andrews, what is *wrong* with us?'

Dr Andrews finally smiled, an unheard-of softening of his hard-lined face. 'Ah, Miss Quincy. Haven't you ever noticed that criminologists never do a study on criminologists?'

'We're sick, aren't we?'

'We're intellectualists. Our desire to understand why things happen outweighs our rage at the events.'

'Rage is purer,' she said bitterly.

'Rage lacks constructiveness. Think of it this way: Cops are doers. They get angry at what they encounter. They make arrests. In that way, they help control crime, but their intervention is always after the fact. Criminologists, sociologists, criminal behaviorists, are thinkers. We get curious. We do studies. We come up with things like profiling, which enables law enforcement to prevent future atrocities.'

'When I was growing up,' Kimberly said, 'I used to think of my father as a general, off fighting in some foreign land. It made me proud. Even when my feelings were hurt, even when I was mad because he missed my soccer game or my birthday, I was proud.'

Dr Andrews leaned forward. He said gently, 'You say you're proud of your father, Miss Quincy, and I believe that you are. But lately, you've also been distancing yourself from him. Why is that?'

She stiffened. 'I don't know what you mean.'

'The anxiety attacks. You've mentioned them to me, but I get the impression you haven't mentioned them to him.'

Kimberly bowed her head again. Her fingers fidgeted in her lap. 'I didn't . . . I don't know. I tell myself I don't want to worry him. But I don't think that's it. I think . . . I don't want to seem high-strung. You know – like Mandy.'

Dr Andrews winced. He sat back, and for the first time, Kimberly noticed how troubled he appeared. The lines were deeper in his face, his eyes didn't have that stern stare she'd grown accustomed to. For a moment, he almost appeared human. 'I have a confession to make, Miss Quincy. I think I might have led you astray.'

'What do you mean?' She sat up straighter. Her heart began to pound again.

No, she thought. *No mistakes from you.* No mere mortality from NYU's most-feared professor. Her world was falling apart and even if it was immature of her, she needed the gods in her life to remain gods.

'I'm the one who originally attributed your anxiety attacks to stress,' Dr Andrews said.

'My sister had died, it made sense.'

'But now we have additional data points. Think of what your father said. Someone has targeted your family. That someone has been at this for at least two years.'

'Yes.' She looked at him quizzically, then it suddenly clicked. The blood drained out of her face. Oh no. Oh no, oh no, oh no. 'My feeling of being watched. You think . . . you think it's him.'

'We can't rule it out,' Dr Andrews said quietly. He added with the most kindness she'd ever heard from him, 'I am truly sorry, Miss Quincy. I rushed to the most obvious conclusion. Perhaps it's time to listen to my own lectures.'

'He's stalking me.' She couldn't get over that idea. The concept was a curious one. It made her feel at once violated, yet relieved. Violated because some unknown predator had invaded her life and hunted her down like cattle. Relieved because the violation was real, not just in her head. All those times. The goose bumps, the cold chills creeping up her spine. She hadn't gone mental. Strong, logical Kimberly was still strong, logical Kimberly. Oh thank God . . .

'It fits his MO,' Dr Andrews was saying.

'Goddammit, he's been stalking me!' She was mad now. The rage brought desperately needed color to her cheeks, and stiffened her spine for the first time in weeks. Hunted? She would not be hunted.

Dr Andrews was studying her. He must have liked what he saw, because he nodded encouragingly. 'Remember what we were saying. Get curious. Put yourself in the predator's shoes. What makes him tick?'

She took a deep breath. 'Games,' she said after a moment. 'He likes playing games.'

'That is consistent with what we know. What else?'

'He doesn't want a quick kill. It's not about the murder, it's about the process. Personal. He wants it to be personal. Intimate.'

'He won't be a stranger to you.'

'But I might not have met him yet,' Kimberly said slowly. 'That feeling of being watched . . . If I had already met him, he wouldn't have to monitor me from a distance; he'd already be part of my life.'

'Reconnaissance,' Dr Andrews theorized. 'When did the sensation begin?'

'A few months ago. So he's been doing his homework. Looking for an opening.'

'New boyfriend,' Dr Andrews offered.

'Too obvious. He's done that ploy, first with Mandy, and then with my mother. Though he upped the ante with my mother – we think he also posed as someone who received one of Mandy's organs.'

Dr Andrews blinked. 'Brilliant.'

'I'm supposedly the smart one,' Kimberly murmured softly, still thinking out loud. 'That's what Mandy and my mom would have told him. I'm the serious one, the one who's always wanted to join law enforcement. The one who started taking martial arts at the age of eight, who likes tackle football and guns . . .' Her voice trailed off, her mind already forming a connection with one new person in her life. A charming gun pro who just happened to join her rifle association six months earlier. Doug James.

'You have an idea?'

'I don't want to jump to conclusions.'

'Better to be safe than sorry, Miss Quincy.'

She smiled. 'That's the first platitude I've ever heard from you. I didn't know that you knew any. Then again, duly noted.'

Dr Andrews smiled. 'You're leaving, yes? I assume that is what you're here to tell me. Strategic retreat is a perfectly valid option.'

'I don't know how long I'll be gone.'

'Understandable.'

'I can't tell you where I'm going.'

'Did you hear me asking?'

'You . . . you should probably find another intern. I mean, I would understand . . .'

'At this late date? Bah. I can read my own notes for a change. Might do me a world of good. Jumping to obvious conclusions. Next thing you know I'll be dreaming of the Washington Monument and blaming everything on my toilet training.'

'Dr Andrews . . . Thank you.'

'Miss Quincy, it has been a pleasure.'

There was nothing left to say. Kimberly rose. Held out her hand. Across the desk, Dr Andrews also stood and extended his hand. Kimberly was touched by how grave he appeared.

'One last piece of advice?' he asked solemnly.

'Of course.'

'Law enforcement, Miss Quincy. This man, he seems to specialize in identifying his victim's vulnerability, the thing she thinks she needs or admires most. For you, it's law enforcement. You have an inherent trust and respect for anyone wearing a badge.'

'Point taken.' Kimberly hesitated. It was silly to say what she was going to say next. But then, she felt that she must. *Day One*, she thought. *My sister is gone, my mother is dead, and I am learning to question everything.* Her gaze went to the window, now robbed of the light of day. Outside, a car backfired, sounding like a gunshot on the crowded streets.

'Dr Andrews,' she said quietly. 'If anything should happen, can you tell my father something for me? Tell him the last person I saw this evening was a newly hired instructor at my gun club. Tell him I met a man named Doug James.'

21

William Zane's Office, Virginia

'I want a name.'

'Anonymity is the spiritual foundation of AA; we don't give out that kind of information.'

'Fine. Screw the name; it's probably just an alias anyway. I want a description.'

'And one more time, anonymity is the spiritual foundation of AA. We don't give out that kind of information.'

'Mr Zane, this is a homicide investigation. You give me information now, quietly, or to the police later as part of an official investigation that will be reported to the press. Now, do you want to provide one man's description as a private exchange between you and me, or do you want word to get out that some psychopathic killer is using AA meetings to select his victims?'

William Zane, president of Mandy's AA chapter, finally hesitated. He was a big guy. Six one, two hundred and forty pounds. He wore a suit that screamed investment banker and carried himself in a way that suggested he was accustomed to people doing exactly what he said. Rainie figured he had at least three ex-wives and one helluva cocaine habit somewhere in his past. In theory, he was clean now and did an impeccable job of running the AA meetings. Someday, she'd be sure to send him a Hallmark card congratulating him on being such a nicely reformed human being. At the moment, however, she simply wanted the name and description of Amanda's 'friend' at the AA meetings.

It was six P.M. Thursday, nearly twelve hours until departure to the relative safety of Portland, and for no good reason, Rainie was increasingly worried about Kimberly. In other words, she didn't feel like dicking around.

William Zane sighed. He'd agreed to see Rainie upon hearing that Amanda Quincy's car accident had been re-opened as a murder investigation. Now, he clearly regretted that decision. He got up from his chair in his posh office, moved his impressively clad bulk to the door and shut it firmly.

'You have to understand what you're asking,' he said. 'The key to AA's effectiveness is its simple operating principle – we provide confidential support to anyone willing to stop drinking. We aren't beholden to the courts, or to the police, or to anyone. We're an equal-opportunity support organization. And for a lot of people, we're the only lifeline they've got.'

'Amanda doesn't need a lifeline anymore.'

'You're not asking about Amanda. You're asking about current members.'

It was Rainie's turn to sigh. 'Here's the kicker, Mr Zane. I'm a member of AA. I confess that I wouldn't have walked into my first meeting if it hadn't been anonymous and I wouldn't have continued to attend meetings after I became a police officer if it hadn't been anonymous. So as a matter of fact, I see your point. But this man *murdered* Amanda

Quincy. He set up a scenario that sent her face crashing into a windshield at thirty-five miles per hour. And then there's what he did to her mother. Would you like to see the crime-scene photos?'

'No, no, no, no.' Mr Zane shook his lily-white hands emphatically and managed to go another shade of pale. To the image of the three ex-wives, Rainie added the picture of him pacing *outside* the delivery room with a box of Cuban cigars. She wondered if he ever did manage to change a diaper.

'I'm looking for a killer, Mr Zane,' she pressed. 'You want to be a lifeline, be a lifeline for the other women who are doomed to die unless you help me stop this guy. Be a lifeline for the future victims. Because at this moment, you're the only chance of finding this guy that I've got.'

'Perhaps,' Mr Zane said finally. 'Off the record. *Way* off the record—'

'Deal. Sit, Mr Zane; let's talk.'

Mr Zane sat behind his big desk. She got out her notebook.

'Do you remember Amanda Quincy?' Rainie asked.

'Yes, she joined our meetings nearly a year and a half ago.'

'Did she have a sponsor?'

'She had a sponsor. I don't see the need to give out his name unless absolutely necessary.'

'Yeah, and here's a photo of what happens to the human skull when it hits the rim of a windshield—'

'Larry Tanz,' Mr Zane said. 'Nice guy.'

'How did Amanda know Larry Tanz?'

'He owned the restaurant where she worked. Larry's been an AA member for ten years and has sponsored a fair amount of his staff in that time.' Mr Zane slid her a look. 'It's amazing how many bartenders are drunks. And then there're the cooks . . .'

Rainie rolled her eyes, then jotted down a quick note. Larry Tanz, manager where Mandy used to work, which meant by definition, manager where Mary Olsen used to work. Interesting.

'Did Mandy and Mr Tanz seem to have any other kind of relationship? You know, beyond the sponsor-sponsee kind of thing?'

'Our chapter suggests that people wait at least a year before dating,' Mr Zane said promptly. 'As I'm sure you know, quitting cold turkey is very hard. You don't want to risk the additional stress of having a serious relationship end – it might send even the strongest person back to the bottle. We don't recommend dating until the initiate celebrates his or her one-year anniversary.'

'Sounds romantic. So was Mandy fucking Larry or what?'

Mr Zane said stiffly, 'I don't think so.'

'Why not?'

'One, Larry is a good guy. And two, while he felt sad and disappointed by Amanda's accident – perhaps even guilty – I wouldn't call him crushed. Her death was tragic, but certainly not deeply personal for him.'

'How nice for Larry. What about someone else? Someone she might have befriended at the meetings?'

'She befriended lots of people—'

'New members who may have joined around the time she did who seemed like particularly close friends.'

Mr Zane hesitated. Rainie stared at him. He picked up a laser-etched paperweight, a souvenir from some exotic vacation. She stared harder.

'Well, there was one guy . . .'

'Name.'

'Ben. Ben Zikka.'

'Description.'

'I don't know. Older. Late forties or early fifties, I would say. Not tall, five ten, maybe. Thinning brown hair. Soft around the middle. Not good taste in suits – definitely off the rack.' Mr Zane ran a hand down his own tailored jacket with authority. 'I think he said he was a police officer or something like that. I could believe he'd eaten a lot of doughnuts.'

Rainie scowled, then began chewing on her lower lip. This wasn't what she'd expected. 'Older, kind of frumpy-looking guy? You're sure he was with Mandy?'

'Fairly sure. They started leaving the meetings together. At one point, I noticed they now came in the same car.'

'And we're talking about the same Amanda Quincy, right? Twenty-three, slender, blond hair, big blue eyes? If the star quarterback hadn't dated her in high school, it wasn't from lack of trying.'

'She was pretty,' Mr Zane said with more enthusiasm.

Rainie was getting a headache. 'You're sure Zikka and Amanda were an item?'

'I don't know. You asked about new members she'd befriended. He was the new member she'd befriended. To tell you the truth, however, he only came the first few months. Then he stopped coming. She showed up a few more times, but each time was farther apart. Larry Tanz was going to call her about it, when she had the accident.'

'So she comes to AA, meets this guy, and slowly trails off.'

'Yes.' Mr Zane shrugged. He said, 'It's often like that in

the beginning. Admitting you're an alcoholic is tough. Staying sober is even tougher. Most of our members end up starting and stopping a few times before it sticks.'

'Was there anyone else at this meeting who seemed to know Mandy? Say, someone six feet tall, well dressed, trim build, late forties, early fifties?' Rainie was working off Bethie's neighbor's statement to the police that she'd seen someone resembling Quincy enter the townhouse. But Mr Zane shook his head.

'Are you sure?' she persisted.

'You haven't been to an AA meeting lately, have you, Ms. Conner? You spend half your life overindulging in alcohol and drugs and you're rarely the well-dressed, trim-build type. Maybe a Hollywood star can pull it off, but the rest of us, we've abused ourselves and we look it. Even Amanda Quincy was becoming harsh around the edges.'

Rainie scowled again. One name and description later, she was more confused than when she'd started. She studied good old William Zane. His gaze was clear. He met her eye. Dammit, just when you were hoping someone was feeding you a lie, he went and told the truth.

She glanced at her watch. T-minus ten and still two stops to go. She rose, shook Zane's hand, and tried not to take his obvious relief at her departure too personally.

At the door, however, she was struck by one last question. 'At your meetings,' she said, 'you talk about some very personal things, right?'

'Yes.'

'What did Mandy talk about?'

He hesitated.

'Crime-scene photos, Mr Zane. Crime. Scene. Photos.'

'Mandy had self-esteem issues. Mandy . . . had a *lot* of

self-esteem issues. She talked about how famous her father was. She talked about how beautiful her mother was. She talked about how smart her sister was. And she talked about – Let's put it this way, she often categorized herself as a disposable blonde.'

'A "disposable blonde"?'

'Mandy had this obsession with violence, Ms. Conner. She liked to see slasher movies, to read true-crime novels. She told the group that when she was younger, she used to sneak into her father's office and look through his homicide textbooks, even read his case files. They terrified her, but she still came back for more. It wasn't a healthy thing. It wasn't a face-your-fear kind of thing. She did it to punish herself. You see, most of us identify with the crime solver when we watch slasher movies or read mystery novels. Not Mandy. She identified with the pretty, blue-eyed, blond victims. Disposable blondes, Ms. Conner. Beautiful women who exist simply for the deranged killer to savage first.'

Rainie was still shaken by the time she pulled into the tiny commercial real estate building that housed Phil de Beers's office. Clouds had rolled in. The air crackled with electricity. A nearly full moon had to be up there somewhere, but the night had taken on a dense, suffocated feeling. Even the crickets had gone quiet.

She got out of her car hunch-shouldered and skittish, ready to shoot first, question later. Nine P.M. Kimberly should be back in the relative safety of her apartment. Quincy had probably wrapped things up with his boss at Quantico and was now returning to New York City. Rainie just needed to finish up two last chores, then it would be her turn.

Instead, she stopped in the middle of the empty parking lot and searched the inky black depths for something she couldn't name. Beyond her line of sight, she could hear cars humming by on the distant freeway. Four streetlamps bounced puddles of light off shiny black asphalt. The scent of honeysuckles and blackberries came to her, cloying and thick.

'Howdy, ma'am.'

She startled, then whirled, her right hand already reaching for her Glock.

Phil de Beers stood in the doorway of the building, the spitting image of his Internet photo as he gazed at her curiously. 'Want to come in?' he asked politely.

She shivered violently and nodded.

'Brewed some coffee,' he said a moment later as he gestured her inside the building. 'Don't know what it is about thunderstorms, God knows they generate enough humidity to drown a rat, but they always make me feel in need of a good hot drink. Or whiskey. But on account of this being a professional visit, I thought I'd stick with coffee.'

'Bummer,' Rainie said, and earned a wide, flashing smile from the small, neatly dressed black man.

'You caught me. I do have some good ol' sour mash . . .'

'Yeah,' she said gloomily, 'but I'm an alcoholic. I only get the coffee.'

'Bummer,' he echoed solemnly, and she decided that she liked him very much.

They went first to the tiny kitchenette shared by all the clients in the building. Phil splashed a delicate mist of whiskey into his brew. Rainie poured in cream and sugar until the private investigator began to laugh.

'I see some dependency issues,' he commented.

'Sugar and fat are socially acceptable drugs.'

'And you carry them well,' he assured her, conducting an unabashed sweep of her figure before leading her into his office. He took a seat behind his desk in a positively sinful red leather chair. That left a hard, spindly old kitchen chair that she figured was designed to discourage lengthy visits.

Phil held up a small glass dish. 'M&M's?' Rainie shook her head. He took a large handful. 'I got some dependency issues, too,' he admitted cheerfully and munched on the candy while she finished taking inventory of his office.

The space wasn't large but it was adequate. One wall contained two rows of bookshelves bearing thick volumes of *Virginia State Law* as well as piles of magazines. The other wall contained a gallery of framed prints. A diploma from the Virginia police academy. A variety of black and white photos showing de Beers with various men in suits. Probably important men in suits, Rainie thought, but now she was merely showing off her powers of deductive reasoning.

'Important person?' she asked, picking one photo at random.

'Director Freeh,' he said.

'Director Freeh?'

De Beers flashed her that wide grin. 'Head of the FBI.'

'Oh yeah, *that* Director Freeh.' Rainie shut up and drank her coffee. It would've been better with whiskey.

'So,' de Beers said. 'I've been watching Mary Olsen as you requested. Damn boring woman, Mrs Mary Olsen. Didn't leave her house yesterday or today.'

'That's not very helpful.'

'No, but I got a contact at the phone company. I'll pull her records, give 'em a whirl. If you rattled the woman, she's probably not passing the time merely watching TV.'

'She's checking in with people.'

'There you go. I can get names, numbers, and addresses. Then what do you want me to do?'

'Fax me the phone numbers and names of whomever she's called the most. I know a state trooper who can check them out.'

'I don't mind doing it.'

'I want you to stay on Mary, in case phone calls are no longer enough. Oh, and here's a new name for you. Larry Tanz. He supposedly owns the restaurant where Mary Olsen used to work, and where Amanda Quincy worked up until the time of her death. I'd be curious to know if he suddenly paid his former employee a personal visit.'

'Frightened women can be consoled long distance for only so long . . .'

'Absolutely.' Rainie hesitated. 'You carry, right? All the time? Heavily?'

De Beers gave her a look. 'Uh oh. Now is when I get that not-so-fresh feeling anymore.'

'We have evidence that my client's daughter didn't die in an automobile accident as originally reported,' Rainie told him. 'It was murder. Then last night in Philadelphia . . . Most likely the same man murdered my client's ex-wife. Brutally.'

De Beers arched a brow. He got up. He found a folded newspaper on the side bookshelf. He tossed it on top of the desk so Rainie could see the headline. 'High Society House of Horrors.' Some enterprising photographer had managed to snag a crime-scene photo of the hallway and its endless rows of bloody handprints.

'I'd call this brutal,' de Beers said.

'That would be the one.'

'Says here she was the former wife of an FBI agent. Which would make your client—'

'I can see how you've succeeded as a private investigator.'

De Beers sat down again and studied her face. 'Let me recap, darlin'. You want me to tail a woman who will hopefully meet a man whose current hobby is taking on the Federal Bureau of Intimidation and murdering the ones they love?'

'Just one man's loved ones. It's personal.'

'Personal?' His gaze strayed to the gruesome newspaper photo. 'Hell, you're talking a psychopath with balls of steel.'

'Before you kick him, make sure you put on combat boots.'

De Beers sighed. 'I wished you would've told me yesterday that I should be carrying around kryptonite.'

She shrugged. 'I've been busy.'

De Beers sighed again. 'Okay. Looks like I'm breaking out my TEC-DC9 and leaving my thirty-eight Special for backup. Anything else you can tell me about the biggest badass in town? Name, age, description?'

Rainie got out her notebook. 'We have record of two aliases. Tristan Shandling, used recently in Philadelphia to approach Elizabeth Quincy. Then the name Ben Zikka, used approximately twenty months ago here in Virginia, to approach Amanda Quincy. I haven't gotten to run down Ben Zikka yet, but the name Tristan Shandling wasn't backed up. We knew it was an alias the minute we tried to run it through the system.'

'You'd think a man taking on a Feebie would be more careful.'

'He uses the aliases to approach women outside of law

enforcement. What normal woman bothers with something like a routine security check?'

De Beers nodded his agreement. 'Makes my life easier. I'll get a list of names from the phone records and find out which ones stand up to scrutiny. Then you sic your state trooper on the ones that don't.'

Rainie was struck by another thought. 'Actually, to get an account with the phone company, the man will have to document the name, and we do know one ID that's fleshed out.'

'That name?'

'FBI agent, Pierce Quincy.'

De Beers gave her a look. She smiled tightly. 'He stole my client's identity. No one realized it until two days ago. The Bureau has a whole case team on it now, but given the murder in Philadelphia . . . The fraud investigation is probably slipping through the cracks at the moment.'

'Balls of steel,' de Beers muttered. 'Balls of steel. Well, let's return to what we do know. Subject's description?'

'I have two. They don't match.'

'Of course.'

'As Ben Zikka, recovering drunk twenty months ago, our guy was described as being five ten, overweight, balding, and frumpy. According to members of AA, Zikka claimed to have some sort of tie with law enforcement. This information is only two hours old, so I haven't gotten very far with it.'

'Other descript?'

'In Philly, he used the name Tristan Shandling. According to a witness, he's tall, well-built, and sharply dressed. In fact, he looks very much like an FBI agent. At least the age is the same. Mid-forties to early fifties.'

'So I'm looking for a middle-aged white male. That's what you have for me?'

Rainie thought about it. 'Yep,' she agreed. 'That's about it.'

'Well, there you go. At the first sight of a middle-aged white male, I'll shoot to kill. Darlin', you've just made my day.'

'I try. Listen, I have to leave town. You can reach me at this number on my business card, but I'm going to be three thousand miles away so don't consider me the cavalry. You get into real trouble, call state trooper Vince Amity. He's handling the investigation of Amanda Quincy's MVA. He's a good guy. And Phil – don't put yourself on the line, okay? Just watch, take notes. If Mary meets this guy in person, feel free to keep a very low profile. I went into the house in Philadelphia. That picture is not the half of what this man did.'

'What are you going to do?'

Rainie smiled. 'My client has one daughter left. I plan on keeping it that way.'

Two minutes later, de Beers watched from the doorway as she got into her rent-a-wreck and started the engine. She appreciated his diligence. But then she was out of the parking lot, onto the freeway, heading for her motel. The sky broke. The rain poured down in sheets as thunder rumbled off in the distance. Rainie drove alone through the torrent, listening to the rhythmic sound of her windshield wipers, and periodically tugging on her seat belt. The tension held.

Ten-fifteen P.M. Eight hours until departure and still, at the moment, safe.

22

'I'm here to see Doug James.'

'He's with a student.'

'He's an instructor of mine. I just need to speak with him for a second . . .'

'Would you like to leave a message?'

'Can't. Needs to be in person. I swear it will only take a moment.'

The teenage boy working the front desk gave Kimberly a long-suffering sigh. He was new here, or he would have recognized her as a regular and given her less hassle. Instead he was trying to be diligent new employee of the month. Kimberly's hands were shaking. She was on the verge of losing her nerve. She wished Diligent New Employee would diligently do what she asked. Otherwise she might be forced to reach across the desk and wring his new-employee neck.

Maybe her thoughts showed on her face, because he started to look at her nervously.

'PMS,' she told him curtly.

Geek boy turned bright red and quickly scurried off. She'd have to remember this strategy for the future. *Day*

233

One, she thought again, advancing her mental notes. *I realize that even I can be a homicidal maniac.*

Four minutes later, Doug James walked from the shooting gallery into the gun club's lobby. He looked right at her and Kimberly had to catch her breath all over again. Doug James was handsome. And not in that slick, preppy sort of way. She would've been able to see through that. Instead he was older, gray hairs blatantly sharing space with sun-bleached brown. His face was weathered. He had the squinted, deeply peering eyes of a man who'd spent his life outdoors, staring into the sun. Some days he was clean-shaven, but by evening he almost always sported a five o'clock shadow and even with the gray stubble mixed in with the dark, he looked good.

He wasn't too tall, but he possessed a solid, broad-shouldered build. And he was well muscled. She'd felt the rippling band of his arms around hers as he'd adjusted her aim. She'd felt the hard plane of his chest as he'd shifted her stance. She'd felt the heat of his body, standing mere inches from hers.

He also wore a gold wedding band on his left ring finger. She'd thought of that often when he'd first started as her instructor. She'd thought of him as older, married, and way out of her league. And it had made her even more aware of each and every touch.

'He won't be a stranger to you.'

Kimberly thought of Dr Andrews's warning and her stomach churned. She looked at Doug James, ruggedly handsome Doug James, and she felt desire sweep over her again, even as her body was swamped with fear. Was this how her mother had felt about the man who had butchered her? And poor Mandy?

'Kimberly, how can I help you?'

She gazed at Doug blankly. Her mouth opened, but no words came out.

He smiled. 'I'm sorry, I didn't mean to startle you.'

'I have to cancel all my lessons,' she said.

He stilled, then frowned. She searched his gaze for anything sinister. He simply appeared concerned, and somehow that frightened her more. *He makes himself into what the victim wants*, Dr Andrews had theorized. Kindness. That's what all women wanted. Someone who was kind.

'I'm sorry to hear that, Kimberly. Is everything all right?'

'Where were you yesterday?'

'I was sick. I'm sorry. I tried to reach you at your apartment, but apparently you had already left.'

'And last night?'

'I was at home with my wife. Why are you asking?'

'I thought I saw you. Somewhere. At a restaurant.'

'I don't think so. I did come here briefly to pick up some paperwork, but then I went straight home.'

'To your wife?'

'Yes.'

'What is her name again?'

'Laurie. Kimberly—'

'You don't have any kids, do you?'

'Not yet.'

'How long have you been married?'

'I don't like this conversation, Kimberly. I'm not sure what is going on, but I don't think this is appropriate.'

'I thought we were friends. Friends can ask questions, can't they? Friends can talk.'

'We are friends. But I don't feel that you're asking these questions in a friendly way.'

'Does that make you nervous?'

'Yes.'

'Am I asking too many questions?'

'I think so.'

'Why? What are you trying to hide?'

Doug James didn't say anything right away. He stared at her, his peering eyes impossible to read. She returned his look inch for inch, though her pulse was fluttery and her hands had fisted at her side.

He said slowly, 'I'm going to return to my student now.'

'I'm not coming back.'

'I'm sorry—'

'I'm leaving this state. You won't be able to find me.'

'Okay, Kimberly.'

'I'm not as easy as my mother.'

'This other student *really* needs my attention.'

'She was a lovely woman, did you know that? Maybe she was raised out of step with the women's revolution. Maybe she should have tried harder in her marriage. But she loved us, and she did her best and she never stopped trying to be happy. Even when it was hard, she never stopped trying to be happy—'

Her voice broke off. She was crying. She stood in the middle of the threadbare lobby with its trophy case, stuffed animal heads, and sagging couch, weeping while other gun club members began to stare. Doug James slowly backed away, his hand fumbling behind him for the door connecting to the shooting gallery.

'I miss my mother,' Kimberly said, and this time her voice held as her tears stopped. She stood there dry-eyed, which she knew must be worse. The other members looked away. Doug James fairly bolted out of the lobby.

After a moment, she turned back to the front desk where the new, diligent employee of the month was regarding her with unabashed terror.

'What time did Doug stop by last night?' Kimberly asked.

'Eight P.M.,' the boy squawked. 'Stopped in the office, grabbed paperwork and left. His wife was waiting outside for him.'

'You saw her?'

'Yes.'

'What does she look like?'

'Not nearly as pretty as you,' the boy said hastily, still not understanding the situation.

Kimberly slowly nodded. Her mind was still trying to make the pieces fit. What had the witness said about her mother last night? Her mother and the strange man had pulled up together at ten P.M. in a fancy red car. According to the neighbor, her mother had been out all day.

'Was the woman a blonde? Mid-forties, slender, nicely dressed?' she asked.

The boy frowned. 'No. Doug's wife is a brunette and she's kind of big right now. I think they're expecting a baby.'

'Oh.' It definitely wasn't her mother who'd come here at eight. Which meant it might indeed be Doug James's wife. And hey, he might be telling the truth and he might be an actual gun instructor, happily married and now expecting his first child.

Day One, I don't know what to believe anymore. Day One, I've grown so afraid. Day One . . . Mandy, I'm so sorry I never realized before how life must feel to you.

Kimberly walked out the door. The air was black as pitch outside and just about as heavy. Nine-thirty P.M. She thought there was going to be a storm.

Quantico, Virginia

Quincy left Quantico shortly after ten P.M., as the first fat drops of rain hit his windshield. He peered up at clouds so thick they obliterated the moon. The wind was whipping. It was going to be a good, old-fashioned thunderstorm. He turned toward I-95 as the first bolt of lightning lit up the sky.

Not much longer, he kept telling himself. Not much longer.

Everett didn't like Quincy's decision to leave town. He demanded full accountability – where Quincy would be staying and who he would be with at all times. It did not give Quincy the level of security that he would've liked, but he couldn't very well tell the Special Agent in Charge that he didn't trust him, not when the man was going out of his way to help Quincy salvage his family and career. Both of them gave up what they had to. Neither of them was happy. It was the usual sort of compromise.

Quincy had packed up his laptop. He'd put a box of old case files in his trunk. He still had his FBI-issued 10mm, which he planned on keeping until the bitter end. He did not feel ready, but he was as prepared as he was ever going to get.

Not much longer.

Wind howling fiercer now. Trees starting to bend. He had to slow the car, but he did not get off the road. Ten-thirty P.M. His daughter needed him.

Not much longer.

He stared in his rearview mirror at the approaching headlights and he felt an incredible sense of doom.

Motel 6, Virginia

Ten forty-five P.M. Rainie dashed from her car to the entrance of her motel. The rain was coming down in sheets and the four-second sprint left her soaked. The night manager looked up as she bolted through the door, spraying raindrops and bits of tree leaves that had gotten stuck in her hair.

'Ugly night,' he commented.

'F-ugly night,' she amended. She stalked down the hall, shivering as the blast from the motel's air conditioner cut her to the bone. She needed to grab her things and check out. A hot shower could wait. Dinner could wait. All attention was focused on making it to New York. T minus seven.

In her room, the message waiting light was blinking. She glanced at it apprehensively. Then she sighed, sat down, and prepared to take notes.

Six calls. Not bad considering hardly anyone knew this number. Four were hang ups. The fifth was Carl Mitz. 'I'm still trying to reach Lorraine Conner. We need to talk.' She gave anxious Carl the credit for the hang ups as well, though she could be wrong. The sixth call surprised her the most. It was from her former fellow Bakersville officer, Luke Hayes.

'Rainie, some lawyer is calling all over town with all sorts of questions about you and your mom. Name is Carl Mitz. I thought you should know.'

Rainie glanced at her watch. She didn't have time for this now. Mr Mitz, on the other hand, didn't seem inclined to back off. Asking questions about her and her mother. All these years later, and the memory still gave her a chill.

She called Luke at his home, but got his machine. 'It's Rainie,' she informed the digital recorder. 'Thanks for the heads-up. I'm out of town, but I'll be back in the morning.

Do me a favor, Luke. Set up a meeting with Mitz. Just you and him. Then let me know when and where so I can crash the party. The man has spent the last three days hunting me down like vermin. It's time he and I had a chat.'

She hung up the phone. Rain ran off her short hair and splattered onto her T-shirt. She caught her reflection across the room, and was startled by the broad, pale lines of her face, the deep shadows hollowing out her rain-dampened cheeks. Her lips appeared bloodless. Her chestnut hair was spiky and wild. She looked like a punk rocker, she thought. Or maybe a vampire's latest victim. She gazed at her own reflection, felt no kinship with that beat-up woman, and was nearly struck dumb by sheer exhaustion.

Bethie had fought in the end. She'd seen her attacker and she'd tried desperately to escape. What did a woman feel in those last moments? Did the mind give you the luxury of feeling betrayed? Or was the terror only physical? Adrenaline and testosterone. Pure animal instinct to fight, to live, to breathe?

When she was younger, she'd watched wild cats stalk field mice. The cat would catch the mouse in its mouth, then let it go. Then scoop it up, then let it go. And the mouse would squeak and squeak and squeak, first shrill, then, as the game wore on, with less and less volume. Until finally, even after being released, the mouse rolled over on its back and very clearly surrendered. Dying had become preferable to living. Maybe that was nature's way of taking pity on the smaller members of the food chain.

She thought of Mandy, willing to get drunk again even after those hard-fought months of AA, then willing to get behind the wheel without a working seat belt. She thought of Bethie and how after years of isolation she'd agreed to allow a strange man through her front door.

Dying becomes preferable to living.

Rainie got off the bed. She threw the last of the toiletries in her bag. Eleven P.M. Seven hours until liftoff, and two hours left to drive. Life's a battle, she thought. Time to rejoin the war.

Quincy's House, Virginia

Special Agent Glenda Rodman was curled up on the floor in a corner of the cologne-smelling office. Outside the wind howled. Rain scoured the windows. Trees beat against fellow trees. Thunder still growled ominously, but the lightning struck further and further apart.

The alarm had shrieked five times, power punching in and out. Apparently, the backup system had not been properly wired. Every time the power failed, so did the alarm. She had the security company on speed dial now. Special Agent Montgomery was still nowhere to be found.

While in the kitchen, the phone began to ring again and the answering machine picked up.

'Death, death, death, kill, kill, kill, murder, murder, murder,' a voice sang. 'Death, death, death, kill, kill, kill, murder, murder, murder. Hey Quincy, check your mailbox. I disemboweled that puppy, just for you. Death, death, death, kill, kill, kill, murder, murder, murder. Death, death, death, kill, kill, kill, murder, murder, murder. Death, death, death . . .'

Glenda wrapped her arms around her knees. On the floor of the office, she rocked back and forth as the power went out again, and the state-of-the-art alarm system once more began to shriek.

23

Greenwich Village, New York City

'Mace.'

'Mace.'

'Firearms?' Quincy asked.

'I carry a Glock forty,' Rainie replied. 'I have to check it, though. Private investigators don't qualify to carry onboard.'

Quincy nodded, then turned toward his daughter who was standing over her open suitcase, having just handed her father her canister of Mace.

'I have a Glock, too,' Kimberly said, which caused her father to do a double take.

'You have what?'

'As long as you're armed, you might as well be well-armed,' she replied seriously. 'What can you really accomplish with a twenty-two?'

Quincy raised a brow. He brought out his own pistol, a stainless steel 10mm Smith & Wesson, standard FBI issue. The Smith & Wesson held nine .40 caliber cartridges in the magazine and one in the chamber. Clipped to his belt in a brown leather holder, he carried two additional magazines, giving him total access to thirty rounds. Firepower would not be a problem.

'As the only person in this room qualified to carry on a plane,' he said, 'I'll cover us during transit. I'll also take the Mace. Otherwise, pack up, Thelma and Louise. Upon arrival in Portland, I want you carrying at all times.'

'I have to meet with Luke Hayes once we get to Portland,' Rainie said. 'I can ask him if any of the deputies would like to moonlight as bodyguards. That would give us more coverage.'

Kimberly's face brightened at this suggestion, but Quincy shook his head. 'Too conspicuous. Plus, I don't think bodyguards will do us any good. He's not going to strike long distance. Drive-by shootings, sniper fire, isn't his style. He'll create an elaborate ruse, something to get up close and personal. Bodyguards can't protect you when you're the one letting the UNSUB through the front door.'

'Dr Andrews said he'll be someone I know,' Kimberly said quietly. 'The man . . . the UNSUB, works on identifying what the victim needs or wants. Mandy always wanted someone to take care of her. Mom wanted Mandy. Me . . . I have an instinctive trust of anyone wearing a badge.'

Quincy had been folding one of his daughter's shirts. Now his hands stilled. He looked down at the blue-and-white-striped top as if he didn't see it.

'Kimberly . . .'

'It's not your fault, Dad. It's not your fault.'

Quincy finally nodded, though both Rainie and Kimberly could tell he didn't believe her. He finished placing the shirt in the single duffel bag. It was a little after one in the morning. None of them had slept much in the last two days and they were working off a list to keep their minds functioning through a sleep-deprived haze.

Lisa Gardner

'What's next?' Quincy asked.

'Toiletries,' Kimberly announced. She went into her bathroom, and a moment later, they heard the clatter of the medicine cabinet as she started throwing things into a waterproof bag.

'Did you meet with the private investigator?' Quincy asked Rainie under his breath, his gaze on the open bathroom door.

'Yes. Nothing. You?'

'They don't know about the note yet. It's a big crime scene; it will take the technicians several days to process everything. If I'm lucky, they'll get to the note last.'

'How can it be your handwriting? You didn't write it!'

'I don't know, but that's my handwriting. The loops, the slant, the dot over the I's . . . He's obviously been practicing.'

'Isn't there a way of telling that it's forgery? Hesitation marks, something like that?'

'Depends on how good he is. Depends on how good the handwriting analyst is. In all honesty, I doubt the forgery is perfect, but I also doubt that will help me in the end. All the UNSUB needs is an initial report that the handwriting *appears* to be mine. The Bureau will follow up, but by then I will also have been arrested, disarmed and discredited. This UNSUB is not only clever, but efficient. He knows just how half-assed he can be, and still get the job done. In a perverse way, I admire that.'

Kimberly walked back into the bedroom. She tossed the plastic bag into the suitcase. 'What's next?'

They didn't have any items left on the list. They zipped up the small collection of bags and piled them by the door. In three hours, Rainie would drive them all to JFK airport where they would return her rental car and board the six

244

A.M. flight to Portland. Outside the storm still raged and from time to time Quincy glanced nervously at the window. Rainie knew he didn't care about thunder and lightning. He was extremely concerned, however, about their flight possibly being delayed.

They huddled around the small kitchen table. Kimberly poured fresh cups of coffee, though they were already twitchy from too much caffeine. The roommate Bobby was gone. Quincy had suggested it might not be safe for him to be in the apartment either. Given the option between being terrified of every sound in his apartment or having unlimited sex at his girlfriend's place, Bobby had decided to stay at his girlfriend's. Bobby was a smart guy.

Rainie drank more coffee, her hands wrapped around the steaming mug. She'd gotten a chill running around in wet clothes, and now nothing she did made her warm.

'So what else did Dr Andrews say?' she asked Kimberly at last.

The young girl shrugged. She was holding up remarkably well, Rainie thought. Pale, jumpy, but functional. Rainie supposed they'd all hit the edge where you either kept moving or completely collapsed. Dying was not preferable to living at this point, so they kept moving.

'He . . . he told me I should tell you something,' Kimberly said abruptly. Her gaze flicked to her father, before becoming locked once more on her coffee mug. 'I um . . . a few months ago, I started having what I thought were anxiety attacks. I felt as if someone was watching me. I'd get goose bumps, find it hard to breathe. The hair would stand up on the back of my neck.'

Quincy set down his mug hard on the old table. Hot coffee sloshed over the edges. 'Why didn't you tell me?'

245

'At the time, I thought it was stress related. The situation with Mandy, I've been carrying a heavy course load plus the internship . . . It doesn't matter. What's important is that I'm telling you now and that maybe it wasn't all in my head. Maybe it wasn't stress induced—'

'He's been watching you,' Quincy said flatly. 'Some man has been stalking my daughter and you didn't even tell me!'

'I carry Mace! I pay attention to the people around me. I make eye contact. You can't hold my hand, Dad, and you can't always protect me—'

'Like hell! It's my job and what's the purpose of all these years of training if I can't protect my own family?'

'No father can protect his family. All children grow up. It's what we do.'

'I'm a professional—'

'You're human, just like all other fathers.'

'You should have told me—'

'So, I'm human, just like all other daughters.'

'Dammit, I'm sick of this!' Quincy roared.

'Good, I am, too!' his daughter yelled back. 'So let's catch this son of a bitch, so I can return to my classes and finish up my degree. Then I'll join law enforcement, neglect my own family, and the cycle will be complete!'

Quincy pressed his lips into a thin line. He opened his mouth, shut it. Opened his mouth, then shut it again. Finally, he picked up his mug of coffee and stared at the rain-splattered window.

'You know,' Rainie said, 'these family moments are very touching.'

'I may have a lead,' Quincy said thirty minutes later. The clock had now struck two. By some unspoken agreement, it appeared that none of them were going to bed. Quincy's 10mm sat on the kitchen table for easy access. They'd drawn all the blinds, then dimmed the overhead lights to prevent their silhouettes from standing out against the shades. The storm still raged. They'd tried the Weather Channel once, which told them things should clear up by morning. In their current mood, Rainie wasn't sure any of them believed that.

'What did you learn?' she asked Quincy. Kimberly was no longer making eye contact with her father. Rainie decided they could all use some rest.

'An agent working this case, Albert Montgomery, has a bone to pick with me. He worked the Sanchez case first. He screwed up, however, and the Bureau gave the case to me.'

'What was the Sanchez case?' Kimberly asked.

'Fifteen years ago, California. Sanchez and his cousin were murdering young prostitutes. Eight of them. Sometimes . . . they held the girls for a while.'

'Oh,' Kimberly said. 'The cassette tapes.'

'*You listened to them?*'

Kimberly shrugged. 'Mandy did. She had an obsession with your work. When you were gone . . .'

'Oh for God's sake—'

'So,' Rainie interjected, in her new role as peacekeeper. 'Montgomery is on the case, but not in your corner.'

Quincy turned back toward her. His gaze was blazing, his face gaunt. 'In Montgomery's view, my success with the Sanchez case made his own failings even more glaring. Let's just say that when the supposed "evidence" reports finally come in from Philadelphia, I wouldn't count on his support. In fact, I'm relatively sure he'll be the first to lead the lynching.'

'Not much time,' Kimberly whispered.

'No,' Quincy said bluntly. 'I give it three days. Then the first wave of lab reports will arrive and Everett will call me in. That's that.'

'Well,' Rainie said briskly. 'Let's keep focused then. I also managed to make progress today. I met with the president of Mandy's AA chapter, William Zane. He confirms that she befriended someone at the meetings, but the man doesn't sound anything like what I expected – he's described as being five ten, balding, overweight, and prone to rumpled suits.'

'I thought Mom's neighbor reported a guy who was tall, well-dressed, and handsome,' Kimberly interjected.

'Exactly. But the sightings were twenty months apart, which could mean the man has the ability to dramatically change his appearance.'

'Ted Bundy was notorious for changing his look,' Quincy reported. 'His weight often fluctuated more than fifty pounds, changing impressions of his face, and also of his height – heavier people are often perceived to be shorter. Then we have Jim Beckett, who pursued his victims and eluded police for over a year by significantly altering his appearance. He would wear padding, stuff his cheeks, things of that nature, to change the contours of his build.'

'So one implication is that this guy is a master of disguise,' Rainie said. 'The second is that he's patient. Twenty months apart . . . that's not someone who is committing a rash or random act.'

'He's planned this for quite some time,' Quincy agreed.

'When we get to Portland, I'm putting you two into a hotel room under aliases. And then we go on the offensive. I have Officer Amity reopening the investigation of Mandy's crash. Investigator Phil de Beers is tailing Mary Olsen and should have word for us shortly. Even if we don't trust Montgomery, Everett seems to be on your side, Quincy, and Special Agent Rodman appears to know what she's doing. She may be able to help connect the dots from the inside.'

'We sit,' Kimberly murmured. 'We wait. We wonder where he'll strike next.'

'We're ahead now,' Rainie rebutted firmly. 'He had the advantage with Mandy because she was his first victim. He continued his advantage with Bethie, because we didn't know any better. We know now. And in exactly' – she glanced at her watch – 'three hours, we'll be out of strike zone. We'll finally be ahead of his game.'

Kimberly and Quincy nodded tensely. Rainie returned to her notes. 'Now then, I have another person for us to pursue. According to the AA president, Mandy's sponsor at the meetings was her boss. Larry Tanz owned the restaurant where she and Mary both worked. Now, I don't know a thing about Mr Tanz, but given Mary's strange behavior and the fact that Mr Tanz knows both Mary and Mandy . . .'

'He's worth considering,' Quincy said.

'I told my new best friend Phil de Beers to work on it. You know,' she added seriously, 'he makes his coffee with sour mash. I think my cream-and-sugar habit is now looking quite respectable.'

As a unit, Quincy and Kimberly rolled their eyes. They looked just like father and daughter when they did that. Huh.

Rainie flipped the page of her notebook. 'Finally, I have the two aliases that the UNSUB has used thus far. He used Tristan Shandling in Philadelphia – we should run that through a database of names from your past cases, Quince, to see if it rings any bells. Then, twenty months ago in

Virginia, he used the name Ben Zikka to approach Mandy at her AA meeting.'

'What?' Quincy spoke up sharply.

'Ben Zikka,' Rainie repeated. 'The name Ben Zik—'

'No! *Son of a bitch. No, no, no!*'

Quincy bolted from the table. He grabbed the cordless phone, fumbled it for a moment, then got a hard grip. His knuckles were white. Rainie didn't even recognize his face. Something bad had happened. She didn't understand what. She glanced at Kimberly and saw the girl's face turn the color of bone.

'Grandpa,' Kimberly whispered.

'Oh no.' Rainie closed her eyes. None of them had even thought about Quincy's father. He was a sick old man, stricken with Alzheimer's, tucked away in a retirement home. 'Oh no . . .'

'Shady Acres Elder Care,' Quincy barked into the phone. 'Put me through!' And a moment after that, 'Abraham Quincy, please. What do you mean he's not there? Of course he's there; he requires full-time medical attention. His son picked him up? His son, Pierce Quincy, picked him up earlier this afternoon. Of course you made him show ID. Of course he had a driver's license. His son, Pierce Quincy . . .'

A horrible stillness had come over Quincy's face. Rainie couldn't move. *Go to him*, she thought. *Touch him*. But she knew she couldn't. She knew Kimberly couldn't. Because they were watching a man in the throes of something terrible and it had only just begun.

He punched off the phone. He lowered it, cradling it against his neck as if the plastic receiver were something special.

'Ben Zikka was my father's best friend,' Quincy

murmured. 'They grew up together, went to war together. He used to tell stories . . .'

Kimberly and Rainie remained silent.

'He's an old man,' Quincy whispered. 'Seventy-five years old, can't even remember to piss in a toilet, for God's sake. He's sick, he's easily frightened. He doesn't recognize his own reflection, doesn't know he has a son. He doesn't even remember the name Pierce Quincy.'

Kimberly and Rainie didn't say a word.

'He worked hard his whole life. Built a farm, raised a son, helped pay my way through college when money was tight. Never even wanted a thank-you. He did it because that's what he did. Seventy-five years old. At the stage where he deserves to die with dignity.'

'Quincy . . .'

'*He doesn't even know he has a son! How can the man kill him? He doesn't even remember I exist. Goddammit, goddammit,* GODDAMMIT!'

He hurtled the phone receiver to the floor. It shattered into bits but it wasn't enough. He grabbed a chair and smashed it into the stove. He hurtled the coffeepot into the sink. He flipped over the table with a roar.

'Dad . . .'

'I can't go I have to stay he might be alive you never know. I can't leave him he's my father and he doesn't even know he has a son. He's going to be tortured and murdered and oh God did you see what that monster did to Bethie and he's just a sick old man he doesn't even know he has a son. Jesus Christ, Rainie, he doesn't even know he has a son . . .'

'You're coming to Portland.'

'NO!'

'You're coming to Portland, Quincy. We won't let you stay. It's exactly what this sicko wants.'

'My father—'

'Quincy, he's dead. I am so sorry, but he's dead. You know he's dead. I am so sorry . . .'

Quincy's knees buckled. He went down on the floor, surrounded by glass and wood and fragments of plastic phone. He went down on the floor and he looked at Rainie with an expression she hoped she would never have to see again.

'My father,' he whispered. 'My father . . .'

'Daddy, I'm scared. Please Daddy, I need you.'

Quincy turned toward his daughter. She had begun to cry. A heartbeat passed. Rainie didn't know what he was thinking. Looking at his daughter and seeing traces of his rapidly vanishing past? Or looking at his scared, stricken little girl, and seeing a future that could still happen?

Quincy held open his arms. Kimberly flew into his embrace.

'It's going to be all right, Kimmy,' Quincy murmured. 'I promise you, it's going to be all right.'

Then he closed his eyes, and Rainie knew why. He didn't want any of them to see that he had just told a lie.

24

JFK International Airport, New York

Friday morning, five thirty-five, eastern standard time, they
boarded the first flight for Portland, Oregon, proud owners
of three tickets purchased with cash the day before. They
had shown ID to pick up the tickets, then Quincy had used
the power of his FBI creds to get the woman at the counter
to change their names to aliases so there would be no record
of their flight. The attendant had looked secretly excited to
be involved in some sort of covert law enforcement
operation. The three of them had remained pale and drawn,
exhaustion making them sway on their feet.

The thunderstorms had finally passed, though the sky
was still dark and the runway slick with rain. Ground crews
in yellow windbreakers ran around the plane, loading bags.
Onboard, Rainie watched them shout orders at each other,
but could not hear their words.

Kimberly sat next to the window. She had taken her seat
and almost immediately fallen asleep, her head slumped
against the bulkhead. Rainie had the middle. She'd passed
the threshold where sleep was still possible and now she was
too awake, unbearably aware of the world around her.

Quincy sat on her right. His face had become a mask. Once, she'd touched the back of his hand. He had moved it away from her. She had not tried again since.

'When my mother died, I hated my father,' he said.

'What caused her death?'

'Heart attack. She was only thirty-four. No one saw it coming.'

'Doesn't sound like it was your father's fault.'

'I was a boy. My father had the power to make everything right, ergo he was also responsible for everything that went wrong. I used to ask him why she died. He always gave me the same answer. "Because she did."'

'Shit happens,' Rainie said.

'Yes, the swamp Yankee version of shit happens. It took me years to realize it was the best answer he could give. Sometimes there's simply no reason for why things happen. What is karma to a little boy? What is the divine wisdom of God? What is the fecklessness of fate? Why did my mother die? Because she did. In his own way, my father was teaching me a very important lesson.'

Rainie didn't say anything.

'Mandy didn't deserve to die,' Quincy said. 'Bethie didn't deserve to die, and my father didn't deserve to die. Shit didn't happen. One man did.'

'We'll find him, Quincy.'

'I'm going to kill him, Rainie. I spent four years being trained to heal as a psychologist, and the thought doesn't bother me. I'm going to find him and kill him. What does that make me?'

She hesitated. 'Vengeful,' she said at last.

He nodded as the plane finally powered up and prepared for ascent. He said, 'I can live with that.'

the Next Accident

Accident

Plan B

25

Bakersville, Oregon

Sheriff Luke Hayes lounged against his patrol car outside of Martha's Diner, looking deceptively sleepy in the midday heat. Standing at five nine, with rapidly thinning hair and a featherweight's wiry frame, he didn't possess the kind of physical presence that immediately struck fear in a suspect's heart. It wasn't a problem, however. For one thing, he hit harder than most timbermen. For another thing, he moved three times as fast. Word generally spread pretty quick. *See that bald guy? Don't go after him or he'll whip your ass.* Hey, it was bad enough to go down in a bar brawl, let alone to be publicly dropped by a guy roughly half your body weight and possessing only a tenth of your hair.

By far, Luke's best feature was his eyes. He possessed a pair of riveting baby blues that soothed enraged housewives, calmed rifle-toting drunks, and pacified screaming kids. A suspect had once accused him of practicing major mojo with his gaze. Luke didn't think he possessed any special magic. He was just a naturally calm guy with a solid, even temperament. You'd be surprised how many women dug that.

His eyes weren't visible at the moment. They were closed

against the white-hot sun, his face turned up slightly as if seeking a cooling breeze. The coastal air was flat today, however. Stagnant. He sighed heavily.

His head came down. He opened his eyes. And found Rainie standing in front of him.

'Another busy day in Bakersville,' she said dryly.

'Gonna be a fight by six. Probably two fights if this heat keeps up.'

'Maybe you should give up law enforcement. Sell air-conditioning units instead.'

'It's not half-bad an idea. I could start by giving myself one. Hello, Rainie. Good to see you again.'

He held out his hand. She clasped it warmly and didn't immediately let go. He thought she looked tired. Her cheeks had that gaunt look she always got when she was pushing herself too hard. She was a beautiful woman, always had been in a striking sort of way. Wide cheekbones, full lips, soft gray eyes. But her body was slimmer now, rangy like a fighter's. And she'd cut off all her rich, chestnut hair, giving herself some spiky city do when he could've told her that half the men in Bakersville dreamed about that long, lush hair. The feel of it in their hands. The look of it, pooled on their pillows. Pipe dreams, of course. But nice ones during the gray Oregon winters.

'Sheriff uniform suits you,' Rainie said.

Luke puffed out his chest. 'I'm a stud.'

She laughed. 'All the nice Protestant ladies are lining up their daughters just for you?'

'Tough to be a hero, but somebody's got to do it.'

'God, I miss this place.'

'Yeah, Rainie. We've missed you, too.'

They went into the diner. Carl Mitz wasn't due to show

up for another hour. By mutual agreement, they slid into their old booth and ordered a late lunch/early dinner.

'How's Chuckie?' Rainie asked after ordering the Friday special – chicken-fried steak with extra gravy and garlic-mashed potatoes. Guaranteed to add an inch to your waistline, or your money back.

'Cunningham has settled down,' Luke answered. 'Bit more confident these days. Plus, I think we've gone a whole month without him drawing down on some poor civvie whose only mistake was daring to run a red light during Chuckie's shift.'

'He's stopped attacking the taxpayers? That is progress. And the rest of the town?'

'One-year anniversary was tough,' Luke said softly. 'Still a lot of paranoia, some bad blood. I hate to say it, but it's probably a good thing Shep and Sandy moved away. I'm not sure folks could've handled it otherwise.'

'What a shame.'

'It's human nature, Rainie. We're all looking for something to believe in, and someone to blame.'

'Still—'

'We're okay, Rainie. That's the joy of small towns – even when we change, we don't change. Now how about you?'

She didn't say anything right away, which he had expected. She had always been a private person, even when it had been just her, him, and Shep, a three-man sheriff's department united against the world. But then, that's what Luke liked about Rainie. She could be moody. She possessed one hell of a temper. But you knew she'd get the job done. She showed up, she delivered, and when things had gotten rocky, Luke had been proud to have her in charge.

He'd been sad – no, he'd been angry – when the narrow-minded town council had demanded that she go. He had thought she'd put up more of a fight, and like a lot of folks in Bakersville, he'd been surprised, maybe even hurt, when she hadn't.

'Quincy's in trouble,' she said abruptly.

'I gathered that.'

'It's . . . bad, Luke. Very bad.'

'Accident wasn't an accident?'

She nodded. 'Amanda was murdered by somebody out to get Quincy. Except it didn't end there. The man then used her death to target Quincy's ex-wife. Befriended her, romanced her, and slaughtered her, Luke. Absolutely butchered her. That crime scene was barely twenty-four hours old, before he kidnapped Quincy's father.'

Luke arched a brow. 'Bureau's got to be involved,' he said tightly. He liked Quincy, seemed like a good guy. At least for a fed.

'Sure, the Bureau's involved. Any day now, we think they'll arrest Quincy.'

'What?'

'He's been framed for the murder of his ex-wife. Did I mention that?'

'When G-men make enemies, they make enemies.' Luke was frowning. 'How's he holding up?'

'I don't know.'

Luke's frown deepened. 'I thought you'd know better than most. Or has something changed?'

'For God's sake, Luke, the man's family is being hunted. We're living Agatha Christie's *And Then There Were None*. Now is not exactly the time to put him on a sofa and say, Hey, Quince, tell me how you *really* feel.'

'That's convenient.'

'And what the hell is that supposed to mean?' Her voice had picked up. Color stained her cheeks. This was supposed to intimidate him. Instead it simply made him feel better. Rainie needed some color in her cheeks. He only wished that he'd brought a box of #2 pencils for her to snap. For old times' sake.

'I'm just saying—' he began mildly.

'Oh I heard what you were saying. Now I'm sorry I brought this up.'

'I would've brought it up if you didn't,' he assured her. 'That's what friends are for.'

'Speaking of which, thanks for telling some Virginia cop that I have the hots for a fed.'

'You have the hots for a fed?'

'Luke Hayes—'

He was grinning and the sight of his amusement sent her temper spluttering. But then his grin faded, and he said a bit more honestly, a bit more gently, 'Face it, you and Quincy have a genuine meeting of the minds. That's serious shit, Rainie. You can go an entire lifetime without finding anyone who matches like that. I know I have.'

'Harumph,' Rainie said. She scowled, but Luke wasn't fooled. He saw something in those wide gray eyes. Gratitude maybe. Or relief. Someone else thought she and Quincy could work out. Someone else believed the scrappy home-town girl was worthy of a fed.

You were bigger than this town, Luke wanted to tell her. *You were too smart to spend your career patrolling Friday-night football games. Damn, I'm proud of you.* But he didn't say those words because he understood that she wouldn't know how to take them.

The waitress came over with two Cokes. Luke accepted

his with a smile. Rainie set hers on the table and proceeded to spin it absently between her hands.

'It's . . . it's insane,' she murmured. 'There's someone out there, Luke. We don't know his name. We don't have a clear description. We don't even know how he ties in with Quincy. We just know he's smart. Methodical. And at least twelve steps ahead of us.'

'Plan of attack?' Luke asked quietly.

'Attack is a strong word. We have a plan of retreat. We fled here with Quincy's surviving daughter, Kimberly. The man knows too much about their lives on the East Coast.'

'You need manpower?'

Rainie shook her head. Then she ran a hand through her short-cropped hair. 'It's hard to explain. This man . . . his system. He's not hit-and-run. This guy, it isn't just about the kill, it's all about the game. We know he's still coming. We know he'll follow us here. But he won't strike out of the blue. Somehow, someway, he'll convince one of us to open the door.'

'Carl Mitz,' Luke filled in.

'You have to admit, the timing is suspicious.'

'I see your point.' Luke sighed. He spread out his hands on the table. 'Well, I don't know what to tell you, Rainie. Mitz started calling four days ago. I checked with the law offices of Avery & Abbott in Portland and they confirm having him on staff. He's also on record with the Oregon State Bar. I don't like his timing either, but at this point . . .'

'Mitz checks out.'

'Mitz appears to be a genuine vermin, er, lawyer.'

'What about his client?'

Luke frowned. 'His client?'

Rainie nodded. She leaned forward. 'This guy – Tristan

Shandling, for lack of a better name – he's been using each family member to learn about the other family members. Mandy tells him about Bethie who tells him about Kimberly. Shandling plays his game and conducts his recon all at once. Except Amanda, Elizabeth, and Kimberly don't know a thing about me.'

Luke got it. 'So assuming he's learned that Quincy has a friend in Portland—'

'Not a big assumption. He seems to know everything about Quincy's life, plus he's stolen Quincy's identity. All you need to check anyone's phone bill is a name and Social Security number.'

'Then Shandling needs a source of information about you.'

'He can't come himself.' Rainie thought out loud. 'He's been too busy with Bethie in Philadelphia.'

'So he hires someone.'

'Someone reputable. Just in case we get suspicious and check the person out.'

Luke nodded thoughtfully. 'You're right, he's smart and methodical. So how do you want to play it?'

'I'm thinking we stick to the basics. I sit in the booth behind this one with a newspaper in front of my face so Mitz doesn't see me when he walks in. You greet him, make him comfortable, and pretend to be willing to cooperate.'

'Good cop,' Luke filled in dryly.

'Exactly. I wait here, eavesdrop, and let you pour on the charm. Then, when he's nicely entrenched in his, "we don't give out information on our clients" speech, I pounce and tear him to shreds.'

'Bad cop.'

'Yeah.' She smiled wolfishly.

Luke shook his head. 'Rainie,' he said, 'damn, it's good to have you home.'

At exactly five P.M. Carl Mitz strolled through the doors of Martha's Diner. In a crowd of plaid western shirts and field-stained jeans, he stood out conspicuously wearing a tan linen suit and carting a behemoth brown briefcase. He identified Luke easily enough – maybe the sheriff's star gave him away – and proceeded straight to the booth.

Rainie opened the newspaper and ducked down against the red vinyl seat. The newspaper easily obscured her face, but she still felt vulnerable. Not that she had much to fear. Her first impression of Mitz was an oversized accountant with bad taste in glasses. Mussed-up hair, ill-fitting suit, pinched white features. Whatever kind of law he did, it wasn't criminal because there wasn't a jury in the world who would take that face seriously. He probably did taxes or corporate deals. Something with really big spreadsheets.

Luke shook the man's hand. Mitz winced.

Oh boy, Rainie thought. When your stalker cares enough to send the very best . . .

Mitz sat down. He slid his briefcase onto the seat beside him. It took up half of the booth, but he seemed determined not to let it go.

'Thank you for seeing me,' he told Luke crisply.

'No problem at all,' Luke drawled, his voice magically two octaves lower and eight beats slower. 'You seemed like an earnest fellow. I figured it would be easiest to meet in person, shake your hand, and address all your questions at once.'

'Well yes, of course. Face-to-face is always nice. I only hate to intrude . . .'

'Oh you know how it is in small towns. We got plenty of time and we're always happy to meet new folks.'

Rainie rolled her eyes. She thought the Andy Griffith routine was laying it on a bit thick, but Mitz seemed to relax a fraction more, his spine actually making contact with the back of the booth.

'It's a simple matter really,' Mitz said briskly. 'I'm running a routine background check on someone who used to live in this town. Lorraine Conner. I understand she was a police officer here.'

'Yes sir. I believe she was.'

'She lived here?'

'Yes sir. I believe she did.'

'For how long?'

'Oh . . . for a long time. Years. Yeah, definitely years.'

'Mmmm, yes. And her mother was Molly Conner?'

'Yes sir. I believe that is correct.'

'Do you know how old Lorraine is?'

'Oh no, sir. I'm much too smart to ask a woman her age.'

'You must have it in the files, though. Personnel records, something like that.'

'We might. But she left with our previous sheriff, Shep O'Grady. You'd have to ask him. He's not here anymore, of course. Lives somewhere else now.'

'Shep O'Grady.' Mitz made a note.

Luke said, 'So what's this all about, sir? We don't often get lawyers asking about our former officers.'

'It's a routine background check.'

'She's applying for a job?'

'Uh . . . no.'

'She's applying for a credit card?'

'I'm a lawyer, Sheriff. I assure you I don't get involved

with credit card applications.'

'Of course, pardon me. So when do you get involved?'

'That's confidential. Something I will share with Ms Conner when the occasion arises.'

'Fair enough. I would never ask a man to compromise his principles. Say, just out of curiosity, what is your specialty?'

Mitz, however, was no dummy. 'That would also be something for me to share with her when the occasion arises. So Lorraine Conner served as a police officer for how many years?'

'Several,' Luke obliged.

'I understand she resigned last year.'

'Yes sir.'

'A bit of scandal or something? About a fifteen-year-old incident?'

Luke shrugged. 'Officer Conner resigned in good standing, Mr Mitz. We're all real proud of her.'

'Well,' Mitz said briskly. 'That's good to hear. Of course, as long as I'm in town, you won't be offended if I ask others the same question?'

'Ask away,' Luke said graciously.

'Yes, well. What about the rest of her family?'

'What about them?'

'She has other family?' Mitz sounded surprised. For the first time, Luke hesitated, clearly caught off guard.

'Not that I know of,' Luke said hastily, abandoning the drawl. 'But you asked the question.'

'So she doesn't have an ex-husband, half-siblings, children?'

'Not that I know of. Why do you ask?'

'Line on the form,' Mitz said curtly. He began to make a note again, but Luke caught his hand. The Andy Griffith routine had vanished. Luke's face was hard set, and his voice had grown stern.

'These are very personal questions for a routine back-ground check, sir, and even if Rainie doesn't live here anymore, she's a good friend of mine. Now I'm asking you one more time, what is this all about?'

'And I'm telling you one last time,' Mitz said stiffly. 'I'm not at liberty to say.'

Rainie decided that was her cue. The conversation was going no place, plus good cop was about to beat the crap out of Mr Mitz, which would give her role a tough act to follow. She came around the booth. She gave the lawyer a big smile. 'Hey, Mitz,' she said. 'Surprise.' Then she slid into the booth and effectively trapped the man between her and Luke.

'What . . . what is going on?' Mitz had started stuttering. Perspiration dotted his upper brow and Rainie figured in the last ten seconds, he'd sweat through his tan linen suit. She scooted in a little closer, letting her hand fall to his prized briefcase and stroking the leather almost lovingly.

'You've been trying very hard to meet me, Mr Mitz,' she said.

'Well, yes. I left several messages in Virginia. I didn't know . . . When did you get back in town?'

'Make you uncomfortable?'

'Well, yes. But, but, it's not bad either!' The lawyer perked up. 'I mean, I wish you would've called first. I would've brought the whole file, been better prepared. But you are here now and I have wanted to talk to you.'

'About my past,' Rainie said knowingly.

'Oh, in all honesty, we know all details about your past. Even the, well, "incident." I assure you, he's not concerned about that. Doesn't bother him a bit.'

'What?' Now it was Rainie's turn to feel confused. She glanced at Luke. He was shaking his head slightly, equally baffled. Shit.

'You've spoken to him, correct?' Mitz was saying in a merry rush. 'I gave him your number in Virginia and he promised to call. After all, it seemed more appropriate for him to personally give you the news.'

The hang ups, Rainie thought. Two days of hang ups she'd naively assumed were Mitz. Why is it wrong to assume? Because it makes an ass out of u and me.

'What news?' she heard herself ask.

'The estate, Ms. Conner. The will. That's what I do, you know. Estate planning. I'm his attorney.'

'Whose attorney?'

'Ooooooooh deeeaaaaarrrr.' Mitz drew up short. He blinked behind his glasses. 'He didn't call you, did he? He said he would, but he didn't. It's the wild card, you know. Estate planning, it is an intense, personal experience. You never know how your client is going to react.'

'Mr Mitz, you start explaining now or I swear I'm going to break every bone in your overly educated body.'

Mr Mitz ducked his head. He blinked again. And he said in a small voice, 'I work for Ronald Dawson. Ronnie thinks – we think – that he's your father. Which would make you, Ms. Conner, his sole surviving heir.'

26

'You have a father?'

'Not bloody likely.'

'You don't seem very happy about it.'

'Happy about it? *Happy about it!*' Four hours later, Rainie stood in the middle of the one-bedroom deluxe hotel suite in downtown Portland and whirled on Kimberly Quincy as if the girl didn't have a brain in her head. Rainie had made the two-hour drive back to the city in one hour and thirty minutes. She'd cut off two semi's, flashed half a dozen cars, and nearly rear-ended a police cruiser. Only the fact that the state trooper was a personal friend of Luke's had saved her from a speeding ticket or worse. She should've taken a deep breath then. She hadn't.

Now she started pacing the living room of the suite, where Quincy and his daughter were registered as Larry and Barbara Jones. Quincy was catching a badly needed nap in the bedroom. Kimberly had been staring blindly at some network's TGIF TV-lineup before Rainie had burst through the door. Far from being wary of Rainie's mood, the aspiring psych student seemed grateful for the distraction. Rainie now understood how guinea pigs felt. If Kimberly gave her that deep, probing stare one more time, Rainie was going to start pushing brightly colored buttons in return for pellets. Then she was going to bounce said pellets off of Kimberly's blond head.

Rainie held up her hand. 'One,' she ticked off crisply. 'Let's consider the father-to-be. Ronald Dawson, aka Ronnie. He's a thug. Better yet, a convicted thug. The man has spent the last thirty years incarcerated for aggravated murder. He was only paroled last year because at the age of sixty-eight, he's too arthritic to be considered a menace to society. In his thirties, however, he gutted two men in a bar fight with a hunting knife. Oh wait, I'm sorry. According to his lawyer, Carl Mitz, there were mitigating circumstances. Good ol' Ronnie was so damn drunk, he didn't know what he was doing at the time. Hellooooooooo, Dad!'

'Still, he hired a lawyer to find you,' Kimberly said mildly.

Rainie scowled at her. 'Two,' she continued. 'Ronnie claims to be looking for an heir to his estate, but it's not like he did anything to earn the estate. His father had a hundred-acre farm in Beaverton. Ronnie didn't help on the farm. He drank, gutted, then went to jail. His father worked the farm. His father built the farm. And when the real estate boom hit Beaverton in the early nineties, his father sold the farm to a real estate developer for ten million dollars. Praise be to Grandpa Dawson. Ronnie still sucks.'

Kimberly smiled sweetly. 'As they say, you can't choose your family.'

'To hell with Tristan Shandling,' Rainie said seriously. 'Keep talking, girl, and I will kill you myself.'

'Come on, Rainie. This is exciting news. Your mother is gone. You don't have any aunts, uncles, brothers, or sisters.

But think about it. You might have a dad! A real, live, anxious-to-meet-you dad!'

'There's no proof he's my father,' Rainie snapped. 'So he slept with my mother thirty-two years ago. Who didn't?'

'But you'll take the blood test, right?'

'I don't know.'

'Rainie . . .'

'I don't know!' Rainie threw her hands in the air. 'You want to know the truth? I don't like it. I just plain don't like it.'

'Because he's a convict.'

'Of course he's a convict. My mother didn't hang out with aspiring astrophysicists. Hell, I'm not surprised my potential sire was in jail. I'm just shocked he was ever paroled.'

Kimberly frowned. 'So . . . it's the money you don't like? Becoming an heiress to ten million dollars? You're right, that's tough.'

'Kimberly, think about it for a moment. What do all children who don't have parents do? They dream about their missing parents, right? They make up exotic stories. "My mommy and daddy are secretly eastern European royalty, forced into hiding to flee the communists. When it's safe, they'll come back for me." Or, "my father was a Nobel prize-winning scientist, killed by evil government agents who wanted to halt his impending discovery of world peace." Kids create fables, caricatures of real life. No one's absent father is ever a thug, or drunken white trash who simply didn't want to own up to his responsibility. He's always handsome, dashing, and frankly, rich.'

It took Kimberly a moment, then she got it. 'You think this is all fake. It's *too good* to be true.'

Rainie finally grew still. She looked at Kimberly and demanded bluntly, 'What does Tristan Shandling do? He *identifies* who the victim wants more than anything in the world. *And then he becomes that person.* I've been without a family for fifteen years, Kimberly. As you said, no aunts, uncles, brothers, sisters. There's a loneliness in that I don't think other people can understand.'

'Rainie, you don't know that it's a ruse.'

'Think about the timing.'

'Just because you don't like coincidences, doesn't mean they don't happen.'

'And just because it walks like a duck and talks like a duck, doesn't mean it *isn't* Tristan Shandling in disguise.' Rainie plopped down on the sofa, then hit a cushion. Hard.

'You're scared,' Kimberly said softly.

'Don't psychoanalyze me.'

'I'm not trying to. It's just . . . You're scared.'

'I was so sure he'd go with law enforcement,' Rainie murmured. 'Or maybe a fellow PI. Even knowing how he works, I didn't see this coming. God, he's good. I'm sitting here now, and half of me is warning, Don't fall for it, you're too smart for this. And the other half of me . . . Christ, the other half of me is already picking out Father's Day cards.'

Kimberly took a seat next to her on the sofa. Her long blond hair was pulled back from her face in a rubber band. She'd slept through the long plane ride and she looked better than she had in days. Rested. More composed. It was interesting to Rainie that as their situation grew more dire, Kimberly seemed to actually grow stronger. Young, but rising up to the challenge. Inexperienced, but definitely determined.

'Let's think about this,' Kimberly said. 'What's the next step?'

'Blood testing. Mitz gave me the name of a lab. They'll take a blood sample from me and ostensibly test for a DNA match with Ronald Dawson's.'

'That sounds reasonable.'

Rainie smiled grimly. 'Do you know how long it takes for DNA testing? We're talking at least four weeks, or more probably, a few months. If this is all a scam, it will be over long before then.'

'We can do some checking first,' Kimberly countered firmly. 'You said that Dawson's father sold a farm in Beaverton. Real estate transactions are public records. We can also search for the arrest record of Ronald Dawson.'

'One step ahead of you. Luke already pulled Dawson's rap sheet. That checks out. Now he's working on the real estate records.'

'Well, there you go!' Kimberly clapped her hands. She seemed genuinely excited. Rainie shook her head. She wished she could share the girl's enthusiasm. There was a numbness inside her, though. A sense of dread she couldn't shake. Or maybe it was simply the stunning realization that she was more vulnerable than she'd ever realized. And even as she told herself she knew better, there was something new and soft growing in her belly. Not numbness. Hope.

Thirty-two years old. The last fifteen years with no plans for Thanksgiving, Christmas, Easter. Always working the holiday shifts because what else was she going to do? Always watching other people go home to their families at the end of the day, moaning about their in-laws, bellyaching about the demands of another family gathering, joking about the bad presents on Father's Day. Sometimes the whole concept of a family seemed like an exclusive club to her. Other people were members. She was the perennial outsider, the guest who got the pity invite, but never really belonged at the table.

She wished Quincy was awake. She wished . . . She would like to talk to him right now. Maybe, she'd even like to lean her head against his shoulder and have him tell her it was going to be okay. You have to have faith, he'd told her. She wished it were really that simple.

'Eight months ago,' Rainie told Kimberly softly, 'a man started calling around Bakersville, trying to find my mother. Luke told me about it a few months later, but never gave me the man's name as it didn't seem important. The man was Ronald Dawson. Luke still had the name listed in his notes. A few weeks after Ronnie's first call, the assistant district attorney dropped the criminal charges against me. At the time, I thought Quincy had intervened. In fact, I was really angry with him for it. But I called the ADA after meeting Mitz this afternoon. Quincy never talked to him. The district attorney himself was the one who asked for the charges to be dropped. He's about to run for office again. And according to the ADA, his campaign recently received a healthy donation from a local citizen – otherwise known as Ronald Dawson.'

'Well there you go, Rainie. The timing isn't coincidental at all. Ronald Dawson started looking for you nearly a year ago, and you have proof.'

'Tristan Shandling's been active for at least twenty months. He could still be part of this.'

'But he was focused on Mandy then, and after that, my mother. He can't be on both sides of the country at once.'

'Sure you can. The magic of the telephone, Internet, cable. Plus, it's just an eight-hour plane ride. You can visit the West Coast for a day. It's not fun, but it's feasible.'

'There are cheaper and simpler ways of targeting you than paying off a DA,' Kimberly countered, 'not to mention meddling in a criminal case.'

'I don't think cheap or simple are particular concerns of Mr Shandling right now. He's on the warpath. So what if he runs up the ol' Visa?'

Kimberly frowned. 'Do you, or don't you, want this man to be your father?'

'I don't know. I just . . . I don't know.'

Kimberly was silent for a moment. Then she said, 'Rainie, I never realized you were so pessimistic.'

'Oh God, we have to get you back to college.'

'It's true! You may be on the verge of something wonderful, but you'd rather steel yourself for the downside than inspire yourself with the good. Oh . . .' Kimberly blinked. 'You and my father, I get it.'

'Oh, no. Don't you go there right now. I really don't need this right now.'

She might as well have not spoken. 'I was so sure my father was the holdout in your relationship,' Kimberly declared. 'I mean, given his distant relationship with his father, his reserve with his own children, his fears of intimacy with my mother. But this time around, it's not Dad, is it? It's you. You're the one who doesn't trust the relationship.'

'Why do you people insist on speaking of trust as if life were a Disney movie? Kimberly, my mother beat me as a hobby. My father was basically a sperm donor, who fucked the town whore and moved on. Seventeen years later, my mother's current boyfriend decided she wasn't good enough and turned his attention on me. I have trouble trusting people? Hell yes, I have trouble trusting people. My mother was a mean, ill-tempered drunk. And I still loved her. That's not Disney; that's a complicated world.'

'My father doesn't drink.'

'Give him a few days,' Rainie said sourly. 'He also didn't curse or plot revenge until three days ago, and he's doing a fine job of that now.'

'He would never hurt you,' Kimberly said seriously.

Rainie groaned. 'God save me from psych majors. Kimberly, look . . . I know your father is a good guy. I know he's different from the others. But knowing isn't always knowing, if that makes any sense. I mean, it's one thing to grasp something intellectually. To tell myself that Quincy's different, that he's okay, that he won't hurt me. It's another thing to change a lifetime way of thinking. To emotionally, really . . . believe. To genuinely feel safe.'

'I tell myself logically that my mother is dead,' Kimberly said abruptly. 'But emotionally, I don't believe it yet.'

Rainie nodded slowly. Her voice softened. 'Yeah, it's kind of like that.'

'I tell myself it's not my mother's fault, or Mandy's fault, or my father's fault,' Kimberly said. 'But I'm mad at all of them. They left me. I'm the strong one and I'm supposed to take it, but I don't want to be this strong. I'm angry at them for that.'

'I keep having this dream,' Rainie said. 'Two or three times a week, always the same dream. This baby elephant is running across the desert. His mother is dead; he's all alone and desperate for water. Then these other elephants come, except instead of helping him, they beat him into the ground because he's a threat to their own survival. He gets up though. He fights to live and staggers after them. Finally they find water. I relax. In my dream, I think the baby is going to be all right. His struggle has now paid off. He will live happily ever after. Then the jackals come and tear him apart. And I wake up with little baby screams still echoing in my head. I don't know why I can't stop dreaming it.'

'We read this study last year,' Kimberly said, 'about how children go through phases when they will want to hear the same story over and over again. According to the scientists, there is an issue or theme in the story that the children identify with. When they have resolved the issue, they don't need to hear the story anymore. But until then, night after night, they'll request the same tale.'

'I'm a four-year-old?'

'You identify with something in your dream. Probably the baby elephant.'

'The baby elephant dies.'

'But he fights to live.'

'Nobody helps him. He's desperate to join the herd. He would've been better off alone.'

'He's following instinct. It's everyone's instinct to be part of something. In evolutionary terms, we are stronger together than alone.'

'But not in my story. In my story, the baby elephant's desire to be with other elephants kills him.'

'No, Rainie. In your story, the baby elephant's desire for companionship keeps him alive. What's he running across the desert for? Why does he get up each and every time? He's not fighting to live simply to live. He's a herd animal. He's fighting to join the other elephants, he's living off the hope that if he keeps on fighting, he will get to belong. The drought will end and they will accept him. Or he'll prove his mettle and they will accept him. Either way, he'll end up with his herd. You did the same, Rainie. Your mother hit you, but you still kept believing it would get better. Otherwise you would've succumbed to alcoholism by now, or even committed suicide. You didn't. Why didn't you?'

'I'm stubborn,' Rainie muttered. 'And stupid.'

Kimberly smiled. 'But in your own way, you're also hopeful. You're just not comfortable with that part of yourself. I understand. I'm hopeful I will kill Tristan Shandling. I'm not comfortable with that yet either, but I figure I have a few days.'

'Kimberly,' Rainie said gently. 'Word of advice – don't go there. Tristan Shandling is a piece of shit. You play by his rules, and you won't ever get yourself back. He will have molded the start of your career, and you'll never get to know the kind of officer or agent you would have become. You'll simply be what he made you.'

'You don't know that.'

'Yes I do. I'm a murderer, Kimberly. Thanks to Ronnie Dawson, I'm free and clear in the eyes of the law, but years ago I killed someone. I'm a murderer. And I'll never know what else I could've been. Yeah, I pretty much hate that. Then again, the other person's dead. That's gotta suck, too.'

'I didn't . . . I didn't know.'

Rainie shrugged. 'Life's about baggage. Think twice before you hang a boulder around your neck.'

'But he's going to keep coming,' Kimberly insisted. 'You know Shandling is going to keep coming and coming until either he, or us, winds up dead. The shark is in the water, Rainie. Now, we need a bigger boat.'

Thirty minutes later, Kimberly was asleep on the sofa, her long blond hair pooled around her. The sun was beginning to wane, the white walls of the hotel room becoming washed in shades of gray. Outside the air was probably stifling. Inside it was cool and for a while Rainie simply leaned against the windowsill, six stories above, looking out at nothing in particular. Jet lag was catching up with them. Kimberly was probably down for the night. No sound came from Quincy in the bedroom.

The room was quiet. It hadn't occurred to Rainie until now how much she both craved and abhorred silence.

Maybe she had a father. It was hard to imagine. Her mother had told her once, with Molly's stunning indifference, that her dad could be any one of over a dozen men, and that she'd already forgotten all of their names. Men came, men went, Molly said. Don't be a fool and expect something more.

Thirty-two years later, Rainie's father remained a perfect blank in her mind. He had no eye color, no hairstyle, no distinguishing features. He was a black silhouette, like the mystery person with a white question mark in the middle they showed in magazines. *I gave you life. Do you know who I am?*

No, she didn't.

Maybe she had a father. Or maybe it was a lie and this was all Tristan Shandling. She had to have faith. Cynicism was more likely to keep her alive.

Rainie pushed away from the windowsill. She crossed the room and opened the door to the bedroom. The blinds were drawn. The room was swathed in black intersected by faint beams of fading light. Quincy sprawled in the middle of the bed, his left arm flung across the dark floral bedspread, his right arm crooked over his head. He'd taken off his shoes and tie. His firearm and shoulder holster were positioned within easy reach on the nightstand. Otherwise he'd fallen asleep fully dressed.

Rainie entered the room. She closed the door behind her. Then finally, fully clothed herself, she crawled onto the bed. Quincy didn't stir.

The collar of his white dress shirt was unbuttoned. She could just make out the first whorls of dark, springy chest hair. She had once run her fingers through that light matting of hair. She had pressed her palm over his breast and felt the strong rhythm of his heart.

'Quincy,' she murmured, so he wouldn't startle awake and try to shoot her, 'it's me.'

He sighed heavily in his sleep. Then he rolled over on his right side, away from her.

She sat beside him. She inhaled the faint, soapy scent of his cologne. A year later she still didn't know its name and she wondered why she'd never asked him. Back when they'd tried dating, she would return home with that scent still lingering in her nostrils. She'd fall asleep smelling Quincy, and burrow deeper into the covers like a contented cat. When she woke up the next morning, alone, fragrance gone, she'd always felt a stab of disappointment.

She reached out now and lightly touched his shoulder. His cotton shirt was soft beneath her fingers, his arm warm. He didn't jerk away.

Rainie lay down at his side. She kept waiting for something. Fear. Discomfort. Yellow-flowered fields. Smooth-flowing streams. The places she'd learned to escape to in her mind. Mostly she was aware of the heat of Quincy's body, pressed against her side. And she remembered now what she'd felt that final evening with him. Desire. Real, honest to goodness desire. She hadn't known she was capable of such a thing.

Quincy would never hurt you, Kimberly had said. Rainie

knew that. She probably even truly knew that. Maybe it was herself she still didn't understand.

People could hurt you. They could beat you with their fists and they could do worse; they could die and leave you all alone with no hope of ever making things right. And people could attack you. They could inflict great physical and emotional harm. And you could attack back. You could even kill them, inflicting its own kind of great physical and emotional harm.

And you could punish yourself then, because your mother was dead and someone had to play the role of the abuser. So you could punish yourself day after day, creating the very lifestyle that got you into this mess because you didn't know any other way to live.

You could do all that, or maybe you could try to change. You could give up drinking. You could stop sleeping around. You could try treating yourself better, even respecting yourself. Except sooner or later, you also had to try believing in yourself, and maybe she still wasn't so good at that. She'd always figured it was better to be hostile and belligerent first, then no one could ever accuse her of hiding her true colors. Truth in advertising, that was her policy.

Dying in the desert. Struggling to survive, desperate to belong, but still not figuring out how to live.

She rolled over on the bed. She pressed her cheek against the curve of Quincy's back. She could hear his heartbeat here, too. It sounded slow, and steady, and strong. She wrapped her arm around his lean waist. He murmured in his sleep. And then his hand came up and clasped hers.

She waited for the fear to strike. Images of yellow-flowered fields and smooth-running streams. Nothing.

She inhaled his cologne. She felt the warmth of his hand.

And she thought. . . . She thought this spooning business felt very nice.

Rainie closed her eyes. She held Quincy and finally fell asleep.

27

Quincy's House, Virginia

'Where have you been?'

A little after six-thirty Saturday morning, Glenda Rodman stood blurry-eyed in Quincy's foyer, watching Special Agent Albert Montgomery finally walk through the front door. It had been forty-eight hours since she'd last seen her fellow agent. Her gray suit was hopelessly rumpled from sleeping fitfully in Quincy's desk chair. Her face looked like death warmed over. Multiple days of listening to threatening phone call after threatening phone call did take its toll on a person.

Now, the gifts had started. Yesterday morning, a disemboweled puppy in Quincy's mailbox. Yesterday afternoon, four rattlesnakes released outside the gate. Two had made it onto Quincy's property. Two had gone to the neighbors, where they had garnered the attention of a pet cat and two-year-old boy. Fortunately, the child's mother had snatched him away and called animal control before anyone got hurt. Last night, Glenda had gotten to listen to a voice cackle with glee on the answering machine, telling Quincy that when the rattlesnakes were done with him, he'd personally come skin the agent and make him into a belt.

When Glenda slept, she did not have pleasant dreams.

Now, she glared at Montgomery, who had managed to shower and change since she'd last seen him. Her resentment felt an awful lot like a wronged wife's.

'I've been in Philly, of course.' Montgomery scowled at her, coming through the door and kicking it shut behind him. He shrugged off his stained overcoat.

'Your assignment was to help me stake out Quincy's house.'

'Yeah, but that was before he turned his ex-wife into a shish kabob. You think the local yokels know how to handle a scene like that? Christ, I had to teach 'em how to analyze the glass shards myself. They really thought the window was broken from the outside. Dipshits.'

'Agent, your assignment—'

'Hey, fuck assignment. The action isn't here anymore, Rodman. It's in Philadelphia. If we want to know what's going on, we gotta focus our attention there.'

'There are still things happening here!'

'What, a bunch of harassing phone calls? Dead pets? Oh you're right, we've learned so much by being here the last three days.' Montgomery gave her a dubious look. Glenda shifted uncomfortably.

Nothing much had happened here. Poor Bethie had been attacked and brutalized in Philadelphia. Yesterday, Glenda had received word from Everett that Quincy's ailing father had been kidnapped from a Rhode Island nursing home. Three agents had immediately been assigned to look for Abraham Quincy; after seeing what had happened to Pierce's ex-wife, however, no one was hopeful.

So yes, there was action. But none of it was here. Glenda

simply sat. She listened to horrible, horrible phone threats. And she felt her nerves fray inch-by-inch, hour-by-hour. Still, this was her task. She believed in her assignment. And it bothered her that Montgomery hadn't had the decency to even consult with her, though he apparently knew as much about what was going on in Quincy's house as she did.

'It's important to learn the source of the information leak,' she told Montgomery. 'And the person might still show up. We can't rule that out.'

'What person? Quincy's phantom stalker? Come on, don't tell me you're still buying his little fairy tale.'

'What do you mean?'

'Look, I'll do you a favor. As the agent who's spent the last forty-eight hours in Philadelphia, I'll give it to you straight. That was no break-in. That was no stranger-to-stranger crime. The whole fucking thing is so staged it could open as a Broadway show. Take the bathroom window, the supposed mode of entry. It was broken from the inside out and the glass shards moved to disguise the fact. Then we have the state-of-the-art home security system – deactivated with proper code a little after ten P.M., same time the neighbor swears she saw Elizabeth Quincy enter the home with a man matching Quincy's description. Even the crime scene – it was a fast, brutal attack, no rape, no torture. Posing of the body, postmortem mutilation, all done for show. All done to make it look like a sexual sadist predator.'

'You think Quincy did it.'

'I *know* Quincy did it. But hey, I have no career track left in the Bureau, so I can afford to look honestly at the reigning golden boy. On the other hand, I'm sure the very notion makes you real uncomfortable. I mean, taking on the best-of-the-best and all—'

'Shut up.' Glenda stalked away from him into the kitchen. Montgomery, however, followed.

'I know you don't like me,' he persisted. 'I know I dress wrong. I know I don't do politics well or play all the little reindeer games. I'm a fat, wrinkled slob. That doesn't mean I'm an idiot.'

'True, your state of dress does not mean you're incompetent – your conduct on the Sanchez case does.'

'Oh.' He drew up short, his hands clasping self-consciously in front of him. 'Figured it was only a matter of time before you heard about that.'

Glenda felt better now, as if she were gaining the upper hand. She had known there were problems with the Society Hill crime scene. Quincy had all but told her that he would end up as the prime suspect. It was still difficult to hear her own doubts pouring from Montgomery's lips. She went on the offensive instead.

'You screwed up the Sanchez case—'

'I made a mistake.'

'Quincy saved the day.'

'I never said he was a bad profiler.'

'Oh come on, everyone knows you blame him. It's bad enough to choke, let alone have another agent come along, get it right, and grab all the credit. How many times do you replay that in your head at night, Albert? How many times do you revisit every little nuance of that case, and feel your hatred for Quincy grow a little bit more?' She stared hard at Montgomery. The agent bowed his head.

'You wanted this, didn't you?' she challenged. 'The perfect opportunity to come in and torpedo Quincy's career.'

'No.'

'Yes!'

'No! Dammit!' Montgomery glowered. He looked trapped and cornered, shifting around his heavy bulk until he finally seemed to realize there was no place left to run. Then he planted his feet. 'You want to know the truth?' he spat back. 'Fine, I'll tell you the truth. Not that you'll believe me, not that anyone will believe me, but I took this goddamn case to save Quincy's butt. I took it 'cause I thought, hey, if you can't be the hero, you might as well save the hero. That's gotta count for something.'

'What?'

'Do I have to put this on a Hallmark card? I figured I could help Quincy. And yeah, I kind of thought that might jumpstart my career. Altruistic, I ain't. But I'm not a total jackass either. My career is in the toilet. Do a good deed, however, and I might escape the eternal flush. I'm fifty-two years old, Glenda. My ex-wife hates me and so do my kids. I got nine hundred dollars in the bank. What the fuck am I going to do if I'm no longer an agent?'

Glenda frowned, wanting to refute Montgomery's argument, but coming up empty. She didn't know what to think anymore. She didn't like Montgomery. His ill-kept appearance did bother her. So did his disappearing act. But he had a point. In the patriotic world of the Bureau, there was no greater currency than saving a fellow agent's hide. If he did find Quincy's stalker, Montgomery's career would get a second chance. Probably, its only chance.

'But now you think Quincy murdered his ex-wife,' she said.

'You bet I do.'

'Because the scene is staged?'

Montgomery shrugged. 'Because of a lot of things. Frankly, the phone calls bother me. If you were out to get someone and you had his private telephone number, would you fool around with prank calls, or would you just go out and kill the man? I mean, we're saying this guy has some connection with Quincy's career. So we're talking about a psychopath. Now, what kind of psychopath wants to talk about killing an agent, when he can attack the agent?'

'We discussed this. It's a ruse, a way of disguising the UNSUB's true identity by creating hundreds of other suspects with opportunity and motive.'

'But it also alerts the victim,' Montgomery countered. 'Seems like a massive downside to me. Especially when you consider that in this day and age, the UNSUB can simply read articles on-line about how to conceal evidence. He has the element of surprise, then has all night to cover his tracks.'

'Maybe the UNSUB didn't want an easy murder. Assuming vengeance is the motive, maybe he wanted to make sure Quincy suffered first.'

'Maybe. Or maybe we're making this all too complicated. Look, from where I sit, there is another plausible theory to everything that's happened: Quincy made this whole thing up. Ran the ad in the prison newsletters himself. Then showed up in Everett's office with his, "The sky is falling, the sky is falling!" routine, knowing that Everett will follow protocol and assemble a case team. Now Quincy has four federal agents swearing to the Philadelphia police that someone is stalking him, and that mysterious person probably murdered his ex-wife and kidnapped his old man. But *is* someone stalking him? Or was this all a cover-up, so that he could kill his ex?'

'Listen to yourself, Albert. You're saying Pierce was willing to dupe the Bureau and harm his own father, simply to cover up an attack on his wife.'

'We don't know that Quincy harmed his father.'

'Abraham Quincy is a bedridden Alzheimer's patient. He's now been missing from the nursing home for over twenty-four hours. That's not good.'

'Papa Quincy was checked out by Pierce Quincy, bearing proper ID.'

'Anyone can get a fake driver's license.'

'Yeah, and anyone can use a real one. Glenda, we got no body. For all we know, Abraham is tucked away at some nice posh resort, courtesy of his son. When the police buy Quincy's story of the phantom stalker, Abraham will promptly reappear, having magically escaped his evil captor. Or maybe Quincy will phone in an anonymous tip and the searching agents can rescue his dad. Either way, no harm, no foul, and Quincy's story is better all the time.'

'It's too far-fetched!' Glenda protested. 'Three *more* reasons: One, you saw Pierce in Philadelphia and there wasn't a mark on him.'

'Quick kill. Plus, police have found blood in the drainpipes. Killer cleaned up at the scene.'

'Two, you still have no motive. Quincy and his wife have been divorced for years. You're talking about a long, complicated scheme leading up to a particularly brutal murder. Why? The marriage is old business.'

'I don't know that part,' Montgomery conceded. 'But it's still early. Maybe she never took him off her life insurance. Maybe he blames her for the daughter's death. Give me time. I'll work on it.'

'Ah-hah,' Glenda announced triumphantly. 'Three, the daughter's death – Quincy has evidence that it wasn't an accident. She was murdered. Probably the stalker's first victim.'

'What?' That brought Montgomery up short. 'I thought the daughter was an MVA. Drunk driving. How does a DUI become murder?'

'Someone tampered with the driver's seat belt, rendering it useless. And there's evidence that someone else was sitting in the passenger's seat. The Virginia state police are investigating it now.'

'Maybe the daughter tampered with the seat belt. Maybe it was suicide.'

'Why tamper with the seat belt?' Glenda asked dryly. 'Why not simply not wear it?'

'Oh.' Montgomery was flummoxed. He shifted around his bulk, then grimaced. 'I don't know,' he said at last. 'Have to think about it.'

'It's a complicated case,' Glenda said softly. 'Three family members of a fellow agent are now dead or missing. We shouldn't be rushing to conclusions about Quincy, or anyone else.'

'That's not what Everett said.'

'You already presented this to Everett?' Glenda's voice raised a notch.

'Sure, I called him last night. If Quincy really is our killer, the Bureau is going to have a little bit of egg on its face.'

'You shouldn't have done that. Dammit!'

'I can't speak to Everett? Christ, you really do hate my guts.' Montgomery wandered over to the refrigerator.

Glenda remained poised in the middle of the kitchen. Her hands were clenched into fists at her side. Her heart was beating too fast. She was angrier than she'd ever been, angrier than she probably should've been. Except . . . Except Everett would now call Quincy back. The SAC would have no choice. He'd bring Quincy back and if there really was someone out to get him . . .

You asshole, Montgomery. Why couldn't you wait? What's one more afternoon, one more day of due diligence? Stupid son of a bitch.

The phone rang; the answering machine clicked on. Glenda raised a hand, and began to slowly and methodically rub her temples. It didn't ease the ache. She didn't know what to believe anymore. Montgomery raised interesting points, and if Quincy had committed the murder then it was her job to track him down.

And yet, if he hadn't. If he'd told the truth . . .

Then they were doing exactly what the UNSUB wanted. Three highly skilled federal agents were dancing to a killer's tune. And Quincy, what could he do if Everett ordered him to come in? The minute he walked through Bureau doors, he would be forced to surrender his creds and his gun. He wouldn't be much help to his daughter then. But what was his other option? Become an outlaw to protect Kimberly? It would never work. The Bureau had long arms, particularly when faced with embarrassing situations such as policing its own.

Two scenarios and neither showing much promise. Jesus, she thought. Quincy was either the most brilliant criminal the Bureau had ever faced, or one truly unlucky son of a bitch.

The fax line rang in the office. A moment later, a faint whir sounded as the machine picked up. Glenda went to retrieve the message, leaving Montgomery alone in the kitchen.

The preliminary report on the hard copy of the ad that had run in the *National Prison Project Newsletter* was coming over the wire. The report was four pages long.

Glenda scanned each page as it came through.

Latent found five fingerprints on the typeset ad, all of which matched with various staff members of the *National Prison Project Newsletter*. Serology found no hairs and fibers, but some dust residue that, again, was traced to the *National Prison Project Newsletter*. To complete the evidence-less trifecta, the DNA unit had also been unable to recover any samples from the paper or envelope.

At least the Document Examination Unit had had some fun. Their findings comprised the last three pages of the report, and were a welcome change from N/A, N/A, inconclusive. The ink on the paper was traced to a standard black laser-print cartridge commonly used in HP printers. That narrowed it down to millions of possible printers. Never fear, they were able to trace the font and graphics of the typeset ad. The UNSUB had used PowerPoint. Oh, the magic of desktop publishing.

Glenda sighed. Investigating crimes had been so much easier when people had no other choice but to write notes by hand. How the hell were you supposed to analyze a computer font? Where were the hesitation marks or angrily slanted T's in a typewritten ransom demand? And how the hell did you narrow the field when even serial killers were using Microsoft Office?

On the last page, she finally found some news. The paper was distinct. Not cheap grade white, but heavy-duty cream stationery, handmade with a watermark. According to the Document Examination Unit, the paper came from Britain where it was sold exclusively by a small store on Old Bond Street. Approximately two thousand boxes were sold worldwide each year. And it retailed for nearly one hundred dollars per twenty-five sheets.

Glenda set down the report. So, they had an UNSUB with computer access, PowerPoint savvy, and extremely expensive taste in stationery. Who in the world sent an ad to a prison newsletter on hundred-dollar stationery? It probably came in some kind of fancy gift box with pressed flowers and silk ribbons tied around the top. Maybe a gift. What a wife might give to a husband, or a boss to a colleague, or a daughter to a dad.

Glenda looked at Quincy's desk. His beautiful, richly finished desk with the state-of-the-art fax machine, the fine leather chair. Everything perfectly matched, such as what a well-bred wife might select for her workaholic husband back when they were still married . . .

She grabbed the first desk drawer. Ripped it open. Pens, pencil, a Louis Vuitton check holder. She tried the drawer beneath that, then the one beneath that. Finally, in the bottom drawer, the location of a man who didn't write much, three boxes of stationery, all hardly touched.

She'd been wrong about the dried flowers and silk ribbons. The stationery came in a beautiful sandalwood box, tied with a leather thong. Geppetto's Stationery, imported from Italy, beautiful to behold, and now down to nineteen sheets.

'Oh Quincy,' Glenda whispered, box in hand. 'Oh Quincy, how could you?'

28

Portland, Oregon

When Rainie woke up, Quincy was gone. She glanced at the red-glowing alarm clock next to the bed. Seven A.M., making it ten eastern standard time. Quincy and Kimberly had probably been up for hours. She dragged a hand through her hair, caught her reflection in the mirror above the bureau and winced. She looked like she'd stuck her hand in a light socket. Then again, her mouth tasted like old socks.

Ah, another beautiful Saturday morning.

She rolled out of bed and into the adjoining bathroom. Toothpaste helped. So did a quick shower. She donned her three-day-old jeans and white T-shirt, wrinkled her nose with distaste, and bravely left the bedroom.

Quincy and his daughter sat at the brown circular table in the tiny kitchenette that comprised the front half of the living room. Quincy was hunched over his laptop computer, while Kimberly leaned against his shoulder to get a better look at the screen. Both held cups of Starbucks coffee, and both were arguing vigorously. Rainie identified a third cup of coffee, probably hers. She scooped it up, while trying to come up to speed on their squabble.

They seemed to be working on the database. Kimberly wanted to focus more on Miguel Sanchez, Quincy thought it was a dead end – the man couldn't exactly do much from the confines of San Quentin. Well what about family, Kimberly argued. What family? Quincy countered. Sanchez's only living relative was a seventy-year-old oxygen-dependent mother, hardly a likely candidate for psycho of the week.

'Touché,' Rainie murmured.

They finally paused, Quincy glancing up from the computer. Something passed over his face, an expression she couldn't read. Then he said evenly, 'Good morning, Rainie. There are croissants in the bag if you'd like.'

She shook her head. 'Been up long?'

'A few hours.' Quincy was avoiding her gaze. That was okay; she couldn't seem to meet his eye either. Had he been surprised to wake up and find her pressed against him on the bed? Pleased? Or had he considered it purely practical – Kimberly already had the sofa. Rainie studiously memorized the Starbucks logo on her cup of coffee.

'Where are you with things?' she asked.

'Working the database.'

Kimberly chimed in, 'I think we need to reexamine the Sanchez case. Miguel's the one who reached Dad by phone, plus, his treatment of his cousin, Richie Millos, proves that he's big on revenge. Then there's the Montgomery factor – that Albert Montgomery also worked that case and happens to hate Dad because of it.'

'That I personally took Sanchez's call was a random event,' Quincy countered. 'There were fifty-six other convicts on the answering machine, whose calls I could just as easily have caught in person. And while the "Montgomery factor" is interesting, coincidence does not equal conspiracy. Bottom line: Miguel is securely behind bars in California. He has no opportunity, and frankly, I don't think he's that smart.'

'What about the cousin?' Rainie asked.

'Millos? What about him?'

Rainie took a seat. Safe on the comforting topic of homicidal maniacs, she could face Quincy again. 'Think of it this way: Your assessment of Richie and Miguel's partnership led the police to focus on Richie. And by focusing on Richie, the police guaranteed his death at the hands of Miguel. Ergo, someone could argue that you were responsible for Richie's death.'

'Ergo, I killed Richie,' Quincy murmured. 'Not bad.'

'Does Richie have surviving family?' Kimberly asked.

'I don't know. Grab the case file.'

Kimberly began digging in the box next to Quincy's feet. Apparently, they'd been through this drill a few times already, because she came up with the manila file in four seconds flat. 'Millos, Richie. Let's see what kind of nuts are hanging from the family tree.' She flipped it open, turned three pages, and began to briskly scan the background report. 'Okay, we got a mother – fifty-nine years old and listed as a housewife. We have a father – sixty-three years old, former janitor, now on disability. Oh, condition is listed as rheumatoid arthritis. That probably rules him out.'

'Any siblings?' Quincy asked.

'Two younger brothers and one younger sister. Jose is thirty-five and comes with his own rap sheet. A B&E guy, but not currently incarcerated. That's food for thought. Mitchell "Mickie" Millos is thirty-three, and hey, no rap sheet. In fact, he's an engineer with a degree from the University of Texas in Austin. So apparently one of the men in the family made good. Finally we have Rosa Millos, the baby daughter, who is twenty-eight. We have no info on her, why is that?'

'Chauvinism,' Rainie replied. 'The feds have a history of underestimating women.'

'I'm not going to comment on that,' Quincy murmured, 'given that I'm outnumbered, and outgunned, in this room. Now, for no good reason at all, tell me more about Mickie.'

Kimberly flipped back through the background report. 'I don't have anything more on Mickie. Once the investigating agent determined he had no criminal history, he seemed to have lost interest.'

'Figures.' Quincy frowned, mulling something over in his mind. Then his gaze rose to meet Rainie's. She'd been staring at the column of his throat, admiring his dark blue polo shirt and wondering why she hadn't gotten him out of a suit more often. The soft cotton fabric draped nicely over his chest, accentuating the hard planes of his runner's body, the deep color of his piercing eyes.

Why hadn't he woken her this morning? He could've taken at least one moment to brush her cheek and say . . . anything.

Belatedly she realized he was looking at her. A fresh flood of color rose in her cheeks. She looked away hastily, feeling not at all like herself.

'Rainie?' he asked softly.

'Ummm, the youngest brother. Yes, let's look harder at him.'

Kimberly frowned. 'Why Mickie? He's not even the right age. Our guy's much older.'

'Age can be faked,' Quincy said, his gaze still on Rainie. 'Plus, people are notoriously bad at estimating age. You put a man in T-shirt and jeans and people will say he's early twenties. You put the same man in a dark suit, and people will say he's early thirties. While eyewitness testimonies remain the number one way of catching suspects, they are very easy to manipulate, especially by someone who's done any reading on the subject.'

'But Mickie's an engineer,' Kimberly protested. 'Educated, no history of crime.'

'Exactly,' Rainie spoke up. 'The UNSUB we're looking for is sophisticated. He has a complex plan, a gift for manipulation, confidence in approaching both a beautiful young woman – your sister – and a sophisticated older woman – your mother. Most likely he is educated, fairly worldly, and with a knack for problem solving.'

'And he has money,' Quincy added. 'At the current pace of development, our UNSUB's most likely engaged in this pursuit full-time. So he must have a nest egg to live off of. He's also been traveling, demanding additional resources. Then there's this new development with you, Rainie. Kimberly told me about your meeting with Carl Mitz. If, as you suspect, your "father" really is Tristan Shandling, then our UNSUB has paid off a DA and hired a lawyer as part of his plan, both actions requiring significant financial resources.

'Now, does a thirty-three-year-old engineer such as Mickie have that kind of money? Generally, I'd say no. But in this day and age of software millionaires and dot-com billionaires, who knows? Mickie could be a very wealthy young man.'

Kimberly nodded slowly. 'I hadn't thought of that. Okay, so we run a complete background check of youngest brother Millos, including his financial assets. One name down.' She looked at the box of files. She sighed. 'Fifty more names to go.'

'With all due respect,' Rainie spoke up, 'I don't think this database project is going to get us anywhere.' Quincy immediately frowned. He and his daughter swiveled to look at her. Rainie shrugged. 'Think about it, Quincy. Is this guy's name somewhere in that box or in this database or in FBI files? Probably. Is it going to help us? No. Why not? Because he knows his name is in there, too.'

She leaned forward, speaking intently. 'What is the UNSUB's major vulnerability? Process of elimination. It's a personal case, not stranger to stranger, so given enough time and resources, he knows you'll be able to identify him. What's his strategy then? In the beginning, it's secrecy. He selects Mandy, the family member in the least amount of contact with the rest of the family. He disguises his appearance, he uses an alias, and he conceals her murder as an accident. And in the beginning, that works. He understands, however, that he can't hide his actions forever. The minute he attacks Bethie, you'll start connecting the dots. You'll start looking for him. And he prepares for that as well.

'Fourteen months after Mandy's accident, he starts a fresh wave of maneuvers. First tactic: Diversion. He spreads around your address and telephone number to every psycho in the continental US. Next tactic: Confusion. He steals your identity, assumes your appearance, and begins to plant evidence that will get your fellow agents off his trail and on to you. Final tactic: *Speed.*'

'Everything is now happening at once,' Quincy said.

'Wednesday, Mom is murdered,' Kimberly whispered. 'Thursday, Grandpa is kidnapped. Friday, we're all on the run and Rainie is approached by some lawyer about her father. He's not going to give us time to think, anymore. He's not going to give any of us time to stop and consider and analyze. Because the minute we do, he knows he's in trouble.'

Rainie was looking at Quincy. 'This guy . . . he's a black hole, Quincy. We don't know who, why, how, when. He's not giving you any information. He's not making the mistake of underestimating you. Why?'

'Because I definitely know him.'

She smiled. 'Because he definitely knows you. You thrive on information, puzzles, games. It's your whole life. So step one was to keep his actions hidden for as long as possible. And step two is to keep you moving, instead of thinking. As long as you're reacting to him, you can't get ahead. Keeping you reacting is keeping you vulnerable. We have to break that cycle, Quince. We need an active game plan, a way of going on the offensive. And hiding out in Portland playing with databases isn't it. He'll find us here – probably a lot sooner than you think.'

Quincy grew silent. Then his gaze rose slowly to meet hers. 'What do you think of Carl Mitz's allegation that you have a father?' he asked.

'I don't know.'

'Just because it's coincidence, doesn't mean . . .'

'I got that!' Rainie took a deep breath, then let it out. 'I just . . . I have to be careful. Mitz seems legit. There are aspects of Ronald Dawson's background that also appear genuine. He was in prison for most of my life, we may very well find public record of the real estate deal that made his father a millionaire. On the other hand . . . Tristan Shandling's MO is to disguise himself as the person his victim wants most. And yeah, I am interested in Ronald Dawson. I'm desperately interested in Ronald Dawson, and frankly, that scares me to death.'

'What if Mitz could arrange for you to meet Mr Dawson in person?'

'No way.' She shook her head adamantly.

That intent look was back in Quincy's eyes, and not his slow sexy look, but his all-knowing professional stare. 'Active game plan,' he murmured.

Rainie closed her eyes. She knew what he wanted. It hurt her, it killed her, but it didn't change the fact that once more, he was right. 'Fine! I'll meet with Ronnie. I'll put my achy, breaky heart at risk. Never say I didn't do anything for you.'

'But you can't meet with him,' Kimberly blurted out. 'If he's the UNSUB, he could attack you, or kidnap you, or worse.'

'I don't think your father intends for me to meet with Ronnie alone,' Rainie said dryly. 'Not that he's opposed to offering me as some juicy little bait.'

'I never—'

'Oh shut up, Quince. For God's sake, I'm the one who just said we needed to be proactive. If Dawson is our favorite stalker, then let's turn the tables on him. I'll contact Mitz and set up a lunch date, with Luke and the boys singing backup. I can drill Ronnie for additional information about his paternity claim. At the very least, I can get yet another description to add to our files. Tristan Shandling, the man of many faces.'

'What if he tries something?' Kimberly protested.

'He won't,' Rainie said.

'How can you be sure?'

'Because it's his MO,' Rainie said flatly. 'If Ronald Dawson is Tristan Shandling, he's not going to come out of the gate swinging. Oh no. Quite the opposite. He's going to sit across from me telling me how much he's always wanted a daughter. He's going to dazzle me with stories of what I could do with a ten-million-dollar inheritance. He's going to tell me that finding me is the single best thing that's ever happened to him.' Her voice cracked. She caught it. 'And I'm going to get to doubt every word he says. I'm going to sit there thinking this man is either the world's most perfect long-lost father, or someone who wants me dead. Hey, all in a day's work.'

'Rainie—'

'I'll do it, Quincy.'

'I've changed my mind. I don't want you to do it. I was wrong.'

'You were right,' she snapped crisply. 'Don't grow soft on me now.'

He fell silent. So did she. His eyes locked on hers. The moment drew out, grew long.

'This is very hard,' Kimberly said at last.

Quincy nodded, his gaze not leaving Rainie's. 'This is very hard.'

'I mean, we don't even know who this man is, and look what he's doing to you. Mom is gone, and Mandy's gone, and now you have to fear for Rainie and me.'

'I've always feared for the people I care about.'

'But not like this. Not this active, immediate, horrible kind of worry.'

'I always worry,' Quincy said quietly. 'It's the nature of my job. I know what can happen, and I do think about it late at night.'

'We're going to be okay,' Kimberly said fiercely. 'We know what's going on now and information is power! We're going to be okay.'

'We'll delve deeper into Mitchell Millos,' Quincy said

softly. 'I'll try to come up with a list of five or ten other names. Then I'll check in with Everett, see if he has any new developments. Perhaps, my father . . .' His voice grew too wistful. He caught himself and said more firmly, 'And we'll move on Ronald Dawson. One way or another, we're going to get a fix on him.'

'We have one last ace in the hole,' Rainie spoke up. 'Phil de Beers in Virginia. He's still tailing Mary Olsen. Think about it. She's alone. She's betrayed her best friend, and she has no self-esteem or she never would've gotten into this mess in the first place. She's probably already reaching out to the guy. And as each day passes, she's only going to get more demanding about meeting him in person. When she does . . .'

'I want photos,' Quincy said immediately. 'Best quality Mr de Beers can get. It's time we develop a better physical description.'

'But he uses so many disguises,' Kimberly protested. 'The two descriptions we have don't match. How will a third help us?'

'He only *seems* to be good at disguise, because we're relying on accounts from laymen,' Rainie pointed out. 'Everyday people get bogged down with eye color, hairstyle, facial hair, clothing – all easily altered elements. What people should look at are standard features such as the amount of space between the eyes, the location of the ears on the head, the shape of the jawline. Those features can't be changed, they're unique. If we can get a photo, then we could have it analyzed by a forensics artist for those elements and then we'd finally have something to work with.'

'You'll contact de Beers?' Quincy asked.

'I'll call him this minute,' Rainie promised. She smiled

thinly. 'And then I'll call Mitz about setting up lunch with Daddy. We gotta get moving – thirty-six hours since Señor Psycho's last strike; I doubt we have much time left.'

29

The Olsen Residence, Virginia

Curled up in the deepest corner of her walk-in closet, Mary Olsen cradled the cordless phone to her ear. Her dark hair was snarled. Mascara streaked her face. On her left shoulder was a fresh bruise she didn't want to talk about. Her icy blue silk robe hid the remains of many more. Her husband had come home this morning from an emergency surgery that had not gone well. Ten minutes after he tore back out of the driveway in his Jag convertible, she had grabbed the phone.

'I know I'm not supposed to call,' she said in a rush, 'but I can't take this anymore. You don't understand how bad things have been. I need to see you. Please, baby, please . . .'

'Shhh, take a deep breath. Everything will be all right.'

'No it won't. No it *won't!*' Her voice rose to a frenzied pitch, then dissolved in a flood of tears. Her ribs hurt. She was going to have bruises between her thighs. Who ever would have thought that a man who looked so soft could hit so hard? 'I'm lonely,' she sobbed. 'It's been weeks of nonstop torment, and now I don't even have you to look forward to. I can't keep living like this!'

'I know, baby. I know it's been hard.' In contrast to her high-pitched pain, he sounded calm, gentle, kind. She let the words wash over her bruised thoughts and strained emotions. She held the phone closer to her mascara-stained cheek.

She had always loved the sound of his voice. Mandy once had commented on his eyes, that it was the power of his gaze that drew her in. For Mary, however, not allowed to see him much, it had always been the sound of his voice. How he could seem to know her anguish from hundreds of miles away. How he could whisper in her ear across the telephone lines and lend her his strength in the middle of the night when her husband had finally fallen asleep but she knew it was only a matter of hours before he awoke and it would start all over again.

'He tells me what to say, what to do, what to wear,' she whispered brokenly. 'I didn't know it would be like this. Why did he want to marry me, if he hates me so much?'

'You're a beautiful woman, Mary. Not all men can handle that.'

'But I never gave him anything to worry about!' she cried. 'I mean . . . well, you know, not before. God, I'm tired! I miss you. I *need* you. I'd give anything just . . . just to hold your hand, see your smile. Make me feel beautiful again.'

'I wish I could, honey,' he said apologetically. 'I really do.'

'Why not? It's been days since the Conner woman showed up. Surely it's safe by now. We can meet anyplace you want. I'll take the precautions you showed me. Please, it'll be all right.'

'But love, it's not all right. Don't you know? You're being watched.'

'What?' She gasped, genuinely surprised.

'I tried to get a note to you two days ago,' he explained. 'But then I saw a small silver hatchback tucked inside the bushes with a clear view of anyone entering or exiting your property. I watched the car for hours, and it never moved. I'm sorry, baby, but I think your husband is having you followed.'

'No! The goddamn jealous prick. I've never given him any reason . . . I mean not before. Oh, fuck him! What are we going to do?'

'What can we do? If he gets even one picture of us together . . . I know you don't want that to happen. Not after everything you've been through.'

'I won't give him the satisfaction!' Mary vowed. 'By God, when I leave the son of a bitch he's going to pay me every dime he's worth. I should leave him today, this instant. I'll just . . . I'll just do it!'

'The shorter the marriage, the less likely you are to receive half his assets,' he said gently.

She started to cry again. 'What am I going to do? I miss you. I am *going insane!*'

He didn't say anything right away. There probably wasn't anything to say, and she knew that even if she didn't want to admit it. She was a married woman. She did need her husband's money. Oh God, her shoulder hurt. So did her ribs. Some mornings she wasn't sure how she made it out of bed. The more her husband beat her, the angrier he seemed to be. Was it himself he hated for hitting her, or herself for never saying no?

How did my life come to this? I don't know, I don't know, I don't know . . .

'I have an idea,' her lover said.

Lisa Gardner

'Yes. Anything. Please.'

'This afternoon, a box of chocolates will arrive. Godiva, I think. The brand doesn't matter. Are you listening?'

'Yes.' Her voice was breathless.

'I want you to take the box and walk down the road until you see the silver car. A black man will be sitting behind the wheel.'

'Oh my God!'

'He's not going to hurt you, baby. He's a private investigator, no doubt the best your husband's money can buy. Tap on the window. Smile charmingly. Then, tell him you know what he's doing. He'll be chagrined, embarrassed about being caught. You become even more charming. Invite yourself to join him, tell him you just want to talk. Then pour out your heart about your evil husband, and while you're at it, offer him a chocolate. If he refuses, take one yourself. Eat it in front of him. Then offer him more. Make sure he eats two or three. That will do it.'

'Are they poisoned?' she asked. A shiver ran down her spine.

'You think I would ask you to eat poisoned chocolates? What has your husband done to you?'

'I'm sorry, it's just—'

'The candies are doctored, love. A chocolate-flavored laxative, that's all, melted down and injected with a syringe. One truffle will have a minor impact on your system. Two or three, however, should, well, give the private investigator more pressing things to do with his time than watch you. When he drives off in search of proper facilities, you can get away.'

'To meet you!'

'I've missed you, too, love.'

'Tell me I'm beautiful.'

His voice was generous. 'You are beautiful beyond compare, particularly in black lace.'

'I'll wear the garters,' she said breathlessly.

'Perfect. I'll wear nothing at all.'

'Oh God, I can't wait to see you!'

'One box of chocolates later, I'll be at your side.'

She smiled for the first time all morning. But then she remembered how she looked, and she hesitated. 'I'm a little . . . sore,' she said softly.

He understood instantly. 'Then when I see you, baby, I will kiss all your pains away.'

She started to cry again, quietly this time, genuinely. He would make her feel better. He always did. The first time she'd arrived with black-and-blue ribs, she'd told him that she'd fallen down the stairs. But he'd known. And instead of turning away, instead of looking at her with disgust, he had taken her in his arms and held her tenderly.

'You poor thing,' he had said. 'You are much too precious for this.'

She had cried that night for hours. The whole time, he simply held her and stroked her hair. In her entire life, she had never had anyone touch her as gently as he did. In her entire life, no one had ever made her feel so special.

Briefly, for one instant, she thought of Amanda. Amanda who had never hurt her. Amanda who had been a good friend. Amanda who had been so excited to introduce her new man . . .

But you kept drinking, Mandy, she thought. You had the world's most perfect beau, and still you hit the bottle. After that, you deserved what happened. Besides, you always had plenty of men. And I . . . I needed him.

She replaced the phone, using the sleeve of her robe to wipe away the streaks of mascara and tears. One box of chocolates later on she would be with him again, she thought. One box of chocolates later. She hoped they came quick.

30

Pearl District, Portland

A little after eleven A.M., Quincy followed Rainie into her downtown loft. She flicked on the lights out of habit, though daylight streamed through the front bank of windows and the space was bright. The air carried the musty scent of a home that had been empty too long. Quincy knew that fragrance – it was how his own residence always greeted him.

'I should check on a few things,' Rainie said nervously. He nodded, walking into the living area while she flitted about the open space. She had been like this all morning. Rarely meeting his eye, skittering away if he moved too close. Soft and still one moment. Nearly frantic the next. He thought he knew what was going on. Then again, his instincts weren't the best these days.

Shortly after their discussion that morning, Rainie had left a message on Carl Mitz's cell phone. She couldn't leave the number for Quincy's cell phone without revealing that he was with her, and she couldn't give the phone number of the hotel room without compromising that location, so she provided the number Mitz already knew – her loft in the

Pearl District. Kimberly had opted to stay in the hotel room, where she was using Rainie's PI license number to access various law enforcement databases for background reports. Quincy and Rainie would wait for Mitz's response at her place. The division of labor made practical sense. If there were other motives, no one was mentioning them.

Quincy walked around the sofa, pausing in various sunbeams. He liked the feel of light and heat washing over his face. He closed his eyes and felt knotted muscles unclench. He took a deep breath and reminded himself that this, too, shall pass. He held on to that thought fiercely these days.

He had called Everett about his father. No news yet, and Quincy knew better than most what that meant. Each hour that passed without finding Abraham decreased the probability of ever seeing him alive. It had been thirty-six hours now. One moment, Abraham had been sleeping peacefully in his antiseptic-smelling bed. The next he was gone, checked out by a stranger posing as his son, not that Abraham would know the difference. A janitor reported seeing Quincy's father being led to a little red sports car, probably the same Audi TT the UNSUB had used to pick up Bethie.

No sign of the car since. No sign of Abraham. No big break in the case to ease the pain steadily building in Quincy's chest. His father's kidnapping was the ultimate failure, worse somehow than Amanda's and Elizabeth's murders, because they had been independent adults. His father, on the other hand, had been vulnerable and utterly helpless. Once a proud man who had single-handedly raised his son, now a dependent. Quincy should've done more to keep him safe.

The realization left him in a strange place. At once bottomed out, yet fiercely enraged. Empty of all emotion, yet desperate to feel alive. Defeated. Determined. Unbelievably angry. Unbearably sad. The academic searching for a reason. The man, knowing there was no such thing.

Why is my father gone? Because he is. Isolation is not protection. No amount of distance numbs the pain.

And then Quincy had a strange memory, a moment he hadn't thought about in years. Little Kimmy coming home from her fourth ballet lesson, walking into the living room where the family was gathered, and with her feet planted and her hands balled on her hips, announcing in her loudest voice, 'Fuck ballet!'

Quincy remembered Bethie's stunned gasp, Mandy's awed expression, and his own desperate attempt to fight a smile. Fuck ballet. Such attitude. Such confidence. Such fearlessness. He had felt so proud.

Had he ever told his father that story? Abraham would've liked that. He wouldn't have said anything, but he would've smiled. And he also would've been proud. Each generation takes the next step forward. From a stoic swamp Yankee to a reserved federal agent to a brash aspiring criminologist, who obviously knew her own mind.

Isolation was not protection. He had lost his father, but maybe, just maybe, he was getting an opportunity to rediscover Kimberly.

'I'm going to grab some clothes,' Rainie called from the walk-in closet. 'If the phone rings, let me answer it.'

'I am not here,' Quincy promised her.

'Do you think Kimberly needs anything?'

He smiled faintly. 'I think you would know that better than me.'

Lisa Gardner

'That's not true. You're not a total idiot savant.'

'Coming from you, I take that as a compliment.'

Rainie exited the closet. He could tell she was happy to be home because there was an extra bounce in her step, a spark of energy that had previously been missing. She'd changed from her T-shirt into a blue chambray button-down. As she walked toward the kitchen, he found himself studying how the soft, well-worn cotton flowed over the curve of her hips.

She is beautiful, he thought, and this time around, the realization stunned him. She was not just good-looking or attractive or sexy. She was beautiful. Beautiful in jeans and a cotton shirt. Beautiful in the way she burst past two homicide detectives at a Philadelphia crime scene simply because she knew that he needed her. Beautiful in the way she stood up to his fellow FBI agents even though she felt uncomfortable and outclassed. Beautiful in the way she was still beside him, when God knows that his life was disintegrating quickly and it would be so much easier to walk away.

She'd told him once that she didn't know anything about relationships or commitment. She was the most loyal, trustworthy person he knew.

'Rainie,' he said quietly, 'I messed up this morning.'

That grabbed her attention. She froze with one foot in the kitchen, and the other in the bedroom. 'I don't know what you're talking about,' she said.

'I was having the best dream, probably the first good dream I've had in months. We were together, on a beach, curled up on white-hot sand. I remember I was playing with your hair. We weren't saying anything. We were simply . . . happy.'

'That had to be a dream.'

'Then I woke up and you really were beside me.'

'Was I snoring?'

'You weren't snoring.'

'Phew.' She made an exaggerated motion with her hand as if wiping sweat from her brow. 'Here I was sure that I'd been snoring so loud, you'd had to run for your life.'

'You had your head on my shoulder,' he said softly. 'And your arm around my waist. And your leg . . . it was curved over my thigh.'

'I get cold when I sleep.'

'It was . . . it was one of the nicest things anyone has ever done for me.'

'Oh, fuck you, too, Quince.' He blinked his eyes in shock. Rainie stalked toward him. Her cheeks were flushed, her finger making dangerous, jabbing motions in the air. Somewhere along the way, his little speech had obviously pushed the wrong button because she was definitely pissed off. Run, he thought immediately. Where? The place had no walls.

'I am not nice!' she spit out. 'Can we get this straight? *I* am *never* nice.'

He watched her finger warily. 'Okay.'

'I did not crawl into your bed to be nice. I did not curl up beside you to be *nice*. And I did not fall asleep to be *nice*. Got it?'

'I didn't mean—'

'Yes you did. I reached out to you. I made a *huge* leap forward for me. And you not only took the coward's way out this morning, but you're taking the coward's way out now, by reducing my act of caring to an act of pity.'

'Are you going to stab me with that thing?'

'With what?'

'Your finger!'

'Quincy!' she yelled, throwing both hands into the air. 'Stop being a smartass. For God's sake, you're acting like *me*! Snap out of it!'

He fell silent. After a moment, so did she. 'I might have panicked this morning,' he admitted.

'There you go.'

'You could be gracious about this.'

'No, I couldn't. Keep talking.'

'It's possible,' he said softly, 'that I fell back on old habits. I woke up, saw you there, liked having you there, and . . . Rainie, now is not a great time to be someone I care about. People I care about are suffering notoriously short life spans.'

'Quincy, boyfriends apologize, shrinks analyze. Which are you?'

He blinked. 'Damn, you're getting good at this.'

'Come on. Mitz could call at any time and then we'll have to get going. So apologize and make it snappy.'

'I'm sorry,' he said dutifully.

She wiggled her fingers. 'For . . . ?'

'For sneaking out of bed like a thief in the night. For not waking you up first. For pretending it didn't happen, when spending the night with me was a monumental step for you and I appreciate your growth—'

'Okay.' She held up a hand. 'Quit while you're ahead. Any moment now, they'll be giving you your own talk show.'

'Rainie, I liked waking up with you by my side.'

Her hands finally came to rest in front of her. She gave him a sideways glance. 'I kind of . . . I kind of liked it, too.'

'I didn't snore?' He couldn't help himself. He took a step

forward. She didn't move back.

'You didn't snore,' she said.

'No tossing and turning, stealing covers, keeping you awake all night?' He kept approaching. She still didn't move back.

'Actually, you were rather cuddly. For a fed.'

He was now only an inch away from her. His nerve endings had flared to life. He could smell the faint scent of her soap, the apple-ish fragrance of her shampoo. He could see every nuance of her face, the direct line of her gaze, the firm resolve of her lips, the way her chin was up as if preparing for a fight. Now was not the time, he reminded himself. Carl Mitz could call at any moment. The world could end.

He wanted to touch her so badly, his fingertips burned. She challenged him. She pushed him. And more than all that . . . She made him dream of white-hot sands when for so long he'd been a shell of a man, methodically analyzing humanity and sacrificing his own somewhere along the way.

'I don't want to hurt you,' he whispered.

'Bad things happen, Quince. Someone I respect explained it to me once. We can't stop all the bad things in the world. We can simply try to enjoy the good.'

'If I lost you . . .'

'You would get on with life,' she said bluntly. 'So would I. We're practical people, Quincy. And we're tough, and we're going to make it through this. Now stop talking. Stop thinking, stop analyzing, dammit, and *kiss me*.'

He obliged.

His first touch was light. In spite of her bold words, he knew she was nervous. He could feel the tension in her spine as his hand settled on the small of her back. He could feel the finite hesitation as she tilted back her head and offered her lips. She expected him to dive right in, and she had steeled herself for the attack. He wasn't interested in a stoic or a martyr, however. He understood her history. Sex for Rainie had been about pain and punishment. Even if she thought it would be easier that way, he wasn't going to rush.

He brushed the corner of her mouth with his lips. He raised his left hand, and feathered back her hair. Her eyes were squeezed shut. He ran the ball of his thumb over her silky eyelashes.

'That tickles,' she murmured.

He smiled. 'Open your eyes, Rainie. Look at me. Trust me. I won't hurt you.'

She opened her eyes. The gray depths were wide, translucent. He had never seen eyes quite like hers, the color of smoky, midnight skies. He bent lower, his gaze still locked on hers, and kissed her left cheekbone.

'Have I ever told you how much I love your profile?' he murmured. 'Such a stubborn jaw and then these dramatic cheekbones . . .'

'I look like a Picasso painting,' she said.

'Rainie, you're the most beautiful woman I know.' His lips came down and found her mouth. This time her gasp was unmistakable. Her spine relented. Her hands curved round his head. Her hips connected with his.

She had full lips, he'd appreciated that the first time he'd seen her. And he'd been struck by the dichotomy of her hard-boned face coupled with an undeniably sinful mouth. Men dreamed about lips like these. Men paid money, wrote sonnets, and sold their souls for lips like these. She should never have gone thirty-two years without appreciating her own sexuality, he thought. And he was honored that she trusted him with it now.

She shifted restlessly. He felt the faint gyration of her body through his hand on her waist. He took that as a signal to move lower, his lips feathering across her jawline, then down the long, smooth column of her throat. Her breathing quickened. He felt her pulse flutter beneath the tip of his tongue.

'Tell me a story,' he whispered as he dipped his head into the V of her soft chambray shirt and inhaled the fragrance of her skin.

'I can't . . . talk.'

'I don't want you remembering, Rainie. I want you in this moment with me.' He picked up her left hand and placed her palm on his chest, where he knew his heart was racing. 'Talk to me about anything you wish. You talk. I'll touch.' His lips returned to her throat.

'Mmmmm, when I was a little girl' – her voice was husky – 'I was . . . going to be . . . a gymnast. An Olympic athlete. Mmmm hmmmm.'

'You have an athlete's body.' He ran his hand down her side, appreciating the taut feel of her form. She was a runner, like him. He had a sudden image of their long, naked limbs intertwined on white cotton sheets and had to catch himself. Breathe deep. Take it slow.

'Did you take lessons?' he asked softly, his fingers finding the first button of her shirt and slipping it free.

'Lessons?'

'Gymnastics.'

'Mmmmm . . .'

He kissed the base of her throat.

'No . . .'

'Watch competitions?' His lips whispered across her collarbone while his leg slipped between hers, supporting her weight and simultaneously making her gasp.

'I watched . . . the Olympics . . .'

'The Olympics are good,' he said. He undid the final button on her shirt. The sides fell open. She shivered as the cooler air hit her skin, but didn't protest.

'Nadia Comaneci is my favorite,' he said casually. He slid his hands inside her shirt. Her skin was warm and silky, stretched taut over her abdomen, tight around her waist. He stroked her sides, and she shifted restlessly against him.

'Favorite what?' she mumbled.

'Gymnast.'

'Oh yeah . . . that. Mmmmm.'

He didn't take off her shirt. Instead, he resumed kissing her mouth, which was opening now, meeting his own advance, and beginning to counter. He trailed more kisses along her jaw, then nuzzled the curve of her ear. Her head turned. She drew him back to her lips, her hips moving faster against his leg, her tongue finally, tentatively, wrapping around his own.

His hands stroked up her spine. They found the clasp of her simple white bra. He let it go, and the undergarment sagged forward.

'I thought you were supposed to do that with one hand,' Rainie whispered against his lips.

'I'm out of practice. Remind me next time, and I'll show off.'

'Quincy?' she said softly. 'Maybe . . . maybe we should move to the bed.'

He didn't need a second invitation. He scooped her up in his arms and headed for the queen-sized bed. At the last moment, he tripped over her shoes. They went down in a tangle of limbs, but managed to land on the down-covered bed. The comforter puffed up. The pillows went poof. Rainie laughed breathlessly. And Quincy found his face between her half-covered breasts. He had to kiss one, then the other. Then his mouth was on her nipple and far from pushing him away, her hands were urging him closer.

'Gymnastics,' she was murmuring. 'In this moment. Gymnastics, floor routines, balance beams. Quincy . . .'

Her sigh undid him all over again. He wanted bare skin against bare skin, moan meeting moan. No rush, take it slow. If he didn't get his shirt off now, he was going to die.

He got his shirt off. He stripped off her loose top and dangling bra, then somehow he was on his back and she was on top of him, her pale white breasts pressed against the tanned expanse of his chest.

'I'm not thinking about the Olympics anymore,' she whispered.

'What?' he muttered thickly.

'Exactly.' She'd found the scar on his left shoulder. She kissed it. Then the small pucker down his arm. The other above his collarbone. 'Who did this?'

'Jim Beckett.'

'Did you kill him?'

'His ex-wife did.'

'I like her.' Her head trailed down. She rained tiny kisses across his rib cage, down to his abdomen, and he sucked in his breath sharply. Her hair tickled him. The good kind of tickle. God, she was killing him.

'Quincy,' she said solemnly, 'I don't want to be like my mother.'

'You're not like your mother.'

'Night after night. Guy after guy.'

'If there's a new guy tomorrow night, I'll shoot him.'

'All right then.'

'Rainie?'

She placed a finger over his lips. 'Don't say it,' she murmured. 'Save something for afterwards.'

She slid off her jeans. She helped him shimmy out of his pants. Then she was on her back and he was poised above her. Her legs parted. Her hips lifted. He couldn't take his eyes off her face, filled with both delicate hope and grim resolution.

'Rainie,' he whispered. 'It's all right to enjoy life.'

'I don't know how.'

'Neither do I. We'll learn together.'

Her legs wrapped around his. He gritted his teeth and eased in slowly. He tried to be gentle, but immediately, her body stiffened. A spasm moved across her features. He stilled, wanting so badly for it to be good for her, trying so hard to make it good for her. Breathe deep. Don't rush. And then a heartbeat later, her expression changed. Her body eased, adjusted. Wonder lit up her face. She shifted beneath him. Then again, then again.

'Easy . . .'

'Please . . . Now. Please!'

He bowed his head. He gave himself over to her and the feel of her hands urging his body. No more control. No more thoughts in his head. Rainie's cries. Rainie's body. Rainie's trusting gaze.

She cried out. Surprised. Ecstatic. He took one moment to enjoy the expression on her face. Then it was too much; he joined her in the dark, shuddering abyss.

* * *

Afterwards, Rainie fell asleep first. Quincy thought he would also doze, but found himself wide awake. The white down comforter was tangled around them. Sun streamed through the bank of windows. He lay on his back with Rainie's head resting upon his shoulder and her arm across his stomach. From time to time, he trailed his fingers down the bare curve of her shoulder and enjoyed the feel of her snuggling close.

He marveled at the sight of her sleeping. Her dark mahogany hair tousled around her pale face. Her long eyelashes like dark smudges against her cheeks. Her shell-pink lips slightly parted, as they uttered small, whispery breaths. Half woman, half child. All his.

His fingers brushed her arm again. She murmured something softly in her sleep.

'I'll never hurt you, Rainie,' Quincy said quietly. Then his gaze went to the phone, which he knew would ring shortly. Back to the hunt, back to a psychopath's killing game.

He thought of his daughter, young and proud, sitting in a hotel room right now, diligently scouring financial records. He thought of Rainie, the tilt of her chin, the way she sparked a room just by sauntering through the door. He thought of himself, older, wiser, and determined to learn from his mistakes.

He reached a conclusion. Time to stop mourning the things he had lost. Time to start fighting for what he had left.

31

The Olsen Residence, Virginia

The chocolates arrived shortly after 3 P.M., marked for special Saturday delivery and borne up the steps by a bouncing, brown-suited UPS man with gorgeous hazel eyes. Mary signed for the chocolates, gave the man a wink, and felt even better when he blushed. She took the plain delivery box inside and eagerly opened it. A small dark green box sat nestled in a sea of gold foil paper. Not Godiva; she didn't recognize the name on the label.

She opened the inside box, and was immediately struck by the scent of bittersweet chocolate and almonds. Twelve truffles, she saw, four rows of three. Each one dusted in cocoa powder and topped with a candied nut. Beautiful box, beautiful truffles. She wondered if PIs got the munchies.

She put the lid back on while consulting her reflection in the mirror. The dark shadows beneath her eyes were now coated with a heavy layer of makeup. A pink silk cardigan covered her bruised arms. Hot rollers had done wonders with her hair. She looked fine, better than fine, actually. She looked lovely. The perfect doctor's wife, swathed in layers of Pepto-Bismol pink.

'Here goes nothing,' she told her reflection. Then she grabbed the box of chocolates and headed out the door.

True to her lover's word, she found a silver hatchback two driveways down with a well-dressed black man sitting in the front. He appeared to be studying a road map. The minute he made eye contact with Mary, however, his gaze dashed frantically from side to side. She marched right up to the driver's side and rapped on the window.

'Howdy, darlin',' he said immediately, rolling down the glass. 'I was hoping someone like you would come along. I have no idea where I am and could sure use some help.' He held up the wrinkled map and flashed a helpless grin. She noticed, however, that his left foot was furiously kicking something beneath the driver's seat. Probably his surveillance camera.

'I know you're a private investigator,' she said.

'I'm telling you, ma'am, you get on these windy back roads and suddenly everything looks alike—'

'Especially when you're seeing the same road for the second day in a row. May I?'

She gestured to the empty passenger seat. He blanched. 'Now darlin', if you could just point out the quickest way to I-95 . . .'

'Fine, I'll show it to you on the map.' She came around the front and climbed into the car before he could utter further protest.

Inside, the air was stifling. The cloth-covered seat pressed her dress uncomfortably against her skin; the dash was warm to the touch. Belatedly, she realized that she should've brought iced tea or lemonade. God knows who'd want candy in the middle of this kind of heat. Live and learn, she thought, and resolutely held up the green-wrapped box.

'I thought you might want a snack,' she said, 'so I brought you something.'

'Ma'am—'

'I'm not an idiot. Please don't treat me like one. And for God's sake, it's only a box of chocolates.'

'Chocolates?' The investigator's voice picked up in spite of himself. He shot her another wary look, then took the box from her hands. The minute he opened it, however, the odor of chocolate and almonds overwhelmed the tiny space. Too sweet, too strong for this kind of heat. He closed up the box immediately. Even she was grateful.

'Thank you, ma'am,' he said politely. 'I confess I have a bit of a sweet tooth, but maybe I'll pass for now. I had a big lunch.' He stuck the green-wrapped box on the dashboard. They both stared at it.

'I'm Mary Olsen,' she said finally, sticking out her hand, 'but then, you must know that.'

The man didn't seem to know what to do. 'Phil de Beers.'

'You work for my husband.'

'Darlin', I'm just a man having a very bad day.' He sighed heavily.

'My husband doesn't like me much,' Mary volunteered. 'When we first met, I was a lowly waitress, and boy was I flattered to meet him. He's a world-renowned neurosurgeon, you know. He saves lives, he helps young children. I'm very proud of his job.'

Phil de Beers nodded miserably.

'When he asked me to marry him,' she continued, 'I thought I was the luckiest girl in the world. I didn't understand then, what it was he wanted. I didn't understand that he didn't like the way I dressed or talked or acted. I guess I was a little naïve, Mr de Beers. I thought my husband asked me to marry him because he loved me.'

'I am so lost,' de Beers said, and this time, he might have been telling the truth.

'He thinks I'm cheating on him, doesn't he?' Mary said. She turned in her seat, looking the man in the eye. 'He thinks I'm sneaking around, dating other men behind his back. Why? Because he leaves me alone all the time? Because he's cut me off from my family and friends? I have no job, sir. No life, no hobbies, nothing to do but flit around some big ol' empty house waitin' for my big ol' doctor husband to come home. Or did he tell you everything?'

She let the pink silk cardigan slip from her shoulder. De Beers's gaze fell immediately to the darkening bruise. His lips tightened, a muscle twitched in his jaw. Surely he felt sorry for her now. They could be allies. She, not her husband, would win. De Beers didn't say anything, though. The silence dragged out, then grew unbearable. Mary turned away, feeling suddenly desolate and overexposed. She pulled her cardigan back up and buttoned it around her neck.

'Maybe . . . maybe I'll have one of those chocolates now,' she said in a small voice.

He handed her the box. She took it without looking at him. And then she knew she had him.

'You must have a chocolate, too,' she said briskly. 'I won't feel so guilty if I'm sharing the box with you.' She handed him a truffle, took one for herself, and then returned the box to the dash. He couldn't back out now. Welcome to southern courtesy. She held up her truffle. He had no choice but to do the same. 'Cheers,' she told him. She popped the chocolate into her mouth. A moment later, Phil de Beers reluctantly followed suit.

She steeled herself for the taste of chemicals or something

327

related to laxatives. It never came. The chocolate was nice – soft and freshly made, melting on her tongue. It was definitely flavored, some kind of liquor maybe, mixed with dark chocolate and almonds. Not bad. She swallowed the candy down, feeling encouraged.

De Beers had also eaten his, but now he was frowning. 'Who makes these?'

'They're good, aren't they? Want another?'

'It's . . . strong.'

She nodded brightly, reaching for the box again, when she became aware of a slight burning sensation on her tongue. Her heartbeat tripled, her cheeks flushed. Suddenly, the car spun sickeningly, and she grabbed the dash for balance.

Across from her, Phil de Beers began to pant. As she watched, sweat burst from his pores. His dark eyes dilated, grew huge.

'Jesus, woman, what's in these things?'

She tried to answer, but her throat had caught on fire and she could feel moisture flecking across her face. Oh God, she was foaming at the mouth. Why? How? So dizzy. Not good. Not good.

'Hot,' she whispered. 'Hot . . .'

She fumbled for the door handle. Popped it open. And he was standing there.

No, she cried, but the word remained in her head instead of uttering from her spittle-spewed lips. She tried to wave him away with her hand. *You mustn't be here. He'll see you and I already got him to eat a chocolate. Another hour, we'll be together. You'll kiss all my bruises away. You'll make me feel beautiful. Please . . .*

Her lover didn't move, however. He was looking at her

strangely. As if he'd never seen her before. As if he'd never held her in his arms or whispered sweet words of encouragement. His lips wore an icy smile. What had happened to his thick, dark hair?

She tried to speak again. She couldn't catch her breath. 'Help,' she tried to say this time. 'Help.' She reached out her hand to him.

Her lover turned away. She slowly followed his line of sight back into the car, where Phil de Beers now lay gasping over the steering wheel. He was looking at the man in horror while his right hand fumbled beneath the seat.

'Al—' the private investigator muttered. 'Stupid bastard . . . Almonds . . . I gotta . . .'

His hand reappeared, his arm trembling convulsively. And then Mary saw . . . a gun. He held a gun.

No, Mary tried to yell to her lover, but couldn't. *Move, run, get away*. The warning never left her mouth. Her throat burned, burned, burned, the car spun, spun, spun. God, she had never felt such pain. *Help me, help me*.

Her hands wrapping around her stomach. *I'm sorry, I'm sorry, I'm sorry*.

Phil de Beers raised his shaking arm. His finger fumbled with the safety. He couldn't get it. He couldn't get it. His arm began to fall . . .

Mary stared at him, and in the spinning, churning, burning car, their gazes finally locked. Funny, how he looked so apologetic, as if he had somehow let her down. An odd gargling sound came from his throat. His eyes rolled back. He slumped over the steering wheel, his gun tumbling to the floor as a wave of white foam gushed from his mouth.

Mary stared at the gun. Stared at the gun. And . . .

Car . . . spinning. *Hot. Can't breathe. Heart too fast*. Her hands clenching her stomach. *Almonds, almonds, why almonds? Hot. Makeup melting. Don't look at me. Don't look* . . . Fading into the seat.

Her gaze rose to her lover's face. She stared at him, with his strange thinning hair, stared at him standing there and not making any move to help.

'It will be over soon.' He checked his watch. 'Another sixty seconds, I'd say. In all honesty, I'm surprised you've lasted this long. Then again, everyone reacts a bit differently.'

Almonds, almonds, almonds . . .

'Oh, did I forget to mention it on the phone? I changed my mind about the laxative. I injected one hundred fifty milligrams of hydrocyanic acid into the center of each chocolate instead. The smell is a bit much, but boy is it quick.'

Her lips moved. He leaned down closer to hear. 'Praying? *Praying?* Why Mary Margaret Olsen, did you forget? You betrayed your best friend. God's not going to have anything to do with you.'

He straightened, the bright sunshine blazing behind him and turning him from a glorious man into an even more glorious avenging angel.

I loved you, she thought as her lungs froze up. And a heartbeat later, *I should've known. What other kind of man would have loved me?*

One last thought. The only thought she had left as her body began to convulse and her lungs fought for air.

'Yours,' she whispered. 'Y-y-yours.'

He frowned. Then he followed the spasm of her hands around her belly and his eyes widened in stunned surprise. 'No! No, no, no . . .'

'Yours,' Mary Olsen whispered one last time. And then her eyes rolled back into her head.

The man jumped forward. He dragged her out of the car. Down on the hot asphalt, he shook her shoulders and slapped her face. 'Wake up! Goddammit, wake up! Don't you do this to me!'

Mary's arms fell limply to her sides. Her pulse was gone, her heart silent in her chest. Cyanide induced a horrible death, but, as he'd promised, it was swift. The man stared at the tiny mound of her belly. Something she would have told him about that afternoon when they were finally together again. She would've looked at him earnestly, so meek and desperate for reassurance. And he would've felt . . .

After all this time. Years of being alone, decades of having no family left.

'Son of a bitch,' he whispered. And then more gutturally, *'Pierce Quincy, goddamn son of a bitch! Look at what you made me do! You'll pay! You'll pay . . . Now, now, now!'*

32

Kimberly reread the Miguel Sanchez file for the fourth time in two hours. Strands of fine blond hair kept working themselves loose from her hastily constructed ponytail and falling over her eyes. She impatiently brushed the strands back with her left hand. She should shower and change now that she had the hotel room to herself. She kept reading the file. Something was in here. She understood her father's point that his personal conversation with Sanchez was purely random. She understood that Special Agent Albert Montgomery's assignment to the case was most likely coincidental. But something was in here. She had her own instincts, and they were screaming at her to revisit Miguel Sanchez.

An odd sound came from the hallway outside her room. Slow, squeaking wheels laboriously rolling down the hall. Most likely some rusted-out metal cart. Kimberly frowned. She continued to read the file.

As a death row inmate in San Quentin, Sanchez now lived alone in a six-by-ten-foot cell. That ruled out the possibility of him having a roommate who might have been released and taken up efforts on his behalf. On the other hand, some condemned prisoners spent up to four hours a day in the rec yard with sixty other inmates, lifting weights, shooting hoops, and doing God knows what.

Kimberly delved deeper into Sanchez's file. According to San Quentin corrections officers, prisoners were classified as two types: Grade A or Grade B. Grade A covered prisoners who had assimilated well to prison life. They followed the rules, didn't give the guards any hassles, and were seen as successfully 'programming'. These inmates were eligible for privileges such as daily rec time with their fellow deviants.

Grade B inmates, on the other hand, were men who hadn't taken to their cells like hens to a chicken coop. They threatened corrections officers, they threatened each other, they actually inflicted physical harm. These men spent lots of quality time in ad seg – administrative segregation, according to the staff, or the hole according to the inmates. Miguel Sanchez was familiar with the hole. According to his file, he'd started out as a Grade B inmate, managed to calm down to Grade A status for about six months in 1997, then went back to his Grade B ways. In other words, Miguel should not have had the opportunity to make many friends in San Quentin. Then again, Richard Millos wound up dead while Sanchez was ad seg, which seemed to indicate that even the most severe type of incarceration had not rendered Sanchez powerless.

That damn squeaking was driving her nuts. Room service should oil the wheels of its carts. Something. Sheesh.

In the good news department, she had found tons of press on the convicted serial killer. Partnerships for psychopaths were unusual, and Sanchez had carved out quite a niche as a professional guinea pig for criminologists writing case studies on famous homicidal duos. The interviews probably helped Sanchez ease the boredom of his now tedious existence. They also allowed him to gloat, reliving the glory of the kill under the guise of an academic exercise.

As Kimberly learned, there had been a couple of male-female sexual-sadist killing teams, but in those cases, the female was completely subservient, more of a live-in victim than a live-in partner. Most psychopaths were loners with no genuine ability to relate to others and thus little need for any kind of relationship. In Miguel and Richie's case, experts theorized that the partnership was based on Miguel's interest in having an audience for his actions and Richie's complete willingness to do as he was told. Plus, Richie Millos genuinely feared his cousin. Most likely, Miguel fed off that, perhaps even found that element even more appealing than an extra pair of hands.

One criminologist had written that Richie represented Miguel's latent homosexual desires. When that criminologist had tried to interview Miguel again, the convicted murderer waited until he was locked in the visitor's room with his shackles removed, then dove at the researcher over the table and tried to strangle the man with his bare hands. Miguel had to be forcibly dragged out of the room by four prison guards. Apparently, Miguel didn't care to be labeled a latent homosexual.

One thing was clear: Miguel Sanchez was not a nice man. Kimberly had found a photo of him on-line. He had dark, wild hair only Charles Manson would love. His eyes were deeply sunk into his forehead, his cheekbones craggy. Tattoos riddled his shoulders, and according to one report, he continued to add to his body art while incarcerated with the aid of a needle and a ballpoint pen. He claimed to be a walking monument to his victims. Kimberly had stared at his photo three times before she realized what the elaborately scrolled design on his shoulder said. Then she had gone cold.

Amanda.

He had the name Amanda permanently etched into his body. Kimberly had to work on easing her heart rate again. She knew Miguel Sanchez's Amanda. A long time ago, she and Mandy had listened to the tape. One more link, however. One more link between a stone-cold psychopath and Kimberly's rapidly disintegrating family.

The squeaking was growing closer. Fuck, she couldn't think.

She got out of her chair, scowling at the door and the noise that was now right behind it. She didn't need this kind of distraction. She had a job to do. And as long as she kept focused, kept determined, she felt like her old self again. Capable, strong, self-possessed.

Funny how Mandy's death had sent her drifting, filled with too many conflicting emotions of rage and grief and fear. And ironic how her mother's murder had anchored her again, taking all of those same emotions and giving them a purpose. She was going to find this bastard. And she didn't care what Rainie said. She was going to kill him. Frankly, if he was anything like Miguel Sanchez, she wasn't going to feel bad about it either.

Darwinism, she thought. *Survival of the fittest. You take on me and my family, you'd better be prepared for the consequences. Because I've been training for this day since I was twelve, you son of a bitch. I won't go down easy.*

A knock sounded on the door. Standing just three feet away in the kitchenette, Kimberly froze. And that quickly, her confidence left her. The color leeched from her face, her heart ratcheted up to one hundred and fifty beats per minute, and sweat burst from her pores.

'Room service,' a high squeaky male voice called out.

Room service. Oldest trick in the book. Kimberly ran into the bedroom. She fumbled through her bag, pulled out her stainless steel Glock, and sprinted back to the living area where she leveled her semiautomatic at the cheap wooden door.

'You got the wrong room, buddy,' she yelled. 'Back away from my door!'

There was a pause. Her hands were trembling so badly, she couldn't sight her gun. She was thinking: *Wednesday, my mom. Thursday, my grandpa. Friday, we're all on the run, and today? Not me! I won't go down easy!*

'Uh, I got an order here for your room—'

'*Get the fuck away from my door!*'

'Okey dokey. I'll be going now. You want your, uh, champagne and strawberries, you can come downstairs yourself, ma'am. Sheesh.'

Kimberly heard squeaking again. Then a moment later, the same high-pitched voice muttering, 'Gotta be a fucking full moon tonight or something. Sheesh.'

She slowly lowered her gun. Her body was still shaking. Sweat had plastered her T-shirt to her skin. Her heart hammered fast, as if she'd been running a marathon.

She took a deep breath. Then another. Then another.

And then, still not feeling good about things, she got down on her hands and knees and peered beneath the door. No dark shadow of feet standing outside her door. She collapsed into a sitting position on the carpet, her Glock cradled in her lap.

'Oh yeah,' she murmured darkly in the empty room, 'I'm doing just fine.'

* * *

'I'm thinking, no sickening-sweet pet names. Phrases that have been used on nighttime soaps do not belong in the home. Plus, if it's been used on a Hallmark card, I don't really think it applies to me. I'm not a Hallmark sort of gal. Though, for the record, I could probably learn to like flowers now and then. Pink roses. Or that champagne color. Yeah, I'm pretty sure I would like that. Of course, that raises the whole issue of chocolates and other special-delivery sweets. I'm going to say yes to the chocolates, no on the heart-shaped box. Things that involve red velvet also do not belong in the home. What do you think?'

Rainie was sprawled next to Quincy in the deep-pile comfort of her bed. They hadn't bothered getting dressed yet. It was a little after twelve, the sun was high in the sky and at any minute, her phone was bound to ring. Screw it.

Her head was on his shoulder and she was doodling little designs on his chest with her index finger. She liked the feel of his chest hairs, crisp but silky. She liked the way he smelled, aftershave mixed with sex. She liked the way he looked, his broad, well-toned chest like a vast plane beneath her hand. She was thinking she'd soon be ready for more talk of Olympic-medal events.

'Green-light flowers and square boxes of chocolates,' Quincy dutifully repeated. 'Red-light sickening-sweet pet names.' His hand was stroking her hair; he was obviously in no rush to get up either. He tilted his head down to see her better. 'For the sake of argument, what qualifies as a sickening-sweet pet name? I'd hate to think I was being cute and adorable, only to wind up dead.'

'Sweetheart, cupcake, sugar pie, honey bunch,' Rainie rattled off. 'Sweetie pie, cutie pie . . . You know, the kind of names that when other people use them, you want to give them a whopping dose of insulin . . . or a smack on the head.'

'No terms of endearment that owe their origin to the glucose family?'

'That's my stance. You don't call me sweet cheeks and I won't call you stud muffin.'

'I don't know,' Quincy said mildly. 'I kind of like stud muffin . . .'

She hit him on the chest. He pretended to be mortally wounded. She was just leaning over to kiss him back to life when the phone rang. She groaned.

'Carl Mitz,' Quincy murmured.

'Gymnastics!' she countered.

'Later, I'm afraid.'

'Spoilsport.' Rainie reached over and grabbed the cordless phone off her nightstand. 'Hello,' she declared grumpily.

'Lorraine Conner. How nice to speak with you.'

Rainie frowned. She didn't recognize the voice. Not at all. 'Who is this?'

'You know who this is. I want to speak with Pierce.'

Rainie looked questioningly at Quincy. If the caller wanted him, that ruled out Carl Mitz or her long-lost father. But hardly anyone called Quincy Pierce. So who . . .

Shit. She bolted upright, covers falling away as her heart began to thud furiously. She knew who this was. 'How the hell did you get this number?'

'Directory assistance, of course. Hand the phone to Pierce.'

'Fuck you, asshole. I'm not doing anything you want.'

'How marvelously childish. Hand the phone to Pierce.'

'Hey, you call my number, you get to speak with *me*. So if you have something to say, I suggest you start talking or

I'm hanging up.' Her words ended in a screech; Quincy had grabbed the phone out of her hands. She was ready to battle him for it, but then she saw the steely look in his eyes.

He put the receiver to his ear. 'Hello,' he said evenly. 'Who is this?'

'Pierce Quincy, of course. Would you like to see my driver's license? Or perhaps a sample of my handwriting?'

'Delusional disorder, subtype grandiose,' Quincy said.

The man laughed. 'As if to be Pierce Quincy is such a grand thing. Your daughter is dead, your wife is dead, and your father is no place to be found. You don't seem so powerful to me.'

'I don't have a wife,' Quincy said.

'Ex-wife then,' the man granted graciously. 'Still demoting her even after she's gone. You are a cold fish.'

'What do you want?' Quincy shifted the phone to his other ear. He caught Rainie's eye and made a circular motion with his hand. She nodded immediately, and slid off the bed naked in search of a tape recorder.

'It's not what I want, Pierce, it's *who* I want. But all in good time. Would you like to speak with your father?'

'We both know he's dead.'

'You don't know that. You're assuming he's dead so you won't feel guilty. I understand he raised you all by himself, served as both mother and father. And yet how quickly you let him go. "My father has been checked out of his nursing home? Goodness gracious, let me run away and hide!" I expected more from you.'

'I doubt it.'

Rainie arrived with the tape recorder. Quincy held the phone out for better audio as she fumbled with the buttons, then began to tape.

'He's alive,' the man said. 'Well hidden from federal minions and quite querulous, but very much alive.'

Quincy didn't answer.

'Maybe we can arrange a swap. You can exchange your daughter for your father. She's younger, but in his current state he's more of a child.'

Quincy didn't say anything.

'Or maybe we should bring the lovely Lorraine into the mix. You can swap your lover for your father. Sure she has a nice ass, but we both know you don't keep women around for long. Does she moan for you, Pierce? Your wife moaned for me. So did your daughter.'

'How is the weather in Texas?' Quincy asked. Rainie looked at him in confusion. Then she remembered. Mickie Millos lived in Texas. Quincy was fishing.

'Texas? You aren't on the right track.'

'And what track would that be? The one where I ruined your career, destroyed your life? Interesting, that I could have such an impact on your life and not remember you at all. Guess it was all in a day's work. I have met so many incompetent criminals over the years.' Quincy's voice was light, goading.

In contrast, the man's voice gained an ugly edge. 'Don't fuck with me, Pierce. There are plenty of people in your life left to kill, and I can make it better for them, or worse.'

Quincy feigned a yawn. 'Now you're boring me.'

'Will I be boring when I touch your daughter? Will I be boring when I rip off her shirt and run my hands over her tomboy breasts? I'm much closer than you know.'

'You won't touch my daughter.'

'Going to protect her, proud papa?'

'I won't have to. Get within four feet, and she'll kick your balls into your throat.'

The man laughed. 'Funny,' he said. 'That's not what Bethie or Mandy did.'

For the first time, Quincy's grip tightened on the phone.

'Pierce,' the man said, 'intermission is over. If you won't go back home for your father, I'll just have to find somebody else to kill. You have one hour to get on a plane headed to Virginia.'

'I don't think so.'

'Then I will make her death very long and excruciatingly painful.'

'You can't touch my daughter—'

'It's not Kimberly I'm going to punish. Get to the airport, Supervisory Special Agent Quincy – you don't have many friends left. Oh, and please tell Ms. Conner that next time she hires a private investigator, she should find one who doesn't like chocolate.'

The line clicked off. Quincy stared at Rainie. There was a fierceness in his expression she had seen only once before – the night Henry Hawkins had tried to kill her.

'He's coming after you,' he said.

She shook her head. 'No, not me. Think about his words, Quincy. He wants you home. He's obviously gotten to de Beers. That means East Coast. He's still somewhere around Virginia.'

'But who . . .'

They got it together. 'Glenda!' Quincy swore.

'We have one hour.'

Quincy picked up the phone and dialed furiously.

33

Quincy's House, Virginia

'Get out of the house.'

'Pierce? I don't think—'

'Glenda, listen to me. The UNSUB just called. He wants me back on the East Coast and he's prepared to kill someone to force me to return. He's targeting you. I'm almost sure of it. Now, please get out of the house.'

Glenda's grip tightened on the phone. Alone in the middle of Quincy's office, she stared at the incriminating box of stationery – one sheet already sent to the document section of the science-crime lab – and she wished . . . She wished she had never taken this goddamn case.

'I don't think I should be speaking with you,' she said quietly.

'Is Montgomery there?'

'That's none of your business.'

'You're alone, aren't you? Dammit, how did he even qualify to be an agent? Glenda, the UNSUB knows where I live. He understands Bureau protocol, so he knows someone is manning my residence. Hell, for all I know, he also has

342

knowledge of the layout of my home, the best way of scaling the fence, accessing the grounds . . . You cannot under-estimate him.'

'Your phantom stalker,' she said.

Quincy fell silent. *Good*, she thought. *Be surprised. I have lived in this house for three days, listening to nothing but hate, and now I have to wonder if it hasn't all been some horrible, twisted game. Are you the hunter or the hunted, Pierce? I don't know anymore, and I'm tired!*

'What's wrong, Glenda?' Quincy asked. He sounded wary now, uncertain. She took pride in that.

'There's no such thing as a perfect crime, Quincy. You should know that better than most. For every little detail that is considered, there is always one or two more that slips through the cracks.'

'The police report came back from Philadelphia, didn't it? They know the note found at the scene matches my handwriting.'

'*What?*'

He fell silent again. She could practically feel his confusion across the phone line. It was nothing, however, compared to the sudden acceleration of her heart. She'd still maintained some small residue of doubt about Quincy's guilt. But now . . . That note, that dreadful note stuffed in Elizabeth Quincy's abdominal cavity, soaked in blood. He had written it. Pierce Quincy, a fellow agent, the best of the best. *Oh sweet mother of God . . .*

'You're a monster,' she breathed. 'Montgomery is right. You're a monster!'

'Glenda—'

She snapped her cell phone shut. She let it fall to the floor where she eyed it as if it were a coiled snake. She had goose bumps running up and down her arms. She had gone nights without sleep and she could now feel it all crashing down on her. She was cold, she was horrified. She had believed in this man. Oh God, she was never going to feel clean.

On the floor, her flip phone started to chime.

She didn't answer it. She wasn't going to let him manipulate her like this. The musical ringing went on for ten seconds, then voice messaging took over and the noise stopped. She had just started to relax, when it started again. And went on and on and on.

Dammit! She snatched back up the phone.

'I don't believe you!' she cried. 'You're making this up. And I am armed, Quincy, so you just stay the fuck away from me.'

'I am in Oregon. I can't hurt you,' he said.

'I don't know that!'

'Listen to me. We don't have much time, Glenda. I did not write that note. I know it looks bad, but I did not write that note.'

'Of course you did. You just said so.'

'*I know my own handwriting!* For God's sake, I recognized it the minute the ME's assistant brought the note into the room. But I did not write it, Glenda. This man, he got copies of my handwriting, he studied it, he did one hell of a superb impression. I don't know exactly how he did it. But *he* did it, not me.'

'Listen to yourself, Quincy. "It's my writing, but I didn't do it." Things are unraveling and you're not even lying very well anymore.'

'Glenda, *why* would I use my own script? I am a professional. I've taken classes on how to analyze handwriting. If I'm so smart, why would I be so dumb?'

'Maybe you're not dumb. Maybe you're arrogant. Besides, it's not just that note. We've also traced the original newsletter ad. We know it was sent on your stationery.'

'The bottom drawer,' he murmured. 'Christ, it's been years . . .' And then, 'Dammit, then he's definitely been in my house. Glenda, I beg you, get out of there.'

'I'm not listening to you.' Her voice was rising hysterically. In spite of herself, her gaze had gone to the uncovered windows. She felt suddenly vulnerable, a lone woman standing in a fishbowl. What if Quincy was already out there? Or the phantom stalker or maybe more rattlesnakes? God knows. She was tired. She was so tired. Where was Montgomery? She was not herself.

'Think, Glenda,' Quincy was saying relentlessly. 'You are a bright agent, you are a brilliant agent. And so am I. So why would I create such an elaborate stalking story, then use my own stationery for the newsletter ads? Why would I stage such a brutal murder in Philadelphia, then use my own handwriting? Why would I even commit these crimes? What would I have to gain?'

'Showing off. Cracking up. Maybe the job has finally done you in.'

'I haven't been out in the field in years.'

'Maybe you resent that.'

'So I butchered my own family? Fifteen minutes, Glenda. Please get out of the house. I'm begging you, *get out of the house.*'

'I can't,' she whispered.

'Why not?'

'I . . . I think someone may already be out there.'

'Oh Glenda . . .' She heard him take a shaky breath. He was murmuring to someone at the other end of the line. She caught the distinct tones of a female reply. Lorraine Conner. So they were in this together.

For the first time, Glenda frowned. They were in this together? What together? Murdering his family? Threatening a fellow agent? It didn't make much sense. And who sent an ad on hundred-dollar stationery anyway? A criminal mastermind who was provocatively stupid?

Holding the phone, Glenda moved out of the office, into the kitchen where she had a better view of the entrance and was framed by fewer windows. She unsnapped her shoulder holster. Then she reached down to her ankle and checked on her backup piece. Quincy returned to the line.

'You're going to be okay, Glenda,' he said firmly. 'I'm going to get you through this. First, I'm going to play a tape for you. Rainie made this recording just twenty minutes ago, sitting beside me in her loft in Portland. This is the UNSUB, Glenda. If you still don't believe me, hear for yourself what he has to say.'

Glenda heard a click. Then a fuzzy recording filled her ear. She needed about three minutes of the conversation. Somewhere about the time the man said, *Then I will make her death very long and excruciatingly painful*, she had had enough. Quincy was right, the evidence against him was too perfect and they had still uncovered no good reason for a highly respected federal agent to suddenly begin butchering his entire family.

Which meant the stalker did exist. A man who thought nothing of killing an agent's young daughter. A man who had viciously slaughtered the agent's ex-wife. And a man who had topped it all off by kidnapping, and probably murdering, the agent's sick, Alzheimer's-stricken father. Oh God . . .

'All right,' she said quietly. 'What do we do?'

'Do you have a car outside?'

'Not on the driveway. Down the street.'

'How far away?'

'Three to four minutes.'

'You can do this, Glenda. Think of it as a training exercise in Hogan's Alley. Take out your Smith & Wesson, undo the safety, and run like hell. You'll make it.'

'No.'

'Glenda—'

'There's no cover, Quincy. He could be out there anywhere, behind a neighbor's bush, up a tree. Your property offers nothing. The minute I'm out of the front door, he has me. No, I'm safer in here than out there.'

'Glenda, he *knows* the house. Inside you're trapped. Outside you have options.'

'Outside he can pick me off. Inside I can at least see him coming. Besides, we changed the security system of your home. He has to have a fingerprint and an access code now. That will hold him up, buy me some time.' Her eyes were on the kitchen window. She had her 10mm out. Working on the safety. Her hands were sweating badly. She fumbled the piece.

'He'll have a plan for the security system. He's had a plan for everything thus far.'

Glenda finally got her pistol secure in her grasp. She forced herself to take a deep breath and steady her nerves. 'Remember his MO,' she told Quincy briskly. 'The UNSUB relies on his gift for manipulating people. Well, the computerized system could care less. It has no deep dark secrets to exploit and it will not accept a severed digit.'

'Call for backup.' Quincy remained urgent.

'Fair enough.'

'How long before they arrive?'

'Five to ten minutes. No more.'

'If he gets there first . . . Remember his strengths. Do not let him talk. Shoot first, question later. Promise me, Glenda.'

Glenda nodded into the phone as she reached for the radio to summon her fellow agents. Just as she was about to click it on, however, Quincy's home line began to ring. Another admirer, she thought. Just what her nerves needed at a time like this. But then the machine picked up, and the voice was not a stranger's. It was Albert Montgomery and he did not sound like himself at all.

'Jesus Christ, Glenda,' he wailed. 'Pick up the goddamn phone. I've been trying to reach you on your cellular . . . I was wrong. Not a phantom stalker. He's here, he's here, he's here. Oh God, he has a knife!'

She heard Quincy screaming something in her ear. She wasn't paying attention anymore. She dropped her flip phone on the marble countertop. She reached over with her right hand. She grabbed Quincy's white cordless phone and . . .

The pain was instantaneous and intense. Deep, searing heat as if someone had branded her hand with a red-hot iron. She cried out. She dropped the cordless phone on the floor. And in the next moment, she heard the *beep beep* of someone disarming the security system, followed by a click as the front door swung open.

She looked over at her 10mm, within easy reach. She looked down at her right hand, seared by some sort of acid, now bubbling up with blisters, her fingers impossible to move.

'I'm sorry, Quincy,' she murmured.

Then she watched Special Agent Albert Montgomery walk into the kitchen holding his cell phone in one hand and his 10mm in the other.

'Surprise, baby! It's me!'

The last sound Quincy heard was gunfire. And then nothing but his own desperate voice, 'Glenda, Glenda! Talk to me. *Talk to me!*'

Quincy hung his head. His breath came in ragged gasps. The disconnected phone had fallen from his fingertips and now lay on Rainie's bed. *He must stay in control*, he thought. Now more than ever . . . Rainie's arms were around his shoulder. She had not spoken, but there were tears on her cheeks.

'I should call Everett,' he murmured. 'Get agents over there. Maybe . . .'

Rainie didn't say anything. Like him, she didn't really believe that Glenda was still alive.

Quincy took a deep breath, and reached for the phone just as it began to ring. He picked it up slowly, figuring he knew who this would be, and already steeling himself for the man's mocking tone.

'I shot Special Agent Montgomery,' Glenda Rodman said without preamble.

'Glenda? Oh thank God!'

'He put . . . something on the phone. Last time he was here, I suppose. He thought it would disable me. Stupid bastard. He should have read my file more closely. My father was a cop – he believed strongly in being able to shoot ambidextrously. You never know which hand will wind up free under fire.'

'You're okay?'

'Albert's shooting skills are equal to the rest of him,' she said dryly. 'My right hand needs immediate medical attention. Other than that, I'll live.'

'And Special Agent Montgomery?'

'I aimed to kill.'

'Glenda—'

'I disabled him with shots to his kneecap and his right hand instead; I know you need answers. Quincy, he says he'll only speak with you. He says he knows where your father is. You need to get back here ASAP. At least, before I change my mind and start shooting again.'

'Glenda,' he tried again.

'You're welcome,' she said. And hung up the phone.

34

Portland, Oregon

Back at the hotel, Quincy swiftly threw his clothes into his travel bag. Rainie was in the living room, talking to Virginia state trooper Vince Amity on the phone. Kimberly, on the other hand, stood watching him from the doorway, her shoulders hunched as if preparing for a blow. She'd had a run-in with room service while he and Rainie had been gone. Apparently, an overworked bellhop had transposed two numbers and tried to deliver someone else's anniversary surprise to Kimberly's room. The bellhop had hoped for a good tip. Instead, he'd encountered a screaming woman who – fortunately unknown to him – was brandishing a loaded semiautomatic.

The hotel had explained the mixup to Quincy upon his return. He'd relayed the story to Kimberly. She'd smiled in an attempt to find humor in the situation, but Quincy could tell the incident had left her shaken, and news of Glenda's attack had only further frayed her nerves.

'So Special Agent Rodman is all right?' Kimberly asked for the third time. Her voice had taken on the anxious edge he remembered from two days ago. Nothing he'd offered in the last ten minutes seemed to change it.

'Special Agent Rodman is an extremely capable woman,' Quincy said, trying a new tack as he rounded up his socks. 'She took her training seriously, and when the moment came, that training paid off. She not only met the threat, but she took out Montgomery with two clean shots.'

'She must be an excellent marksman.'

'I believe she's won a few medals.'

'I'm a good shot,' Kimberly said. 'I practice three times a week.'

Quincy raised his head and met his daughter's eyes. He said firmly, 'You're going to be fine, Kimberly. Rainie is staying here with you, and you're a capable young woman. You'll be safe.'

Kimberly's gaze fell to the floor. She was gnawing on her bottom lip; he couldn't tell if he had reached her or not.

'What about Special Agent Rodman's hand?' she asked.

'I don't know. Montgomery confessed that he sprayed the phone with Teflon to protect the plastic, then applied hydrofluoric acid, which is an extremely corrosive chemical. The acid reacted with the moisture of Glenda's hand, burning her fingers and part of her palm. I'm not sure of the long-term prognosis.'

'It's her right hand. She could be permanently damaged, or scarred.'

'She's receiving the best medical attention you can get. I'm sure she'll recover.'

'But you don't know—'

'Kimberly!' he said sharply. 'Albert was going to kill her. You know that, I know that, she knows that. Instead, she controlled her fear and pain and disabled her attacker. This is a triumph. This is a lesson in the value of hard work and proper training. Don't give this victory away. Don't demoralize yourself like that.'

'I don't want you to go,' she whispered.

Quincy closed his eyes. The irritation drained from his body. He felt simply rotten instead. 'I know,' he said softly.

'It's just . . . So you have Albert in custody. So he went after Glenda. There's still something wrong . . . something else going on. If Albert looks the way you say he does, I can't see him getting anywhere near Mom. Plus, there's the matter of brainpower. If Albert was this clever, he wouldn't have had problems at the Bureau in the first place. Don't you think?'

'He fits the description of the man in Mandy's AA group,' Quincy said, though he knew that wasn't really an answer.

His daughter knew it too. She gazed at him miserably, obviously needing more than he was giving. He wished he knew what to do at times like this. He wished he knew how to make his daughter feel safe and confident and strong. And then he really did miss his ex-wife, because Bethie had always been better at these moments than him. He held a doctorate in psychology. Bethie, on the other hand, had been a mom.

'I love you, Kimberly,' he said.

'Dad—'

'I don't want to go. Maybe sometimes it seems that I do. Maybe we both mistake my sense of duty for desire. But it is duty. Montgomery has information about Grandpa that I need to know and he claims he'll only give that information to me. It's been forty-eight hours, Kimberly. If we don't find Grandpa soon . . .' His voice trailed off. His daughter had taken law enforcement classes; he knew that she understood as well as he did how the probability of finding Abraham alive decreased with each passing hour. The UNSUB had claimed that Abraham was tucked away safely. Quincy, however, had subsequently learned a new detail. He'd called Everett after he'd gotten off the phone with Glenda. The red Audi TT convertible had been found by Virginia state police at four that morning. It had been left parked in the exact spot where Mandy had hit a telephone pole fourteen months before. Forensic technicians found traces of urine in the passenger's seat, probably from Abraham. Extra personnel had now been brought in to scour the surrounding woods. They were also using dogs – cadaver dogs.

'There's a good chance that Montgomery planned this whole thing,' Quincy said now, his voice purposefully firm. 'He hated me because of the Sanchez case, he plotted revenge. If that's the case, then it's over, Kimberly. You're safe now. Everything will be all right.'

'Then why won't you let us go with you?' she protested.

'Because I'm not one hundred percent certain, and I'm not going to risk you without being completely sure! Until we know everything, you're safer here than there.'

'But what about you? You're returning to the East Coast, where some man knows all about you.'

'I've also had a lot of training.'

'Mom is *gone!*' Kimberly exclaimed. 'Mandy is gone! Grandpa is gone! And now you're leaving, and, and, and . . .'

Quincy finally got it. His daughter wasn't seeking reassurance for her own safety. She was terrified for *him*. She'd already lost most of her family and now her good old dad was once again walking out the front door into the face of danger. Christ, sometimes he was an idiot about the most basic things.

Quincy came around the bed. He took Kimberly into his arms, and for once, his stubborn, independent daughter did not protest. 'I'm not going to let anything happen to me,' he whispered against the top of her head. 'I promise you that.'

'You can't make that promise.'

'I am Quantico's best of the best. I can, too.'

'Dad—'

'Listen to me, Kimberly.' He pulled back enough to look her in the eye, to let her see how serious he was. 'I'm a good agent. I take my training seriously; I do not underestimate my opponent. This is a game, but it's a game where the stakes are life or death. I never forget that. And because I never forget that, I'm better at this than most.'

Her blue eyes were still watery. He could tell she was on the brink of crying, but she sniffed back her tears. 'You won't let down your guard?' she pressed. 'You won't be fooled by anything this Albert guy says?'

'I am going to keep myself safe so I can come home to my daughter. And you are going to take good care of yourself and Rainie, so I can come home to you.'

'We'll look out for each other.'

'Kimberly, thank you.'

From the doorway, Rainie cleared her throat. Quincy looked up, and knew instantly from the expression on her face that she had bad news. He took a deep breath. Then slowly, reluctantly, he let his daughter go.

'I have an update from Virginia,' Rainie said as Quincy and Kimberly turned to face her.

Quincy nodded. 'Go ahead.'

'Phil de Beers and Mary Olsen are dead. The police found their bodies an hour ago in a car just down the road from Mary's house. The car was registered in Phil's name. We'll need the medical examiner's report to be sure, but the police are guessing poison. The bodies have white foam around the mouth. There's a strong smell of almonds . . .'

'Cyanide,' Quincy deduced.

She nodded grimly. 'They found a box of chocolates in the car. Two are gone. The rest have that same bitter almond scent. According to the butler, Mary accepted a delivery shortly before leaving the house. He found the empty shipping box in the foyer, no return address.'

'So someone sent Mary a box of poisoned chocolates and she took them to de Beers? But why did she eat one, too? That doesn't make any sense.' Kimberly looked baffled.

'For the sake of argument,' Quincy said slowly, 'let's assume Montgomery spotted de Beers conducting surveillance on Mary. Mary probably knew Montgomery through Amanda, so now Albert has two loose ends. An accomplice who can connect him with the murders and a private investigator watching the accomplice. He doesn't have a lot of time, but he must do something.'

'He poisons the box of chocolates,' Rainie murmured, 'sends them to Mary, and makes up some story that convinces her to share them with de Beers. Not bad really. Eliminates two people without burning a lot of time or resources. You're right, Quincy, this guy is an efficiency freak.'

'Death by UPS,' Kimberly said. Her shoulders sagged.

Rainie shot her a look. 'Hey, Kimberly, if Montgomery is so good, why is he the one in FBI custody? He might be efficient, but we're the ones who won the war.'

'Tell that to Phil de Beers.'

Rainie's lips tightened. She turned on her heels and marched back into the living room. A second later, Quincy heard the sound of wood snapping. She had finally found his stash of #2 pencils in his computer case. From here on out, he would apparently be taking notes in pen.

'I guess I shouldn't have said that,' Kimberly murmured after a moment.

'No, you shouldn't have.'

'I'm sorry—'

'I'm not the one to whom you should be apologizing.' His voice came out too harsh. Kimberly instantly looked stricken. Quincy repressed a sigh. He wasn't used to Kimberly being this sensitive. Then again, she had never lived under the threat of immediate death before.

'Kimberly,' he said more patiently, 'Rainie hired Phil de Beers. She met with the man. She gave him an important assignment, which means she trusted and liked him. She is not going to cry into her coffee right now because she knows the situation is still live and she can't afford that luxury. But don't think she doesn't have feelings. And don't lash out at her, just because you feel helpless.'

'I'm sorry. I'm just . . . I don't know myself anymore!' Kimberly's voice rose, the full force of her anxiety now flooding to the surface. She stepped away from him, rubbing her arms compulsively and shaking her head. 'I'm tense, I'm moody. One moment I feel strong and in control. I can meet this challenge, I can take this man! The next moment I'm shaking in my boots, drawing down on room service and mistrusting every noise I hear. I can't stand this level of uncertainty. I hate doubting myself, I hate worrying about what's going to happen next. I'm not supposed to fall apart like this, Dad. I'm supposed to be *strong!*'

'Are you having panic attacks again?' Quincy asked immediately. 'Do you feel as if you're being watched?'

She drew up short. 'No . . .' she said slowly. 'In fact, I haven't felt that prickly sensation since we came here.'

'Good.' Quincy started breathing again. 'You are strong, Kimberly,' he said evenly. 'You are doing remarkably well for everything you've been through.'

'Do you feel like you're falling apart?' she demanded. 'Are you swamped by anxiety, do you jump at shadows, are you tempted to open fire on room service waiters?'

'No, but I've been doing this kind of work for over fifteen years.'

'Dad, does it frighten you?'

'What?'

'To feel so comfortable in the face of so much death?'

He bent down and kissed her cheek. 'Yes, Kimberly. Sometimes it frightens me to death.' He moved back to his duffel bag. 'Help me pack, sweetheart. The only way out of this is to keep moving forward. So let's keep moving, one step at a time and then one step beyond that.'

Kimberly nodded. She uncrossed her arms. She took a deep breath and picked up one of his shirts. And she looked so determined, it made Quincy's heart ache all over again. He lowered his head so she could not see his eyes.

He had lied to his daughter. He didn't think Albert Montgomery had masterminded this elaborate plan. He didn't think it was safe to head back East. Instead, he was absolutely certain he was once again being manipulated, but he didn't know what else he could do. Damned if he did, damned if he didn't. Fifteen years of being the best of the best and now he was being played like a toy violin.

There had to be another option. There was always another option . . .

'I couldn't uncover anything interesting on Millos,'

Kimberly spoke up. 'He doesn't even have that much money in the bank. Most of the searches I did just kept bringing up Miguel Sanchez. The man has spawned even more case studies than Bundy.'

'His partnership was unusual,' Quincy said.

'Maybe not anymore,' Kimberly murmured.

He didn't pretend to misunderstand her. His bag was full. He zipped it up, then finally met his daughter's waiting gaze.

'Maybe you could do me a favor,' he said casually. 'You have a good memory. Perhaps you could make a list of everyone you knew in your childhood, friends of yours, friends of the family. You know, the people we knew when your mother and I were still married.'

Kimberly looked at him. He hadn't fooled her. After a moment, she nodded wordlessly.

'Hey Kimberly,' he called softly. 'Fuck ballet.'

Her gaze remained somber, but then finally, slowly, she smiled.

Minutes later, Rainie and Quincy rode the elevator down to the lobby to hail a cab for the airport. Kimberly had tactfully agreed to stay upstairs in the room, seeming to understand that they might want a moment alone. Quincy figured there was something profound he should say to Rainie. All he could think was no sickening-sweet pet names.

In the lobby, Rainie glanced at her watch. 'Two hours,' she said, 'not one.'

'And yet I'm heading home.'

'Intermission is over,' she agreed.

'Rainie—'

'I won't let anything happen to Kimberly,' she interjected quietly. 'You have my word.'

Lisa Gardner

He nodded. He had figured that Rainie also realized that Montgomery was a long shot for a lone gunman.

Say something. Do something. Learn from your mistakes. Quincy heard himself murmur weakly, 'Take care of yourself.'

'I'm not the one walking into the lion's den.' Rainie jerked her head toward a cab that had just appeared on the street. Quincy flagged it down, and before he was really ready, the driver was out of the car and taking his bag.

'I'll call you,' he said.

'At my loft, not here. Just to be safe.'

'Agreed.' The cab driver had the back door open. He looked at Quincy impatiently. Quincy, however, was still gazing at Rainie. His chest felt tight. He knew now what he needed to say, then realized he couldn't utter the words. They would make the moment too final. They would reveal too much of his fear.

Rainie seemed to understand. She leaned forward and before he could react, she kissed him quick and hard on the mouth.

'Hey Quince. See you soon.' She walked back into the hotel. A moment later, Quincy got into the cab.

'Airport,' he told the driver.

Then, alone in the backseat . . . 'Hey Rainie,' he whispered. 'I love you, too.'

At three P.M., Rainie finally heard back from Carl Mitz on her home answering machine. She listened to it from the hotel room as she called in to check messages. Kimberly sat at the table in the kitchenette, hunched over Quincy's laptop and rereading some report on Miguel Sanchez that was making her scowl. Rainie occupied the sofa in the adjoining living room, restless since Quincy's departure, feeling not at all like herself.

Mitz informed her answering machine that he'd just gotten her message on his cell phone. He would be available for the next few hours if she wanted to call back. Rainie hung up, then glanced at Kimberly.

'What would you think if I arranged a meeting with Ronald Dawson for tomorrow?' Rainie asked quietly.

Kimberly looked up from the computer. 'I think Special Agent Albert Montgomery is a putz,' she said.

'Me, too.'

'I think he couldn't have reached my mother with a ten-foot pole, which means while he might be an Indian, he's definitely not Chief.'

'Agreed.'

'And I think . . . I think if Ronald Dawson *is* the head honcho, well, if you invite him here, then he can't be there in Virginia.'

'My thoughts exactly.'

'Set up lunch,' Kimberly said firmly. 'Then call your sheriff friend and get out your gun.'

Rainie grinned. 'Girl,' she said, 'I like your style.'

Three-thirty P.M., Rainie reached Carl Mitz. Three-forty P.M., Quincy arrived at the Portland International Airport. Three forty-five P.M., Sheriff Luke Hayes received a phone call. He spoke for approximately fifteen minutes, then hung up the phone, told Cunningham he was leaving him in charge, and got into his car.

It wasn't perfect, but it was a plan.

35

'Here's what you need to know, Quincy.' Glenda snapped
open a manila file, stuck a pen behind her ear, then resumed
pacing the eight-foot length of the narrow conference room.
He watched her restless movements without commenting. It
was nearly 3 P.M. Sunday afternoon, almost twenty-four
hours since Montgomery's attack, and they were still denied
access to the disgruntled agent. First Montgomery claimed
he needed immediate medical attention. Given the state of
his kneecap and right hand, that was hard to dispute. The
trip to the emergency room had been followed by surgery to
repair the damage to his leg. The doctors had then said he
needed time to recover from the anesthesia. The anesthesia,
however, had been followed by large amounts of morphine
personally requested by Montgomery. He was in a significant
amount of pain, he claimed. He needed drugs, he needed
medical assistance, he needed rest.

He couldn't be properly interviewed while under the
influence of medication and they all knew it. Even if they
forced the issue, the first judge who heard the case would
toss his comments out of court.

Albert Montgomery had an aptitude after all. He could stall like nobody's business. And as each hour passed, they grew increasingly nervous. Something big was brewing. They could feel it.

'Stop fidgeting,' Glenda said.

He looked down to find himself methodically twisting the top button of his suit jacket, and instantly jerked his hand away. Glenda had met him with fresh clothes first thing this morning. As a general rule, wearing a nicely tailored suit made him feel polished, more in control. Not today. As hour grew into hour, he could've sworn the necktie was conspiring to strangle him.

He wondered how Rainie was doing. He wished it felt safe to call.

Glenda had returned her attention to the manila file. Her right hand was heavily bandaged. Late last night, she'd been treated for third-degree burns, then released. She couldn't move her fingers yet, and the doctors had warned her that the deep-searing acid might have caused permanent nerve damage. Time would tell and at this stage of the game, she didn't seem to want to talk about it.

'Albert first crossed paths with you fifteen years ago on the Sanchez case,' she said briskly. 'For the record, he'd already received a less-than-stellar review for his prior work, but it was his inept profile of Sanchez that officially torpedoed his career. He fought with the locals, pegged Sanchez as a lone gunman, then lost all credibility when you came aboard, identified the work as part of a killing team, and cracked the case. Albert's wife left him three weeks later, taking the two kids with her. Doesn't look like they were big fans of weekend visitation either.'

'He fits the profile,' he said hoarsely.

'The *circumstances* fit the profile,' Glenda said. 'Now let's look at the man. According to Albert's file, his IQ is a respectable one hundred thirty. The problem seems to be in execution. What do they call that these days? Why an idiot can build a successful business while a genius can't even find his socks?'

'EQ – emotional intelligence.' His voice was still rough.

'Emotional intelligence.' Glenda rolled her eyes. 'That's it. Albert has none. According to four different case reviews, he lacks focus, diligence, and basic organizational skills. In his twenty-year career at the Bureau, he's been written up six times. In each case, he's written a counter opinion stating that he's not incompetent after all, Supervisor So-and-So is simply out to get him.'

'Albert Montgomery, a walking advertisement for government downsizing.'

Glenda finally smiled. 'If you can get that made into a bumper sticker, I'll put it on his car.' Her expression sobered. 'Before we write off Albert completely,' she said, 'there is another factor to consider: While Albert may not be the sharpest tool in the shed, he has had plenty of free time on his hands. The estimated time of death for Elizabeth is ten-thirty P.M., Wednesday. Albert has no alibi for that time. Furthermore, he claims he spent Thursday and Friday in Philadelphia assisting the local detectives. Not true. I followed up with the detectives – they only saw him Friday morning. The rest of his time – basically Wednesday after-noon through Saturday morning – is an open question. Which means he could've visited Mary Olsen in Virginia or shown up at a Rhode Island nursing home, or flown to the West Coast for a Portland rendezvous. We simply don't know.'

'Travel records, plane tickets, hotel stays?'

'Checked with his credit cards – nothing. Checked with the local airport, nothing. Of course, there are roughly half a dozen airports within a three-hour drive of here. He could've left from any one of those, paying cash and/or using an assumed name.' Glenda smiled. 'Welcome to the convenience of the Eastern Corridor.'

'And even if he lacks focus, seventy-two hours provides plenty of time for misdeeds.' He grimaced, then caught himself and said more crisply, 'What about financial resources?'

'Albert is currently proud owner of nine hundred dollars in his bank account, so while he's had time to run around the country, financially I'm not sure how he could've pulled it off. On the other hand, if he has been traveling he's been paying in cash, so it's possible a second person has funded his venture with a briefcase of money. Without access to the second person's accounts, it's impossible to know.'

'Smart, but lazy. Poor, but possibly funded by vengeful deviants-R-us. Wonderful.'

'At the very least,' Glenda said, 'we know Albert has been actively involved in positioning you as a suspect. He called Everett Friday night, saying that he's convinced you killed your ex-wife. Then he made a point of visiting me first thing Saturday morning to let me know all his doubts about the Philadelphia crime scene.'

'Poisoning the well.'

'He was extremely persuasive,' Glenda said quietly. 'Everett was strongly considering calling you in. In fact, the only reason he didn't is that Albert's credibility is an issue. That wouldn't have mattered much longer, however. Albert got me wondering, which is what he intended. I found the stationery in your desk, messengered a sheet over to the lab ... That report should come back any time now, confirming the original ad was sent on your stationery. Once that report arrived, Everett would have no choice but to ask you to turn yourself in. Plus, Albert's accusation and the subsequent finding of your stationery made me seriously doubt you, which set everything up for act two.'

'You turning up dead.'

'In your home, protected by a state-of-the-art security system to which you have access. And, if that wasn't damning enough, the casings from the two shots Albert fired both bear your fingerprints. It would appear Albert helped himself to your ammo during one of his visits to the house.'

'What?' He was so startled, he momentarily forgot himself and exclaimed, 'Son of a bitch!'

Glenda frowned. 'You can't say that,' she said sternly.

'I'm sorry,' he said immediately.

'Stop fidgeting.'

The button was getting to him again. He forced his hand away, then caught his reflection in the room's long mirror and felt even more discouraged. He looked tense and uncomfortable, not at all like a ruthlessly competent federal agent. When word came down that he could finally interview Montgomery, he needed to walk into that room appearing 100 percent calm and in control. *You messed with us, Montgomery, now let me mess with you.*

He did not look calm and in control. He looked like someone who hadn't slept. He looked like someone who was deeply worried. He looked like someone who was, for the first time in his life, out of his league.

Albert Montgomery is nothing, he reminded himself firmly. Not even the real deal. Just a hired hand.

'He wants to talk,' Glenda said softly, as if reading his

mind. 'Don't forget, Albert is driven by his need to prove himself smarter than you. All you have to do is sound skeptical, and he'll hand you the keys to the city simply to prove he can. You hate him. You want to lean over the table and kill him. But other than that, Quincy, this interview shouldn't be too hard.'

He nodded, then glanced once more at his watch. Three thirty-two P.M. Twenty-four and a half hours since the attack on Glenda . . . Enough time for someone to cross the country. Enough time for someone to assume any manner of disguises. He wished once more he could talk to Rainie. Goddammit he had to leave this button alone!

The door opened. A young agent poked his head into the room. 'They're escorting Special Agent Montgomery to the interview room,' he reported.

Glenda nodded. The agent closed the door.

He took a deep breath. Then, he squared his shoulders and ran a hand down his jacket. 'Well,' he said, 'how do I look?'

Portland, Oregon

Twelve-eighteen P.M., Pacific standard time, Rainie and Kimberly were sitting side by side on the tiny sofa. From this vantage point, they could see into the adjoining bedroom on their right, or through the kitchenette area to the front door of the small suite on their left. They weren't doing anything. They weren't saying anything. They both simply stared at the phone.

'Why doesn't he call?' Kimberly asked.

'He must not have anything to say.'

'I thought something would've happened by now!'

Rainie glanced at the hotel-room door. 'So did I,' she murmured. 'So did I.'

Virginia

Sitting in the dimly lit interrogation room, Special Agent Albert Montgomery looked pretty good for a man who'd been shot. He wore light-blue surgical scrubs in lieu of his customary rumpled suit. His mussed hair was combed, his face freshly scrubbed and slightly less jaundiced. His right hand, heavily bandaged, rested on the table. His left leg, with its recently repaired kneecap, was encased in a cast and propped up on a chair. All in all, he appeared quite comfortable and at ease.

They eyed each other steadily for the first thirty seconds, neither one of them wanting to blink first.

'You look like crap,' Montgomery said.

'Thank you, I worked on it all night.' He walked up to the table, but didn't sit. From this vantage point, he could look down on Albert Montgomery. He could cross his arms over his chest and stare at this man as if he were the lowest form of life on earth. Albert simply smiled up at him. He'd also attended interrogation classes and knew the tricks.

'You sound like shit, too,' Albert said. 'Catch a cold on the airplane, Quince? Those things are nothing but petri dishes with wings. And you've had plenty of time to incubate. East Coast, West Coast, East Coast. Tell me, Quincy, how does it feel to be a puppet on a string?'

His hands clenched. He almost rose to the bait, then remembered what Glenda had said. He couldn't afford to kill Albert. Too much depended on what the man had to say.

He pulled out a chair and took a seat. 'You wanted me here: I'm here. Now speak.'

'Still arrogant, huh Quincy? I wonder how arrogant you're gonna be when the Philly detectives get through with you. Have you checked out their prison system yet? Maybe you can get a tour of your future home.'

'I'm not worried about the PPD.'

Albert stared at him. He stared back. Albert broke first. 'Son of a bitch,' he rasped.

'What's his name, Albert?'

Albert didn't answer right away. His gaze flickered to the clock on the wall. 'I don't know what you're talking about.'

'You acted alone?'

'Sure I did. You don't think that I hated you enough? You fucked my career, Quincy. You took my family, you ruined my life. Well hey, guess who has the last laugh. Where's your beautiful daughter, Quince? Where's the mother of your children? Where's your own dear old dad who desperately depended upon you? And I don't care what you say, when that report from Philly comes in, where's your precious fucking career? The bigger they are, the harder they fall.'

'You didn't do this.'

'Like hell.'

'You don't have the brains.'

Albert's face turned red. 'You think you're so smart, Quincy, consider this: Revenge. Fifteen long years of desperately wanting revenge. I could try to get the same case as you, set you up to fail, but that would be risky. I could try to get on the same case as you and shoot you in the back, but that would be no fun. So one night it comes to me—'

'Comes to him.'

'Comes to *me*. Why go for the direct attack? On the job is where you're in your element, where you do good. But you don't do everything right, Quincy. Hell no, you're not perfect. In fact, when it comes to being a husband, being a father, being a son, you pretty much suck. Once I realized this, I knew I had you.'

'You approached Mandy at her AA meeting.'

'I started looking up your father, your ex-wife and daughters. Didn't take me too long to figure out Mandy was the weak link. Shit, you must've done quite a head job on that kid, Quincy. She's a drunk, she's promiscuous. She's the perfect, insecure wreck. What do you have your PhD in again?'

He thinned his lips. Montgomery smiled, happy to feel he had the upper hand and as Glenda predicted, now expansively verbose.

'Yeah, I approached Mandy, pretended to be the son of an old acquaintance of your dad's, Ben Zikka, Jr. That's the nice thing about AA meetings. They build a sense of camaraderie, allow even perfect strangers to bond. Three meetings later, I had her.'

'You introduced her to him.'

'I *had* her.'

'Mandy had standards. You never so much as held her hand.'

Albert scowled, so he'd struck a nerve. But the disgruntled agent quickly scrambled to make up lost ground. 'Your daughter was a real friendly girl, Quince. Lunches, dinners, breakfasts. Didn't take any time at all to learn all about the rest of the family. And so many fascinating details about you, Pierce. Your habits, your home security system, your pathetic letters trying to keep in touch with your oldest daughter and build some kind of relationship.'

'Handwriting samples,' he deduced. 'Material to copy as the UNSUB prepared the note for Philadelphia. For that matter, stationery.'

Albert merely smiled. His gaze flicked once again to the wall clock.

'I was at Mandy's one night when you called,' Albert said. 'Got to hear one helluva stilted conversation, that was for sure. Really, Quince, you never did understand your own daughter. You ought to be ashamed of yourself.'

'He milked her for information,' he said softly. 'And then he killed her.'

'*I* came up with the idea. Get her drunk and behind the wheel of the car. It was a little risky. Maybe she didn't die right away. Maybe she regained consciousness. In the end, who cared? She was so damn drunk, she'd never remember what really happened, and we could always arrange a little accident in the hospital.'

'We?'

'I,' Albert said hastily. '*I* could arrange a little accident. I considered her murder a little test, Quince. Would you catch on? How good was Quantico's best of the best? But, true to form, when it comes to your family your instincts are a complete zero. Hell, you didn't even stay at her bedside. Just showed up and agreed to pull the plug. You helped kill your daughter, Quince. Not that I mind, but how do you feel about that?'

He ignored the question. 'You used her to approach Bethie.'

'Sure. Mandy told us . . . me! all about her mom. Favorite restaurants, favorite music, favorite food. It's not rocket science after that. And I do have my charm.'

'Bethie hates charm. He approached her as an organ recipient. He disguised himself as part of Mandy.'

Albert's eyes widened. He clearly hadn't known they knew that much. His gaze dashed to the clock. The time seemed to soothe him. He took a deep breath and eyed his interrogator more warily.

'When I'm brilliant, Quincy, I'm brilliant,' Albert tried.

Quincy merely shook his head. 'He had to wait over a year for Mandy to die. Did that make him anxious? That couldn't have been part of his plan.'

'Patience is a virtue,' Albert said.

'No, he got nervous. He needed my attention for the game to be interesting. So he used Mary Olsen to raise my suspicion.'

'I didn't want destroying you to be too easy,' Albert said. 'After fifteen years of planning, a guy's gotta have a little fun.'

'Mary Olsen is dead.'

That shocked him. Albert's gaze widened again and this time, he distinctly paled. 'Ummm, yeah.'

'How'd you kill her, Albert?'

'I . . . uh . . .'

'Gun, knife?'

'I shot her!'

'You poisoned her, asshole!' He felt a spark of anger, then checked himself, and said more sternly, 'She received a care package in the mail, chocolates from her lover, laced with cyanide. Horrible way to die.'

'Stupid bitch,' Albert muttered. He was definitely uncomfortable now. His fingers drummed on the table.

'How do you think he'll kill you?'

'Shut up!' His eyes shot to the clock.

'Poison? Or something more personal? You're a liability, Albert. A big, fat liability who, thanks to Glenda, is in no shape to run and hide.'

'Shut up, shut up, shut up!'

'Or did you forget that from the Sanchez case? Psychopaths can have partners, but partners are never equal. Miguel Sanchez lived. His partner, Richie, died on a prison floor with his balls crammed down his throat.'

Albert shot up from his chair. The movement jarred the supporting chair from beneath his injured leg and his cast fell heavily to the floor, making him yelp. Albert gripped the edge of the table to keep himself from falling, then glared at him with a face mottled with rage.

'You just fucking blew it!' he roared. 'I was gonna tell you where your father is. I was gonna take pity on the pathetic old man. But not now. Now he can rot where he is, tied up, starving, shitting in his own pants and getting bedsores from his piss. How do you like them apples, you arrogant prick!'

'My father is dead,' he said quietly, though he really didn't know that and his heart had begun to beat hard in his chest. This was the big risk. The life-or-death gamble. If he was wrong . . . *I'm sorry. Lord have mercy, because I cannot.* 'My father is dead,' he repeated more forcefully. 'We already found his body.'

'Impossible!'

'Would you like to go to the morgue to see him?'

'But he shouldn't have washed up for days, not after all the weights we put on him.' Albert suddenly heard his own words. He drew up short, then burst out, 'You tricked me. *Goddammit, you ice-cold son of a bitch*, you gave up on your own dad!'

373

'All in a day's work,' he murmured, though his throat felt tight now. He had an ache in his chest. Montgomery was a monster. The UNSUB was a monster. God, he was sick of all of this.

'It's over, Albert,' he said hoarsely. 'You're nothing but a liability now. You either talk to us, or you die for him.'

'You don't know shit!'

'Tell that to Mary Olsen.'

'Dammit, *I'm* the one in charge here.'

'Then prove it! Tell us something we don't know. Dazzle me!'

Albert froze. He suddenly smiled. He drew himself up straight. His gaze was on the wall clock again, but this time he made no attempt to hide it.

'Hey Quincy,' he said. 'Here's something interesting. Mandy wasn't the first target. Mandy didn't give up her family. Kimberly did.'

'What?'

'Oh, look at the time. Four-fourteen P.M. Why don't you call your daughter's hotel room, Quincy? Reach out and chastise Kimberly who's staying right where Everett told me she would be. Oh wait, I'm sorry, you won't be able to reach your daughter anymore. Four-fifteen P.M. Time's up, Agent. And your daughter is *dead*.'

36

Portland, Oregon

When the phone on the coffee table finally rang, Rainie nearly jumped out of her skin.

'Shit,' she said, then glanced hastily over at Kimberly.

'Shit,' Kimberly agreed. One P.M. Much later than they had thought and they were both now wound too tight. Rainie scooped up the phone before it could ring again.

'Hello.'

'Rainie? It's Luke. I got a problem.'

'What problem?' she said without thinking. Then her eyes widened and she motioned furiously to Kimberly. The girl got the hint and ran for her Glock.

'I'm not convinced this afternoon's meeting is the way to go, Rainie,' the man was saying. 'Maybe too risky. Can we meet ahead of time and talk about it?'

'My God, you're a perfect mimic,' Rainie murmured. 'If I didn't know any better . . .'

'What's that?' He sounded friendly and still so much like Luke Hayes that even knowing better, one part of her kept thinking it was him. But it wasn't. He was simply a person with a superb aptitude for mimicry and an extremely cruel sense of humor.

'How did you get this number?' she asked.

'I looked up the hotel.'

'I never told you where we were staying, *Luke*.'

'Sure you did. When we met with Mitz.'

'No, I didn't. And Luke knew better than to ask where I would be. Nice try, Super Freak. Wanna try again?'

The voice changed instantly, from an almost dead-on impression of Luke Hayes to the silky, smooth voice Rainie remembered from yesterday on the phone. 'Why Ms. Conner, you don't trust your own friends. How interesting. You know Bethie surprised me, too. She actually requested a background check on me. What do you suppose it means that all the women in Quincy's life are so suspicious?'

'That he values common sense. Where are you?'

'Now Rainie,' the caller chided. 'After all this time you wouldn't take this fun from me, would you? I truly deserve an A for effort.'

'You did deserve an A for effort. But Glenda Rodman lived, and I got you pegged.'

'Glenda Rodman was supposed to live.'

'What, you got a weakness for stern gray suits?'

He laughed. 'Come now, we both know Albert Montgomery is incompetent. You were a police officer, Rainie, you know the importance of understanding your fellow officers' strengths and weaknesses. I let Albert have Glenda. He really has such a deep-seated rage for anyone in law enforcement. I think it goes back to his father, a washed-up security guard. A little too strict, Albert's father. He produced a son who desperately needed to prove himself better than his own dad, and yet despised himself all the more for following in his father's footsteps. But that's neither here nor there. Albert's conflicted, Albert's incompetent. Therefore, it stood to reason, Albert would fail.'

'You bet against your own pawn,' Rainie said.

'Of course, although it hardly matters. If Albert succeeded, Pierce would stand accused of Glenda's shooting and would have to return to Virginia. If Albert failed, Pierce would need to question Albert and he'd have to return to Virginia for that. Either way, I win my game.'

'You lured Quincy back home so you could kill him.'

'No, I lured Quincy *away*, so I could kill *you*.'

'Oops, I'm sorry. But now that I've given it some thought, I don't feel like dying today.' Rainie made another motion to Kimberly. The girl nodded, and headed straight for each window, cautiously raising the sash and inspecting the outdoor fire escape. Kimberly looked both up and down. When she was done, she left the windows open as they had planned, nodded to Rainie that the fire escape was clear, and headed for the bedroom to do the same with those windows there.

'Are you afraid of hell, Rainie?' the man asked. Rainie could hear static now. He was definitely calling from a cell phone, which meant he could be anywhere. Riding up the elevator. Creeping down the hall. He thought keeping her talking would keep her distracted. He would learn soon enough that talking was his mistake.

'I'm not afraid of hell,' she answered. 'I pretty much figure that's what life is for.'

'Suffering here on earth? Come now, surely you have some notion of spiritual reward and punishment. Given everything you've done, that must make you wonder where you will spend your end of days.'

'You're one to talk. Your whole life is about punishing Quincy. To do that you've killed how many people? It *therefore stands to reason,*' she mocked him, 'that you're not one for religion, since your eternal punishment is gonna be one helluva long suntan session.'

Kimberly returned from the bedroom, shaking her head. So far, nothing on the fire escape. She started toward the door, but Rainie hastily waved her away. She'd read of people getting shot as they peered through the peephole. She didn't know if that could really happen, and she didn't want to find out. She gestured to the carpet. Kimberly got the hint and peered beneath the door instead. No sign of feet.

'Are you going to kill me, Rainie?' the man asked.

'I'm thinking about it.'

'Oh, thinking's not good enough. You have to commit to the act, Rainie. Visualize the goal, imagine yourself as the victor.'

'Wonderful, *Chicken Soup for the Serial Killer*. Just once, I'd like to be attacked by a mute.'

Kimberly was looking at Rainie for new instructions. The girl was clearly nervous. Despite her cavalier tone, Rainie was increasingly nervous, too. He was close. He craved intimacy with his victims. He liked to be there for the kill.

'Is Kimberly with you?' the man asked.

'Why? I'm not good enough for you?' Rainie was desperately looking around the room. The fire escape was clear, the hotel-room door clear. Where else could he come from? What had they missed?

And then she got it. Simultaneously, she and Kimberly both looked up. Jesus Christ, there was the tip of a drill bit coming through their ceiling. How the hell had he done that?

'Go!' Rainie yelled. Kimberly dashed for the front door just as the man said, 'Thank you, Rainie. I'd love to come in.'

Too late, she realized her mistake. If he'd been actively drilling, they would've heard it, so it had to have been sometime earlier. And peering beneath the door was never foolproof. All the person had to do was stand to one side. Rainie shot to her feet.

But Kimberly had already flung open the door and his gun was already pointed at her chest.

'Carl Mitz,' Rainie snarled.

And Kimberly whispered shakily, 'Oh my God – Dr Andrews.'

'I'll take your guns, please,' Dr Andrews announced, stepping into the hotel room and kicking the door shut behind him. He was dressed plainly today. Tan chinos, white-collared shirt. He looked like anyone walking down the street, except that in addition to a large black canvas bag slung over his left shoulder, he also carried a 9mm semi-automatic. The barrel was now four inches from Kimberly's heart. The girl couldn't take her eyes off of it. Her face had gone bone-white.

'You don't surrender your weapon,' Kimberly told him in an unnatural tone of voice. 'An officer should never surrender her weapon!'

'Hand over the gun, Kimberly,' Rainie told her tersely. 'For Christ's sake, this isn't the police academy's final exam and you're not bullet-proof!'

'One of us will live,' Kimberly insisted in that same tone of voice. 'He'll fire, but he can't kill us both.'

'Kimberly—'

'It's all my fault. Look at him. Don't you get it? *It's all my fault!*'

Dr Andrews smiled. He let the large canvas bag slide from his shoulder. It landed heavily on the floor. 'Very good, Kimberly. I was wondering when you were going to figure that out. After all, I did tell you that I wouldn't be a stranger.'

'But my anxiety attacks—'

'I tailed you. Just because I was willing to confess that you would know your own killer, didn't mean I wanted you to know that you'd already met him. Frankly, didn't it ever occur to you that you hardly saw me after your sister's funeral? You thought I was giving you time off to recover. But I was really buying myself time to destroy your family. We all have our priorities.' He gestured to his sharply pressed pants and white linen shirt. 'What do you think of my new look, by the way? The right wig, nicely tailored clothes, contact lenses . . . I wasn't always such a wreck as a professor, you know. I just thought you'd find me more comforting in tweed. So over the years, I became more and more dowdy, and you became more and more trusting. Interesting that for your mom and Mandy, I had to reverse the process. Now drop your gun and kick it over to me slowly.'

'*I thought you were my friend!* My mentor! I told you so much about my family. My father, my mother, my sister . . . And all along . . . All along . . .' Kimberly's body convulsed. She looked like she was going to be physically ill, yet she still didn't lower her Glock.

'Kimberly,' Rainie growled. She was sweating profusely, reluctant to let go of her own pistol and feeling the situation spinning dangerously out of control.

Andrews looked at her. Kimberly noticed the change in

his gaze and followed his eyes toward Rainie. No, Rainie started to yell, but she was too late. The instant Kimberly's focus left Andrews, he chopped his left hand down hard on her right forearm. The girl cried out, her gun slipping from nerveless fingers onto the floor. Rainie jerked up her own pistol, but found Andrews's weapon already trained at her body.

'I trust you'll be more reasonable,' he said, twisting Kimberly's arm behind her back and positioning her as a human shield.

Rainie nodded. Slowly, she lowered her gun to the carpet, her gaze falling on the black canvas bag. Why such a big bag? What would he bring with him?

'Now, kick the firearm toward me.'

Rainie complied, jabbing at her Glock .40 with her toe but not putting much effort into it. The heavy pistol stopped three feet away, under the glass coffee table. She made a show of shrugging helplessly, and waited to see if Andrews would push the issue. He frowned at her, but with his hands already full with one female, seemed content to let it go.

Rainie took a deep breath. *Remain calm*, she instructed herself, though her hands had begun to shake and her heart hammered in her chest. She'd kept him on the phone for a decent interval. Now if she and Kimberly could stall him just a minute or two more. The open windows. The unwatched fire escape with easy access to their room. Come on, cavalry . . .

What was in that bag?

Kimberly was weeping. Trapped against Andrews, her shoulders had slumped, her spine was bowed. She didn't seem to have much fight left.

'Perfect,' Andrews said. 'Now that everyone is feeling

more agreeable, we have a lot of work to do, ladies. Bombs to build, detonating devices to wire to telephones. Your father is going to call at precisely one-fifteen, Kimberly. I don't want to miss the opportunity for him to blow his own daughter and his lady love into tiny little bits.'

Oh shit, that was what was in that bag. Rainie closed her eyes. Andrews had brought all the ingredients for a home-made bomb. God knows it wouldn't take much to blow up a room this size and who cares if Andrews took out a fair portion of the hotel and other unsuspecting guests with him? It would be the ultimate triumph for him. Restraining Kimberly and Rainie. Then rigging a bomb to the telephone, so that the first ring triggered the blast. Quincy would not only lose the only family he had left, but when the first forensics report came in, he'd get to learn that he'd basically pulled the trigger. He'd killed his own daughter. He'd murdered Rainie. Oh, Quincy. Oh, poor, poor Quincy.

Rainie's eyes came open. She felt the breeze from the open window on her face, but she no longer knew if they had enough time to wait. She and Kimberly could not let Andrews build that bomb. Under no circumstances could they let Andrews take out half a hotel simply to spite Quincy.

Rainie looked at Kimberly, trying to catch the girl's gaze. They needed some kind of plan. Maybe Kimberly could get the professor talking, keep him focused on exchanging banalities with his former student so Rainie might ease her way toward her Glock. Three feet. That wasn't much. Right?

Kimberly, however, had her head down. Her slender figure appearing despondent. She was so young, after all. And under such terrible stress.

'I blamed my father,' Kimberly whispered, maybe to herself, maybe to Andrews. 'All along, I blamed my father, but in reality, I'm the one who betrayed my family.' Another thought seemed to strike her. Her head jolted up, her eyes suddenly growing wide. 'Oh my God, the Sanchez case. I've been going over it and over it, thinking there was more of a connection. Of course. Dr Andrews's research work at San Quentin.' She twisted toward Andrews, straining to see his face. 'You knew Sanchez! You're the connection! How could I be so blind? *Dammit!*'

'You failed to ask the right question in the very beginning,' Andrews said matter-of-factly, yanking Kimberly's arm more savagely to quell her movements. Rainie saw her chance. She eased forward an inch.

'If this was revenge, why now?' Andrews postulated for his former student. 'You could theorize that it was a felon who finally got out of prison, but I trust you already explored that option and found it to be a dead end. Then you could look at family of felons but again, why, after all this time? Interestingly enough, I think Quincy was finally getting on the right track, that it wasn't a past FBI case at all. So if it was from his pre-FBI days, then truly, why now?'

'Because you found me!' Kimberly spat at her captor.

'Because you fell into my fucking lap!' Andrews roared. 'Nearly twenty years after that man took my own daughters from me, and here you are! Beautiful, smart, poised to become everything a father could want for his girl. Why should he be so lucky? Why should he have everything that I deserved? Goddamn interfering *shrink!*'

His gaze suddenly shot back to Rainie. She froze, having made it two steps closer to her gun, and wanting that to be progress, while knowing it wasn't enough. Andrews was frowning at her. Had he figured out that she'd cut the distance to her discarded handgun? He studied her hard.

'You were one of Quincy's patients,' Rainie said quickly, seeking to distract him again, and holding perfectly still now that his attention was back upon her.

'I was not!' Andrews replied indignantly. 'My stupid ex-wife was. She went to him for help. She had all sorts of outlandish stories that I was an unfit father and that my children were terrified of me.'

'You abused your kids?' *Your turn, Kimberly*, she thought frantically. *I'll keep him talking, you think of something brilliant.*

'I did not, I did not, I did not. They were my girls! I loved them, I wanted what was best for them. It was their mother who could not appreciate their potential. She wanted to coddle them, give them time to play, give them time to grow. For God's sake, you do not get anywhere in life by playing!'

'Quincy testified against you in the custody hearing, didn't he?' Rainie persisted. 'His opinion helped sway the judge.' *Come on, Kimberly. We have to do something here. Fast.*

'He told the judge that I suffered from severe personality disorder! He told people that in his professional opinion I was manipulative, egocentric, and totally lacking in genuine ability to empathize. In short, I exhibited psychopathic tend-encies, I used my children as pawns to get what I wanted, and should they ever try to exert their own personalities, he couldn't vouch for their safety. And I never saw my children again. Do you realize what that does to someone? One day, I'm a highly respected family man. The next, I'm a name on a restraining order! If I so much as said boo, they would've taken my license from me. I would've been totally ruined!'

'You haven't done too badly since then.' Rainie shrugged dismissively, working on prolonging Andrews's diatribe.

'After I moved from California to New York and started all over again,' Andrews countered. 'All alone. With no one. Having nothing. You know, I might have had a second chance with Mary Olsen. She was pregnant with my child, maybe we could've been happy. But Pierce fucked even that up for me. Forced me to kill her before I ever knew.' Andrews's voice changed. 'Son of a bitch. Everything I ever wanted, he's taken from me. No more! I'm the one calling the shots, I'm the one in control. He wants an expert opinion? I'll give him an expert opinion. An expert in explosives. Goddammit, it's *time!*' He suddenly yanked on Kimberly's right arm. The girl had just raised her foot to stomp down on his instep. Now her foot fell to the floor harmlessly as he jerked her off balance. She grimaced and sagged despondently against him. Rainie grimaced along with her, her gaze going longingly to her Glock, so visible beneath the glass tabletop, and yet still so far out of reach.

They had to do something. No more time. Think, think. Come on, come on . . .

'Oh thank God! Luke!'

Rainie jerked her eyes to the space behind Andrews. It was a desperate act, a stupid gamble. Andrews twisted around, feeling the breeze for the first time and thinking he'd left himself vulnerable to a flank attack. No time for digging around under the coffee table for a gun. Rainie darted left and grabbed the best weapon she could find. One of the metal kitchen chairs.

'What the . . . ?'

'Kimberly, *now!*'

The girl dug her elbow into Andrews's exposed side and lashed out with her foot. Twisted and off balance, Andrews released his hold on her instinctively, struggling to bring his gun up and around. Rainie whipped the metal chair into Andrews's neck and shoulder. He howled as his gun and the chair both went flying and he realized too late he'd been duped by the oldest trick in the book.

'*Bitch!*' he roared.

'Kimberly,' Rainie cried out again. 'Gun, now!' They needed to find a weapon. Now, now, now.

Her Glock, under the coffee table. Rainie scurried over on all fours. Andrews saw her movement, and cut her off with a brutal kick to her chin. Her jaw cracked. She collapsed on her back, seeing stars. Dimly she was aware of Kimberly diving across the room reaching for Andrews's fallen gun. Andrews saw her. He had the chair. Raising it over his head, towering above Kimberly.

The chair slammed down. Kimberly made a heavy, wet sound Rainie had never heard before.

Andrews smiled in triumph. Then he flung down the chair and crouched for the 9mm Rainie could now see lying just inches from Kimberly's body. The girl had been so close . . .

One last chance. Rainie flipped onto her side, looking, looking, looking. The Glock, there against the brass leg of the table. Come on, Rainie. Dying is not preferable to living. Dying is not preferable to living! Damn, she'd be an optimist in the end. *Reach!*

The startling sound of a cartridge being ratcheted into a gun chamber. The sound of death.

'Bye-bye, Rainie,' Andrews said.

And Quincy said, 'Hey Andrews. Get your fucking hands off my daughter.'

Virginia

Albert Montgomery was still feeling calm and controlled fifteen minutes later when Quincy returned to the dimly lit interrogation room. Four thirty-one P.M. The agent probably had just confirmed his daughter's death. Albert wondered if he'd get to see him cry. He would like that.

His interrogator stopped in front of him.

'Howdy Albert,' the man said in a crystal-clear voice Albert had never heard before. 'It's my turn to tell you some things you don't know. One, I'm sure Kimberly is just fine. And two, I'm not Pierce Quincy.' The man reached up and ripped off the salt-and-pepper wig it had taken Glenda and an FBI makeup expert two hours to apply. Then he stepped out of special shoes with two-inch lifts. And he removed his navy blue suit jacket, custom-tailored to mirror Quincy's taller, broad-shouldered build. 'The name is Luke Hayes,' the stranger said calmly. 'And I'm a friend of Rainie's.'

Portland

Andrews's face paled. He snapped around toward the bedroom door, the gun in his right hand dipping down toward the carpet, but his left hand still on Kimberly's shoulder. 'Who? How? But you're in Virginia!'

Quincy stepped into the living room from the adjoining bedroom. He had his 10mm out, but down at his side. His gaze was locked on Andrews. He'd wasted fifteen minutes relentlessly searching the lobby for a man talking on a cell phone before he'd realized his mistake. The man was already upstairs. The man was already in his daughter's room. Plan B had always been the fire escape. Six floors up, rung over rung. Quincy should be tired. He should be exhausted.

He stood looking at this man who was heavily armed and crouched over his daughter, and he felt unbelievably calm. Time had slowed. All was manageable. The UNSUB finally had a face. And like so many killers before, the face wasn't even that impressive. He was just a man after all, average height, average weight, average age.

'You killed Mandy,' Quincy said. He kept approaching. Andrews still hadn't brought his gun back up. He hadn't shot any of his other victims. Chances were that he wasn't that comfortable with guns, Quincy decided. An ambush was one thing. A genuine face-off, another.

'Easy pickings,' Andrews snarled. But his voice wobbled. Behind him, Rainie was slowly extending her arm again, reaching for a pistol Quincy could just make out beneath the glass table. Quincy quickly looked away, not wanting Andrews to follow his line of sight. He focused his gaze on Kimberly instead, who was beginning to moan at Andrews's feet.

'You killed Bethie,' Quincy said.

'More easy pickings.' Andrews shifted suddenly, wrapping his arm around Kimberly's neck and dragging her up against him. Kimberly's eyes fluttered open. She looked disoriented, bewildered. Then her gaze met her father's and she simply looked heartbroken.

'It's okay,' Quincy told her automatically. He wanted to comfort his daughter, erase the pain from her gaze. He wanted to reach out to her. He kept his hands at his sides. Kimberly was strong. He would trust her strength to carry her through, just as he hoped she trusted his strength now. *Believe in me*, he willed his daughter. *I will always take care of you.*

Andrews smiled cruelly, and jerked Kimberly closer. 'On your feet, Sleeping Beauty. Time to say bye-bye to Daddy.'

Andrews jerked them both upright. Quincy didn't make any move to stop them.

Out of the corner of his eye, he discerned another movement in the background, but once again he resisted the temptation to look. He homed in on Andrews, focusing now on narrowing the man's universe. There was just Andrews, Kimberly, and Quincy. Just one vicious predator, one daughter, and one father determined to keep his child safe. If he had eyes only for Andrews, Andrews would have eyes only for him. Rainie . . . The rest must be a leap of faith.

'How does it feel, Quincy?' Andrews demanded, twisting Kimberly's arm savagely and bringing her even closer against him. 'How does it *feel* to lose everything and never even understand why!'

'You're not a real person,' Quincy said conversationally, moving slightly to the left, away from the living room, and drawing Andrews's gaze with him. 'You're a shell of a man, lacking genuine feelings, connections, compassion. You've spent your whole life acting at being a human being, molding yourself into other people's images because otherwise you don't know how to be. You don't know *who* to be. The greatest justice in life was that your little girls never had to see you again.'

Andrews jerked up his pistol. He pointed it at Quincy's head. 'Fuck you,' he screamed, causing Kimberly to flinch. 'I'm going to kill you! I'm going to blow out your goddamn brains!'

'You can't,' Quincy said, his voice as calm as Andrews's was angry. He looked at his daughter, willing her to remain strong, willing her to be all right. *Trust me, trust me, trust me.*

Lisa Gardner

'Yes I can!'

'You can't. Without me, your life has no purpose. When I'm gone, who will you be, Andrews? What will you do? What will you dream about at night? As much as you hate me, you *need* me even more. Without me, the game ends.'

Andrews's face grew red. His eyes dashed from side to side. The rage was building inside him, the implosion imminent. From rational act to crazy reaction. This was what Quincy needed. For Andrews to finally lose control. For Andrews to unleash the monster he kept locked inside.

Andrews's finger wrapped around the trigger. Quincy kept his eyes on Kimberly. He tried to tell his daughter how much he loved her, and he tried to apologize for what she would have to watch next. Rainie. Kimberly. Rainie.

God give them both strength.

A movement out of the corner of his eye . . .

'Kimberly,' Quincy murmured. 'Fuck ballet.'

On cue, she sagged heavily in her captor's arms. Andrews howled in surprise and pulled the trigger, but her unexpected movement had rocked him off balance. Gunfire spit low across the wall. Quincy dashed left. He brought up his 10mm to return fire but Andrews and Kimberly were too tangled together. He didn't have a shot. He didn't have a shot.

'Kimberly,' he yelled, though he didn't know why.

'Daddy!'

'Hey Andrews,' Rainie called. 'Look here.'

The man jerked around. Kimberly broke free and dove to the floor just as Rainie racked back her Glock.

'No!' Andrews howled. He pointed his gun at her –

And Quincy very calmly, very coolly shot the man point

390

blank in the chest. Andrews dropped to the floor. He did not move again.

'Is it over?' Kimberly asked when the echoes of the gunshot faded away. She was trying to raise herself off the floor. Her left arm wouldn't bear her weight. Blood and gray matter streaked down her long, fine hair.

Quincy went over to her. He took his injured daughter into his arms, feeling the tremors rocking her slender body. He cradled her against his chest, holding her as gently as he had when she was a newborn. Oh God, she was infinitely precious to him. He had saved her, but he had also hurt her, and he knew it would take them both years to sort out the difference between the two. All he could do was try. Isolation was not protection. No amount of distance kept you safe in the end.

His gaze went to Rainie, now bent over Andrews.

'He's dead,' Rainie said quietly.

Kimberly clutched his shoulders more tightly. And then she began to cry. Quincy rocked his daughter against him. He stroked her blood-splattered hair.

'It's over,' he said to Kimberly, to Rainie. And then more firmly, to all of them, 'The game is over.'

A loud knocking on the door. 'Hotel security,' a voice barked.

And the aftermath began.

Epilogue

Pearl District, Portland

Six weeks later, Rainie Conner sat hunched over her desk in her downtown loft, ostensibly trying to make her budget love her, but really eyeing the phone. Damn thing wasn't making a sound. Hadn't made a sound for days. She was really starting to hate that.

She picked up the receiver. 'Well, what do you know, dial tone.'

She set down the receiver. She went back to studying her Quicken file. It didn't do a thing to improve her mood.

Quincy had paid her. She'd yelled and screamed and put up a fuss. When they were both satisfied that she'd made all the appropriate noise, she'd accepted his check. A girl had to eat, and all those cross-country plane tickets had just showed up on her AmEx card. Conner Investigations got to have a profit. For about seven days. Then she started flying to Virginia again. She kept telling herself it was all for good reason.

First she had to join Quincy to finish picking Albert Montgomery's brain. The agent had finally admitted that the esteemed Dr Marcus Andrews had approached him two and a half years ago. Andrews had wanted revenge against Quincy. His wife, Emily, had hired Quincy as an expert witness in the bitter child-custody hearing between her and her ex-husband. Quincy's testimony had been pivotal in the judge's decision to deny Andrews access to his children permanently. While the case had been important at the time, Quincy hadn't thought about it now in years and the name Andrews had been too common to make Quincy think twice when Kimberly began talking about her highly respected professor.

Funny how Bethie had always thought it was his career at the Bureau that would put Quincy's family in jeopardy. None of them had considered that mental health professionals also faced dangers in the form of unbalanced patients and disgruntled families.

Andrews had interviewed Miguel Sanchez as part of his prison research study. As he became familiar with the killing spree and the officers involved in the Sanchez investigation, he'd identified Montgomery's role and realized here was someone else who probably hated Quincy as much as Andrews did. Dr Andrews tracked down Montgomery in Virginia, introduced his cause over dinner, and a few beers later, had enlisted Montgomery in a joint quest for revenge.

Montgomery had been playing the inside man ever since. First he helped Andrews understand how the Bureau worked. What would happen if an agent seemed in jeopardy? What if an agent's family was in jeopardy? How fast could the Bureau review past case files? What if an agent was suspected of a crime? From there, Montgomery had simply sunk in deeper. From introducing Mandy to Andrews to confiscating Quincy's stationery to attacking Glenda because his hatred had festered and grown that insane.

Nine months ago, Montgomery had searched the Oregon corrections department data banks to find a good candidate for Rainie's father. Yes, Ronnie Dawson existed. He went to jail at the right time, he was paroled at the right time. And upon personal investigation, he was a five-foot-two aging redhead, who'd never heard of Molly Conner and was as shocked as anyone to hear that a fat donation had been made to a county DA in his name.

Easy come, easy go. Rainie dedicated three days to feeling kind of funky. Then she surprised herself by getting over it. It was hard to miss something you never had, and she hadn't even truly lost her dream. She did have a father. He was somewhere out there. You never knew.

Attorney-at-law Carl Mitz existed, too. A good lawyer, and as Rainie had learned over lunch, a genuinely nice guy. Just one more person who had the right credentials, so Montgomery got his Social Security number, mother's maiden name, and date of birth. Andrews took over from there.

Rainie was not feeling so good anymore about the electronic age. She'd ordered a copy of her credit report the other day. She found herself checking it compulsively.

Special Agent Albert Montgomery wasn't going to stand trial. Apparently, Andrews had left one last present for him: Cyanide in his blood-pressure medication, which some kindly agent retrieved for him from home. Shortly after Quincy's final interview with him, Albert opened the bottle. Both he and his guard smelled the odor of bitter almonds immediately. The guard dived forward. Albert downed half the bottle. Sixty seconds later, Albert didn't have to worry anymore about how he was going to live with himself.

For Quincy and Kimberly it wasn't quite that easy.

Kimberly spent forty-eight hours in the hospital with a broken arm and severe concussion. Fortunately, she was young and strong and recovered quickly from her wounds. The physical ones, that is. Quincy tried to get her to return to Virginia with him. She insisted on going to New York, however. She wanted her apartment back. Her classes, her routine, her life. Rainie and Quincy called her every day for the first week. Kimberly liked that so much she took her phone off the hook. She was an independent girl and as Rainie understood from personal experience, she needed to deal with things in her own way, in her own time.

Two weeks after Albert committed suicide, the Philadelphia police got the handwriting analysis back from their crime lab and tried to arrest Quincy for his ex-wife's brutal murder. Rainie definitely had to return to Virginia for that. She'd yelled at the detectives, yelled at the district attorney, and made a general nuisance of herself. Glenda, on the other hand, finally convinced the DA to send the incriminating note to the FBI lab, which promptly verified the presence of numerous hesitation marks – a classic sign of forgery. Quincy thanked Rainie for coming. Glenda got a promotion.

Rainie returned once again to Portland. She had her business, Quincy had the case to wrap up and his daughter to think about. Of course they spoke by phone. Rainie told him she understood he had a lot going on. She practiced being sympathetic, supportive, and all around undemanding. He couldn't be there for her, but she could be there for him. This is what relationships were about. Real, adult, mature relationships. If she became any more well adjusted, she was going to have to beat someone.

Two weeks before, a fishing vessel off the coast of

Maryland pulled up Abraham Quincy's body in its nets. Montgomery had already revealed that Andrews had ordered the body heavily weighted and dumped in such deep water that it would never be found. He wanted Quincy to never know what happened to Abraham, to always have to wonder if his father was still out there, maybe still alive, maybe still waiting for his son . . . Not even Andrews could control fate. A fishing vessel happened to be active in the area. The fish happened to eat through the ropes bearing the weights. Abraham Quincy was found.

Rainie heard the news from Kimberly, who called her sounding quiet and much too old. They were going to have a small family ceremony for Abraham later in the week. Perhaps Rainie could come?

Rainie bought a third ticket to Virginia. Then she waited to hear from Quincy and waited to hear from Quincy and waited to hear from Quincy. Finally, she picked up the phone. He didn't return her call.

Rainie had had enough. She drove to the airport, flashed a ticket that wasn't valid for another two days, told them she had a family emergency and boarded the plane. Eight hours later, she knocked on Quincy's door. He opened it, looking tense, then shocked, then genuinely grateful. She jumped his bones before he ever made it to the bed. She decided she was getting pretty good at this sex thing.

Later, they went out to Arlington and simply sat next to Mandy's and Bethie's graves. Didn't talk. Didn't do anything. Just sat until the sun had sunk low and the air had grown cold. On the way back to the car, Quincy held her hand. Funny, she was thirty-two years old and she'd never walked hand-in-hand before. Then he opened her door for her, and by the time he got around to the other side she had this strange ache in her chest. She wanted to touch him again. She wanted to take him into her body and wrap her legs around his flanks and hold on tight.

Instead, when they were back at his house, she put his exhausted body to bed. Then she stayed awake for a long time afterwards, stroking the lines on his face, the ones that didn't go away, not even when he slept. She fingered the salt in his pepper hair, the scars on his chest. And she finally got it. All of it. The enormity of it. Why people sought each other out and formed families. Why baby elephants stumbled relentlessly through drought-stricken deserts. Why people fought and laughed and raged and loved. Why people, at the end of it all, *stayed*.

Because even when it hurt, it felt better to hurt with him, and when she was angry it was better to be angry with him, and when she was sad it was far, far better to be sad with him. And damn, she didn't want to get back on that plane. So silly. They were two adults, they had independent lives and demanding jobs, and it's not like there wasn't the telephone, and damn she didn't want to get back on that plane.

She stayed through the funeral. She held Quincy's hand. She patted Kimberly's shoulder as the young girl wept. She met extended family and played nice with everyone. Then she went back to Quincy's house where they came together as if they'd never touched before and would never touch again.

Monday morning he drove her to the airport. She had that tight feeling back in her chest. When she tried to speak, nothing came out.

Quincy said, *'I'll call you.'* She nodded. Quincy said, 'Soon.' She nodded. Quincy said, *'I'm sorry, Rainie.'* And she nodded, though she wasn't really sure what he was sorry for.

She got back to Portland. Five days, six hours, and thirty-two minutes ago. Her phone did ring. But when she picked it up, Quincy was never there.

'I can't be this well adjusted forever,' she told her computer screen. 'You know this isn't my style. Are women supposed to change everything for men? I mean, I was hostile, insecure, and stubborn before and he wanted to get to know me better. Now I'm honestly trying to be a mature, productive member of society, and I haven't heard from him since. On the one hand, the man is under enormous amounts of stress. On the other hand, that's just plain rude.'

Her computer screen didn't reply. She scowled. 'Do you think it was the sickening-sweet pet names? Maybe if I had called him stud muffin . . .'

Her buzzer sounded. Her head bobbed up, her gaze going to her TV/security monitor. A man was standing in front of the outside doors. He wore normal clothes, but she would've known that salt-and-pepper hair anywhere.

'Shit!' Rainie yelled. 'Why doesn't he ever give me a chance to shower!'

Screw the shower. She buzzed him up, ran to the kitchen sink, and hastily splashed water on her face. Two sniffs. Hey, at least this time she'd done deodorant. He rang the doorbell of her loft just as she dragged on a clean white shirt. One last hand through the hair, and she was at the door.

'Hello, Rainie,' he said.

She just stood there. He looked good in his Quincy-like way. A little uptight, a little too smart, a little too much weight of the world resting upon his shoulders. But he was wearing slim khaki pants with a navy blue open-collar shirt, the first time in weeks she'd seen him out of a suit.

'Hey,' she said. She opened the door a little wider.

'Can I come in?'

'It's been known to happen.'

She let him in. SupSpAg had something on his mind. He walked all the way to her family room where he promptly paced back and forth while she gnawed her lower lip. Six days ago they'd been so close. Why did they suddenly feel like strangers?

'I've been meaning to call,' he said.

'Uh-huh.'

'I didn't, though. I'm sorry.' He hesitated. 'I didn't know what to say.'

'"Hello" is always a good start. Some people like to follow that with, "And how are you?" I find that works better than, "Drop dead."' She smiled.

He winced. 'You're mad.'

'Getting there.'

'You've been very understanding.'

'Oh God, are you breaking up with me?'

He finally stopped pacing, looking genuinely startled. 'I didn't think so.'

'You didn't *think* so? What does that mean? I asked if you were breaking up with me. If you're not, for God's sake say no, with authority!'

'No, with authority!' he said.

'Five days, six hours, and thirty-seven minutes!'

'What's that?'

'How long since you promised to call. Not that I'm counting or anything.' Her hands flew up into the air. 'Oh God, I've become one of those women who waits by the phone. I swore I would never be one of those poor saps waiting by the phone. Look at what you've done to me. You ought to be ashamed of yourself!'

'Rainie, I swear I haven't been trying to torture you. I swear, last week when you arrived, I've never been so happy to see anyone. I've never . . . *needed* anyone the way I needed you. When I drove you to the airport, all I could think was that I didn't want you to go. Then I had this image of us – driving to and from airports, the high of getting together, the low of splitting apart, trying to be a couple, but still leading separate lives and . . . And in all honesty, then I thought that I was much too old for this shit. There are so few things that make me happy, Rainie. There is so little I have left. So why was I driving you to the airport?'

'I had a ticket?'

He sighed. She could see the tightness around his eyes. He stood too far away, half of the loft looming between them, but she couldn't bring herself to close the gap. He had more to say. That was the problem. He'd said the good stuff, so if he still had more . . .

'I'm no longer an FBI agent,' he told her quietly. 'I tendered my resignation to the Bureau two days ago.'

'No way.' She rocked back on her heels; she couldn't have been more surprised if he'd suddenly announced that he could fly.

'I've decided to reinvent my life. Kimberly has returned to school and is saying she's perfectly fine, so we know she's going to need help. Even if she's too stubborn to let me hold her hand, I think it would mean a lot to her to know that I'm really there for her this time. Not out in the field where I could get hurt. Not running back to the job as I've always done. But close. Say in New York, somewhere by NYU, where she could drop in for dinner if she liked or simply show up to chat. I'm thinking I'll get a loft, put up a shingle and work as an independent consultant for law enforcement agencies.'

'Profiler for Hire?'

He smiled. 'You'd be surprised how many profilers retire to become consultants. You get to pick your cases, choose your hours, and best of all, ignore all the politics because they're no longer your problem. It's a good setup. Of course, there is one problem.'

Rainie eyed him warily. 'I'll bite. What problem?'

'I'd like to have a partner.'

'You came all the way here to tell me that you're offering Glenda a job?'

He rolled his eyes. 'No Rainie, I came all the way here to offer you a job. With full benefits I might add.'

'What?' Far from being calmed, she became incensed. 'Five days, six hours, and thirty-seven minutes later, this is what you're offering me? *A dental plan?*'

He finally appeared uneasy. 'Well, maybe not dental. The company is a start-up.'

Rainie stalked toward him. Her eyes had narrowed into slits. Her finger jabbed the air. 'What are you doing, Quincy?'

'Apparently once again dodging your finger.'

'You fly across the country, you come to my home, and you offer me employment? Do I look like a woman who needs a boss?'

'Not boss,' he said immediately. 'Oh no, I am not that dumb. I said partner, and I meant partner.'

'*It's a professional arrangement!* Five days, six hours, and thirty-seven minutes later, I do not want a professional arrangement. I have not flown across the country three times in six weeks looking for a professional arrangement. I did not jump your bones just last week, looking for a professional arrangement. So help me God, Quincy—'

'I love you.'

'What?' She drew up short. Her finger froze in midair.

'Rainie, I love you. You don't know how many times I've already said that because it was always after you'd fallen asleep or left the room. I didn't know if you were ready, or maybe I didn't know if I was ready. But I love you, Rainie. And while I need to stay on the East Coast for my daughter, I don't want to drive you to airports anymore.'

'Oh.'

'Now would be a good time for you to say something more than, oh.'

'I get that.'

'You're making me nervous.'

'I have a mean streak. And you made me wait five days.'

'All the casework you can handle,' he offered quietly. 'Never easy, nothing boring. You know how it is in my world. I've waited so long to be happy, Rainie. I've made so many mistakes. I want to do better this time. And I want to learn to do better with you.'

She sighed. She had that tight feeling back in her chest. So that was what this was about. So this is what everything was about.

She leaned forward. She wrapped her arms around his neck. 'Hey Quince,' she murmured. 'I love you, too.'